CHOSEN OF THE DARK REALM

The Great Plan
Book 1

David Cornford

This book is dedicated to my wonderful wife.
Thank you for understanding when my mind was in this world.
This book could not exist without you.
My person x

Contents

Part Two

Part Three

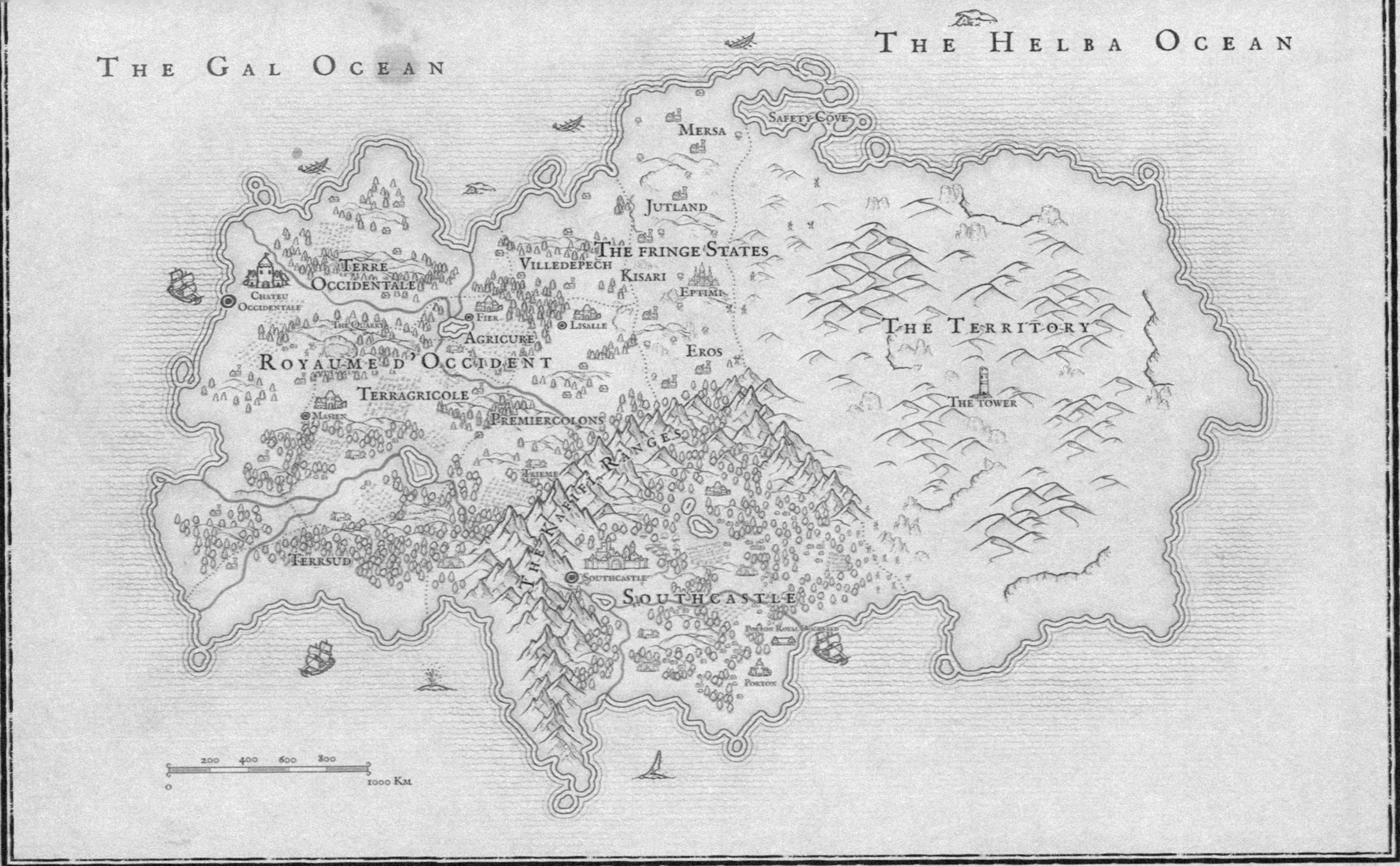

THE HELBA OCEAN

THE GAL OCEAN

SAFETY COVE

MERSA

JUTLAND

THE FRINGE STATES

KISARI

VILLEDEPECH

EPPING

EROS

LISALLE

AGRICURE

THE TERRITORY

THE TOWER

PREMIERCOLONS

THE NATTEN RANGES

SOUTHCASTLE

TERRE OCCIDENTALE

CHATEU OCCIDENTALE

ROYAUME D'OCCIDENT

TERRAGRICOLE

MASREE

HERKSUD

0   200   400   600   800   1000 KM

Part One

I needed something to believe in.

I thought the Church of An would give me what I needed. The Church was eager for my yearning and in return, wrapped its arms around me. Instead of the pain and despair of my former life, An gave me one full of hope and righteousness.

As you know, I have been a priest for a while, but the more time I have spent here cocooned from normalcy and comforted by its teachings, the more I have realised this is not what I need. No matter how deep I have buried myself, I have never found contentment. I need more than just a soothing balm for the wrongs I have suffered. I need something to redress the balance of my life.

I know you do not agree, but I believe the answers lie in Migru, and I intend to travel there at first light. By the time you read this, I will be well on my way.

I need this, Usemi. I cannot go on pretending my life is complete; it is anything but that, so I am leaving the Church, leaving the priesthood.

I have such a burning desire for... retribution, for satisfaction. For vengeance. There, I have said it. I have denied it for years, suppressed it, but it grows stronger all the time, and now it will not be denied. I do not want to deny it.

Do not follow me.

Adaru

A letter from the former priest Adaru to the alchemist Usemi, claimed to be from before The Great Collapse and preserved in the Museum of Darisam Artefacts in Salamu.

Chapter One

1003 Years After The Great Collapse.

The lack of windows and the dark surface of the mud-brick walls made the tavern gloomy and full of shadows. Woven pastel-coloured rugs covered the floor, worn thin by the passage of many patrons over the years. A fine layer of dust and sand from the world outside was scattered on those rugs. A yellowish herbal mist softened the interior lamplight as men blew fragrant smoke dragged from the many hookahs available. The tavern smelled of sweetness, spice, and sharp spirits.

A short, round man with thick, black hair down to his shoulders, and a similarly coloured beard, leaned casually back in his chair as he sipped a glass of arak. He wore a kandora, a loose, long-sleeved beige robe that hung to the floor. It was made from fine cloth with precise stitching that showed its value. A medallion hung around his neck, upon which was the seal of the Association of Fringe State Merchants. Even though he appeared relaxed, the tightness of his eyes and the slight fidget of his hands said that his demeanour was a mask.

The man in front of him noticed. He was lean, his dark-brown hair cut just above his ears, his beard stretching almost a foot below his jaw.

He was also dressed in a kandora, but one of clearly cheaper material, though still more finely made than most.

"I am Omar," he said. "You petitioned The Guild, and I am here to understand what you are looking for and to see how we might help."

The merchant smiled, though it did not touch his eyes. "Many thanks for meeting with me, Omar. I am Jabir. I am a merchant with an interesting request. It involves a tower—"

The tavern door opened fast and wide with a slight *crack* as if forced, capturing the attention of both men. The man that entered had bright blue eyes that almost blazed in their intensity. A cream keffiyeh was draped across his back and shoulders. The cotton head cloth was not wound about his face, so his black beard and dark hair were on display. His hair was pulled back and tied into a tail with its curling ends pulled over his shoulder to lay across his chest.

"Omar," he said with a slight mocking smile as he walked toward the two men. His long, loose, white tunic billowed with each step, and a sleeveless dark cloak flapped as a light gust of wind slipped through the closing door, catching it.

Omar's eyes were hard and angry. "Baraka."

As Baraka walked, his eyes darted to a nearby dark-haired serving woman, and he flicked a coin to her. *Thank you, Aya*, he mouthed. The woman smiled coyly and dipped her head. Baraka did not see her expression. His eyes were full of anguish as they watched the coin spin through the air.

Four left. Just four.

He bowed to Jabir. "I understand there's a job on offer."

"Welcome, stranger," Jabir said, dipping his head. "I would be happy to talk with you, though I am in discussions with this man at this time."

Baraka shrugged with mock nonchalance. "With a nobody who has a tenth of my clients and a fraction of their buying power."

Omar slammed down his glass, the drink splattering across the stone table. "The Guild has been petitioned, Baraka, and that gives me first rights."

Baraka shrugged again. "The Guild's a long way away, Omar. Bet this man here doesn't give a rat's ass about their laws and would rather get the best value for his money."

"The Guild provides assurances and guarantees for any transactions that pass through them," Omar said. "What can you offer *treasure hunter?*" He turned back to Jabir. "You were saying about a tower?"

"I'm the best," Baraka said.

Omar growled and jabbed a finger at Baraka. "I am warning you." He turned to the merchant. "This treasure hunter can talk the hump off a camel, but make no mistake about who he is. He is not part of The Guild and cannot offer any service guarantees, cannot verify buyers for anything secured." Omar snorted in derision. "He does not even have any men!"

"So, where's this tower?" Baraka said, ignoring Omar. He kept his tone light and casual but could not hide the sharp intensity in his eyes.

"In The Territory," the merchant said. "An acquaintance has come into possession of a rare item, a map that points to—"

Baraka's fragile façade cracked at the mention of the desert. "Nothing that enters The Territory returns," he muttered. His hand unconsciously grasped the coins in his pocket.

I needed this to be a real job.

Jabir caught Baraka's change of mood and raised his hands in the air. "I know how this sounds-"

Omar finished the last of his arak and stood. "Thank you for the opportunity," he said before turning to leave.

"Wait!" the merchant called out. "Why are you leaving?"

I should leave, too, Baraka thought, but he was acutely aware of the four coins in his pocket, the sum of his wealth.

Omar looked, wide-eyed, back at Jabir. "Why? Do you even know what you are talking about?"

The merchant nodded. "Of course, I do. An unforgiving, difficult desert that—"

"Unforgiving? Difficult? The Territory is impassable. No one can travel more than an hour, at best, without falling ill."

"Two weeks," Baraka said.

"Two weeks?" Jabir repeated, turning to look at Baraka, who was picking at his teeth with a small toothpick.

Baraka nodded. "Two weeks in The Territory without as much as a cough."

The merchant turned back to Omar, who was glaring at Baraka.

"The Guild's told you before about telling lies to get jobs."

Of course, I am making it up. Nothing can last two weeks in The Territory!

"Still prickly about the run to Safety Cove, eh?" Baraka said.

Omar loomed over the table, his hands curling into fists clenched so tight the bones of his knuckles gleamed white. "I lost a lot of money when that woman pulled out."

Baraka raised first his eyebrows, and then his hands in the air.

"You pulled the rug out from under me. You—" Omar took a deep breath as he ground his teeth. "Pah!" he spat. He walked away, throwing the door open to slam against the far wall with a deafening crash.

"You have history," the merchant remarked.

"It's a ruthless business."

"And he does not trust you. He makes many good points. Why should I trust you?"

Baraka gestured to Aya, and once he had caught her attention, he motioned to the empty glass Omar had left before returning his eyes to the merchant. "Because I am the only one who can do this job. Omar is many things, but he is not a fool, and he is right—The Territory is a deadly place. The only people you'll find who want a job involving The Territory are either trying to scam you or trying to steal from you."

"And which are you?" the merchant asked with narrowed eyes.

Baraka smiled. "Neither. I'm the person you want for this job. I can do this."

Aya approached and refilled the glass with arak. Baraka's fingers were trembling as they curled around the four coins in his pocket. *This is everything. This is all I have.* He hesitated. *This is insane. The Territory! Nothing survives in that desert. If I take this, I'm almost certainly a dead man.*

He cupped the four coins. *There has not been another job in months. Four coins will barely buy me food, and I'll be sleeping on the streets. If I don't take this, I'm definitely a dead man.*

He made-up his mind. *Some chance, no matter how slim, is better than no chance at all.* He placed all four coins on the table. *I'm all in now.*

Aya swept the coins away. Baraka felt an acute sense of loss as they left him.

The merchant frowned. "And just why would I choose a lone treasure hunter rather than someone from The Guild?"

Baraka sat back and gestured to himself. "What you see is what you pay for. I go in, myself, bring back what I find, myself. You deal with me and me only. There are no hidden fees, no politics, no additional agendas." He smiled and leaned forward. "And besides, I don't think The Guild is going to pick this one up, so what options do you have?"

"Without a support team, how can I be certain you will deliver? What assurances can you provide?"

"First of all, I don't even know if this tower exists. You want to know how I can deliver? I don't even know if there is anything *to* deliver." Baraka shook his head. "It doesn't matter." He gestured between them. "This is about trust. I trust in you, and in return, you trust in me. You give me just enough to make the trip and return. Don't pay me gold, just give me the supplies I need. If I don't come back, your losses are negligible."

The merchant pursed his lips as he considered Baraka's words.

The treasure hunter appeared calm as he waited, but his stomach was cramping with anxiety.

I need this job. After Safety Cove, The Guild will do whatever it takes to stop me from getting a lucrative opportunity.

Baraka forced his hand to stillness as he took a sip of arak. "Where in The Territory is this tower?" he pushed gently as he set the glass down.

The merchant's eyes flickered. "In the centre."

Baraka let out a long, slow whistle. "That is a long way, my friend."

"It is," Jabir agreed.

"If I take this—"

"If you take this," the merchant interrupted, "what is to stop you from running away with what you find?"

"Eptimi is a small place. Sure, I could make a return route via Eros or Jutland, but a man returning from The Territory with discovered treasure?" The hunter shook his head. "I don't think I would last that long. I come back here, and we complete the job with no fuss, no aggravation."

"How can you do this? How can you travel The Territory when no one else can?"

Baraka leaned across the table. "I never give up. I keep going when everyone else stops. When I feel like I can't do any more, I go that bit farther. That is why I can do this. Besides, no one is going to take a job to go into The Territory and especially not one going that deep into it."

Jabir nodded slowly.

Baraka's eyes narrowed. "I would hazard a guess that you paid a substantial amount for the information about this tower. How many hunters did you go to before you went to The Guild?"

Jabir did not answer.

Baraka nodded. "Thought so. I am the only option you have."

And you are the only option I have.

Jabir cleared his throat. "What is the catch?"

"A fifth of the value found."

"Absurd. A fiftieth is the best I can offer."

Baraka smiled as he prepared to negotiate. *It's happening.*

Weeks Later.

Baraka clutched the weathered stone of the ruined tower with arms shaking in protest.

"Don't give up," he said to his body. Words spilled through cracked lips and muffled by the shemagh's cloth ends that were wound around his face and neck.

His lungs refused him a deep breath. His fingers and toes screamed at this ordeal he forced upon them, sending jolts of pain from their bloody tips. Sweat abandoned him in favour of a quick death on the desert over one hundred feet below.

"Just a little farther."

The wind moaned a promise to pry him away from the ruin and shatter his body on the sand below.

Baraka could feel his fingers slipping as he pulled himself closer to the stone. He hissed in pain as his foot cramped, and he longed for the foot-spikes he had been forced to sell a month ago to feed himself.

"It is just a little farther."

His overworked and underappreciated back spasmed at the lie. He was barely half-way.

"Please don't give in now." Trembling fingers reached for his next handhold.

"I just need to reach the top. I just need to see what's inside."

If there is anything inside.

Sand-laced wind howled in hateful incredulity that he was here. It wrapped its hands around him and tried to rip him away from the wall he climbed.

"Please just let me make the climb," he pleaded to the wind as it fought him.

As if enraged by his audacity to try and bargain with it, the wind intensified. It came at him like an enraged brawler, pounding his body with fast hard punches.

"If there is nothing here, if this has all been for nothing, then I will gladly give myself to you because I have nothing left. Please, I have to try!"

How dare you! Baraka heard the wind shriek as it beat and raked his body. *Die!*

Pain throbbed in his thighs, in his calves, in his forearms, in his biceps, and across his shoulders.

A cry of desperate longing to be anywhere but here burst from Baraka's parched throat. As if sensing victory, the wind struck again, changing tactics and trying to wrestle him away from the wall. Baraka's toes started slipping from the niche they were barely lodged into. The fingers of his left hand lost their grip. His right hand started to slip. He began to fall backward. His fingers and toes slipped some more.

Die! the wind shrieked.

His cry of desperation became a scream of denial. He snatched at the wall with his left hand, and his fingers found a grip. He pulled himself closer to the wall, pushing his toes back into the niche.

"I will not give in!"

Die!

"No!"

With a howl of frustration, the wind realised it was beaten. It lashed out with one last spiteful blow before rushing away to find easier prey.

Baraka let out a shuddering breath, and then reached up, searching for his next handhold. His fingers slid over stone that had been weathered glass-smooth until they found a space between two blocks. He gripped the edge and pulled his body up.

Please hold.

It held.

Inch by inch he rose, scraping up from a reality of nothing toward a dream of something. It was a journey of blood and pain. It was a near impossible climb on something broken that brutally resisted his advancement and promised to break him.

It was the physical embodiment of his life.

It will not break me.

He raised one knee and reached out with a leather boot, searching for the space he had used as a handhold a moment before. Cracked leather scratched against the wall as he sought it once, twice, three times. His eyes grew wide as his fingers started slipping.

He found the opening on his sixth attempt, higher than he had thought. He shoved the toe of his boot into the crack and settled his weight with a gasp and a moan. After a few moments, when he had regained a measure of strength, he reached up with his left hand for his next handhold.

Without warning, the stone he gripped in his right hand crumbled. He snatched at the wall with his empty, reaching hand as he started to fall back, his heart pounding. His fingers found a stone edge and clutched it tight. His body continued to twist away from the wall, and he lost purchase with his right foot, leaving him hanging from just his left hand.

His feet scrabbled at the wall as he tried to find purchase. He swung his right arm around to scrape at the stone with that hand as the bloodied fingers on his left started to lose their grip.

He cursed himself for taking this job. He cursed the tower he climbed. He cursed the wind, the sand, the sun, the world.

Just as he was about to fall, his right hand found something to hold on to, then his left foot found something to stand on. He pulled his body flat against the wall and took several deep breaths.

Please let there be something here...

After a moment, he started to climb once more. Rest would only be found by finishing the ascent.

Search for something to grasp, grasp what was found. Search for something to stand on, stand on what was found. Step-up. Pull-up. Search for something to grasp, grasp what was found.

Over and over.

He stretched for his next grip, but where there should have been stone, he found nothing except air. His hand flailed around for a moment before settling on a worn, thin, raised surface. Adjusting his feet, he reached up with his other hand and took hold of it. He traced its surface and found the edge of an opening a little wider than he was. Gripping with blistered fingertips, he moved his legs until he found places he could put his weight on, and both pulled and pushed to get himself up and onto the edge's opening.

Protesting muscles hauled him over, and he leaned forward to feel down and find what was on the other side. His hands touched sand. He manoeuvred himself through with the last of his strength, then rolled onto his back. He lay panting, looking up through a gaping hole in the floor above into a cloudless sky of deep blue. He pulled the shemagh off his face so he could breathe properly.

Once he had caught his breath, Baraka sat upright, and with one hand on the nearest wall to steady himself, he took in the ruin's interior.

Sand.

Even as high as he was, being open to the elements had enabled the desert to invade and consume whatever had resided in this room. Sand lay in sweeping dunes throughout a space just over two hundred square feet. A cylindrical stone core rose from the sand into the wooden floor above.

Taking small steps, Baraka walked onto the piled sand, and then around the buried room. The sand was particularly high at one point, and he was able to reach up into the floor above. He pulled himself up into that next level on protesting, painful muscles and with a groan that came from deep in his exhausted core.

This level had no ceiling, and sand piled in corners here, too, but he could see a closed door in the central stairwell. The floor he had pulled himself onto had many gaps. The one he had gained entry through was one, another was just after it, and another before the stairwell door. A landing of about a square foot stretched in front of it.

Baraka stared at that door. It was maybe six feet high and had a curved top with a wrought-iron ring pull as its door handle. He stepped back, and then took a running leap over the space to the door. He landed on groaning wood. Grasping the iron ring, he pulled hard.

It did not move.

Baraka cursed and took a moment to compose himself before pulling with all his strength. Inch by inch, and with grinding protest, the door opened to reveal stone stairs leading down into darkness. After he had caught his breath, he walked inside.

Baraka found what he had hoped for after several steps down: A small copper oil lamp hanging on the wall. He reached up and felt around the base to check how it was attached to the wall. Satisfied that it could be removed, he lifted it off its fixture, twisting its base so the lamp was vertical.

The glass chimney was cloudy and dirty from use, but thankfully, still intact. Baraka sat on the stone step, checked the oil font: half full. He removed the chimney and found enough of a wick to use. After setting the glass down beside him, he reached into his sling bag and took out his flint and steel. In moments, the lamp was alight. He replaced the chimney, and then sat with a weary sigh.

He dipped into his sling bag again and pulled out a water skin, then took a slow, measured drink. He closed his eyes and licked his lips, savouring the moisture on his cracked lips and his parched throat. He sealed the skin closed and replaced it, then twisted his neck one way, then the other, grunting as his spine cracked. He massaged his biceps and forearms, then did the same to his thighs and calves.

He stared into the darkness. A sense of foreboding filled him, and he hesitated to take the next step.

Taking a deep breath, he rose and, holding the lamp before him, started down.

The first few doors he came across were impossible to open, and Baraka assumed the desert had found a way into the spaces beyond and filled them with sand. He descended, stopping only when he found other lamps to collect oil and replacement wicks from.

The lower Baraka went, the colder it became, until he was shivering, and his teeth were chattering. He paused and took a moment to wrap himself in his shemagh before continuing.

Finally, he managed to open a door, and he stepped into a wide corridor that encircled the central stairwell. There was no sand on the floor. The dark was oppressive, and the air was thick with the smell of things left discarded and forgotten.

He made his way around the corridor by the lamp's dim glow and found doors set into the outer wall. He could not open the first, but the second was open, and he walked inside. The flickering lantern flame illuminated a small library, its walls covered by shelves that stretched from floor to ceiling and were full of books of every colour and size.

Several tables and benches were scattered throughout the room, as were splendid, upholstered armchairs with accompanying sculpted side tables. Rugs and animal skins covered the floor in a haphazard patchwork, and lanterns hung on the walls.

Baraka walked to one of several tall, narrow windows set within deep recesses. He saw they were split into two halves that were sealed together by three handles—each the size of one of his hands—running up the centre edge of one section. Thick lines of lead crisscrossed the surfaces of each half, and by the light of his lantern, the treasure hunter could see closed wooden shutters on the other side protecting the windows from the sand piling against them.

He searched the chamber.

Nothing of value.

There was an open door in each interior wall leading to rooms beyond. He picked one at random and walked through.

This seemed to be a classroom with desks, chairs, and blackboards as tall as he was and equally as wide on each wall. All of them were covered with intricate shapes and explanatory scribbles, but in a language he did not recognise.

Again, nothing.

He returned to the small library room, and from there passed through the other door and found another classroom.

Please say there is something here!

Baraka returned to the stairwell and descended deeper into the oppressive darkness.

Opening several other doors revealed similar corridors leading to similar rooms and the same distinct absence of anything valuable.

Was this all for nothing?

The arched top of a doorframe several floors down caught his eyes and made him pause. It was covered in strange signs that sat deep in the stone with blackened edges as if they had been burned into the rock.

This is no ordinary room.

Baraka grabbed the iron ring pull. Sparks burst from between his fingers and lit the stairwell. He fell back, cursing and rubbing his skin. He looked at his hand, expecting the worst, but it was not even singed. Baraka tentatively touched the iron again, but this time, nothing happened. He took a firm grip and pulled. The door did not move. Taking hold of the ring with both hands this time, Baraka pulled as hard as he could. The wooden door groaned in protest, but as Baraka continued to pull, it grudgingly surrendered. Licking his lips, he walked inside.

Unlike the other levels, there was no corridor on the other side.

Instead, it opened into a single windowless room that filled the entire level.

It was full of bodies.

Each was dressed in clerical robes. They had mummified in what must have been a considerable number of years since their deaths so that their genders were unidentifiable.

The treasure hunter walked around the room, turning up his wick to let more light illuminate the space. There was little to be found, apart from the bodies. A few overturned braziers and a couple of broken chairs. A narrow, single-column stone lectern stood in the room's centre. Baraka hurried to it.

A thick book stretching three-feet tall and almost the same wide lay open on its slanted top. Baraka brought up his lantern to study it. Symbols were scrawled across the open pages in dark, thick lines. His eyes traced the shapes, and as they did, the room seemed to get even colder. Baraka could not look away, even as he tried to control his shivering. A faint scratching gnawed at the edge of his mind. As his eyes continued to slide along the dark lines that blotted the page, pressure began to build inside his head, pushing against the inside of his skull and making his temples throb with sharp pain.

The scratching grew louder, shifting from a formless background noise to something he could almost identify.

Baraka began to drip with sweat, and puffs of steam came from his mouth with each breath even though his fingers and toes were blue from the freezing temperature. A low whine slipped through his lips at the building tension. Just before he reached the end of the drawn symbols, he realised what the growing noise was.

It was laughter.

Chapter Two

Chill mountain air tussled the woman's long, curling blond hair as she pulled her light, violet shawl around herself and stared out over the balcony crenelations and across the city. The breeze tugged at the bottom of her pale-yellow, sack-back gown. The fabric pulled against the small hoop underneath her petticoat, over which hung a skirt that pushed out from her hips to then fall to the floor, hanging suspended over the hoop skirt. It was modest compared to the exaggerated bowls that hung from the hips of most other women, but Nanaya still felt uncomfortable.

This might not be the strangest fashion I have experienced, but I will be happy to see the back of it.

At first glance, her smooth, wrinkle-free face, slender arms, and voluptuous body showed her to be a young woman. Her bright green eyes, however, had an intensity well beyond those apparent years and seemed to hold the wisdom of ages.

Nanaya walked back into her sparsely yet elegantly decorated sitting room, the main feature of which was a detailed map of the island continent, which covered one wall. From there, she crossed into her bedchamber. Whereas light spilled through twin glass terrace doors and brightened her sitting room, her bedroom lacked windows, and thick stone walls gave off a chill.

She approached a four-foot-long chest with a padded lid that could be used as a seat, turned, and carefully sat, smoothing her skirt as she settled. Nanaya closed her eyes and slowed her breathing. She turned her thoughts away from what surrounded her to focus on what was inside her. She focused on the pulsing of her heart, the rhythm of her breathing, attuning herself with her body until her mind and breath and heart were one.

As she prepared to use a whisper of her power, the terrors of her past made her hesitate. Just like every other time she did this, she wondered if this would be the moment when what had slaughtered her brothers and sisters of The Academy, and what had forced her into hiding for centuries, would sense her.

Her vow would not let her rest, however. She had made a pledge to safeguard the tower, and that was a profound and sacred binding of herself to that cause. Breaking that would be an unforgivable sin.

Now is not the time for doubt. He has never sensed me before. He might not even still be alive.

She concentrated on focal points in her body specific to the nature of her powers. Warmth grew in her throat. The heat stretched to the centre of her forehead and then to her crown and an intense euphoria rippled through her being as her energy awakened.

She released her awareness from her body.

Nanaya looked down at herself. Three soft pure glows pulsed from her body. For the first time in a very long time, she considered the woman below.

It was not always like this. I was not always like this.

She still remembered the innocent, anxious girl she had been and the happy, light-hearted woman she had developed into. She remembered being full of wonder, excitement, and most of all, she remembered being full of love. She stared at the hard face of the woman before her.

That was before. Now, there is only my duty. Nothing else matters.

She swept through her rooms and passed through the open terrace doors. Higher and higher Nanaya rose, until she was looking down at the capital, then she was speeding north-east. The land flashed beneath her: lakes, farms and villages, towns and factories, roads and woodlands. Before long, she was racing over the Kafifi Ranges; passing over, at first, big mountain pine trees and huge boulders of bare moss and lichen-covered stone, then deep blankets of unbroken snow as she reached the higher elevations. The Ranges dropped as she passed over them, and the snow gave way to stone once again. Then there was only sand, and The Territory filled her vision, endless dunes of dusty orange sweeping as far as she could see. A lifeless, barren ocean.

The tower first revealed itself as a blemish, an abnormality amid the endless rolling dunes. Its summit was broken, a shattered remnant of dark ambition.

Nanaya stared at its weathered stone with hate-filled eyes.

This place took everything from me.

She longed to destroy all memory of what it was, of what had happened here and the inconsolable loss she had suffered, but she never could. She could never have peace.

Amid the debris of the highest level, the door to the central stair-well, closed for over a thousand years, lay open. Terror seized her with paralysing claws, suffocating in its fierceness.

It is breached.

She cast her eyes back to the desert. The tower stood in the centre of a broken world. Reality flowed like the sand the deeper into The Territory one travelled. Dunes rose, fell, and moved without the wind, as if they existed in one place one moment, and then existed in another place a breath later. The only constant was the tower standing untouched in the midst of the fractured desolation.

Nanaya rushed through the opening and made her way down the stairs. She passed several open doors that had always been that way and several others she remembered had been closed. She did not pause to look through them and continued downward.

Please let it remain sealed!

She descended level after level until she jumped the last step and was staring at a narrow doorway filled with stone. Four triangular shapes were on its surface, formed like the points of a compass. Running through them all was an unbroken ivory circle.

The triangle at the top was a twisting, churning pillar of yellow smoke, a noose of which curled around its tip.

The shape to its right was deep red, blazing with writhing, spitting flames and also pointed upwards. The stone around it was blackened and scorched.

Directly below the yellow shape was one that had a wide base at its top, making it appear to point downwards. It was a mass of cracked vibrant green stone, a line of which ran horizontally just below its tip just like the noose that hung around the top of the shape above it.

The last shape was opposite the one of flames and had its base at the top and its tip at the bottom like the green stone shape. Its sides were thick, soft and flowing, and a deep dark blue.

Their colours bled into the ivory circle where they touched.

Sigils representing the fundamental energies of the realm.

She released the breath she had not realised she had been holding.

Unbroken. Just as we left them. The seals between the realms remain safe and untouched on the other side.

Turning away, Nanaya climbed back up the stairwell and froze as she noticed another open door.

She glanced at the arched top of the doorframe. It was blackened.

Something broke the wards we placed.

Nanaya moved closer to the arched doorframe, step by cautious step. She peered inside.

Long-dead bodies lay among debris, but her eyes were drawn to a narrow, single-column, stone lectern and the book it held.

She looked at the dark lines on the pages. *Blood.* She studied the lines. *The fabric of this realm was parted. Something was bound into the book but has now been released.*

She stared at the book for a moment before fleeing back to her body. Opening her eyes, she breathed in deeply before standing and leaving her chambers for the corridors of Southcastle.

Even though the fortress had high towers where one could survey the land, gatehouses to control who could enter, and crenelations on every wall where defenders could fire through the crenels and take cover behind the merlons, Southcastle was more of a fortified palace than an actual castle.

It stood on a flattened hill, overlooking the walled city with the same name, and was arranged in a distorted, tiered, and inwardly sloping pentagonal shape with its point away from the city. A courtyard easily seventy feet wide sat in its hollowed centre, accessible from wide, fortified entrances in each wall. Balconies hung off most rooms on all sides, offering unrestricted views of the city or mountains, depending on the side of the building, and those on the highest levels had views of rivers running from the Kafifi Ranges into deep, freshwater lakes. The balconies also grew more expansive on each level, until the highest had open terraces and even some small gardens.

Southcastle had eight floors with over a thousand rooms, including four mess halls, seven vast banquet halls, over one hundred royal and guest suites, three hundred staff quarters, numerous reading rooms, and countless themed lounge rooms. Around them all wound long, pedestal-lined corridors, and dotted throughout the palace were art galleries and rooms to showcase rarities, heirlooms, and treasures. The main audience chamber containing the Southcastle throne was on the third floor with a ceiling that stretched up to the sixth floor. It was to this room that Nanaya headed.

"And the recent trade delegation from The Fringe States brought with them a revised renewal proposal, which we will be reviewing next week."

King Edward Harolden cocked his shoulder-length brown-haired head to one side, his hazel eyes narrowing, his face tightening. He had a soft face that gave him a youthful appearance, however, the lines around his eyes and on his brow spoke of stress and tension.

"Revised?" The king's voice wavered slightly. He gripped his right hand with his left as it started to tremble.

His wife, Margaret, the queen consort, sat in a throne beside the king, and she reached over to lay her hand on his arm. A few years older than the king, her brown hair was gathered and pinned on her crown. Her green eyes were full of concern.

The prime minister noticed the king's agitation. Eight years older than the king, Prime Minister Martin Stations looked at least a decade older still. Heavy-set with a red face etched with creases born from over a decade of governance.

"Minor concessions," the prime minister said quickly, to calm the king. "A few new requests. Nothing unexpected."

King Edward nodded and took a deep breath. His shoulders dropped, and he opened his hands. "Keep me advised, Martin. The Fringe States has maintained a solid bond with us even in the face of the West's aggressive pursuit of trade concessions. I don't want anything to jeopardise that."

The prime minister bowed.

King Edward smiled and waved his hand, indicating the audience was at an end.

Martin left the audience chamber through twin gold-edged doors that opened without a word as he neared and closed without sound after he exited.

Bernard Forges, the elderly royal physician, who was never far from the king's side, had also taken note of Edward's shifting mood. He approached the king's throne and bowed deeply. "Is there anything I may get you, Your Majesty? You have not taken any tonic for a few days."

Edward shook his head. "No, thank you, Bernard, I—"

The king's attention was caught by the audience chamber doors opening to admit the Officer of The Chamber, a senior member of the palace staff, who stood as gatekeeper to the audience chamber.

As the household staff bowed and departed, the Officer of The Chamber approached and also bowed. "Lady Nanaya, Your Majesty."

"Please," the king said without hesitation, "let her in."

The man bowed once again and crossed the room to depart between the gilded doors. After a moment, they opened again, and Lady Nanaya strode in.

Margaret sat forward on her throne, her eyes frosty as she regarded the other woman.

Edward motioned to the Master of The Chamber, a man responsible for the household staff who worked in the audience chamber. The man acknowledged the king's command and clapped his hands, then turned to each of the attending men and women and made short, curt motions with his hands. Without a word, each turned and bowed or curtsied to the king before exiting through one of the many working passages that connected the staff areas to the royal places.

"If you will excuse me," Margaret said in a hushed voice to her husband, "I will speak with Martin about The Fringe States's proposal."

Edward smiled at her. "Thank you. I would very much appreciate that."

Margaret smiled back and patted his arm before rising and walking past Nanaya, each woman dipping their head to the other in a slight gesture of greeting that did not have the slightest warmth.

When Nanaya had reached the king, they were alone.

"My Lady," Edward said as she curtsied.

"Your Majesty," she replied. Her voice was tight.

"Shall we retire to the Royal Consult?" the king asked, noting her mood.

Nanaya nodded, and together, they walked around the throne and toward three small doorways in the far wall. Each led to a private chamber where the king held closed discussions with selected persons. One led to the Inner Council Chamber where the king sat with senior advisers on major matters of state governance and security. A long, thick slab of wood stood in the centre of the room, around which sat seven chairs for the seven heads of church and state. A more ornate chair sat at the head of the table for the king. Maps of the city, kingdom, the continent, and of their Royaume d'Occident and Fringe States neighbours hung on the walls around that table.

Another doorway led to the Chamber of Treaties, where matters of domestic policy and foreign pacts were discussed with the prime minister, senior politicians, diplomats, and, when appropriate, foreign envoys. This room had a more casual feel, with a thick rug on the floor, two dozen comfortable chairs arranged around a low circular table and an open fireplace.

The third room was behind a thick, dark, fur pelt that covered the doorway, and this was where the king and Nanaya went. Called The Royal Consult, this was a small room with enough space for two thickly upholstered chairs and a small, high table to one side, where wine or other refreshment sat. This was an intimate room where the king sat in one-on-one consultation with his most trusted advisers. Without the formality and detail of the Inner Council Chamber, and the expectation of long discourse that sat heavy in the Chamber of Treaties, the Royal Consult was a private place where the king could give and receive delicate advice.

"You are troubled," the king said as he took a seat and indicated Nanaya should take the other.

Nanaya nodded and sat at the edge of the other chair so that her hoop skirt rested comfortably and modestly around her. She steepled her hands and gazed blankly over her fingers as her mind worked through her feelings.

Edward remained silent as she thought.

"Something has happened," she said after a moment.

Edward leaned forward, frowning. "What has happened? I have rarely seen you this concerned."

"I am not sure," Nanaya said. She took a deep breath. "Something has happened in The Territory."

The king frowned and shook his head. "I don't understand. The desert? What—?"

"I cannot explain it at the moment, but trust me when I say something has happened there that concerns me. You must let me know if you hear anything concerning The Territory. No matter how insignificant it might appear to you, you must tell me."

"Of course. But will you tell me at least something about what has happened?"

"I will," Nanaya said as she rose and slowly smoothed the fabric of her skirt. "I will in time," she corrected. "I need to learn more. I do not understand what this means. Yet."

The woman pushed aside the fur pelt that closed off the room from the chamber beyond but paused in the doorway. She turned back to look at the king intently. "Anything, Edward. You must tell me anything you hear about The Territory."

"Of course. Whatever you need is yours."

Nanaya nodded, and then walked out of the room, leaving behind a bemused king.

Chapter Three

The sky was full of clouds that were thick and black and through which raced bright, jagged, forked lightning. They moved in a circular motion as they churned against one another, and below the centre of the vortex stood the tower.

Dark stone reached for the heavens from what had been a lush forest but was now a barren plain of mud pounded flat by the boots of thousands of soldiers. In gleaming, black-and-burgundy armour, they stood stiff at attention, all facing the tower, weapons sheathed, their eyes wide, and their faces taut with inner turmoil.

Here at the end, they doubted themselves. Their queen had commanded them to defend this place of learning, and they had eagerly obeyed. Those who cried for the destruction of this place were from The Academy, a place that taught magic, and therefore, could not be trusted. Queen Su was right to be suspicious of the ambitions of The Academy, with its unnatural creatures and powers, and her soldiers had marched to Migru in full support of her, their belief in her unquestioning.

That belief had started to waver when the unnatural storm had begun to form, however, and had cracked when the day had turned to night.

They had questioned then, but it had been too late. Every soldier *stood powerless, held immobile by unseen forces. None believed in their righteousness any longer. All wanted to flee what was happening and were terrified about what might be coming, but there was nothing they could do. Thousands of men stood awaiting their fate. Not a single word was spoken as hundreds within their ranks suddenly dropped lifelessly to the ground, the only sound a slight, high-pitched whistling that seemed to ebb and flow with the wind.*

The clouds churned faster and more violently, and as they did, the whistling revealed its nature: a whisper of a scream, the last gasping agony of a tortured soul.

Rain pelted the metal breastplates and angular helms of the army in loud, fat drops, but it was not water that streaked down uniforms and the skin left uncovered by the low brow and nose guard. What fell was a sticky, oily liquid.

Lightning struck the tower. Once. Twice. More and more, until a twisting serpent of white energy ran around the stone and spider webbed back up into the convulsing sky.

A mist formed at the top of the tower, a shimmering sheet of grey. A shadow appeared at its core, a shadow that grew darker as the wind grew stronger and the clouds spun faster.

Something broke.

The world changed.

Something pushed through the portal, and as it did, the bodies of the dead soldiers lifted from the ground, gripped by eddies of dark energy and sped toward it. The bodies snapped and pulled apart as they moved through the air until streams of flesh and bone poured into the portal. Clawed feet formed from the raw material and gripped a reality it was never meant to see.

A wolfish snout formed and sniffed the air before opening a jaw filled with rapidly growing long, sharp teeth and shrieking its arrival.

Baraka screamed himself awake.

He lay on his back, panting, with his heart pounding as the last vestiges of the dream left him.

He pushed himself up, breathing hard. He looked around. The star-filled night sky illuminated his surroundings. He was in a deep muddy hollow with long, twisting tree roots stretching above him like a thick canopy.

Where am I?

Baraka climbed his way out of the hollow and saw that he was in the middle of a dense wood. The land sloped down to a small stream before rising back up on the other side.

A breeze rustled the leaves and sent violent shivers racking his bones and setting his teeth chattering. He pulled his cloak around himself.

He tried to climb to his feet, but his thighs cramped and sent him sprawling to the leaf-covered mud. He lay there, curled into a tight ball, trying to find the strength to move, but the cold sapped the last of his energy, and the world dissolved into blackness.

~

"Catch me, Baraka!"

Laughing, he ran through dusty alleyways after... someone. Who was that? He felt like he should remember. He felt a slight pressure, a warmth in his head as he ran after... Clarissa! That was her name! A girl he had grown up with.

The sandstone walls around him dissolved, and he was in another place, sitting behind a small, chipped wooden desk in a timber room with over half a dozen children around him. He remembered this place. He had been here as a child. He opened his mouth—

His dream changed. He was in water now, and it was cold, but he ignored the temperature as he swam harder and faster to reach...

He was no longer in water. He was lost. The light fell as evening approached, and the cold of the desert night pushed the warmth of the day away. This was one of the darkest memories of his childhood. The shadows of the empty bazaar stalls stretched and twisted in frightening shapes just as they had so many years ago, and he thought he could hear things moving around. He wanted to cry out for his mother, but his voice failed him, and the shapes continued to grow, reaching for him.

Again, things shifted.

His mother cried and clutched at him, but then that memory was cast aside, and another filled his mind, one of a tavern maid moving closer, her lips meeting his. The kiss was soft and wet, her tongue light and caressing. Her body was firm, yet full and...

He wanted to hold on to that memory, but the decision was not his, and it was discarded for another where he landed on his arm and felt the snap even as the shocking pain leapt—

Baraka woke to sharp edges pushing into every part of his body. He lay for a moment, trying to collect his thoughts.

He landed on his arm and felt the snap.

He clutched at his arm; it was unharmed, as he knew it must be because that break had been years ago. He shook his head and shifted, trying to get more comfortable as he sifted through the images now fading in his mind. Loves, losses, celebrations, pains, and despairs. Scenes from his life, yet he could not understand what had made him think of any of them.

As the memories fled back to the recesses of his mind, he dimly remembered climbing a small stone wall and staggering across a ploughed field toward a round hay bale, which he had then burrowed inside. He shuffled around. The straw was sharp and itchy, but at least it was warm and dry. He wrapped his arms around himself and sobbed.

What is happening to me?

Hunger pains wracked his stomach, and he felt lightheaded. Exhausted, Baraka cried himself back into dreams of his past.

He stood in a cobbled street.

Frowning, Baraka turned around, eyes roaming the grime-covered walls, trying to make sense of... that heat in his head again—he was late!

Master Stevens of the Archaeology Institute would have his hide if he was late again!

The heat abated.

Darting out of the alley, he ran through the wider main street, hopping over pools of refuse and piles of excrement and trying to avoid the early morning tradesmen, throwing belated apologies in response to their curses when he knocked into them. He heard bells tolling somewhere in the distance and picked up his pace. If he hurried, he might...

Baraka tossed in his sleep and clutched his head in pain.

He watched as Henri Francois, the tall and well-set Archbishop of Royaume d'Occident, smiled and turned over a small wooden figurine, a delicate carving of a woman carrying a basket of herbs. Baraka could see the muscle of his youth was still there to some degree, but now layered with soft fat. What had once been a thick head of hair was now a bald scalp, but a thick fall of dark curls dropped from the back of his head to lay across his shoulders.

Baraka snuck a glance around the room, noting the gilded mirror, the finely woven rug, and countless other items of obvious value. He smiled. Making the long journey to the West had been a gamble, but he was glad he had done it. He was confident it would pay off handsomely.

The archbishop placed the carving at the edge of a slab of polished, deep-mahogany wood, four feet wide and seven in length, that served as his desk. "Thank you, it is quite exquisite, and you are quite correct, I do love such items. Where did you say it came from again?"

Baraka frowned and gestured dismissively. "The exact location escapes me, Your Eminence. Suffice to say, it was in a forgotten place of the Old World I explored to great personal danger. However, I am, as you are, a lover of antiquities and valuable historical artefacts, and I could not just leave that there for someone else to find who would not see its value."

Henri pursed his lips and opened a drawer under his desk. His eyes moved between the few tied velvet bags of coins that sat inside. He picked out the smallest and tossed it to Baraka, who caught it deftly in one hand.

Baraka's smile faltered as he hefted the bag in his hand and judged its contents. He opened his mouth to speak.

"Now, you must excuse me," the archbishop said. "Matters of State occupy my time."

~

Power. Position. Wealth.

The voice that whispered through Baraka's mind was not his. The memory of meeting with the archbishop froze.

Perfect.

The scene dissolved, and with a weary moan, Baraka finally found rest.

Chapter Four

The young man slammed his walking pole into the ground as he crested the hill he had just climbed and winced as an icy wind buffeted his face.

Where is that sheep?

Samuel sighed, ran a hand through his mop of dark, curling hair, blue eyes gazing at the land around him. He stood at the western steps of the Kafifi Ranges, a lush green land fed richly by the waters coming down off the mountains. Wheat, barley, oats, and a wide range of vegetables filled the neighbour's fields, whereas his family's four hundred acres had livestock. Seven hills of various gradients and sizes dominated the rangelands of the farm, the one he had just crested being the longest and steepest and sat at the edge of their land. Grassland, shrubland, and woodland pockets dotted the fields that swept east from where he stood through the region of Premiercolons toward the Fringe State of Eros. Samuel imagined the land losing its richness as it neared the Fringe States, becoming a punishing stretch of coarse grasses with sparse cover and ever-increasing stone.

I'll see it for myself one day, Samuel thought. *My life will be bigger than this farm.*

The young man tucked his chin into his coat's sheepskin collar as his eyes searched across the sloping pastures in the dwindling light. He found the lost sheep far below, lazily grazing in a slight hollow that offered protection from the wind. He looked up.

Rain clouds moving closer. There is no way I can get back to the farmhouse before night.

Samuel stared across his family's land. There was a shelter not too far away. He walked a little down the hill he had just climbed and returned to the mare he had tied to a remnant of a lightning-struck tree. Whispering words of encouragement, he untied his mount and led her toward the sheep.

The shelters located at the farthest edges of farmland were supposed to be places where a shepherd and flock could take refuge if they were unable to get back home. Their nature, though, meant they were seldom used, and their maintenance was often overlooked, reducing them to ruins. The one where Samuel took cover had enough room inside for himself, his horse, and his sheep, but was little more than a broken shell. Stone had been piled to form four walls, but without any mortar, the wind whistled eagerly through the gaps between them. The roof was a mix of old fence posts, patchy thatch, and bark strips, either lying atop one another or roughly woven together and held down by a number of heavy blocks of stone. Rain poured through countless holes, and at times, entire sections threatened to peel away as gusts of wind swept under them. There was also no door, so Samuel used what had fallen away from the walls and had collapsed from the ceiling to fashion a crude barricade to keep the sheep inside.

Pushing himself into a relatively dry corner, Samuel pulled his legs to his chest and closed his eyes to wait out the night.

Bleary-eyed, and his body aching, Samuel herded the sheep back into its field and fixed the broken fence to prevent another escape before trudging back to the farmhouse, the smell of freshly baked bread urging him on.

"Samuel!" His mother rushed from the stove, where she had been preparing a vegetable stew, wiping her hands on her apron as she moved, and then throwing her arms around her son. "I was worried sick!"

She was slightly shorter than he was, of average build, and had curling brown hair that hung just above her shoulders.

"What happened, son?"

Samuel's father was taller and leaner than his mother and had a kind face aged by both the elements and the rigours of farm life. A thick mop of grey hair topped his head.

Samuel's stomach growled loudly before he could speak. His mother tousled his hair, then strode back into the kitchen and to the fireplace. She wrapped a cloth around her hand, and then grasped an iron handle protruding from a mound of ash. She shook it, and the ash fell away to reveal an inverted pan. She lifted it, and underneath was a small, round, flat loaf of bread. She grasped it with her covered hand and moved it onto the wooden kitchen table, where she carved it into thick, steaming chunks. She took a stoneware pot from the pantry and sat it next to the bread, then lifted the lid to reveal soft, churned butter.

"The count was off, so I went looking for the missing sheep," Samuel told his father as he ripped apart the chunks of bread and used a dull knife to lather them with butter. "Found the last one about as far as it could go, near the shelter," he mumbled as he ate. "With the storm, I decided to stay 'till the morning."

"How's the shelter?" his father asked. "Haven't been out there for a bit."

"I did what I could, but it needs a bit of work."

His father nodded as he dropped vegetable ends into the stew. "I'll get out there in the next few days to pull it together." He walked to Sam, leaned down, and hugged him. "I'm glad you got home safe."

Samuel nodded as he ate his bread.

"The storm came in strong last night," his father said. "Lot of fencing needs to be checked, barn needs a good look." His father gestured above his head. "And the roof here."

Samuel stifled a groan.

"Let him eat his breakfast first, Rickard!"

Rickard chuckled. "Yes, dear." He leaned in close to Sam so he could whisper into his ear. "Finish up, and I'll see you out front."

A few hours later, Samuel and his father were inspecting a broken post and rail fence at the edge of the property.

"Top rail looks to have split and fallen on the one below and broken it," the young man said. He gestured to a nearby copse of trees. "Sure to find some decent wood in there. Let me have a look."

Rickard nodded as he untied a saddle bag and took out a small hatchet. The butt of both broken rails were still inside the post mortises, and he set about levering them out.

Samuel rode his horse to the edge of the trees before dismounting and taking his hatchet from his saddlebags. He saw a lot of fallen branches, but none were either thick enough or long enough to use. A little way into the trees, he found what he was looking for, however: A long, sturdy bough in the crown of a tree had broken close to the trunk but had not detached. It now hung from the remaining wooden fibres, almost reaching the ground.

Samuel walked around the roughly twenty-foot tree and smiled at his good fortune. It was a cypress, perfect timber for fencing. After some consideration, he decided on his climbing route and clambered up the trunk and into its boughs. He made his way up to the broken end of the branch, and a few good swings of the hatchet brought it down.

"Perfect," his father called out when Samuel emerged from the trees, dragging the branch behind him. Before long, they had cut it into two rails and shaped tenons at each of the ends so they fit snugly into the post mortises.

"One down," his father said as they finished. He laughed as Samuel yawned. "Let's ride on."

~

It was dark when father and son made it back to the house. They had travelled the perimeter of the farmland and fixed seven fences, with two more holding up for now but needing some work before the next storm.

By the time they turned for home, Samuel's horse was as tired as his rider. He was heaving, unwilling to gallop, and taking little notice of anything Samuel did to direct him. The horse trudged its way home and into the stable, staggering when he stopped.

"I think it's time for a big rest, my friend," Samuel soothed after removing the tack and brushing him down. He picked out the hooves and tidied the mane and tail before making his way into his own home.

After devouring two bowls of stew, Samuel washed and collapsed into bed. He was asleep in moments.

Chapter Five

The light *clink* of crystal glasses as the prime minister and king cheered was the rich sound of deep friendship.

"I have to say, Your Majesty, that was perhaps the worst chicken I have ever tasted," the prime minister declared.

The king choked on his white wine as he laughed. "You are more than welcome, Martin," he croaked. "My worst is, as ever, far superior to your best."

The prime minister chuckled and shook his head. "Oh, that's a low blow, Edward!"

A tall man in a fitted, long-tailed suit entered the room. "Your Majesty, My Lord, the Hunting Room fire is stocked, and brandy will be served at your pleasure."

"Very good, Charles," the king said as the prime minister dipped his head in thanks.

"If the men are going to talk about hunting, then I think we should take our drinks to the reading room, Margaret," Christine, the prime minister's wife declared.

As both women departed, the two men rose and left via a door in the opposite wall to the one their wives had just walked through.

It was a short walk to the Hunting Room. A fireplace laden with logs crackled and spat at the chill night as the two men entered. Two oversized, leather loveseats sat side-on to the fire, a small, dark wood, side table next to each, upon which sat a selection of small bites and an empty crystal brandy glass ready for the evening liqueur. Seven great stag heads, each fourteen-pointers, adorned the walls, and between them hung hunting weapons from various ages, ranging from bows to crossbows to muskets.

"We should hunt again, Martin," the king said, gesturing to the walls as he and the prime minister sat opposite one another.

"I would love that, Your Majesty," the prime minister said as he drained the last mouthful of wine. He savoured it in his mouth for a moment before swallowing. "Anything of worth been seen lately?"

"Maybe up in the higher Ranges. I remember hearing something from one of the forts. I'll ask the rangers tomorrow."

"Please do. It feels like an age since we have been out."

The king nodded as he finished his wine. "It does, indeed, and for no good reason. We are well past the errors of your predecessor. Things are better than they have been in decades." His eyes turned distant. "I always feel better when I am away from it all," he said in a quiet voice.

"I know, Edward," the prime minister said, noting the king's mood. "We will get away from it all as soon as we can. Catch our breath. Refresh ourselves."

A thought came to him to change the subject and avoid the king descending into the bleakness that never lay far from the surface. "I almost forgot, have you heard the latest rumour out of The Fringe States?"

The king shook his head.

"Word has it that a man walked out of The Territory a few weeks back! What a ridiculous story—can you believe it?"

Something has happened in The Territory.

Edward choked on a mouthful of brandy. "What?" he spluttered.

"It's absurd, of course." Martin chuckled. "The man was probably homeless in The States's outskirts, and hunger drew him in."

The king smiled, but the smile did not reach his eyes. His fingers went to his chest and rubbed the pendant that used to be his father's, a simple metal crook, the sign of the Shepherd.

"Martin, I want this checked out."

The prime minister frowned. "Check what out? A mad rumour that sprang up from Shepherd-knows-where?"

The king gestured to his friend. "Use our network and contacts in The Fringe States. Find out all there is to know about this tale."

The prime minister's frown deepened. "You are serious, aren't you?"

"Quite serious."

"Edward, you know how this works. We have an arrangement, you, Margaret, and I. You have empowered your wife to assist me in matters of state, and I manage things like this so that you are not burdened with them. Please, just leave things like this to me."

Edward's eye twitched, and his mouth tightened as he was reminded of how things worked.

He cleared his throat. "Martin, I do not ask much of you."

Martin sat back in his chair and stared at the king. "You want us to use our assets to chase this story? We will be a laughingstock, and besides, we will be pulling resources from actual valuable work."

The king sighed and leaned forward. "I know what it sounds like, but—"

"It sounds absurd—"

"Please," the king said, massaging his head with a slightly shaking hand, "please just do it."

"You are ordering me in this matter?"

The king took a deep breath. "I do not want to order you, Martin, I just need you to trust me that I need this looked into, not for me, but—"

Martin held Edward's stare. "It's Nanaya, isn't it?"

The king involuntarily bit his lower lip, and Martin's eyes widened. "It is!" He shook his head. "That woman—"

"She has asked to be informed of anything involving The Territory, and I have no reason to deny such a request," Edward said.

Martin took a deep gulp of the brandy and leaned forward. "Edward, I have always been worried about how much control she has over you. Especially given your condition. What next? Will she want to know about our foreign policies? Will you tell her information about our allies? How much do we really know about her? What her intentions are?"

The king stood and downed his drink with a slightly shaking hand before setting it down firmly on the table beside his chair. "She is someone who has helped and advised my family for generations. I have no reason to believe she has any intentions except continuing to do so. There is no harm looking into this and informing her of what we find. Please, just get it done, Martin." He turned and left.

The prime minister watched him go with a sad expression.

His wife walked into the room, glancing behind her where the king had just departed. "What just happened?"

Martin shook his head. "Nanaya is meddling in things again."

Christine huffed. "She has far too much influence, if you ask me."

The prime minister nodded. "I agree. It concerns me greatly."

Christine laid a hand on his arm. "I fear her meddling will one day cause a confrontation between you both."

The prime minister patted her hand and shook his head. "I am sure it will not come to that. Edward and I have been friends for a very long time. We will work things out."

Chapter Six

"Your Holiness, a man from The Fringe States wishes to see you."

Henri Francois, archbishop of the western kingdom of Royaume d'Occident, did not look up. "Why are you bothering me with this, Claude?" He shuffled a handful of papers together, dipped his quill into a wide ink jar, and added his signature to the last sheet. Reaching across the table, the archbishop took hold of a curling pounce pot and dusted the fine powder contained inside over the wet ink. He placed the paper within a slim leather sleeve faded from use. Without a word, a young man standing nearby stepped forward and took the sleeve from the table before walking out of the room. Henri finally looked at Claude and frowned.

"Well, Claude?"

The thin man rushed to the archbishop's side and dropped to one knee. "Your Holiness, if I have upset you in any way—"

"By the Shepherd, Claude! Just turn this man aside. I am far too busy to be concerned with whatever he wants to sell."

"Holiness, this man, Baraka, is a procurer of antiquities, and your greatness has a few items from him already."

Henri frowned. "I do?"

Claude nodded.

The archbishop waved a hand in the air. "Find time later in the week."

Claude fidgeted but did not leave.

Henri dropped his hands to bang loudly on the table, scaring a loud yelp from his aide. "What is it, man?"

"He is here now, Your Grace, and well, he is eager to see you."

The archbishop sighed. "Fine, fine, I will see him. Show him in."

Returning to the papers before him, the archbishop lost himself in matters judicial. Feeling a chill enter the room, he looked up to find Baraka standing over him.

The treasure hunter was sickly thin, the rags of clothes hanging from a frame with the barest of muscle. A ragged beard hung from a face of sores and lesions.

"Claude!" The archbishop pushed himself as far back from the man as he could. "What are you thinking letting this beggar..." His words trailed away as his gaze was drawn to the man's eyes. Set deep in sunken black pits, they gleamed unnaturally.

Henri opened his mouth, but before he could utter a single word, Baraka lurched forward and gripped his neck. He dimly heard Claude's cries for guards to protect the archbishop before everything dissolved to blackness.

Chapter Seven

The sheep bleated in noisy protest as Samuel hauled on the ewe's forelegs to pull her off her feet and onto her side. Sitting on her shoulders, he reached under her upper foreleg and began shearing her fleece with hand shears that had been used by his family for generations. The ewe was due to lamb sometime within the next two months and needed to be sheared now rather than later to prevent it causing distress to both the ewe and her unborn lamb. The barn had been checked and re-insulated so that after she had lost her coat, she would be safely and comfortably sheltered and ready for her lambing.

The ewe chewed nonchalantly as Samuel worked, first cutting away the fleece from the ewe's belly, then moving to the hind legs, the crotch, then tail, working up across her side before flipping her over and continuing on her other side. Making the last cut, he pulled away a single stretch of wool.

After making sure the ewe had enough feed, the young man returned to the farmhouse to wash, and after another hour, was on his way to The Plough. It was later than he would have liked, but on a farm you worked to its schedule; it did not care for anyone else's.

The inn was a good fifteen miles from Samuel's home. The first half-dozen miles Samuel rode were simple dirt tracks worn in and maintained by his family. A cart's width, they stretched from the farmhouse up and over hills, between woodland copse, and alongside a small stream before meeting what was considered the area's major route: the Main Road. This was another rustic track, but one lined by small stone walls and where regular passage had long since scraped away the soil to leave the underlying stone. Samuel kicked his horse to a trot as soon as he reached it.

The sharp *clack* of the horse's hooves on the road played a steady beat that filled Samuel's ears and mind. He closed his eyes and breathed deeply, filling his lungs with the cool air and savouring the smells of grass, dirt, wood, and leaf that filled his nostrils. The wind around the horse's hooves jostled nearby trees, and distant dogs barked. Samuel lost himself in the natural melody.

The lights of The Plough sparkled ahead as the young man crested a small hill. He had still not passed a single person, but given the later hour, that was not surprising. People were either inside the inn, enjoying a hearty meal or inside their homes, enjoying something similar. His stomach growling, Samuel urged his horse to quicken its step.

It was always a bit of a shock when the door to The Plough was opened, and the quiet, tranquil environment outside was shattered by the raucous environment inside. The cacophony was eagerly welcomed by all, however. The world outside was full of daily strife and struggle, and the world inside the inn offered a respite from that.

Samuel made his way to the far corner of the inn, pausing as he passed various people to answer questions about how his family was doing, how the farm was faring, the amount of damage they had suffered in the storm, and what he thought of the weather to come.

"Ah, the lost lamb finds his way home!"

Samuel smiled as he walked toward his friend, James. The two young men were virtually the same age and of similar build and temperament. Their family's farms adjoined one another, and so the boys had grown up together. Each a single child, they had both found the brother they never had in one another and were inseparable.

James gestured to a tankard full of frothy ale. "Got you one already. You can get the next."

~

A couple of hours later Samuel was sitting on a rise near Main Road. He pointed toward the moonlit peaks of the Kafifi Ranges. "Over there is Southcastle, and I want to see it one day."

James laughed. "How? By herding sheep all over the mountains?"

Samuel stared at the distant mountains. Some rose so high they had snow all year round, their white tips cascading in brilliant white sheets to deep-blue brooks below.

Samuel shook his head. "No, I *am* going to see it one day. You watch, I'm going to travel all over this land."

James sniggered. "You gonna run away, join the circus?"

"Maybe." Samuel chuckled. "Running away, not the circus bit," he said, remembering the last time a circus had visited Trieme. "You remember The Great Alfonso's Spectacular Animal Extravaganza?"

James groaned. "I thought we were the luckiest people alive when they came. I didn't know the only reason they were here was to fix a broken axle on the great cat wagon."

Samuel's lips curled in distaste. "The animals were malnourished, the performers were tired and uninterested, and the great top was dirty and patched with worn rags. No, I am definitely not joining the circus, but somehow, I'm going to get out of here and see more. Be more."

"Same," James agreed. "Got to be more to life than this, right?"

Samuel dragged a stick through the dirt. "You ever read that adventure book The Plough has?"

James snorted. "I reckon we have all read that."

"Remember the passage through the jungle? Discovering the lost tomb?"

James laughed. "*The Romance at the Palace!*"

Samuel burst into laughter with his friend, and the sound of their happiness carried on the breeze to twitch the ears of cattle downwind.

"Don't you just want it?" Samuel asked after a moment. "Even just a little of it? To live like the stories, instead of just—"

"Instead of just this every day?" James finished.

Samuel dragged his stick through the dirt again. "Yeah." His sigh was soulful.

James shrugged. "Both our families have farms, and our parents aren't getting any younger. In the next few years, they will need us more and more." The young man pulled a tuft of coarse grass from the ground and began to tear each blade apart. "I think we missed any chance to get out."

The two young men sat in contemplative silence for a while.

"I mean, we are luckier than a lot of people," James said. "We have farms, and when our parents move on, those farms will be ours. We have land and crops and livestock and decent homes. A lot of people have a lot less."

Samuel nodded. He knew the truth behind the words, but he could not dissolve the knot of unsettlement that was still inside. "Can you imagine, though?"

James nodded. "All the time."

The wind blew, the clouds moved across the night sky, and the two young men sat in contemplation.

"I mean it can't just be this, right?"

James shrugged. "I don't know. Maybe? What else do we do? Do we walk away from our family when they need us? Packing-up whatever we have and walking off to find something?" He tossed his handful of ripped grass. It caught upon the wind and scattered around him, then he threw his hand in the air. "And where do we go and what do we do? We have money for now, but we need to work. Do we work on someone else's farm? What else?" He tore another handful of wild grass from the ground, but this time threw it as far as he could. "I don't know much, Sam. I know some of what my da knows and that's just about the farm. I don't know I can do much else."

Samuel opened his mouth to argue they could do anything they wanted, but his words died on his lips. The world was so much bigger than they were, and maybe they were just not ready to throw themselves into it.

"But imagine if something happened to take us away," he said, voicing his thoughts.

"Just as well imagine finding a pot of gold in your field. It is not going to happen, Sam. This is our lot."

"If something happens, if that opportunity comes around, I'm taking it."

"Sure, Sam."

Samuel looked at his friend. "I know you will be right there beside me."

"Ain't going to happen."

"But if it did?"

"Ain't gonna—"

"But what if it did?" Samuel pushed. "If something happened and you could get away, would you?"

James looked his friend in the eyes and sighed. "Yeah, of course, Sam. I'd take it."

Samuel stared up into the sky. "Just got to hope it happens then."

Chapter Eight

"There..." Edward took a deep breath to settle himself. "There is something. A rumour regarding The Territory."

Nanaya's heart pounded.

"What is it?"

Edward shook his head. "It is probably nothing."

Nanaya pursed her lips, narrowed her eyes, folded her arms. and kept a tight rein on her impatience as she noted Edward's trembling lips and wide eyes. *I can see he is fragile today, but I need answers.*

"Tell me what you have heard."

King Edward stared at her for a moment before walking to a small table, where he poured himself a glass of watered red wine from a small glass pitcher. Her tone stoked the embers of disgruntlement that had been smouldering ever since Martin had reminded him of his place. He took a long slow sip from the glass as he sought composure.

"I have great respect for you," he said. His eyes locked with hers. "But you need to remember that I am the king and afford me at least a little of the respect in turn."

Nanaya ground her teeth. *I don't need you to assert yourself now!*

Her eyes flashed. "You also need to remember who I am. I was here long before your ancestors arrived, and I will be here long after Southcastle is nothing more than a distant memory." She smoothed her dress, taking the time to settle her anger. "I have advised your family in varying capacities for generations, and I have never asked anything of you or your forebears before except some confidentiality and a residency here at the palace. All that I am asking now is that you let me know what you have heard."

The king drained the goblet before placing it back on the side table. "There is a rumour from The Fringe States that a man was seen walking out of The Territory."

Nanaya shivered, her eyes widening.

"I have asked the prime minister to look into this," Edward continued.

"You cannot just ask! You must make sure he does!"

Just leave things like this to me.

Martin's words echoed in Edward's mind, and with them, the resentment of being reminded how weak he was. He gave Nanaya a hard look.

She ignored it. "I must know the truth of this. It will be better for Southcastle if you handle things, but I will get involved if I must."

Edward frowned. "What do you mean?"

"I do not know what will happen if I reveal myself." Her eyes grew distant. "There was once a creature that hunted people like me. If he is still out there, he will come for me, slaughtering anything that gets in his way. Then there is whatever has escaped the tower. That could be worse. Far worse. I must know what is out there."

The king threw his hands in the air. "What tower? What are you talking about?"

The woman looked up at the king, her eyes delving deep into the man before her, assessing and judging how much to say. "You must trust me."

The king shook his head. "This does not make any sense." He filled his glass again. "What is going on, Nanaya? I need more information."

"Edward, please just trust me, and believe—"

You know how this works. I manage things like this. Martin's words flashed in Edward's mind, and anger came with them. His lips trembled. "I can do things, you know. I am not entirely useless!"

Edward sat back down and regarded her with hard eyes. He took a deep breath, and then exhaled slowly, a fragility entering his gaze. "I don't understand. Just explain it to me."

The silence stretched and deepened as Nanaya regarded him. She nodded. *I will not reveal myself. Yet. But I will force Edward's hands. This will terrify him, but that will be a good thing. I need him to do what is required.*

A small part of her, the part that remembered the young woman she used to be, was horrified at the notion of intentionally manipulating and using someone. A shiver of revulsion rippled through her, and as it did, the image of a stout woman with flowering vines for hair filled Nanaya's mind. She wore a cloak of glossy leaves, and her green lips were parted in a warm smile. The woman vanished and was replaced with a much younger petite girl with slightly curling, bobbed, dark hair. Aqua eyes sparkled with amusement from above accentuated cheekbones. Nanaya's heart ached at the memories.

Ninsar. Aru. My dearest friends. Both gone. Both murdered.

A faint sound swam through her thoughts. It was abrasive, yet something about it pulled at her.

What is that?

It grew louder as she focused on it, and then it was suddenly clear. It was the sound of a baby crying.

Nanaya gasped and shook her head to cast away the sound. It fled to the furthest reaches of subconscious.

So much loss.

The cold, hard woman she was now returned.

I will do whatever it takes to stop the past from repeating itself. If that means using one man, I will do it, and if that is not enough, I will confront whatever is out there, regardless of the cost.

Nanaya's eyes narrowed. "I can show you, but it will be confronting. It will aggravate your condition."

The king looked at her for a long moment before nodding.

His world exploded, Nanaya and the room around them shattering like a mirror struck by a hammer.

For a moment, the king was left in a void of absolute darkness and a total absence of sound, then the shattered parts of his vision retreated and pieced themselves back together.

He was looking at a war.

Men screamed as they died and screamed as they killed. Horses screamed as they rode into battle and screamed as they were hacked down. Around and through it all there was another scream that sliced into his mind, the scream of a realm being torn apart.

It was all too much. The noise, the chaos, the intensity. Edward felt as though he was going to burst.

The chaotic symphony of discordance abruptly ceased, and Edward watched the war continue in eerie silence.

Be calm.

Nanaya's voice was close and settling, and Edward felt anxiety bleed away from him.

Where am I?

You are watching the past through my eyes, Nanaya said. *Be calm. This has already happened.*

Edward's vision turned from the battle below, and a dragon filled his sight. It towered perhaps thirty feet above him and was covered in overlapping scales of cloudy white that caught the light and shimmered with oily colour. The dragon stared at him with glowing blue eyes, and the king was transfixed by the absolute raw power that shone within them. With a flex of its mighty wings, it took to the skies.

The king's gaze moved again, and now a huge bipedal figure made from slabs of moss-covered stone gestured toward the assembled masses. It dipped its head and strode away with ground-trembling footfalls.

Look closer.

A section of the fighting grew in his vision. Men in black-and-burgundy dented armour fought against others in the same-coloured armour, but these were sporadically adjourned with dull ivory embellishments.

As he watched, Edward saw that the soldiers without embellishments were hopelessly outmatched. Where they fought with a sense of self-preservation, their opponents fought without thought for their own defence. Hacking and slashing, they were wild storms of blades and scythes and axes that rained down blow after blow on their opposition.

What kind of soldiers are they?

Watch closer.

Again, Edward seemed to move closer to the battle, and he could now see individual figures fighting. Those without the ivory ornamentations were exhausted. Fatigue filled their eyes, laboured their breaths, and slowed their swings, stabs, and blocks. By comparison, their enemies were galvanised. They bounded joyously from one attack to another, tirelessly swinging, jabbing, and hacking with abandon.

One of the disturbing figures filled his eyes. Its head jerked one way, then the other as it searched for its next prey. Its hands flexed on the swords it held in its eagerness to use them. The way it moved was almost feral. It sniffed the air, and as it did, its jaw stretched unnaturally wide to reveal triple rows of small sharp teeth.

As the king stared at it, he realised the ivory adornments to its armour were not embellishments. They were bone. Growths pushing out of its skin and through its armour.

What are these things?

They were once men, now twisted into little more than beasts.

The king watched the armoured creature search for its next victim. With a shriek of joy, it bounded away.

The Fall of Darisam, Nanaya said.

Edward looked around him. The soldiers were being slaughtered. *It's a massacre.*

The world rippled, and then changed. He was now farther away than he had been, and the army was gone, a broken, smoking ruin of a tower stood alone in a land that was, as far as the eye could see, ash.

What happened?

His eyes were drawn to the tower. A curl of black smoke wound up into a storm-laden sky from a ragged, broken top where the upper levels had been destroyed.

The scene abruptly changed, and now the tower stretched out of an ocean of sand.

Once again, his vision fractured and then restored, and he was back in Southcastle.

Edward clutched his head for a moment, massaging his temples and breathing heavily. His hands shook, and he was sweating heavily.

"What you just saw took place a very long time ago," Nanaya said.

"I saw a dragon!"

Nanaya winced as if struck.

"I have heard that ancient texts overseas describe them as once being among us, but they have not been seen for—"

"Over a thousand years," Nanaya finished with a sigh. "I only ever met one; Annungal was his name. He never told me why, but no others came to our aid."

She took a deep breath. "Annungal is gone. What you need to know is that there is another realm, another reality that exists parallel to this one; it is called Kur."

The king's eyes widened at the name of the netherworld from the holy books. "The domain of the Deceiver," he said in a low voice that quivered. He went to the pitcher of wine and poured himself a full glass, from which he took a long drink.

Nanaya shook her head. "The Shepherd, the Deceiver—your religion has produced these characters. What is truth is that Kur is in many ways a mirror, or perhaps a better description would be a shadow, of the reality we live in. Where this realm is material, the other realm is incorporeal. Where this is a place filled with light and life, the other realm is an absence of those. There are things that reside there. I cannot say that they live there, for life does not exist in that realm. *Gallus*, we call them.

"The gallus are pure hate, savagery, and unquenchable desire. They hunger for what they don't have; they hunger for this reality. The memory I shared with you was a battle that took place over a thousand years ago, after the seals between this realm and Kur were breached, and many of them were able to cross from their realm to ours. We stopped them, just, but through our actions, the kingdom of Darisam, and the land where that battle took place, was annihilated. Every living thing, every structure, every natural formation. All that was left was a corrupted blasted land, what you call The Territory, and the remains of the tower that stood over the nexus, inside of which were the seals between the realms."

The king felt anxiety's claws ripping at him as he struggled to make sense of it all.

Nanaya noticed Edward's distress and rose to stand beside him. She placed her hands together and stared into his eyes. "Breathe, Edward. Take a deep breath."

The king nodded and did so.

"Good, and again. Slowly. Breathe in for ten, out for ten. In for ten, out for ten."

Edward closed his eyes as he breathed. Gradually, the tightness in his chest eased, his heart pounded a little less. He opened his eyes again and nodded at Nanaya. The woman gestured back to where they had been sitting. Edward nodded, and the two retook their seats.

Nanaya closed her eyes and grimaced. "I have kept watch over the tower ever since Darisam was destroyed. A few days ago, I found that a door had been opened, and something sealed inside had been released." She fixed Edward with a firm gaze. "I need you to order an investigation into this and send our people into The Fringe States to—"

The king shook his head and took another deep breath to remain calm. "Even with what you've told me, I cannot send Southcastle citizens into another nation without the proper diplomatic discussions and agreements. Besides, such an act must come from parliament."

"They will never do that. You know that. Martin is a cautious man; he would never agree to such a thing."

Edward sighed and rubbed his brow as he tried to find a way forward. "If what you showed me did happen, then you should show Martin, show them all. That would surely convince them an investigation is warranted."

It was Nanaya's turn to shake her head. She walked to the window and stared out at the snow-capped peaks surrounding them. "You know Martin does not trust me. None of them do." She sighed. "Besides, few really know about me. If I show them, then word will spread, and that could bring terror to Southcastle, the likes of which you could never imagine. No. For now I will not act openly."

Her eyes narrowed as she thought.

"Are you sure the rumour is of a man? Not some sort of creature?"

Edward nodded.

"That would mean what has escaped is not a gallus, but one of those that ruptured the seals before. A kishpu like me."

"A what?"

"A kishpu. Someone able to manifest and manipulate certain energies of this realm. Those that broke the seals were very, very strong. If it is one of them..." Her words trailed away. "If it is one of them, I don't know if what I can do is enough to stop it. I don't know if I am strong enough by myself. My powers are protective and spiritual. Before, I had allies, and together, we were strong. We complemented one another."

The woman licked her lips, dropping her eyes and rubbing her hands together in anxious contemplation. "Now that there is only me..." She turned thoughtful for a moment. "Do I dare wake her...?" She shook her head. "No, at least not yet. She will still be healing."

"Can't you just learn to do something else?"

Nanaya shook her head. "It does not work like that. A kishpu's power is aligned with one of the fundamental energies of this realm, and what we are able to do is restricted to the properties of that energy. Some kishpu have a pure affinity for one of those energies and are called elementals, capable of manipulating air, water, fire or stone. Other kishpu have a variant of those powers. I knew an illusionist long ago, and my dear friend Ninsar had an affinity with plants and the natural world. Some kishpu, though it is rare, have powers that are an amalgamation of aligned energies. Ishkur was called the guardian of storms because he was able to manipulate the energies of both water and air. A kishpu only has powers associated with their specific aligned energies though. It is impossible to do something aligned with a different energy."

Nanaya turned away from the window to face the king. "I need to know what is out there."

The king thought for a moment. "I will speak with Martin to see what has been uncovered so far, and then see to putting something to parliament."

"I don't think it will be enough to—"

The king's gaze turned firm, and he drew himself upright. Nanaya's heart fell.

"It must be. There is a way to do things, and this must be followed. I will speak with the prime minister."

Nanaya sighed but nodded. The king dipped his head and left the room.

Nanaya watched him leave. *I will only wait so long, Edward. If I must intervene, I will do so, even if that means the end of Southcastle.*

Chapter Nine

A sickly thin man with a ragged beard and a face of sores and lesions seized his throat—

Henri woke with a start. Heart pounding, he fought to rise through the disorientation of lingering sleep.

It was dark, but enough light was seeping through the window shutters to announce that dawn had just passed.

Dark mahogany wood was above his head, a delicate fat-leafed ivy carved into its surface that wound across the upper rectangular panel to each of the four posts that held it aloft, then twisting down each to come together in the form of a thick block of dense foliage.

A polished shepherd's sceptre, the symbol of the Church, had been carved out of the bed's backboard, and thick drapes hung between each post, almost blocking out the room the bed sat within.

Henri rubbed his eyes and pulled aside the linen covering his night-shirt-clad body before pushing through the curtains.

Bare, thick, wooden beams stretched across the stone ceiling from wall-to-wall, and worn wooden boards covered the floor, with several rectangular rugs of various sizes, weaves, and colours atop them. Each wall was hidden behind a hanging tapestry depicting a significant event from one of the holy books.

A waist-high table stood against the wall opposite the bed with a wide bowl of water sitting in its centre. Henri walked to the bowl and splashed his face with its cold contents.

The chamber door creaked open, and Claude walked in. He gasped as soon as he saw the archbishop. "Your Eminence! I apologise! I did not know you were awake!" Claude rushed over to the religious leader and scrutinised his face, reaching out to touch Henri's brow.

"What are you doing, man?" Henri said, leaning away from him.

"Your Eminence, you have been unconscious for four days!"

Henri stared at his aide. "Four days?"

Claude bobbed his head. "It's true! You cried out when the man attacked you, and then collapsed on your desk. The apothecaries could not find anything that was wrong. They tried smelling salts and leeches and letting your blood, but nothing would rouse you. They were at a loss, and the only thing they could think of was to get you here to your chambers."

Henri shook his head. *Four days?*

A sickly thin man with a ragged beard and a face of sores and lesions grabbing at his throat.

The archbishop gripped the table edge with both hands as the memory vividly filled his mind. He squeezed his eyes shut to force away the image of the emaciated man coming for him, the feel of his skeletal fingers tightening around his throat.

"Your Eminence?"

Henri waved Claude away. "I am just tired."

As he uttered the words, the archbishop felt his strength leave him, and his eyes grew heavy. He weakly gestured at Claude and mumbled a dismissal before climbing back into bed.

He was asleep as soon as his head touched the pillow.

The archbishop stared at the huge trees surrounding him. They stretched high into the sky, far taller than anything he had ever seen, and their trunks were thicker than five or six of the thickest oaks or yews standing side by side.

"Giant burntbarchs. Over three hundred feet tall, thirty feet wide."

Henri turned toward the voice and found a tall man standing next to him. He had short-cropped brown hair and was dressed in a long, tightly buttoned, calf-length blue jacket, the high collar of a white shirt poking out the top, and bright-red stockings stretching from underneath. Henri had seen similar outfits around Château Occidentale. The man smiled. "My name is Adaru." He gestured behind him, and something tall and dark began to appear. "Welcome to the tower."

Of dark, almost black stone, the tower sat fat and wide at its base and tapered as it grew smoothly up, its peak visible but without discernible detail. Lead and stained-glass windows of various sizes dotted the structure at various levels, and both moss and creeping ivy had coloured its majesty, lending a sense of longevity to the structure.

"I am dreaming."

The man smiled at the archbishop. "More or less."

The tower vanished and was replaced by a vaulted ceiling. He blinked and looked around himself. He was in a room among a dozen people, both men and women, all staring at a sheet of slate covering the wall in front of him. On it was drawn a circle above another circle with their edges joining. A thin, horizontal line had been drawn where they joined. A young and slender woman with long, dark hair pulled into a tail behind her head, wearing the dress and shawl of a teacher, stood before the slate and gestured at what had been drawn.

"You know this," she said. "A world of light that we live in and its opposite, a world of darkness called Kur."

Henri hissed. "Kur, a place of corruption, despair, and sin!"

"We have been taught the place of light is good and the place of darkness is bad, even evil. We have all been taught a lie. This representation is incorrect because it has been warped by a lack of comprehension. What is not understood often becomes stylised, exaggerated, or even fabricated. Truth and fact are lost and become fiction and often superstition. This is the reality. There is no *good* place or *bad* place.

There are different places. Different realities, neither better nor worse than another, just different from one another."

"What is this?" the archbishop asked Adaru.

"Lessons," the tall man said.

"These are not lessons! This is blasphemy!"

Adaru gestured to the woman. "Listen."

"Contrary to common teaching," the teacher continued, "we know there are places in this world where this other realm can be felt, even touched—"

Henri shook his head. "I will not listen to any more of these lies!"

"As you wish." The man sighed.

The world fractured, and then dissolved to nothing.

Chapter Ten

"Unverified, unfounded, and if I am honest, I think it's just untrue." The prime minister rifled through a handful of handwritten papers piled on his desk until he found the one he was looking for and waved it before the king. "This has seven eyewitness accounts of the man who supposedly walked out of The Territory. When investigated, they put him in seven different locations, hundreds of miles apart, in a timeframe that would have meant he walked that distance without rest for weeks on end." Martin shook his head as he took a deep breath. "There is nothing here, Edward."

The king rubbed his brow and sighed. He brought his hand before his eyes. His fingers were trembling.

Martin saw. "Are you well, Edward?"

The king waved a hand dismissively. "Bad dreams. I... I am tired, that is all. It is always worse when I am tired." He cleared his throat. "We should look deeper. To be sure."

The prime minister cocked his head to one side and looked at the king. "Why? What do you know?"

Men screamed as they died and screamed as they killed. Horses screamed as they rode into battle and screamed as they were hacked down.

Edward screwed his eyes shut and tried to dispel what Nanaya had shown him. It scared him, stressed him. His hands clenched into fists. He could feel his self-control slipping.

Martin looked at the king with concern. *He is bad today.*

"Edward," he said with cautious tenderness. "What has Nanaya said to you?"

A white dragon staring at him with glowing blue eyes...

The king gripped the sides of his head.

It's too much!

"What is it?" Martin pushed.

"There was a battle."

Martin frowned. "What battle?"

Edward gasped. "She showed me... there was a dragon. A tower."

The prime minister's eyes widened. "What?"

Edward opened his eyes, and Martin leaned back in his chair as he saw the anguish filling them.

"A door in the tower has been opened. Something has escaped."

"Edward, you are making no sense."

"Something has escaped the tower and—"

"Stop, Edward," Martin said as he pushed his chair back and stood. "You are not well. I think I should call for your physician."

"I don't need my physician!"

The prime minister raised his hands in the air. "Easy, Edward."

The king's hands curled into fists. "We need to be sure. We need to know if something has escaped the tower."

"What tower?"

"In The Territory. It's in The Territory."

Martin lowered his hands and shook his head. "Nothing is in The Territory, Edward."

"She showed me!"

"Edward, I am worried about what Nanaya has done to you. You are not yourself."

"You don't believe me?"

"Edward, you are not well today. I will call for your physician. Now, let us leave this matter—"

"No! We need to investigate this further. We—"

The prime minister threw his hands in the air. "Listen to yourself! This is nonsense!"

"Damn it, Martin, I don't need you fighting me on this! Just use our people—"

"I am sorry, Your Majesty," Martin interrupted, "but I cannot do any more without placing a motion before the cabinet to formally activate our intelligence assets, and I am not going to do that. Please calm yourself. You know stress exacerbates your condition."

Edward shook his head. "I just need a reassignment of—"

"They are not there to verify stories, Your Majesty," the prime minister declared in a raised voice." He composed himself and held his hands out to the king. "Edward, let this go."

"I am still the king," Edward snapped. "I am telling you what I need you to do."

Martin shook his head. "This is not how we agreed things would work."

The king ground his teeth as he stared at his friend of years. "I need—"

"No, Edward."

The king and prime minister stared at one another, and with each passing moment, their friendship frayed.

Edward took a deep, ragged breath and turned away.

"Please, Edward, see your physician."

The king ignored the words and left.

Chapter Eleven

Henri sat near the tower, gazing at the lush forest surrounding him.

"Hello, Henri."

The archbishop started at the voice and swung to stare at Adaru. He frowned and then turned away. "I don't want you here."

"That may be, but this is my place, not yours."

Henri ground his teeth together. "Blasphemy," he muttered.

"The holy books tell of miracles, yes?"

The archbishop glanced at Adaru.

"People healed from near death," Adaru continued, "even resurrected."

Henri dipped his head in acknowledgment, even as he frowned. "They do, but—"

"It is all true." Adaru gestured around him. "Lamadu spoke of places where the power of the other realm could be felt. More accurately, there are places where the energies of both realms can almost be tasted. These are the places where miracles can happen. This is such a place."

Henri shook his head. "Miracles are the blessed acts of the Shepherd, they cannot happen anywhere but by his hand. To suggest such a thing is—"

"Blasphemy again?"

Henri threw his hands up in the air. "Well, yes! And to say that it is possible to feel the other realm—"

"Kur," Adaru interrupted. "Using its name—"

"Brings its attention upon you!" Henri, in turn, interrupted.

Adaru scoffed and shook his head.

"Kur," Henri said, his lips curling in disgust at saying the word aloud, "is the Deceiver's place, a place of pain and evil, where the damned are sent to exist in torment for eternity. If it were possible to feel such a place when in this world, then surely only the foulest, the most perverted of people, would be able to do so."

Adaru sat next to the archbishop. "I can see this troubles you. Would it help to know I was once in your position?"

Henri frowned.

"I was a priest once. Not as advanced in position as you, but a member of the Church, nevertheless." Adaru stared off into the distance, and his eyes lost a little focus as memories of the past filled his mind. "I was searching for the truth when I found this place, well, the tower did not exist then, but I found this location. I was lost, always searching for meaning, meaning for my life and everything that happened to me and meaning for the world being the way that it was. When I first heard about what was happening here, it was like a lantern had been lit in the darkness. The sick were being healed, the weak were made strong."

Adaru turned to Henri, and his eyes sparkled with intensity. "What I found was so much more and gave me answers to questions I did not know I needed to ask." He leaned in close to the archbishop. "Absolute enlightenment, Henri. This is not a place that should worry you; this is a place that can give you everything you want. Don't you want more than a life full of administration and politics? Don't you want to get back to what brought you to the church in the first place? What brought me to my church? Make strong what is weak. Ensure the mistreated and downtrodden are never harmed again."

The archbishop stared at the man. "Of course, that is what I want," he admitted.

"You can realise it, Henri. You can make that happen."

The archbishop shook his head. "There is no place that will deliver that. Only by guiding and teaching—"

"In order to teach you need to learn, Henri."

Henri's eyes narrowed as he considered Adaru's words.

"Just as you did when you first entered your church, open your mind to what you do not know. Learn the truths behind your holy books, Henri."

The archbishop licked his lips. He could not help himself; his curiosity was piqued. "How?"

Adaru smiled and reached out his hand. "Take my hand. Let me show you. Let me all the way in, Henri."

Henri raised his hand. Adaru grasped it.

The archbishop woke and stared at his ceiling. He sat up in his four-poster bed and rubbed his eyes. He sighed. "Just a dream."

He lay back down. As sleep welcomed him back into its embrace, he felt a slight chill from somewhere deep inside that stretched throughout his body.

Chapter Twelve

The rhythmic rocking of the sedan chair stopped and snapped the archbishop's eyes up from a recent court report. He rapped his knuckles on the wooden panel beside him. "What is it, man? Why have we stopped?"

A small square in the centre of the sedan's door unlatched with a rattle of chain and dropped away on small metal hinges to reveal the face of one of the archbishop's guards.

"My apologies, Your Grace. A beggar blocks the way. We are moving him on."

Go to him.

Henri's retort to the guard died on his lips as Adaru's voice caressed his mind.

Adaru?

Flames of fear surged in his chest but were immediately smothered by a numbing wave of peace.

Do not be afraid. All will become clear. Now, go to him.

Adaru was more than just insistent. The words were a command that Henri was powerless to refuse.

"Let me out."

"My Lord? We will shortly be—"

"Now."

"At once, Your Grace."

The sight of the archbishop stepping from his sedan stopped people in the street, and a buzz of excitement grew. Nobility were rarely seen in these streets out of their sedans, and within moments, a sizable crowd had gathered.

A figure wrapped in dirty rags lay in the centre of the road with guards standing their distance and prodding it with the butts of their rifles. Henri gagged and held a hand to his nose and mouth as a gust of air swept between the buildings to either side of him and brought a putrid stench of urine, faeces, and stale sweat.

Go to him.

Henri approached the figure and waved away the guards, who happily and hurriedly moved away.

"You must move, my son," Henri called in a muffled voice from between his fingers.

The figure moaned as it tried to rise, but it was weak, and it fell back to the cobbled street. As it hit the stone, its rags fell open, revealing an emaciated male body covered in weeping sores.

"Leper!"

The assembled crowd gasped and scrambled over each other to back away.

Touch him.

Henri hesitated.

Touch him!

The voice was hard, demanding to be obeyed.

The archbishop reached out to the leper.

The guards yelled at him to stop.

The archbishop's hands closed around the man's swollen head, his fingers resting against the growths that distorted the man's face. He felt something stir inside himself, like something was uncoiling. It made him want to vomit. He gritted his teeth as whatever was inside stretched through his arms to his fingertips.

~

Nanaya clutched her stomach as sudden pain convulsed inside her. It was as if the core of her being was violently reacting to something.

"Lady Nanaya, what is wrong?" King Edward called from his throne, the petitioner before him staring curiously at the woman.

~

The leper's eyes rolled back into his head, and a harsh, guttural growl escaped from his lips, growing in pitch and volume until he was howling and shaking uncontrollably.

The crowd shifted uneasily.

Henri gripped the man's face harder, the tips of his fingers turning white as the skin beneath them turned dark red with the pressure he applied.

"Stop!" someone in the crowd yelled.

Harder.

"You are hurting him!"

Henri ignored them and pressed harder.

~

Nanaya fell to her knees, gasping and clutching her body.

"Nanaya!" Edward jumped up from his throne and ran to her side.

Nanaya's eyes were wide with not only pain, but also with the memory of feeling this before.

~

The leper stopped howling and sat, panting, staring at the archbishop with wide eyes.

Henri's lips pulled back in an acute grimace as sharp stabs of pain rolled up and down his arms.

The crowd erupted into exclamations of surprise.

The man reached up to his face with trembling fingers and touched his sores. His mouth fell open as he felt the swellings flatten and then disappear.

"He is healed!"

The man fell forward into Henri's arms and began weeping.

He is the first, Adaru whispered. *This cannot be mine to do alone. I need hands. Tools. You must find more.*

"Tell me your name, friend," Henri asked, stroking the man's hair as he continued to cry into the archbishop's sleeve.

"Diers, Your Grace," the man managed between sobs.

"Diers," the archbishop repeated. "Are there more poor unfortunate souls like yourself?"

"Oh, yes, My Lord," the leper said eagerly.

The archbishop did not correct the improper use of the lordship title. To his surprise, he quite liked it.

All around him, the crowd whispered in awe at what had just happened, and many reached out with trembling hands to touch him reverently.

"We are in the quarry," Diers said.

Go there. Now.

"Take me there."

Nanaya continued to hold herself as the pain subsided.

"My Lady, are you well?"

She looked to the source of the voice and was surprised to find the royal physician crouching beside her and staring at her with a worried expression. She had not noticed him arrive. She glanced around and saw that the chamber had been cleared of petitioners, and only the king, his physician, and the foot guard remained, all looking at her uneasily.

She stared at the king with wide, fearful eyes. "I was wrong."

"My Lady," the physician pressed, "please tell me what happened. What is wrong?"

Nanaya ignored him and stared at the king as she brought trembling fingers to her lips. "I felt it, Edward. Something *has* escaped the tower, and it is in the West."

The royal physician frowned at the lack of formality, but the king waved him away. Bowing, the physician gave Nanaya a last curious look before leaving the chamber.

The king took his place, crouching beside her and offering his hand to help her stand.

"It's Kur," she gasped. "Something is using its power." Nanaya's eyes grew wider with each word. "I was wrong. What has escaped is not a kishpu. It is something else."

Chapter Thirteen

The quarry sat in the country regions of Terre Occidentale near Terragricole, the agricultural centre of the Royaume d'Occident. The journey there would take about a month. The archbishop made his way back to the basilica so that he could transfer from his sedan chair to a horse-drawn carriage more suitable for the extended travel.

The basilica stood within the high fortified walls of Château Occidentale. When the capital had been settled and work had begun on the castle, the archbishop at that time had demanded a majestic building of his own on the same site. After a period of years, the tug of war between church and state had been won by the then Western king, as while the basilica was built on the same site as the capital castle, it was set lower down the slope, upon which the castle had been built, and closer to the main gate. The castle, therefore, loomed over the basilica, something that had annoyed the Church ever since.

Twelve men-at-arms, permanently stationed at the basilica to accompany the archbishop on any extended travel, hastily emerged from the nearby buildings as he approached. The marshal of the castle also appeared and ordered horses from the stables and clerks to bring a carriage for the religious leader to travel in. By the time the archbishop's sedan chair had come to a stop, the horse-drawn carriage was prepared and waiting.

"Come," Henri invited Diers as he climbed in. As soon as they were seated, the carriage set off.

~

Henri stared out of the carriage window into the passing countryside, but it passed him by unseen. Only two things filled his mind. The first that somehow Adaru was speaking with him and the second that it did not concern him at all.

The archbishop knew he should be terrified at what was happening, yet he was far from feeling that way. In fact, he felt completely calm and at ease. He closed his eyes and took a deep relaxed breath, letting himself be rocked by the constant rhythmic sway and bounce of the carriage over the stone road.

The road and the carriage were gone, and Henri was standing on a small hill, staring out over a vast forest. The trees started about half a mile away from the last buildings, marking the town outskirts, and stretched as far as the archbishop could see. Here and there, he could see woodcutters hard at work, felling the mighty trunks, and on newly created paths, he could see wagons transporting timber to the sawmill for preparation.

His perspective shifted to wide clearing. Newly erected wooden scaffolding towered above ancient stone foundations.

"The tower will be magnificent when it is finished."

Henri turned and found Adaru standing beside him.

"How were you able to talk to me before when I was awake?"

Adaru smiled. "We are close now."

Henri opened his mouth to speak.

"How do you feel about what happened to Diers?"

Henri found the words he was just about to utter catching in his throat. "That was the Shepherd working through me."

Adaru chuckled.

Henri gestured to the tower. "What is it for?"

"A place of learning. A means of enlightenment and enablement. A place of power to usher in a new era."

"What is going to happen at the quarry?"

"Diers is not the only miracle you are going to perform today."

"How did that happen?" Henri asked with genuine wonder in his voice. "I felt—"

"It is time," Adaru said.

Henri startled awake as the carriage hit a series of rocks, and without any padding, the shock was sent painfully straight into the base of his spine. For a moment, he didn't know where he was.

"Your Holiness," Diers said. "We have arrived."

Looking out of the carriage window, Henri saw walls of yellow rock rise alongside him as they descended into the quarry. After a moment, their forward motion stopped, and there was a sharp rap on the door.

"We are here, Archbishop," one of the men-at-arms announced.

Pulling his robes up to bare his pasty ankles, the archbishop unlatched the carriage and stepped out into a sunlit world of dust and rock.

Henri squinted in the bright daylight and fell into a coughing fit as perpetual dust eddies swept ground sandstone into his throat. Holding a pale-yellow handkerchief to his lips, the archbishop hacked into the cloth for a moment before the irritation had subsided, but even after he had finished coughing, he left the cloth on his lips to breathe through.

"You don't notice it after a while," Diers said from beside him. "The coughing, the dry itchiness in the back of your throat. The film that covers whatever there is to eat, that covers your face when you wake, and becomes a thick consuming sludge when it rains. It becomes part of you."

"This place is awful."

"Awful? This is paradise!" Diers moved to face the archbishop. "Imagine, if you can, having leprosy. Being a leper. Your skin thickens in lumps all over your body, you lose your sense of touch; your nose, ears, fingers, and toes deform. It becomes harder and harder to talk, to hear, and to taste anything. You are ill all the time. You become a monster, and worse, if people come near you, they become monsters. So not only are you repulsive, but you are also feared and hated by everyone because you can take loved ones away. You destroy lives. You take lives."

The leper reached down and scooped up a handful of broken stones. "So you hide. You keep to the dark places, the places people don't go. You push yourself apart from everyone and everything, not because you want to—far from it! You crave a kind touch, a kind word, an embrace, a warm fire, and a warmer conversation. You go alone into the dark because you have to, because if you don't, someone will kill you. Filth and despair become your loved ones because they are the only constants in your life." Diers tossed the stone to the ground. "Until you come here."

He stood and walked a little way away from the archbishop before turning back and reached out a hand. "Let me show you."

Henri hesitated for a moment before nodding and taking the man's hand.

A guard gasped. "Your Holiness!"

They cannot harm you.

Henri waved the worried guards away as he walked with Diers down a slight incline and around a boulder that stood to his shoulder. The quarry floor opened before them, and filling the basin were sandstone buildings of various sizes, clotheslines fluttering different coloured cloths, and the noise of many people.

Shuffling figures began to emerge from between the buildings, men and women of all shapes and sizes. Each was covered from head to toe in loose sheets and clothes that hid their appearance, and every one was bent forward and hunched to some degree.

A light breath of air swept the potent stench of decay to his nostrils. Henri gagged and clutched at his mouth and nose.

"It's the sores," Diers said. "They weep continuously. The worse the affliction becomes, the more sores a person gets, and the more those sores weep. It soaks into clothes, bedding, everything. The skin around the sores becomes so inflamed that it's incredibly painful to the touch, and many stop changing their clothes as they stick to the pus, and removing them tears the sores."

Henri watched more and more shuffling figures appear until he was surrounded.

"Diers?"

The rasping, slurred, yet still distinctly feminine voice came from a short, slight, and twisted figure that moved awkwardly away from the others. Diers moved to meet it.

"Diers, is that you?" the woman asked again from within the countless layers of stained cloth that covered her head. Her words were deliberately spoken yet distorted.

Diers held out his hands toward the woman, who shrank back away from him. The light of a nearby torch shone on the blemish-free skin of his hands, and gasps came from the lepers.

"It is me, Marion."

"How is such a thing possible?" Marion whispered in a voice full of awe as she inched a little closer to the young man.

Diers turned and pointed to Henri. "The archbishop healed me!"

The lepers that could speak all did so at once, those who could not grunted and made what noises they could, turning to one another as they tried to make sense of what had just been said.

"It is true!" Diers said. "He touched me and healed me!"

Marion moved toward Henri. "Is it true?"

Henri nodded.

The woman turned around to look at the other lepers around her. They had all fallen silent and were watching. Waiting. Hoping.

Show them.

Henri's arms rose with his hands spread wide as if Adaru's words had moved them.

Marion moved within reach.

Henri tenderly placed his hands on her head. A pressure built inside him, and as it did, words that were not his tumbled from his mouth. "Watch me, Diers," Henri said. "You must learn how I do this so you can do similar things."

Diers stared at the archbishop. "I will be able to heal?"

The archbishop wanted to shake his head, and he was confused at the words he had spoken, but instead, he felt his mouth twitch as if a smile had been smothered. "Of a fashion."

Just as Diers had done, the woman moaned and thrashed under the archbishop's touch, but unlike in the city, here, no one cried out in concern. These people had lived with their death sentence for years, and what was happening before their eyes offered hope.

After a time, the woman's cries and violent movements ceased, and she collapsed.

No one spoke. They watched with bated breath as Marion stirred. Trembling fingers on bandaged hands reached up and tugged back the thick hood that hid her face.

A striking young woman looked out on the world for the first time in a very long time. The cataracts had disappeared from eyes that now shone bright green. Her face was no longer red and bloated by thick skin growths; it shone smooth and unblemished by no more than a few wrinkles of age. Indeed, the woman looked at least a decade younger than she was.

She pulled the hood off her head. Her dry and mottled shaved scalp, once covered in bloody cuts and sores, was now blemish-free and smooth. Her flat nose, caused by the erosion of nasal cartilage, was whole once again. She stretched, closing her eyes, and a breath escaped perfect parted lips as a whispered sigh. For the first time in over a decade, she could stand tall.

She opened her eyes and stared at Henri, tracing every line of his face. "I am healed!" Her voice was rich and strong. She slapped a hand over her mouth in shock as her eyes widened at the sound of her own voice. Tears flooded her eyes.

The lepers reached for the archbishop.

Henri wanted to back away, but he was not in control of his body.

Be at peace.

Adaru's words washed away Henri's anxiety.

And so it begins.

Chapter Fourteen

Nanaya dried her face of the water she had just washed it with and took a deep breath as the pain that had wracked her body subsided. She walked out to her balcony and stared toward the mountains, but the peaks were not what she thought about.

I remember...

What had happened to her before in the audience chamber had been bad, but this had been far worse. The use of power from the other realm had not just assaulted her, it had battered her without pause, to a point where she had almost lost consciousness. When it had eventually subsided, she lay curled and moaning on her chamber floor.

Just as I did over a thousand years ago. Then it had been the floor of my home that I pulled myself up from. She could almost hear, again, the cries of her baby daughter, which had filled her ears, and she gasped with the acute agony that the memory brought.

The energies of Kur have been used to transform something in this realm just like before, Nanaya thought. *Many things,* she corrected herself as she thought on how relentless the assault had been. As her mind turned to what had happened before, the image of a tall, muscular man with twin antlers stretching from his head appeared in her mind.

A painful sense of loss rippled through Nanaya. She wrapped her arms around herself. Her composure cracked. She was overwhelmed by terrible sadness, and for a moment, she was once again the vulnerable young woman she had been. She placed a palm on her stomach as long buried grief unexpectedly broke free of its bonds.

No. I will not think about that.

Nanaya took a deep breath and stood straight. She walked into her sitting room and stared up at the map covering one wall. She pictured the land, the verdant woods and crop-filled fields, the dusty roads, the hamlets and towns. The people, the farms with their animals and crops, the Helba Ocean with its abundance of fish, the Kafifi Ranges and their wildness. Her eyes swept further, into Royaume d'Occident.

That's where it is, whatever has escaped the tower.

She gazed at the western kingdom.

This is where I felt Kur's energy being released.

She shivered as she recalled the agony that had seized her moments ago.

There is no way I can stand against what caused that. She shook her head. *I have truly failed in my duty. Kur is loose in this realm again, and this time, there is nothing to stop it.*

Nanaya leaned forward, placing her brow against the map, and considered what she should do.

The armoured creature jerked its head from side to side, sniffing the air. It turned toward Edward and opened its mouth impossibly wide, shrieking as it lunged for him.

Edward jerked up from sleep with a sharp cry.

"What is it?" his wife gasped as she was shocked from sleep.

The king took several deep breaths and tried to calm himself. He ran a hand through hair dampened with night terror sweat. "A bad dream," he managed after a while. "Just a bad dream, that's all."

Margaret sat up and stroked his arm. "That is the third this week, and you had them last week, too. Will you tell me what is happening?"

Edward shook his head. "Nothing. Please go back to sleep." He swung his legs over the side of the bed. "I need to walk this off," he said as he threw his night robe around himself, and then left the bed chamber.

"May I assist you, Your Majesty?"

Edward forced a smile onto his face as he nodded at the foot guard. "Just some trouble sleeping. I think I will take a walk."

The guardsman nodded and remained at his post.

The king plodded through the silent inner corridors of the palace, trying to shake the image of the creature from his mind, but it would not go. He scrubbed sleep from his face with one hand.

He came near a small reading room and reached out to open the door.

"May I get you something, Your Majesty?"

The king turned sharply at the sound of the voice.

"I am sorry, Your Majesty," a young woman apologised with a deep curtsy. "I did not mean to startle you."

Edward waved away her concern. "My fault for being awake and not being in bed where I should be." He gestured at the door. "I am going to sit for a while. Please ensure I am not disturbed."

The woman curtsied again and made to leave.

"Wait," the king said. "On second thought, please bring me a brandy."

"Of course, Your Majesty," the woman replied and departed as Edward opened the door and stepped inside.

The room was dark, with shutters pulled closed over each window. Leaving the door open so that light from the corridor could spill inside, Edward walked to the fireplace. It had been cleaned and stacked with fresh kindling, and thick logs were piled neatly to one side. He picked up a curved piece of iron called a *strike-a-light* sitting next to the wood in one hand and a piece of flint in the other. A few purposeful strikes later, a small fire was burning.

A knock on the door heralded the woman returning with a glass of brandy. Edward thanked and then dismissed her and sat in an armchair by the fire, staring into the flames.

The creature in blood armour that was punctured by sharp growths of bone jerked its head from side to side.

Edward screwed his eyes tightly shut and then took a big gulp of brandy, willing the burn of it down his throat to scour away the image of the horror.

Nightmares, magic, dragons, and Kur.

Edward swirled the brandy in his glass with a trembling hand, staring into its illuminated amber depths. His heart was pounding. His chest felt tight.

He drained his drink and stared into the flames.

Chapter Fifteen

"And for a number of reasons, I firmly believe a review of regional taxation is required. Let me elaborate on each one."

The archbishop sat in his customary position along the long, wooden table in the narrow room where the Conseil du Roi, or King's Council, of Château Occidentale met. Around him sat the heads of noble houses with hereditary rank, lands, and titles, and the head of the royal army, General Didier Bron. With himself they represented all of the seats of power in the West. Henri took a sip of cognac as Count Terragricole spoke.

"My lands are already taxed heavily by the Crown, my people already impoverished by the rates they are forced to pay..."

Terragricole continued to talk, but the archbishop did not hear him. All he could think about was what had happened in the quarry. After Marion, the lepers had eagerly come to him, and one by one, he had healed them all. The archbishop glanced at his hands as he rubbed them together. He had felt power coursing through him as he had healed them, an energy that came from somewhere deep inside him and reached out through him to restore the health of the unfortunate men and women.

More, Henri, Adaru whispered. *They are more than they were before. You will see.*

"I know you are concerned for the well-being of your people, Count Terragricole, and I sympathise." The king's voice broke the archbishop from his thoughts and pulled him back to the present. "I seem to be hearing of this suffering of our common folk often."

The archbishop inwardly groaned at the king being so easily manipulated yet again.

You are hearing about this so often because lords raise this at every council meeting. A review of taxes is a thinly veiled call to either reduce royal levies or reform their method of collection, either way, introducing an opportunity for Terragricole to increase his income.

"I think if everyone agrees, there is a case to review—"

"If I may," the archbishop interrupted as a hungry, eager gleam entered the eyes of each of the assembled lords. "This is indeed an important matter. As you know, the tithe the Church collects is a tenth of available income, and therefore, we would welcome any review of taxation that might enable our children to give more freely without fear of hunger or impoverishment."

The counts fidgeted in their seats and glanced at one another nervously. The flames of greed died in their aristocratic eyes as they saw their additional wealth diverted into Church coffers.

"I would also imagine that General Bron would welcome any review that would enable the lords to spend more on the preparedness of their feudally required soldiers for his forces. Moreover, a review of royal levies might enable an increased income to bolster the standing royal army under the general."

A broad smile grew on the general's face, and his eyes twitched toward Count Premiercolons, who flushed in anger at the prospect of his military superiority being threatened.

Count Terragricole also glanced at the other count. Premiercolons held a powerful position in the kingdom and had unbridled ambition. He was not someone to antagonise.

"More thought is probably required, Your Majesty," Count Terragricole mumbled to the grunting agreement of the other nobles.

The archbishop's lips twitched into a slight smile of satisfaction.

"Well, that is settled, then," the king said with a smile, oblivious to the political undercurrents. "My lords, if there is nothing else, I will let you have your leave."

Henri stood with the others as the king departed.

"Archbishop," the king called over his shoulder as he left. "Please come to La Chambre des Lys when you are ready."

Henri bowed to the king, who left the room without another word, followed by the counts.

"Nicely done, Your Eminence."

Henri looked at the general, who dipped his head in acknowledgment.

"The counts are balanced," Bron said. "Perhaps more precariously than we would like, but they are balanced nonetheless, and that ensures peace and stability. Let us try to maintain that as long as possible."

The archbishop leaned on the back of his chair and gestured to the general. "I would have thought the prospect of growing your forces to surpass those of Premiercolons would have been appealing."

Didier chuckled. "Premiercolons is an ass to be sure, and I would have immense satisfaction stamping military authority in the West and cowing his lauded army." He shook his head. "But unless something catastrophic happens, Premiercolons will never do anything more than posture. He knows, as we all do, that even if he were to unite the other houses, which is incredibly unlikely, especially after Villedepêch's independence and his elevation to count, any conflict would be bloody beyond measure and have no surety of victory." The general knuckled the small of his back and groaned. "Besides, I am well into my later years and no longer have a younger man's appetite for conflict and bloodshed."

Oh, I doubt that, Adaru said.

Henri smiled and bowed. "We are aligned, My Lord."

Didier dipped his head.

Henri suddenly felt a chill expand from somewhere deep inside him and fill his body.

"General."

Henri heard himself speak, but he had not intended to.

"I would appreciate it if you could visit my chambers at your earliest convenience."

Henri felt terrified. It was not him speaking.

Relax, Adaru soothed, and the words brought with them numbing tranquillity.

"I have something I would like to discuss with you," Adaru said through Henri's lips.

Bron raised his eyebrows with obvious curiosity. "I will indeed, Your Eminence."

King Louis popped a grape into his mouth as he regarded the archbishop. "What happened, Your Eminence?"

Henri blinked. His mind was foggy. "I'm sorry, Your Highness?"

"The leper, Archbishop. It is being called a miracle."

Henri looked around La Chambre des Lys, the Room of Lilies, as he tried to collect his thoughts. Dozens of the large flowers were collected in vases of various sizes scattered around the room. He took a deep breath, and his nostrils were filled with the flowers' rich fragrance that also cleared his mind.

"It was indeed a gift from the Shepherd."

Adaru chuckled in Henri's mind.

"I am at a loss to explain what happened," Henri admitted. A thought came to him, but he was not sure where it had come from. "It is not without precedence, however."

"How so?" The king leaned forward.

"Saint Masier was said to have restored sight to a pilgrim from Southcastle in the founding days of Royaume d'Occident, and in more recent years, Saint Barome de Kovi was widely reported to have healed a child's palsy."

"Amazing," the king said in wonder. He yawned loudly. "I apologise, Your Holiness. I have been feeling quite strung out of late."

The archbishop bowed low. "How may I be of service, My Liege?"

The king huffed and cast him a withering look. "I wish I knew. Master Pierre is petitioning a new performance for which there seem to be a myriad of requirements. Mistress Belange requires my patronage for the theatre, and—" He shook his head. "The list is endless." The king rubbed his brow, and for a moment, the two men sat in silence. "Did you really heal that man, Your Eminence?" the king whispered.

He does not need to know about that, or what happened at the quarry. Stall him. It will all be over soon.

Henri paused as Adaru's voice spoke in his mind. "I don't know, Your Majesty," he said with a little hesitation as he chose his words. "There was no conscious thought or act. I was just there, and then through me whatever happened, happened."

The king nodded thoughtfully. "Where is that man?"

"I have him cared for close by, My King. I visit him regularly and hope to see his apparent rejuvenation remain for good."

Well done, Henri.

The king nodded. "Amazing. Keep me informed, Archbishop," he said before returning his gaze to the platter of fruit in front of him.

Understanding the audience was at an end, the archbishop bowed and left, but as he walked away, he could not help but dwell on Adaru's words.

It will all be over soon.

Chapter Sixteen

It was silent in the chapel.

King Edward stood before the altar and stared at its pitted surface.

Was this the altar the Shepherd was sacrificed on?

The king took a deep breath and then sighed.

Of course not. Was there ever a Shepherd in the first place?

The king walked to the stone alcove behind the altar where seven ornate leather-bound books, *the* holy books, were shelved. He stared at the first.

The story of creation, he remembered. *When the great leviathans ruled the seas, the behemoths the land, and the skies belonged to the dragons.*

Overlapping scales of cloudy white, glowing blue eyes.

Edward shuddered at the recollection.

He traced a finger across the spines of the books until he reached one with *IV* stitched into it and slid it out of its resting place. He placed it on the altar and opened it. He had not read this book since childhood.

When the barrier between the realms is weak, the dark entities of Kur are able to cross from their reality to ours. First are always the sukkal, the emissaries, insidious and seductive things that whisper promises to fulfil any desires. They entice first a taste, and then an indulgence in the foul power of the other realm, every use of which corrupts our world and weakens the barrier between this place and Kur.

Edward delved further through the book.

After The Crossing, when the evil of Kur had seeped heavily into this place, turning father against son and mother against them all, when the crops twisted and decayed yet grew strong in their poison and spread their malignant seeds across the land, when the doorway between this place and that place trembled and splintered, that was when one of the nagiru appeared. A herald. Men and women gave their flesh to it, giving their bodies so that it could step from its dark place to ours. It gazed upon this place with eyes of damnation and bent its will to own it. As it worked, the voices of The Choir could be heard from the dark place, rejoicing that the malku, the princes of Kur, were coming.

The king turned to the end of the book.

Those who had danced on the edge of damnation watched their world burn from the few ships that had escaped the apocalypse, ships that the Shepherd had protected, even though those huddled on their decks had cast him aside. Everything fell to dust before their eyes: trees, buildings, mountains, rivers, and the people who ran screaming for the shores. Those on the boats knew at the end that they had been wrong, and they had been used. They begged the Shepherd for forgiveness, and he forgave them, holding a simple crook high in the air as he shielded them from destruction and shepherded them toward salvation.

Edward closed the book and lay a hand on its cold cover. His fingers trembled with a quiver of anxiety.

The Fall of Darisam.

Images of the battle that Nanaya had shown him burst vividly into his mind. Edward shivered, and it was not due to the chill of the air in this still place.

"Troubled, my son?"

The king turned at the sound of the elderly voice. The Dean of Southcastle walked down the aisle between the pews toward his monarch. A heavy, deep-red silk cape hung over his shoulders, open at the front to show a white, double-breasted cassock buttoned at the neck and held at the waist by a cincture dyed a rich, deep red. The cape was fastened at his breast by a simple metal brooch in the shape of the Shepherd's crook.

"Dressed formally today, Father?"

"Matthew. Call me Matthew, Edward. I have known you for almost all the twenty years that I have been dean." Matthew smiled fondly at the king as he approached, hazel eyes shining in the light of the candles that illuminated the dim interior. "Truth be told, I feel the cold more each year, and this cloak helps keep me warm. What brings you to your chapel, Your Majesty?"

"Oh, if this is anyone's chapel it is yours, Matthew," Edward said. "Besides, I would not want Bishop Gartner hearing that said."

The dean chuckled. "Quite," he agreed. "A precious man. I think the fact that this chapel is a Royal Peculiar, and as such, is under your jurisdiction rather than his diocese often inflames his gout."

Edward smiled, but his eyes remained pained.

"You rarely visit here," the dean said as he walked around the altar. "After your formal year of service in the church, I have only seen you on days of celebration or at special events. I know you are not a religious man, My King." He gestured to the books. "But I saw you reading from these. Was there anything in particular you were looking for?"

"There is a lot I am looking for at the moment."

The dean nodded. "I understand. You have a lot of responsibility."

Edward sighed. He looked at the books. "Where do you think those tales came from?"

Matthew raised his eyebrows. "*Tales?* I thought I taught you better than that, Edward."

The king shook his head. "Not today, Matthew. I am not here for a lecture." His eyes narrowed. "The way these books are written is like the writer was there." The king gestured to the book before him. "Like the events in this one."

The dean looked at the pages Edward had been reading. "Ah, the Fall of Darisam."

Edward nodded.

"You are a smart man, so I ask you this: Who could possibly have been at the events described in each of these books?"

The king took a deep breath. "You are of course referring to the Shepherd."

Matthew raised a hand to stop the king saying anything further. "Yes, I am talking of the Shepherd. Did he write each text? Maybe. Or he may have told another who then wrote down the Shepherd's words." The dean shook his head. "It does not matter who wrote the books; what matters is what is written. These books are our guide away from the Deceiver to a just and righteous life where the weak are protected, the infirm cured, and where spite and anger and hatred are pushed aside for love and a desire to see everyone live in peace and harmony."

"I understand that," Edward said. "I understand their value." He rubbed his brow and licked his lips as he thought. He took a moment before looking the dean in the eyes.

"What if it is all real?"

Matthew shook his head. "I am not following you."

"What if everything in these books is not just a lesson, but a true account of something that happened?"

The dean smiled. "That is, of course, what they are."

"But if that is true, if something like the Fall of Darisam did happen, then the Shepherd is real. The Deceiver is real."

The dean motioned for the king to join him on a pew in the first row. "It sounds like this is the first time you have considered such a possibility."

"It is," Edward conceded. "I have always thought of the books as works of fiction, stories and fables to scare people away from doing what has been decided to be wrong and into doing what has been decided as the right way to live."

"Decided by whom?"

Edward gestured at the dean and then all around him. "The Church." He pointed at himself. "The monarchies. People of power. That is not important. What—"

"But it is important," Matthew interrupted. "It is not us who have arbitrarily decided what is right and what is wrong. Rather, it is through the Shepherd and the Deceiver that we have learned those truths. The people of Darisam believed in many gods. There were gods of the air and sea, fertility, and even livestock. People named their children after them. There are texts that describe tales they believed in, such as the war god Ninurta entering Kur, but in doing so, caused destruction and famine to wash over the land. Others speaking of seven princes of Kur, of huge sea monsters called leviathans. These are stories. They hold no moral guidance. They are just tales. Only the Shepherd guides us along a path where our actions enrich ourselves, those around us, and indeed everything that lives in this world. It is a path of fulfilment, longevity, and renewal. The Church exists to help people find that path and to walk it when, at times, it can seem impossibly hard and its rewards painfully out of reach."

"And what of Kur?"

The dean held his hands up before him. "Edward, we do not speak of the Deceiver's realm carelessly in any place and especially not here in the Shepherd's house."

"I mean no offence, Father," the king said, leaning forward. "But I must know."

The dean stared at the king, scrutinising his face and looking deep into his eyes as he sought the reason for the curiosity. "What has happened to make you ask about that place?"

The king took a moment to consider how to respond. "Something may be happening," he said. "Something—"

"Something connected to Darisam?"

The king nodded.

Matthew's face grew sombre. "Darisam fell to its folly. It succumbed to the Deceiver and lost itself. At the end, Darisam looked to follow it rather than the Shepherd and paid the ultimate price."

All sand. An entire civilisation not just destroyed but eradicated.

"I know," Edward said under his breath.

Matthew looked at the king and raised his eyebrows.

The king shook his head. "It is nothing."

"Whatever you think is happening, if you believe it to be somehow similar in nature or substance to the Fall of Darisam, then it has the

Deceiver's touch on it, and you must be wary. Remember, the Deceiver covets this world more than anything. The Shepherd stopped him once, but the Deceiver is ever waiting to try again."

"In Kur," the king whispered.

The dean took a deep breath. "That is his domain, yes. Those who worship him are taken there when they pass, twisted into things of nightmares so they may serve him better."

"So they may help him cross," the king said under his breath.

The dean caught Edward's words and nodded. "Yes, that is the Deceiver's final ambition, to return here from the place he was banished to." The older man smiled. "But the Deceiver was banished deep into the other realm, and even though it is possible in the darkest of times for some of his minions to cross from there to here, it is impossible for him to return. The Deceiver is one with that place, and it would take the utter corruption of our realm to enable him to cross, something the Shepherd would never allow to come to pass."

"And where is the Shepherd, Father?"

Matthew's smile became a little warmer. "He is all around us. He may not be visible to us, but he can be felt in every breath of air and every ray of sunlight."

The king took a deep breath and smiled wearily at the dean. "Thank you, Father. I did not expect to find answers here, but it is good to talk to you." He rose, and the dean rose with him. The king turned and began walking out of the chapel.

"Your Majesty."

Edward turned back to look at the dean and saw his expression was troubled.

"The Fall of Darisam is a lesson on deviance, corruption, and the price that must be paid when vice is indulged and morality lost. Whatever has you so worried, remember the Deceiver is called that for a reason; he is deceptive. Manipulative. The enemy you are facing may not be the real enemy."

Edward thought for a moment. "Father, if you had to choose between two voices, one guiding you in a true and trusted way and the other directing you down a path never trodden, which would you choose?"

The dean nodded as he walked toward the king. "You are of course talking about the prime minister and Lady Nanaya?"

The king was momentarily lost for words.

"When the prime minister and the king argue, people take note," Matthew explained. "Just as they do when someone like Lady Nanaya is scared and mysteriously afflicted. While it is true that I and the rest of the Church are wary of Lady Nanaya and her... background and capabilities," he said, choosing his words carefully, "we are also cognisant of the fact that the Shepherd and his closest allies were also able to do such things."

He regarded the king. "Edward, I would never advise going against your prime minister. A division such as that leads to a fractured kingdom." He took a deep breath. "However, when someone like Lady Nanaya is worried about something, you should take note and also be worried, and follow her advice. She knows things that perhaps no one other than the Shepherd himself knows."

"But what if I must make a hard choice between them?" the king asked in a voice thick with uncertainty and concern. "What if, to follow one I must lose the other?"

The dean placed a hand on the king's shoulder. "Your Majesty, only you can make that choice. I will repeat, though, if Lady Nanaya is worried about something, then you should take note and also be worried, and if she is offering advice and guidance on such a matter, you should listen to her."

"Thank you, Father," Edward said in a sombre voice and walked away with a heavy heart.

Chapter Seventeen

Pressure grew at the base of Henri's spine, a formless weight that increased until he felt like his back would snap. He fell against the cold stone wall of the inner palace corridor, the savage sensation tearing a surprised and painful cry from his lips before vanishing as if torn away.

Possession is such an... involved process, Adaru said. His voice was strong and clear in Henri's mind. *The first part is the hardest. You see, we were not meant to exist outside our bodies. This is a physical realm; we are anchored by our bodies. So, that first act of separating myself from my body was... Well, excruciating does not even begin to describe it.*

Henri tried to cry out again as another surge of pain assaulted the base of his spine, but nothing came. He could not form a word or make a sound, as if the very ability to do so was being ground away.

When I returned from my exile, I needed another body to anchor myself to.

The pressure swept out from Henri's spine.

Not just any body can be a vessel, of course. Those with the right strength can resist. A vessel must be weak or weakened to be occupied, and even then, it may not work. I tried to possess the first body that I encountered, but for some reason, I could not do so fully. Maybe it was not weak enough, but Henri, you are so weak.

Henri's body shook, and his skin prickled with intense sensitivity.

Once inside, even then the deed is not done. You see, Henri, in order to possess a body, to take it over, there are a few other factors. The first is that the body must be alive with power, rich in the energy of this realm. For most, like you, that power is barely an ember, just a trickle flowing through your veins and just enough for you to live. While that will enable your body to survive, it is not enough for another to take it over. For that to happen, the power of that body must be flowing. As I have just enabled it in your body.

The sensation that had swept into his body from his spine settled at the root of his penis where it became crashing waves of liquid agony. The archbishop silently screamed and clutched between his legs.

Focal points, Adaru explained. *Energy centres in your body.*

The pain flowed into his navel where it turned into flames. Henri fell to his knees, groaning and clutching his belly as his insides burned. Its fingers reached for his heart. As the flames ensnared it, they twisted and changed, becoming violent turbulent air that clutched, whipped and pounded his heart. The archbishop's body shook.

One shaking hand scratched against the floor while the other gripped his chest as if to tear his heart free. As he ripped at his clothes, Henri felt a sheer and utter powerlessness seize him. There was something else, too. In the utter desolation of his soul, something began to manifest.

Yes, Henri, I am here. Another factor to enable possession is invitation. Occupation without invitation is meaningless. A vessel must willingly open itself for something to move inside its body.

Henri remembered his dream, before Adaru had been able to talk to him when he was awake. *Let me all the way in, Henri,* he remembered Adaru saying.

"No!" the archbishop gasped as he remembered grasping Adaru's hand.

Yes, Henri. You let me in.

Henri's mouth opened in a wordless scream of broken sadness edged with hatred, and what he felt as air swelled until an uncontrollable storm raged in his chest. Abruptly, his heart was released, the storm collapsed, but rather than bringing relief, it ushered sheer terror. Where there had been sensation, there was now a vacuum of feeling that gaped with its totality. He also couldn't breathe.

Both hands clawed at his throat, fingernails scratching his skin as he tried to take a breath. The sense of emptiness stretched into his skull, and an intensity grew between his eyes. Henri's vision dimmed as his body began to shut down.

Nearly there, Henri, Adaru whispered. *You are almost ready for me.*

The feeling between Henri's eyes became more acute and reached for his crown, and Henri felt a kind of euphoria building. His body trembled.

Goodbye, Henri.

The archbishop's eyes widened, and then he was no more.

On the floor of the palace corridor, what had been Henri rose to his feet and stretched his arms.

Adaru smiled.

It's good to be back.

An hour later, Adaru was in Henri's chambers, holding his hands before the fire and sighing contentedly as the heat from the flames warmed what was now his skin. He saw beyond the flames, however. His thoughts filled with the moment he had been imprisoned.

The tower shook as energy from its foundations was funnelled up through its structure and manipulated to form a gateway at its peak. Adaru gazed in wonder at the stone ceiling above him, as if he could see what was taking place outside. "When both seals are torn, the way between the realms will be open, and the power of Kur will be ours!"

"This will fail," Lamadu declared.

Adaru frowned. "But look at—"

"Shut up, Adaru. The dragons were not supposed to be aware, and now there is not just one of them, but also an elemental and guardians. Together, they are too strong. There is no way we can succeed." She slammed the outside of her fist against the wall. The woman returned her gaze to Adaru. *"We must plan for the future."*

"But," Adaru spluttered, *"but we are so close!"* He gestured above him. *"The portal opens, the seals—"*

"The seals will be healed," Lamadu said as she walked around the shaking chamber to a stone lectern that stood in its centre. She caressed the edge of an open book that sat upon it. *"The nexus they reside inside will be whole once again. The tower will not fall, however. There is so much energy in this stone I think it could withstand anything."*

She sliced her palm with a ragged nail, and blood seeped from the cut. She dipped a finger into it and began to draw on the pages before her. *"This is only possible here. Even before the seals were torn, this place was one where the fabric of reality was worn thin and frayed."* She paused and glanced at him for a moment before continuing. *"You have power, Adaru. This may fail, but this is just one piece of a grander plan. There will be another chance to complete our goal."*

To complete my *goal,* Adaru thought as he rubbed his hands together before the fire.

I will get what I want. What I need.

Adaru's thoughts moved through some of what he had learned since moving into what had been Henri's mind.

So over a thousand years have passed, and kishpu are the stuff of stories and legends in this land. Well, that may make things easier.

He stared into the flames.

Ah, Lamadu. You were all about some grand scheme of epic proportions. I cannot deny that it intrigued me, but my ambition is quite simple really, to ensure no one can ever hurt me as they did at the orphanages and the seminary.

Adaru shivered as long buried but never forgotten feelings of pain and despair resurfaced.

Never again. I will make it so no one can ever take anything from me again.

He clenched a fist as he recalled his release from the book. *It had been so close!* The flames disappeared, and once again, he was back at the tower, looking at the lectern through the eyes of the body he had just possessed.

He slowly stretched through it, feeling it become his.

Almost.

He had never possessed something before, but this did not feel as he thought it should. The body was his to command, but it was not wholly his. He could not fully take it.

Perhaps I am too weak, he thought. He struggled to his feet and stood, swaying as something in the body pushed back against his mastery of it. After a moment, it subsided, and Adaru felt confident to take one hesitant step after another.

The catacombs!

He staggered from the room into the stairwell.

I must get to the seals. I must have the power of Kur!

Leaning against the wall, Adaru made his way down the stairs until he reached the bottom. The narrow doorway to the catacombs was there just as he remembered it, but now it had been filled with stone.

No!

Carved into the stone were triangles of various sizes, through which ran an unbroken circle.

NO!

Adaru tried to summon the energy from Kur that was inside him, but nothing happened.

He howled in frustration and tried again and again to manifest the dark energies, but nothing happened.

Once again, he had been denied.

Adaru pounded on the stone with his new body's fists as he shrieked with desperate need to get through before finally dropping to the ground in abject misery.

What was the point of returning if the nexus, and through it the power from the other realm, was unreachable?

As he knelt, drowning in despair, he felt the body he inhabited weakening. He could feel its vitality seeping away.

If I stay here, I will die.

The fierce desire for survival that had enabled him to live through everything he had suffered in the past ignited in him.

I will find a way to come back. I will break the seals and feed on the energy from Kur!

A knock at the door brought Adaru back to the present. "Enter."

"The general," Claude announced.

"General, please, take a seat," Adaru said, turning around and smiling at the man who had just entered. He gestured to a gilded couch that sat opposite the burning fireplace.

General Bron dipped his head and sat to one end as Adaru sat at the other. "So what can I do for you, Your Eminence?"

Adaru inspected his fingernails for a moment as he sifted through Henri's memories. "You were quite a legend in your youth."

Bron chuckled. "I had my moments, for sure." He leaned forward toward Adaru. "Now, what is this about?"

Adaru walked to a side table, lifted a square, cut crystal, brandy decanter, poured himself a drink, and then another for the general. "Do you know why you were so successful?" He passed the drink to the other man.

Bron shrugged. "I'm good at what I do."

"Yes, you are, but do you know why?"

Bron opened his mouth to reply, then frowned as he thought better of speaking and sipped the brandy.

Adaru turned back to face him. "You are a killer, Didier." He put a hand in the air and shook his head with a wry expression on his face as the general's face stiffened, and his jaw clenched.

"I know, Didier, and no amount of false protestation will convince me otherwise. When you indulge, when you allow yourself to let go, you feel alive, don't you? And all the time you don't, all the time you deny yourself, you feel, well, unsatisfied."

The general's eyes were cold and hard as he stared at the archbishop. "Interesting ideas, but you have no idea what you are talking about." He took a slow deep breath and put his drink down. "It is time for me to—"

"Let me show you."

The general's eyes widened, and he gasped as a shiver rippled across his body. A burning throb pulsed in his chest, and his throat went dry. "What—? What have you done?"

"I have particular skills." Adaru's lips twisted into a slight smile. "I've released what you have tried to cage and given you a little... gift."

Bron groaned and bent over as cramps assaulted his body. He glared at Adaru. "What's happened to you Henri? I can't claim to know you well, but from the time we have spent together, I know this is not like you."

Adaru sipped his brandy. "I have changed."

Bron took a deep breath as the muscle spasms eased and stood tall. His eyes narrowed. "I hear that you can heal now."

Adaru's eyes sparkled. "I can do a lot of things, General."

"How?"

Adaru ignored the question, took hold of a small hand bell sitting on his desk, and rang it. "Let's reignite that appetite for violence and bloodshed, shall we?"

Didier shook his head, balled his fists, and gritted his teeth. "No! I will not let this take over me again!"

Adaru shook his head. "You have this all wrong, General. Nothing is taking you over. This is who you are. You have been diminishing yourself by denying yourself."

The door opened, and Claude walked in. "Your Grace?"

"You have dismissed the staff?" Adaru asked Claude. "Told everyone this area is to be vacated until I say otherwise?"

Claude nodded.

General Bron grunted and doubled over, moaning and clutching his gut. He fell forward and lay curled on the floor.

Claude gasped. "Holiness! Should I call for help?"

"No," Adaru replied. "Go to him. Help him sit."

The general looked up, and bloodshot eyes locked with the arch-bishop's. "Don't do this."

"I must."

Claude rushed to Didier's side as Adaru closed the door. He

grasped the general's arm to help him. Bron looped one arm over Claude's shoulder as the younger man helped him back onto the couch.

"A little more, I think," Adaru judged, his eyes narrowing.

Didier moaned and clutched at Claude.

"That should do it," Adaru declared with a smile.

"Do what, Your Eminence?" Claude asked in confusion. "What is happening here?"

The general's hand tightened on the aide's back, fingers curling and digging into Claude's flesh.

The younger man yelped. "General Bron, you are hurting me!"

Adaru walked to his desk and sat behind it. He took another sip of his drink as he watched.

Claude choked as the general's arm tightened around his neck.

"I have a plan, General," Adaru said, "but it is rather involved and quite precarious. I need support in order for it to succeed, and you have a part to play in that."

The general growled through clenched teeth. The hand on Claude's back clenched harder.

"General, please stop!"

"Embrace it, General," Adaru commanded. "Be what you were meant to be."

The general threw his head up and roared. It was the terrible sound of something savage that had been caged finally finding release. Flexing his muscles, he jerked Claude off the couch to the floor. He grasped the young man's face with his other hand and squeezed.

Claude screamed.

The general's eyes widened, his breath quickened, and his lips stretched thinly as he bared his teeth and hissed through them.

Claude's screams rose in pitch as his skull cracked.

Adaru closed his eyes and reached into Bron, changing him.

The general's fingers had lengthened and were now wrapped around the young man's face, their new, long, tapered nails digging into the shrieking man's flesh. With a cry of savage eagerness, he clenched his fist, and Claude's head burst in his palm, blood, bone, and brain splattering him and everything nearby.

The room was filled with the general's ragged breath and Claude's heels knocking on the floor as his legs spasmed.

After a moment, the general raised his bloody head and cast a wary look at Adaru. Decades had washed away from the old soldier, and a tighter, smoother, and more youthful face looked at the archbishop. His eyes were brighter than they had been before.

As Adaru regarded him, the glow in his eyes faded but did not disappear. Adaru smiled. "Perfect."

General Bron looked at one gore-coated hand, turning it as he examined it. His fingers were shortening, and his nails were receding to their normal size. He returned his gaze to the man sitting behind the desk.

"The body mirrors what is inside," Adaru said. "How do you feel?"

The general thought for a moment, and then shook his head as he smiled and wiped his hand on Claude's clothes. "I should feel anything except what I am feeling. I feel amazing." He frowned. "What have you done to me?"

"I have changed you," Adaru said. "Well, *started a change* would probably be more accurate. I have taken away the cage that held your rage and aligned your being with it. Where before this was a part of you that you ostracized, now it is your core. Feels better, doesn't it?"

Bron nodded and took a deep steadying breath.

"It is fundamentally who and what you are," Adaru said. "The more you release it, the more you express your anger and indulge in violence, the stronger you will become."

The general shook his head. "I don't know how you knew, but you have the right of it. It's my mother's side. They all have a quick and violent temper, a tendency for extreme anger and an eagerness to inflict pain." The general refilled his brandy glass and took a long deep drink. "I've always known something is wrong with all of us."

"Not wrong, just different."

"Before, you said that you have a plan."

Adaru nodded, rose from behind his desk, and walked toward the general. "There is a place, a place of power. The same power that has enabled me to make you strong. I plan to take more of it, and I plan to make you stronger still."

"Where is this place?"

Adaru's eyes narrowed. "That's a bit of a problem. It's in what you call The Territory."

The general scoffed. "That's not a problem, that's impossible."

"Not entirely. Like I said, I have a plan."

Chapter Eighteen

The tang of ocean salt lay thick on his tongue as King Louis took a deep breath of fresh air and leaned out one of his bedroom windows.

The king stared over the battlements of Château Occidentale and the castle wall beyond, past the courtyard filled with guards and servants going about their evening duties, and past the narrow, twisting, walled path that wound up the sheer cliff from the treacherous rocky beach where many a ship had met its demise. Even at this vast height, the clamour of castle life came to his ears, though it was a faint background noise to the louder snapping of flags in the wind and the raucous calls of sea birds.

Louis closed his eyes, and his mind was filled with a sonnet he had heard earlier that day about a princess's unrequited love for a captain of the guard. He imagined her standing at a window similar to the one he stood before, her heart aching as she tried to see the object of her affection, and knowing they could never be together. He sighed with the romantic drama of it all.

"Will there be anything else, Your Majesty?"

The king turned to face the old man finishing with turning down his bed. "Not tonight, Gregier. You may go."

The man bowed low in acknowledgment and left.

The king returned his gaze to the ocean. The clouds parted, and the light from a crescent moon shined brightly on the waves below. The king watched the light illuminate the water, staring at the undulating waves for a moment before closing the window and pulling the curtain closed, the heavy fabric sealing away the outside world.

Louis rubbed his eyes and walked to the four-poster bed. He pulled back a thick, rich-claret-coloured blanket and climbed under it. He took a deep breath and pulled the blankets up over his body.

Four small gas lanterns illuminated the room in a warm glow, but the king was content to let them burn. As always, someone would check on him in a few hours and would extinguish them, as well as take out any used chamber pot.

With a deep sigh, the king closed his eyes, and after a moment, was sound asleep.

He woke from a carefree dream of running through the palace gardens with the young painter he had met a few weeks ago and lay confused as his mind moved from that blissful afternoon courtship to the chilly, dark reality of early morning. The king closed his eyes and tried to slip back into sleep. He slowed his breathing, cleared his mind of all thoughts.

A floorboard to his right creaked.

Louis's eyes snapped open, and he saw a dark figure advancing toward him. He yelled and sat upright just as the figure swung wildly at him. The king screeched in pain as something sliced across his arm and chest.

Muffled shouts came from the corridor outside as the guards reacted to his cry for help.

Louis began to get out of the bed, but then something speared into the flesh just above his hip, grating against his spine and bursting out of the other side of his body. He fell back to his sheets, screaming in agony.

The royal bedroom door was flung open, light spilling from the lanterns in the outside corridor and illuminating a thin man in dirty rags rushing for the window.

The first guard inside the room fired his flintlock pistol at the escapee, a shower of sparks spraying forward from the muzzle and another sideways out of the flash-hole. The figure howled as a musket ball buried itself into his shoulder blade. All but one of the guards fell upon the assassin as he scrambled toward the window. The other rushed to his liege's side.

"We have him, Your Majesty!" yelled one of the men as they bent a thin arm of wasted muscle behind the assassin's back.

"Save it, Pierre," the guard leaning across the bed muttered, staring at the king's glazed, open eyes. "The king is dead."

General Didier found Count Premiercolons in one of the servants' corridors that ran between the rooms of the left guest wing. There were few visitors at the moment, and so these service-ways were deserted. It was the perfect place for a tryst. A low-burning gas lantern hung every few metres, creating soft pools of yellow light and deep, dark shadows that stretched between them.

The count was partially hidden from view near one such lantern, standing within a small recess. A young girl was between him and the wall, giggling as he mumbled suggestively and chuckled under his breath.

"Premiercolons?"

The count staggered back and into view, his breeches undone, and his shirt untucked. "General!" he spluttered. "What are you doing here? Get away, man!"

The general smiled as he walked closer. He pulled open his dark, full-skirted, knee-length coat, reached inside, and withdrew a foot-long blade that glinted as the gaslight caught it.

"What are you doing?" Premiercolons demanded as he stared at the blade.

The general licked his lips and darted forward.

Premiercolons stepped back, but the general was too fast. He plunged the blade into the count's stomach and leaned in close as Premiercolons's eyes widened, and he opened his mouth to scream.

Bron put his hand over the lord's mouth to silence him, pulled out his dagger, and plunged it in again and again and again.

The serving maid took a deep breath, but before she could utter a sound, the general's arm snapped out, and his open palm hit her head to send it cracking against the wall.

As she slid to the floor, Bron turned back to the gasping count and stabbed and stabbed, his smile widening with each savage thrust. His breath quickened, and he began to pant as he continued to ram his blade into the count. When his muscles started to burn, he stopped, and Premiercolons's bloody, torn body dropped to the cold and dusty corridor stone.

The general's hand and sleeve were slick with warm blood. Reaching down, he ripped the lord's shirt open so he could grasp a handful of material to clean himself with. He took a deep breath. The rich, metallic blood was thick in the air and coated his tongue. Swallowing, he savoured its taste as his skin prickled with sensitivity. Heart pounding, he made a fist and felt long atrophied muscles bunch. A broad grin stretched across his face.

"I totally disagree," Count Terragricole slurred as he leaned across the table toward Count Terrsud, his tankard spilling as he slammed it down. "There is a precedent for…"

His voice trailed off as he noted three royal guards entering the inn. Turning, he saw another two emerge through the kitchen. All were watching the two lords. He stood clumsily as one of the guards approached.

"Count Terragricole and Terrsud, you are under arrest for being in league with The Fringe States and committing the murder of the king."

Terragricole laughed and turned to his companion. As he did, the guard stepped forward and grasped one arm, twisting it behind his back and slamming his face down onto the table.

"What the bloody Shepherd!" Terrsud yelled.

The guard turned to his companions. "Arrest that man!"

Adaru turned as the door opened, and then looked away when he saw that it was General Bron. Guards were running behind him, and the pounding of boots and raised voices filled the corridors.

"It's done, I take it?"

The general smiled. Adaru noticed the youthful vigour as the military man walked into the room and closed the door behind him.

"Premiercolons is dead, Terrsud and Terragricole are in the dungeons, and the other matter has been dealt with."

Adaru nodded. "Good. From here, we will need to move fast." Adaru paused. "You are confident Terrsud and Terragricole will say what's needed?"

Bron nodded. "I will look after it personally."

Adaru nodded and rang the bell on his desk. At the sound, the doors to his chambers opened, and a servant directed inside a very distressed Count Villedepêch.

"Is it true?" he asked in a rush.

"That the king is dead?" Adaru queried as he beckoned the count toward the couch upon which General Bron was already sitting. "Yes, I am afraid so."

"Premiercolons?" Villedepêch asked in a voice that quivered.

"Also dead."

The count dropped onto the couch and took several deep, shuddering breaths.

"Premiercolons's son is not mature enough to keep the barons of his region united," the count muttered, "and they will never heed the countess—"

"And, therefore, you have a number of leaderless nobles who cannot be held in check, each with their own well-trained armed force on your doorstep," Bron commented.

The count stared at the general for a moment before nodding agreement to his summation.

"Fear not, Count Villedepêch," Adaru reassured him in a calming voice. "We believe we have a solution."

"My Lords, please be seated," Adaru welcomed.

Twenty-five impressively dressed men of various ages took their seats around the circular table with varying haste. Each represented a major house within Royaume d'Occident's regions, and each had been a subject of their respective counts, who were now either dead or incarcerated.

The death of the king and the incapacitation of the next most powerful figures in the kingdom had created a unique situation. Power and status were ripe for the taking, and each was eager to seize what he could.

"These are terrible times, My Lords," Adaru continued. "Not only are we bereft of our liege lord through savage and treacherous murder, but we also stand on the brink of war."

The room erupted into commotion as those present turned to one another in worried confusion.

"General," Adaru said, inviting the military man to speak.

General Bron stood as Adaru sat, and more than one lord noticed his increased bulk and the dark streams of hair in a mane once silver. "Thank you, Your Eminence," he said, his powerful deep voice lacking its former rough edge.

"My Lords, the murder of our king and the murder of Count Premiercolons was orchestrated by Counts Terrsud and Terragricole and at the direction of The Fringe States."

The chamber erupted as the barons of Premiercolons turned on those of Terrsud and Terragricole, who vehemently denied such accusations.

The general slammed his fist on the table, and the barons abruptly fell silent. "The assassin—for we can only call him such—has been identified as a citizen of Eptimi, who arrived here in Château Occidental but a few months ago."

The barons glanced at one another. A few muttered, but none dared raise his voice.

"Terrsud and Terragricole have confessed their participation in what appears to have been a *coup d'état*, supported by The Fringe States."

The Premiercolons barons leapt to their feet, hurling abuse at their counterparts, several of which pushed away from the table and looked to leave.

At a gesture from the general, the guards by the chamber entrance closed the doors and stood before them, blocking their exit.

A stunned silence filled the room.

A baron from Premiercolons stood and gestured at the guards. "Stand aside. I must return to Premiercolons and confer with the new count."

"He is dead," Adaru said.

The baron stared blankly at Adaru.

"It seems Terrsud and Terragricole were quite thorough in their plans to take control of the kingdom," he continued as he walked around the room to stand before the sealed doors. All eyes were on him, hushed whispers hissing through the thick apprehension. "The Premiercolons estate has been razed. No one survived, not the countess, nor the son and heir."

Three loud knocks on the closed doors startled oaths from most assembled.

The general nodded to the guards, who opened the doors.

Count Villedepêch walked into the room. He dipped his head to Adaru. "Your Eminence." Turning, he did the same to the general.

Both returned the gesture.

Villedepêch faced the assembled barons. "Sit, My Lords."

The barons glanced at one another. Villedepêch was rarely seen outside of his lands and little ever heard from him. Most had assumed him to be content with his elevated status and uninterested in the machinations of the capital.

"Sit!" the general barked.

After a quick glance at one another, all did so.

"We are at a precipice," Villedepêch began. "We face war without, but if we are not careful, we also face the very real possibility of war within. Civil war. Many of your minds are no doubt already turning to this possibility—"

Voices rose from the barons.

"And I do not blame any of you for doing so!" Villedepêch finished in a near shout, quieting angry voices to disgruntled mutters.

"Royaume d'Occident was born of such discontent. Our forebears settled this land after the Southcastle civil war. Then followed The Tribe War, The Massacre of The Tribes, The War of The North. Our history is filled with bloodshed. King Fredrique bested all who faced him, and through his dominance, this kingdom was born, but ever has it been a tenuous alliance between the most powerful houses. We have all sought to rise above one another."

"As you have done so yourself, sir!"

The count smiled at the angry, red-faced Premiercolons baron, who had spat the accusation, and he nodded. "Indeed, I have." He pointed around the table. "As has every one of you."

The mutters rose in volume, but they were half-hearted and drifted away.

"Royaume d'Occident has ever been a kingdom at war with itself. Now, The Fringe States seek to pry open the cracks between us."

"Yours is the highest-ranking noble house, Count," Baudouin de Dubois, a Terrsud baron, said through clenched teeth. "Do you presume to rise higher? Do you presume the throne now, Villedepêch?"

The mood in the room darkened and became thick with imminent violence.

"I presume a motion the likes of which has never happened before," Villedepêch said. "At this moment, we need unification in the face of external threat. We need to remain together and push aside our differences for another day. I don't believe we can do that, any of us, while our houses jockey for position."

Grim, assenting silence filled the room.

"I propose we, the nobility of Royaume d'Occident, set aside our agendas until this crisis is over, and in our place, and only for the duration of this extraordinary period, we place our faith *in* the Church to look after the realm and its people."

"What are you suggesting, Villedepêch?" Baudouin asked, his eyes darting to the archbishop.

"I am saying that until the threat of The Fringe States is vanquished, Villedepêch will support the Church standing in place of the Crown, while we direct our efforts wholeheartedly to defeat the true enemy."

"The army stands with Villedepêch, supporting the Church and a declaration of war against The Fringe States!" General Bron declared loudly.

The barons cast wild glances between the count, the general, and the archbishop, and then at one another as they tried to fathom what was happening.

Baron Masien of Terragricole narrowed his eyes as he regarded the count and the general. Villedepêch was small, but its armed force was well above anything any other baron could bring to a field of battle. The royal army was second only to the combined forces of all. Together, Villedepêch and the royal army could take on anyone except a union of many, if not all the baronies, and now that the House of Premiercolons was no more, there was nothing to unite the barons. What benefit could be gained from standing against such a force without assured support?

The baron glanced around the table. No doubt many of those here were already sizing-up their neighbours and making plans for expansion. The only way to survive this was to be allied with a force the others feared. He made up his mind and stood. "Masien stands in support of the Church."

The other barons at the table cursed and called for Masien to sit down, but the baron had seen where this was going and refused to meet eye contact with any except the general.

"Lisalle stands in support of the Church."

Heads swung as the Premiercolons Baron of Lisalle stood.

Lisalle, in northeast Premiercolons, sat on the border with The Fringe States, and if anyone needed allies, it was them, as they would be the first hit in any expansionist invasion by The States.

Baron Baudouin ground his teeth and looked nervously around the room.

Another man stood. "Siera'mon stands in support of the Church."

Baudouin cursed and screwed his eyes shut. *Of course, they would fold. Petty little backwater...*

The tide broke. One by one, the barons stood as both their neighbours and their rivals sided with the combined force of Villedepêch, the Church, and the Royal Army. As the gulf between the forces supporting the Church and those yet to declare widened, more barons stood until only Baudouin sat. Reluctantly, he stood, though the look he gave the archbishop was one full of animosity.

Adaru smiled.

"Now, while the Church will devote itself to the governance of Royaume d'Occident and its people, we need to address our security and specifically what must be done about The Fringe States. General, I believe this is your time to speak."

Chapter Nineteen

"What's he doing?"

James looked to where Samuel gestured and watched a man he did not recognise hammering a proclamation onto the town square notice board. He carried another tucked under his arm. He was of medium build and wore a long, crisp, dark-blue coat covered with dirt and dust that hid his other clothes. A similarly coloured tri-pointed hat, with its forward tip longer than the others, sat firmly on his head. A horse was tethered nearby and looked tired.

Four feet square, the town notice board was made of several weathered ash boards and stood at the very centre of town. On it were the official notices of the town approved by the mayor, such as building works, levies, sanitation notices and town-wide events, like the upcoming trade apprenticeship open days.

"No one adds anything to the board except the town crier!" Samuel said. "Piers is going to be—"

The door to the town hall swung open and crashed against the wall inside. Out strode a red-faced Piers Mason, the town crier. Half-dressed, with his bell of office clutched in one white-knuckled fist, his other hand righting his yellow wig, Piers stormed across the town square with his eyes fixed on the man defacing his notice board.

"This is going to be good," James sniggered.

"By the Shepherd, what are you doing there?" Piers bellowed, face flushed and nostrils flaring as a crowd gathered around him.

The man finished attaching the second notice to the board and turned away without saying a word to the town crier. He strode to his horse and untied it as Piers stared at him with a deepening frown, swung into the saddle, and with a kick of his heels, rode away.

"What in the Shepherd does he think—?" Piers began as he started reading the first notice, but he never finished the sentence. His mouth dropped open.

James and Samuel exchanged glances and moved closer to the growing crowd.

"That can't be right," they heard someone say. A handful of women were either sobbing or crying.

"What is going on?" James asked Samuel, who just shook his head.

The crowd was growing more agitated as the young men approached. Several people pushed their way free from the others and ran for their horses, one woman hitching her dress well above her ankles so she could run faster.

James smiled. A man turned to face him, his face as pale as the town crier's. James's smile fell from his face. "What is it?"

The man opened and closed his mouth several times but could not find the words. "Got to get back to my boys," he managed to say before turning and running away.

The crowd continued to thin as James and Samuel approached the notice board. Those who had not rushed away had come together into distinct groups, some drowning in misery, some climbing in anger, and others wallowing in numb inaction.

Pushing his way forward through those still surrounding the board, James managed to see what the man had attached. The first notice made him take a sharp intake of breath.

People of Trieme

and Subjects of Royaume d'Occident:

As of this day, Royaume d'Occident is at war with The Fringe States.

James's eyes darted to the other notice.

The Military Service Act:

All men no younger than eighteen years and no older than forty-one years, that are not excepted or exempted as described in this notice, will be deemed enlisted for the duration of the war.

James turned to stare at Samuel. "This has got to be some kind of joke, right?"

"No joke, lad," a man standing next to him said. "These are up in every village centre around us."

"We are at war?" Samuel asked in a whisper.

"We are, lad," the man said. "I hear temporary barracks and training grounds are being set up nearby." He looked each of them up and down. "Better get home to see your ma and pa. Unless you got something wrong with you, the barracks are where you will be by the end of the week."

Chapter Twenty

"Diers, tell me, how are things in the quarry?"

The young man licked his lips.

"When you told me that we would be... different after the healing, I had no idea quite what you meant."

Adaru steepled his fingers and leaned forward onto the archbishop's desk. His eyes sparkled. "And now?

Diers raised a hand in the air and took a deep breath. He concentrated, and wisps of smoke seeped from his skin, winding around and between his fingers before disappearing.

"And how do you feel about these... changes?" Adaru's voice was low, intense. His eyes piercing.

Diers paused for a moment. "For the first time in forever, we are free. We are free from leprosy, and we are free from oppression, from subjugation. We are more than we ever have been." He smiled. "No one will ever dominate us again." His eyes grew moist and tender. "And it is all thanks to you, My Lord."

Adaru nodded thoughtfully.

"Each of us is different," Diers continued. "We all seem to be able to do different things. It is..." He shook his head. "It is amazing. We are all so strong. Marion and myself, in particular."

"And you shall grow stronger," Adaru said, rising from behind his desk to stand before the young man, who nodded.

"The Chosen already are. We are growing in power daily, but I feel we could be growing faster."

"*Chosen.* I like that. Yes, we are all indeed chosen." Adaru mulled over what Diers had said. "I need Château Occidentale secured, and that requires the Chosen to be strong. There is a journey ahead of us, and a great deal of planning needs to be done. I want the Chosen close to me. They are all to move from the quarry to here at the basilica. We will make changes that will enable them to use their power more freely. After we do, collectively using so much power will cause... change. There will be a shifting of the environment caused by the use of so much energy. I need that change to happen in Château Occidentale. It will empower us and weaken any who might oppose us."

Diers bowed. "At once, Your Eminence."

Adaru nodded. "Good. Once you are all here, I have specific tasks for you and Marion. I also need one other, one that has an ability to inflict pain in others."

"Antoinette, Your Holiness," Diers said without hesitation.

Adaru cocked his head to one side. "Tell me about her."

"There was a guard. A young man just recently posted to the quarry. He was walking past her. Antoinette saw him, and then I felt her reach out to him. Not physically. She just stared at him, and I felt her use the power inside her. The man..." Diers paused.

"Continue," Adaru commanded.

"The man collapsed. He wilted like a dying flower. His head fell to his chest. I saw his breathing quicken and go shallow. I saw his eyes widen as he tried to understand what was happening, and I saw them tighten in pain. Antoinette smiled and then walked away, and as she did, the man fell onto his back, moaning and shaking. He lay there for a long time. When he climbed to his feet and walked away, he was stooped over, dragging a leg behind him. Like an old man."

Adaru clapped his hands in delight. "Perfect! Bring her to me as soon as she arrives here."

"At once, Eminence."

Adaru nodded. "Use the time here to get used to your new abilities. I need everyone to be strong. When our troops leave for The Fringe States, the next stage begins. I want Chosen in each platoon. Their new powers will react to the war, they will grow stronger still when they are close to the conflict. They are to use their skills to heal and… strengthen the soldiers. It will not be long before the men react to their actions, and the Southcastle soldiers will be helpless before them. Remember the quarry?"

Diers nodded.

"That is why you needed to watch me and learn what I did. You need to train the Chosen to heal men of their wounds and change them as they do, making them stronger and fiercer. I also have tasks for you to perform here in the capital. Those I will tell you when the time is right. That is the need I have of you."

"Of course, Your Holiness," Diers said, dipping his head.

"Go now," Adaru commanded. "Make the necessary preparations for the Chosen's relocation and their training. I want them here as fast as possible, and I want them ready for the war."

Diers bowed low, and then hurriedly left the room.

It is all coming together, Adaru thought.

Chapter Twenty-One

"The Western king is dead. They have declared war on The Fringe States, and conscription is in force," Nanaya said, her voice carrying on the light breeze that whispered through the garden.

King Edward screwed his eyes closed and felt his heart pound at the words.

Everything feels like it is about to spin out of control.

He turned away from the leaves of the small citrus tree he had been twisting between his fingers and looked at Nanaya with weary eyes. He had hoped for a few hours' respite, some time alone to find a measure of calm.

Set on the fourth floor of Southcastle, the garden was a private royal retreat. Stepping stones and gravel paths wound around heavy fruit trees, brightly flowering bushes, and fragrant herbs. The garden was Edward's refuge, a place to escape.

"It's in Royaume d'Occident," Nanaya said abruptly.

The king ground his teeth together. In his exhausted state, the frustration, confusion, and uncertainty Nanaya had ignited in him all came together and boiled over. "*What* is? I cannot understand any of this! I do not understand what is happening. You show me" — he shook his head as he tried to put words to the vision she had given him — "you show me horrific things, unnatural things, and you tell me that it happened and could happen again. You show me something I have always believed was a story and tell me that it was real, it happened. You show me a dragon. A dragon!"

Edward's voice rose as he let his emotions vent. His fists were clenched, and his body was shaking. "Do you understand that you just ripped apart everything I thought was real and replaced it with things I cannot understand?" His voice was breaking, his eyes wide. "You need to give me answers. You need to tell me what is happening!"

"I don't know what is happening!" Nanaya took a moment to compose herself. "Something is using power from the other realm in Royaume d'Occident."

Edward frowned. "How?"

Nanaya shook her head. "It is a little difficult to—"

"Damn it, Nanaya! I need to know what is happening!"

Nanaya stroked a nearby fern, giving them both a breath for the intensity to subside. "There is an energy weaving through this realm," she began in a calm voice. "A rich vitality, an essence woven into the fabric of this reality. It fills everything; everything is born from it, and the more something has, the greater it is, the more powerful it is." Her hand dropped away from the green leaf.

"What exists in this realm strives to live. The morality of motivation, and the methods employed to live, are society's judgement, but there can be no argument. Everything in this realm strives to live and prosper." Nanaya drew her cloak around herself as if cold and returned to sit next to the king. "Imagine the opposite. Imagine, for a moment, that instead of an innate yearning to live and grow, there was something that ached for death, to inflict it, to drown in it. Absolute pain, depthless suffering, consuming despair. Not just the destruction of life, but the total eradication, complete consumption of it. That is what exists in the other realm, in Kur."

She looked at Edward and found him staring at her with scared eyes.

"Let's walk."

The king nodded, and they both rose and moved deeper into the Garden.

"What has escaped the tower has energy from Kur, and it is able to use it to corrupt this realm. It has happened before." She shuddered with recollection. "I can feel it happening again." Nanaya's eyes rose to meet Edward's.

"I cannot believe it is a coincidence. Since it moved to Royaume d'Occident, the Western king has been killed, and war has been declared. Whatever has escaped the tower is behind all of it, and the war works toward its aims. As the seals between the realms remain unbroken in the nexus at the tower, it is cut off from the other realm; its power is therefore limited. I believe it intends to return to the tower and destroy the seals so it can grow stronger with the released energies from the other realm. To do so, it needs to be strong enough to cross The Territory. I do not know how it was able to survive its journey from the tower to The Fringe States, but even I am harmed if I stay in the desert for too long, so I would assume that whilst it survived its journey, it was still affected." She paused beside a small bush full of ripening berries and stared at them.

"Kur delights in pain, suffering, and death. Its energy is enriched by such things. There are few things that cause pain, suffering, and death more than war, and I expect that is why this war is happening. I believe this war has three aims: The first is to obfuscate and to give what has escaped time to plan. The second is to create a clear and unobstructed path to the tower, and the third is to enable whatever is out there to grow stronger and ultimately to cross The Territory and reach the tower. Once there, it will try to break the seals between the realms."

Edward took a deep shuddering breath as he fought for composure. "How? How do we stop this?"

"I do not know," Nanaya said. "I do not know how anything can stop what is out there. I need time to think. I need you to buy me that time. I need you to try and stop this war, or at the very least, prevent what is out there from reaching The Territory."

"Stop this war? How can..." The king's eyes grew wide. "You want me to declare war on the West, don't you?"

Nanaya did not say anything.

"You cannot be serious. Declare war? Do you know the impact of such a thing? Forget for a moment the increased taxation to fund such a mobilisation, the fear that would clutch our people at such a decree. Forget for a moment the abrupt cessation of trade, and forget for a moment the farmers and workhands and artisans and bakers and sons and fathers who would be pulled from their lives and families to fight, their fields and livestock left to ruin. Forget it all for a moment and just think of one thing: Royaume d'Occident has the best trained army in this land. By far. We may hold our own for a while, but only for a while." The king shook his head. "Declaring war would be disastrous, almost certainly the end of Southcastle."

"Not declaring war will be the end of everything. You saw what happened the last time the seals were broken."

Edward looked at her for a moment before cursing and turning away. He clutched his hands together and tried to control his breathing.

Silence settled in the garden, each of them lost within their own thoughts.

Nanaya stared at Edward's back.

He is almost certainly right. War could very well be the end of Southcastle, but I need time to think. Nothing matters except stopping whatever escaped the tower. I must make him do this. If the seals are broken, everything is lost. I must frame this in a way he will understand.

"Edward," Nanaya called.

The king turned to face her, his teeth set, his face both angry and anxious.

"Edward, if you do not fight, then Southcastle will fall. Your people will not be impoverished; they will cease to be your people."

Edward stared at her.

"Just listen to me. The Fringe States are rich in metals and ore. If the West gets its hands on that wealth, it will fuel their capabilities to new heights, and their ambitions will soar with it. The peace between West and South has always been fragile and only kept thanks to three factors:

"The first is the Kafifi Ranges separating their military from us. Any kind of assault over the mountains is not just impractical, it is near impossible, especially with our fortifications.

"Second: Any mobilisation against Southcastle would leave them vulnerable to The Fringe States that have always looked to push their borders into the West's fertile lands.

"And third, the West's constant infighting. Their counts constantly scheme against each other, and this prevents any sort of unified front.

"Now, however, they are unified and through that unification are able to overwhelm their troublesome neighbour. Without our intervention, they will win their war, and when they do, two of the three reasons they cannot attack Southcastle will be gone."

The king turned away from the woman and stared into the night as he thought on her words.

"They will not stop, Edward. There will be war," Nanaya said. "The only thing left to you is to take the offensive and try to stop it from reaching Southcastle. Do this, and you save your people and stop what is out there."

The king bowed his head under the weight of her words. "I just don't know. War? I cannot imagine it."

I am sorry, Edward. I must make you do this.

"Look at me, Edward."

The king raised his eyes.

"I know how much you care for your people, and this is the only way. You must listen to me. We must do whatever it takes to stop this, even if that means going to war."

Chapter Twenty-Two

The general clenched his fists and flexed his bare biceps. He stared at the thick bulging muscle and chuckled. That chuckle collapsed into a roar of laughter as he shook his head. *I don't know how he has done this, but I don't care. Look at me!*

He crouched in the sand of the training ground and dug his fingers into the surface beneath him, pulling away a handful of dust and gravel. He rubbed it between his hands, drying them before tossing it away and picking up his practice sword.

Bron rolled his neck, revelling not just in the release that came with each crack of bone, but also in the fact that he could do this without any pain.

The protest of ill-kept hinges turned the general's eyes to a door in the twelve-foot wall that ringed the outdoor sparring area. A leather-armoured, young, well-muscled soldier entered. He stopped abruptly when he saw the general and took another look at the number painted on the outside of the door.

"There must be some mistake," he said with a frown. "I'm sorry, General, I will—"

"No mistake," Bron interrupted. "I asked for you today."

The man's frown deepened, and he shook his head. "Patrick is your usual partner, General. I would be more comfortable—"

The man's words were cut short as he flinched away from a spray of stone Bron had flicked up into his face with the tip of his sword. "I want to spar with you."

The soldier spat grit from his mouth and glared at the older man. "I'm not going to—"

Another flick of stone into the soldier's face stopped his next words. "I want a fight, boy," Bron spat. "What's the matter, not man enough?"

"Fine," the soldier said as he wiped dirt away from his face, "but this is your decision." He walked warily around the older man in a fighting crouch, blade low and ready.

Bron grinned and leapt forward, swinging wildly.

The soldier cursed as he blocked and skipped away. "Easy! This is supposed to be—"

Whatever he was about to say died on his lips as the general lunged forward, and the soldier was forced to turn aside the general's weapon with a frantic parry. Even dulled as it was, the strength behind the blows directed at him would still break bones. The soldier ground his teeth as he danced away to give him space to prepare a proper guard. "You've been working out, General," he grunted.

"I'm strong, boy, stronger than I have been for a very long time." The general's eyes sparkled. "And I am dying to see what I can do."

He came at the soldier with another lunge that when parried, he twisted into an overhead swipe, and when that was turned aside, he spun on the ball of one foot and used the momentum to swing at the soldier's unprotected side. The practice blade crunched into the man's ribs, and he grunted as he felt several crack.

"Shepherd's sake, General! This is practice, not—"

Bron spun again, and his blade came swinging for the soldier's neck. It was blocked, and the soldier lashed out with one foot as the blades met, kicking the general in his chest and knocking him back.

Bron growled and rushed in again.

The blades of the two men clashed again and again, far too rapidly and with far too much weight behind them to be sparring attacks. The noise brought other soldiers to see what was happening, and each who saw the battle between the two men stood stunned. Word spread, and soon, a small crowd of off duty soldiers surrounded the pair, shaking heads and gasping at each lunge and desperate parry. A few called for the men to stop before someone was seriously hurt, but the cries were ignored as that was all Bron wanted to do, and all his opponent could concentrate on was turning aside the next ferocious swing.

The two men skipped and danced around one another as they traded blows, but as time wore on, the soldier's movements began to slow, sweat ran down his face, and his breathing was ragged. In total contrast, Bron seemed ever more energised, and if anything, his blows came harder and faster.

Leaning back to avoid a savage backswing, the soldier stumbled, and Bron was on him. The general lunged forward, and his dull sword tip jabbed into the soldier's chest. The soldier gasped as ribs snapped under the impact, and he staggered backward, his blade drooping. Bron stepped forward and punched the man in the face with his free hand, crushing the soldier's nose in a spray of blood. The soldier tried to raise his sword, but before he could, Bron swung a hook with the fist that still clutched his blade. His fist smashed into the man's jaw with a loud crack of bone that staggered him farther back.

The men watching started shouting for the general to stop.

Bron swung another hook with his other fist into the soldier's kidneys, and he doubled over with a cry of pain. The general swung down with his practice blade, and the crack of the man's skull as the sword hit the top of the soldier's head left no doubt in anyone's mind that the soldier was gravely injured. He collapsed to the ground.

The general's vividly green eyes were wide, and he hissed through clenched teeth, spittle flying. He could feel energy coursing through his body with every strike.

He kicked the man in his ribs and grinned widely as more bones broke. He lifted his sword and swung at the man's head. The skull broke again, and as it did, the soldier mercifully lost consciousness.

Bron lifted his leg and stamped down on the soldier's chest. Sternum and clavicle shattered. He lifted his blade to strike again, but was bowled over as someone tackled him, losing his grip on his sword. He lashed out with a fist and hissed in satisfaction as it hit flesh, and someone grunted in pain. He leapt to his feet and glared at the men surrounding him. His fists were clenched so hard his knuckles gleamed white and spittle flew from his mouth with each ragged breath.

No one dared move, no one dared say anything.

The general stared at each man nearby, demanding they challenge him, daring and threatening someone to stand against him.

Glancing at one another, the men backed away to form a clear path to the open sparring-ground door.

Bron grunted and spat on the floor before striding forward, passing the bloody, broken mess of the soldier as he left.

Chapter Twenty-Three

"When do you leave, son?"

Samuel's words caught in his throat as he saw the tears in his father's eyes.

He could hear his mother sobbing upstairs.

"Tomorrow morning," he managed to croak.

His father nodded, his mouth twisting as he fought to retain his composure.

"How... how will you manage the farm?"

Rickard shrugged. "It's not going to be easy for sure." He cleared his throat roughly and took a deep breath. "But we are all in it, everyone around here. All you kids will be gone, so we will band together and find a solution like we always have."

For the first time in a long time, Samuel did not bristle at his father calling him a child.

His father motioned upstairs. "Go to your mother. Her heart is breaking right now."

Turning away from his father was wrenching, and Samuel heard his quiet sobbing as he walked out of the kitchen and started climbing the stairs. His dad was his rock, was the solidity and strength that underpinned the family. Seeing him like this was beyond unsettling, it was shattering. His father was their strength, his mother their heart. Together, they were his life, and not only was he leaving them, leaving everything he had ever known, he was also breaking them.

His mother was sitting on his bed, clutching the mud-stained shirt he had worn earlier that day. Her eyes were puffy and red. Her breath came in short, ragged bursts. When she saw him, she rubbed her eyes and tried to compose herself.

"You—" Her voice broke. She swallowed and took a deep breath. "You make sure that you keep warm and that you look after yourself." She could not help herself; her face collapsed, and she rushed for him, pulling him into a tight embrace and crying into his shoulder.

He held her for a long time, and at some point, he, too, started crying. Their world was going to be torn apart in the morning, and nothing would ever be the same. Things had already changed. Everything felt different. So mother and son clutched one another and let their tears flow for what had been and would never be again.

"Promise me something," his mother said in a tiny, tired voice when she was able to speak.

"Of course, Ma."

"Hold onto yourself. You are a gorgeous darling boy with a true good heart. I cannot imagine what you are going to see, what pain and what horrors will be inflicted upon you." She clutched the sides of his head and looked pleadingly into his eyes. "It's going to change you. It's going to change you, my boy." She stroked his face, and fresh tears slipped down hers. "Please remember who you are. Remember this beautiful boy who is my son."

Samuel nodded as tears streamed down his face.

His mother pulled him close, and they clutched each other and cried.

A thin frost covered the ground and crunched noisily underfoot the next morning as Samuel walked from the house to the stable. He saddled his horse in silence, but his mind was a riot of eager thoughts.

I'm going to see the world! I'm going to get a gun! A gun! The Fringe States! I wonder if I will see The Territory!

He frowned. His saddle did not look right. He shook his head and unfastened the front and flank cinches.

If I don't concentrate, I'll never get there!

He methodically refastened each cinch.

The saddle secured, Samuel placed both hands on his horse, bowed his head to rest his forehead on its soft, fine hair, and breathed deeply, holding on to this moment in time. Now that the moment to leave was upon him, he suddenly felt uncertain. Other farm smells filled his senses. The straw, the dung, the smoke of the wood fire. He drew it all in and held it inside.

How long before I might smell this again?

"It's time."

Samuel turned and saw his father standing framed by the stable door.

He nodded, grasped his horse's reins, and led it out after his father. He felt a little lightheaded, and he trembled with nervous anticipation of what was to come.

His mother was standing in front of the farmhouse. His father walked to her and put both his arms around her.

"We will say goodbye here; you go on from here by yourself."

Samuel stared at his father for a moment without understanding, and then looked to his mother. Bloodshot eyes stared back beseechingly, and his father was not just cuddling her, he was holding her up as she clutched at him.

"I'm going to stay here with your mum."

Samuel understood and nodded. He took a step toward them, and his mother jerked forward, a wild look in her eyes. His father held her close, and although she pushed against him, she did not have the strength to break free and run to her son.

"Sammy?" she whispered, pleaded.

"Go on," his father said in a broken voice, tears running down his face.

"Sammy!" his mother sobbed, pulling against his father.

Samuel fought against his own tears and pulled himself up into the saddle.

"I love you," his father called as Samuel started to move away. "Come back to us."

Samuel nodded, unable to speak, and kicked his horse to a slow trot, the world ahead dissolving to a blur with tears that could not be held back. As his home and parents fell behind him, however, so too did his sadness, each *clack* of his horse's hooves bringing a rush of excitement.

He met a red-faced James on the way to the muster point. Each nodded to the other and both could not help but grin.

"This is it!" James said with a smile.

Samuel laughed.

The boys paid no attention to their surroundings as they travelled, both lost in their imaginations of what their futures held. Tracks, roads, and fields went unseen as they talked about the sights they would witness. As they crested a hill, they saw a field covered with tents, fires, and one corner busy with corralled horses. They both pulled their mounts to a stop and fell silent. Ahead was their destination. Ahead was their future.

"So, this is it," James said.

Samuel looked out over the gathering. It seemed like every able man from the surrounding farms and villages was here. He spotted the carpenter from two villages over, who had made his bed, walking his horse to the makeshift pen. The town crier was staring around himself as if not understanding what was happening. Maud, the blacksmith's son, was laughing with a group of boys, some of whom Samuel recognised.

"Are you scared?" Samuel surprised himself with the question. The words had been on his lips then out of his mouth before they registered in his mind.

James shrugged. "Maybe. I don't know."

Samuel nodded. "Feels strange."

James scratched at a day's stubble on his jaw. "It's not like we had any choice."

"I know. But we are leaving."

James snorted. "I thought you wanted to leave."

"Yeah, I do. I think. I don't know. I feel strange."

For a moment, both young men sat silently on their horses, alternating their gazes from across the makeshift camp to the world they had grown up in that surrounded it.

"If we are going to do this, we need to go," James said.

The unspoken choice hung in the air and was thick with destiny. Both boys found it harder to breathe, found a sudden pressure building in their heads and pushing down on their chests. Their throats became dry, and their hands shook.

A muscle spasm snapped Samuel's heel into his horse's flank, and its step forward shattered the moment.

James urged his horse to follow, and the two of them left all they had ever known.

The clerk spoke without any embellishment as he worked, dispassionately processing the scared and bewildered who faced him. He did not look up as the next body moved forward in line to face him.

"Name?"

"Ah, Samuel," the young man said.

"Family name?'

"Smithyson."

The clerk nodded as he scratched the name into a ledger, then gestured behind him without looking up. "Move on. Next?"

Samuel moved in the direction the man had indicated and stood behind an older man, who was scratching his head and breathing heavily. The older man looked back and smiled thinly. Samuel judged him about the same age as his father.

"Guess it's been a good run, eh? Haven't had much to do with anything but the farm my whole life. Guess just a matter of time before something happened."

Samuel shrugged and nodded.

The older man grunted, then shook his head. "You're young, lad. Guess this all seems pretty exciting, eh? Get to see the world? Get to experience life?"

"Yeah, I think so," Samuel answered nervously.

"Figures." The man knuckled his back and then turned away. "It's a bit different when you're leaving your life behind," he said under his breath.

"Hey!" James said from behind him.

Samuel turned away from the man in front. He was glad to see his friend; the man's comments had left him feeling melancholy. For a moment, it was his father telling him he had left his life behind, his mother clutching his father tightly with despair in her eyes.

"Hey, you feeling well?"

Samuel smiled though it never touched his eyes. "Of course!"

The line moved forward, and so the two young men shuffled ahead as they talked.

"Where do you reckon we will go?"

Samuel shook his head. "I don't know what will happen now. Maybe we train here?"

James shrugged. "Maybe."

"Name?"

Samuel turned around to see the man ahead had moved on, and there was a space between him and another desk where a man who looked surprisingly similar to the last clerk sat, dressed in the same clothes. Behind him were countless piles of neatly folded uniforms that stretched to the back of the tent.

"Samuel."

"Last name?"

"Oh, yeah. Smithyson."

The clerk scribbled Samuel's name into a book that was a duplicate of the one the other man had used. "Size?"

"Er, clothing size?" Samuel asked.

The man raised one eyebrow. "No, kid, I want to know the size of your cock."

Samuel's mouth opened and closed as words escaped him. James sniggered behind him.

"Of *course*, what size clothes?"

Samuel shrugged. "My mother makes my clothes. I've never asked."

The man shook his head. "Country-folk," he muttered. He sized Samuel up and cocked his head to one side. "Give us a seven-five, Havier."

A man behind the clerk moved to a particular pile of clothes and grasped a bundle tied together with string, which he deposited on the desk. The clerk listed a small tag to note the number marked on it and scribbled that number next to Samuel's name.

"Next."

Samuel took the clothing and walked off to one side, where he paused to wait for James.

"Lad, get over here!"

Samuel started at the shout and turned to see a hard-faced soldier glaring at him. He was standing before a dozen men sitting on shaky, put-up wooden chairs, each with their new clothes on their laps and nervous expressions on their faces. Samuel opened his mouth to explain he was waiting.

"*Now!*"

Samuel hustled over to an empty seat.

"The rest of you still coming will have to listen; I have no more time to wait for you to get processed!" The soldier returned his gaze to those seated before him. "You have six weeks of training, and then you are being sent to the front."

Startled oaths erupted from the assembled men.

"*Silence!* As I was saying. You have six weeks to learn everything you need to survive and take vengeance on those cowardly Fringers. Over these weeks, you will learn how to kill with a musket, you will learn how to kill with a bayonet, and you will learn how to kill with your bare hands. You will learn discipline. You will learn order. You will learn authority. By the end of these six weeks, you will not be farmers or whatever else you sorry lot are now; you will be soldiers, and you will either be ready for the war or not, but you will be sent to the war, regardless. Make no mistake, at the end of the six weeks you will be sent to fight in whatever state you are in. Make sure you are ready. If you are not ready, you will die."

James turned wide eyes to Samuel, who just shook his head.

The soldier glared at the cowed men before him. "That's right, men, be afraid." He smiled. "You are in the army now."

Chapter Twenty-Four

The seagull soared effortlessly over the breaking waves of the Helba Ocean, its wings outstretched and its eyes searching for its next meal.

Harold Cornsten, the newly appointed secretary of war, enviously watched its graceful passage. "After the Royaume d'Occident has finished with The Fringe States, they will come for us, make no doubt," he said, his eyes still on the bird. In his new position, Harold, a former army general, was tasked with keeping an eye on The Fringe States's war, together with assessing Southcastle's readiness if that war should spill into their lands, unintentionally or otherwise.

"No doubt," Captain Robert Hedges, the Resident Commissioner for the Porton Royal Dockyard said, nodding as he watched the activity that bordered on frenetic.

The Porton Royal Dockyard was by far the most expansive of the Southcastle dockyards and where the majority of the Royal Navy was maintained. A series of stone-lined basins had been placed in the dockyard to create stepped-stone dry docks, replacing the former timber dry docks that had been high maintenance, costly, and a significant fire hazard, as the Great Shipyard Fire of a decade ago had demonstrated. The stepped sides were a vast improvement on what had been before and enabled shipwrights to easily and safely work beneath hulls as the vessel rested on the sloping stone steps after the dry dock had been emptied of water. A storage area capable of holding all repair and resupply materials needed in a regular week, a rope-house with an upper story for the repair of sails and rigging, a smithy, and over a dozen homes for the senior dockyard officers completed the site.

"Their appetite for war will have been wetted, not sated," Cornsten continued as he tore his eyes away from the bird and back to the dock-yard. "The forts will hold the mountains. Not if, but *when* they come, they will come by sea."

"No doubt," Captain Robert Hedges agreed.

The clerk of the cheque, William Garrick, was responsible for mustering the dockyard workforce and gazed at the number of men working, inspecting hulls, loading moored vessels, transporting supplies, performing repairs, and completing countless other jobs. "I'm going to need more men," he grumbled.

"The ships that were ready have already been deployed to guard our coastline as a precaution and to dissuade any Western vessel that seeks to enter our waters as they make their way around our lands," Harold said. He gestured to a huge ship resting in one of the dry docks. "I need all my ships of the line out there. When will *The Rock* be ready?"

Garrick raised an eyebrow. "*The Rock of Southcastle* is a first rate ship of the line. Do you know what that means?"

"I—"

"One-hundred guns spread over three decks stretching over one hundred and eighty-seven feet," Garrick interrupted. "Thirty 42-pounders on her lower deck; twenty-eight 24-pounders on her middle deck; thirty 12-pounders on her upper deck, and twelve 6-pounders on her quarterdeck and forecastle. She has three square-rigged masts, and the top of the main mast stands one-hundred and ninety-six feet from the waterline. More than eight-hundred and fifty men will walk her decks. She is a lot of ship."

"How long?"

"Two weeks, maybe three," Garrick said without looking away from the dockyard workers.

"You have one," Harold replied in a tone that declared there was no negotiation. "The other eight first-rates are already either off the Kafifi Ranges dissuading a sea attack from the southwest, bolstering our coastal defence; or off The Territory coast to give us advance warning if Royaume d'Occident's greedy eyes turn our way." He stabbed a finger at the massive warship. "In one week, she sails for The Fringe States."

The clerk of the cheque sighed. "I'm going to need more men."

"No doubt," Captain Robert Hedges agreed.

King Edward rose from the armchair as the prime minister entered the room and motioned to a member of the palace staff, who stood beside the double doors opening out from the sitting room to the small, elevated garden beyond. Dipping his head, the male staff member pulled open each door and latched them securely onto the interior walls.

"Let's retire to the garden, prime minister," the king said.

Martin nodded.

The king's butler stood silently behind the two leaders and gestured sharply to two other male members of the palace staff, who darted from the room. He then led the king and the prime minister toward the garden

'Things were... tense when we last met," Edward said as they walked.

"Indeed, Your Majesty," the prime minister replied.

Edward breathed quickly and rubbed his chest. It felt tight again.

The two men walked in silence for a moment. As they neared the garden, the king's butler stood to one side and paused. "May I bring refreshments?"

"What would you like, Martin?"

The prime minister thought for a moment. "May I ask for a taste of that rich brandy we enjoyed some time ago? I can't remember what it was called."

"The hors d'âge single-barrel aged brandy from the northern steppes of the Kafifi Ranges."

"That's the one."

The king nodded to his butler, who hastened away.

When they arrived at the open doors leading to the garden, the same two staff members who had departed the room previously were waiting for them. They each held a full brandy glass in one hand and a fur cloak draped across the other arm. The brandy was offered to each man and then the cloaks were draped across their shoulders. Edward gestured before him, and the prime minister led them out into the night, the two staff members walking an appropriate distance behind them.

The silence grew as they walked, each man thinking of their last encounter. Their footsteps were heavy, as was the tension around them.

"This garden," Martin began, eager to lighten the atmosphere, "where did it come from again?"

The king shook his head. "In truth, I'm not sure. My grandfather created the garden, but I believe a sea trader gave him the idea. I forget his name." Edward gestured to three cushioned chairs seated before a glowing clay chiminea puffing out wood smoke.

The two men sat, and the prime minister reached over with his glass. "To your health and the fortunes of Southcastle."

Southcastle will fall...

Edward's thin smile faltered as he remembered Nanaya's words. He clinked his glass against Martin's. "Indeed, Prime Minister."

The two men sat without speaking for a moment as they sipped.

"You know this might be the last bottle if this war continues as it is."

"It might well be," the prime minister agreed. "The Fringe States are putting up a good fight, but they are hopelessly outnumbered. Their collapse is just a matter of time."

Martin took another long, slow drink, emptying his glass. He paused for a moment, gazing into the empty depths of his sniffer before holding it out for a refill. The man who had served him before hastened forward and refilled his glass. "But we will see peace again. This war was triggered by the assassination of the Western king. Their revenge should be sated when they conquer The Fringe States."

"I am not so sure."

Martin cocked his head to the side and frowned. "What do you mean?"

The king took a slow sip of his drink as he considered his words. "If we let Royaume d'Occident take The Fringe States, how do we know they will not come for us next?"

"I am confident—"

"Maybe by supporting The Fringe States our combined forces can either defeat the West or convince them that invading the south is a bad idea."

"Edward," Martin gasped, "you are not serious?"

The king narrowed his eyes as he looked at his prime minister.

"Maybe..."

Martin shook his head. "We cannot get involved in this war, Edward."

This is the only way. Nanaya's words filled his mind. "Maybe we do not have a choice."

"We are strengthening our borders, and I believe that is all that we need to do for now." Martin smiled. "Do not worry, Edward. Leave these things to me and you—"

"Without our intervention, they will win their war, and when they do, two of the three reasons they cannot attack Southcastle will be gone," Edward whispered.

"What reasons? What are you talking about?"

Edward blinked several times. "I had just been remembering... I was speaking earlier with Nanaya and—"

"Damn it, Edward! You need to stop listening to her!"

The king rubbed his head. "I don't know. I think—"

"Please, Edward, let me manage this. This is what I do."

The king screwed his eyes closed at the words. *Please, somehow, be on my side with this. Don't make me fight you.*

"I am worried about Nanaya, Edward. First, this thing about The Territory, and now, she is pushing you to go to war."

The king took a deep breath. "You do not understand. What she showed me... And besides, if we do nothing, the West will come out of this war even stronger than it was before it. I have thought a lot about what she said, and she is right."

"Stop dancing to her drum!" Martin took a moment to compose himself. "This is not you talking, this is not you wanting any of this. Going to war? Edward, no matter what the motivation for this is, the West has made no move against us. If—"

"That is irrelevant!" the king interrupted.

"It is not irrelevant!" the prime minister argued. "Edward, listen to reason. Do you want me to strip our fields and factories and families and march them—where? Up and over the mountains where winter still holds? Ship them off across the sea to The States to fight for a land that is not their own?"

Edward felt his chest get tighter, and there was a pain in his head. "I understand what you are saying, but I don't think we have a choice. I think we need to go to war, Martin."

"You are not well, Edward, and Nanaya is taking advantage of you."

"You don't understand," the king said in a weary voice. "If we do not fight, then we will fall. I can see that now. At least by fighting we give ourselves a chance to survive, and we can also stop what is out there."

"And what is out there?"

"What has escaped the tower."

"Edward, there is no tower!"

The king sighed. "I know you do not believe me, but I know what I saw." He shook his head and stood, taking a deep breath. He looked at his prime minister with firm eyes. "Martin, I need you to declare war. Nanaya was right. It is the only way."

"I will not. You do not understand what you are asking."

Edward grunted as the pain pounded in his head. "Don't make me do it, Martin."

Martin's face creased in bewilderment. "Do what?"

"You will do this!"

"No."

A friendship that had lasted decades fractured.

The king glared at his friend.

Martin drained his glass and stood. "I am leaving."

"I have not given you—"

"This is ridiculous, Edward. You need help."

Edward's hands curled into fists. He clenched his jaw tightly. "Do not make me—"

Martin walked out of the garden.

"Martin! Prime Minister!"

Martin did not reply.

"You are forcing my hand!" Edward raged.

Chapter Twenty-Five

A whisper of air where there were no doors or windows to allow such told Adaru that he was not alone. A glint of lamp-light on metal, where a light-dulling coating had not taken as well as it should have, named this other as an assassin, showed Adaru where they were, and said that they had a blade. A grate of stone-on-stone caused by a fragment of masonry being trapped under foot explained how close they were.

Darkness erupted from Adaru's body to enclose him in a shell made from blackest night. The assassin's blade struck it and shattered, the assassin collapsing to the floor with a high-pitched shriek and clutching an arm.

Adaru rounded on the figure, his eyebrows rising in surprise as he saw it was a woman's face staring back. He tutted as he crouched over the fallen, would-be assailant. "It will take far more than that, I'm afraid."

He raised a hand in the air and took satisfaction in the widening of the woman's eyes as she watched streams of twisting darkness like sooty smoke pour from his skin to curl around his fingers. "Your employer did not tell you about me, did he? Not truly. Of course, how could he?"

The woman's eyes were filled with terror as the visible energy around Adaru stretched out to curl around her body.

"A bit of luck, and you would have succeeded." Adaru licked his lips. "But today, that luck was not with you." He gestured dismissively at her. "I am glad you accepted the contract for my death, however, for I would so like to know the traitor in my midst."

The tendrils of darkness around the assassin wound around her head.

"This is going to hurt," he said.

Château Occidentale's guards came running as the assassin's shrieks filled the air. The cloaked woman stopped screaming as they arrived and started shaking.

"Baudouin," she muttered. "Baudouin. Baudouin. Baudouin."

"Your Holiness!" One of the guards rushed to Adaru's side. "Are you hurt?"

"No," the archbishop replied. His mouth twitched as he suppressed a smile. "Thank the Shepherd," he added.

"What is she saying?" another guard asked. "What is that?"

"I was walking," Adaru said. "I do that sometimes, to help me think about all that has happened."

"Baudouin. Baudouin. Baudouin. Baudouin. Baudouin."

"I was walking, and this... this woman tried to attack me."

"Is she saying Baudouin as in Baron Baudouin?" the guard asked as he leaned close to the woman.

"How did you stop her?" the guard holding Adaru's arm asked. "Look at her; she is a hired killer, for sure."

Adaru shook his head. "I don't know."

"Baudouin. Baudouin."

"One moment, I was standing, and then the next, it was like something pushed me to one side. It was like someone was looking over me and trying to protect me."

"The Shepherd," a guard said in a hushed, reverent tone.

"Oh, I don't know about that," Adaru began again with a slightly amused smile.

"Your Eminence, it is true!" one of the guards said. "You healed those lepers. The Shepherd is looking over you. The Shepherd is with you!"

"Baudouin. Baudouin."

"It is! She *is* saying Baudouin. It must be the baron she is referring to, but why?"

"That's the last thing she said to me," Adaru said. "'Baudouin sent me.'"

The guards look at one another for a moment. "Raise the alarm," the guard still holding Adaru's arm said. "Arrest Baron Baudouin."

Adaru stood in the window of the palace tower and rubbed his temples. He felt a little lightheaded, and there was a dull ache in his head after using his power against the assassin earlier. He would need to rest. The dark power of Kur did not easily renew itself.

The war will see to that.

Adaru raised a wide-bowl glass before him so that it caught the light from a nearby oil lantern. He gazed into its mahogany depths, comparing its rich redness with the blood on the dungeon floor he had left a little while ago.

Baron Baudouin had been uncooperative at first, protesting his innocence. Then Diers had done his work, and Baudouin had not only confessed his guilt, but also readily agreed to accuse most of the other aristocracy in the scheme.

Adaru smiled at the memory of Diers embracing his newfound ability to manipulate the bodies of others, recalling the deep satisfaction and pleasure that swam across the man's face as the baron's skin had bubbled and his bones had twisted.

The archbishop swirled the wine in tiny circles and lifted it to his nose, breathing deeply and inhaling its rich bouquet.

Exquisite.

Forces under General Bron were, at this very moment, racing to each aristocratic estate, and by morning, he would be unopposed in power.

Tilting and then leveling the glass, Adaru regarded the legs, watching the streaks of wine slide down the sides of the glass.

What is it they call it here? Ah yes, the tears of a wine. Perfect.

He gazed out the window and over the city as he took a long sip of the red wine. He held it in his mouth, savouring the spice and dark fruits on his pallet before swallowing and tasting its heavy tannins. As he did, his thoughts swept back to a much earlier time, the time he had been given the power of Kur.

The Migru Church was thick with intensity.

What had been an embracing, comfortably silent space was now ominously oppressive. Vapour came with each breath, but it was not cold and had not been for months.

Adaru stood from the pew where he had sat in quiet contemplation for the past few hours and warily looked around. The church was empty. Father Setana was outside, talking with the last parishioner. Adaru walked around the pews, and as he did, he whispered prayers to An and clutched with trembling fingers the small wooden disc painted red, white, and black that hung on the metal chain around his neck. All traces of doubt that there was something here, that there was power in this place, had fled.

The only sound was the crunch of his feet on the floor, his deep, almost panting breaths, and his heart pounding.

He saw the shadowed figure as he neared the lectern.

It was hunched over in the shadows of a stone pillar, a dark form vaguely in the shape of a slender woman, yet it was indistinct, and its outline flickered and tremored.

And it was watching him.

Adaru did not know how he knew it was watching him, but somehow, he knew, and as he looked at it, he felt a scratching in his mind as if something was trying to get inside, and little by little, it was getting in. He could feel slithering alien disturbances through his thoughts.

The shape did not move; it just waited in the dark.

Adaru approached it cautiously.

Each step forward came with a shiver across his skin, a tremor in his heart, and a growing pain in his head.

Adaru....

His name was not spoken aloud but slithered through his mind. As it did, it left a sense of wrongness, like the aftertaste of something unpleasant.

You search for something.

Adaru stood immobile, staring at the dark shape. He tried to speak but was unable to make a sound.

So do we.

"Wha-what do you search for?" Adaru managed. He tasted something vile in his throat as he conversed with whatever had spoken to him.

Something to help us.

"Help you do what? Who are you?"

We are what you have been searching for.

"I don't—"

Don't know what you have been searching for? Yes, you do. It fills you, it screams from you, and calls to us. A purpose. A reason. A direction. An answer.

"A reason for what? What purpose—"

A purpose for everything that has happened to you.

Adaru involuntarily shuddered as his body remembered the beatings and far worse that he had suffered over the years.

You never want to suffer again. You never want to feel helpless again. You never want to be powerless again. You want to be strong. That is why you came here. Came to find us.

Adaru wanted to deny it all. The teachings of An explained such feelings as wrong, as immoral, as against righteousness, but he could not deny what had been said because he knew it to be true. He yearned for those things, and he could not lie to himself.

We choose you. We would give you everything you want. Everything you need. No one will ever be able to harm you again.

Adaru licked his lips. This was everything he had ever wanted. "What do I need to do?"

Open yourself to us, and we will give you a taste. We will start your journey.

A sense of crossroads came to him. In one direction, his life as it was now, as it had ever been, continuing without change. In the other direction? He did not know what lay in the other direction, but that was not daunting. It offered hope.

Tentatively, Adaru reached out a hand.

Just as Henri opened himself to me.

Adaru stared out into the night.

Poetic.

Adaru poured himself the last bit of wine from the decanter.

You are important. You will help us, the apparition had told him after he had asked why it had given him this power. It had been a sukkal, a particular type of gallus, according to Lamadu. An emissary from those that ruled Kur. It had told her that it had given him this power to enable better communication between the gallus and the kishpu as they schemed together to fully break the seals. Adaru had known differently. *We have a plan of our own, and that involves you, Adaru,* it had told him.

Adaru finished the wine, savouring the last mouthful. He had never found out what the gallus really intended for him. The tower had been attacked, and he had been sealed away.

Whatever their intentions, Kur gave me what I needed. They made me strong. He stared out into the night. *I can be even stronger, however. Out there is the tower and the power I need.*

Adaru took a deep breath and closed his eyes.

Not long now...

Chapter Twenty-Six

The air was winter crisp, holding a stark, cold freshness like no other season could. The overnight frost had thawed in all but the darkest of shadows, the moist dirt and mounds of wet, fallen leaves generating an odour that was both cloying and comforting in its fullness.

The wood was a mix of bare deciduous skeletons and dark, thick evergreens, each standing defiantly against the chill with their blankets of decaying foliage pulled up against their bodies.

They all flashed by as he ran.

Arms swinging, breath pumping in time to his stride, Samuel leapt a small stream, ducked under a low tree bough, and then burst out of the woods and into the field.

The tents lay ahead. Thighs and calves burning, his lungs straining for air, his body yearning for rest, the young man pushed himself harder and ran faster.

"First again, Samuel, nice work," the drill sergeant commended as Samuel ran across the finish line.

The young man staggered to a stop, bent over, and placed his hands on his knees as he gasped for breath.

"Suck it up, rookie, beginning tomorrow, you start training with a full pack. You think you're tired now, ha!" The drill sergeant wandered away, chuckling.

Pushing himself upright, Samuel looked back across the field, and despite his exhaustion, smiled with satisfaction. No one else had emerged from the woods. He walked on weary legs to the cold showers.

Samuel was sitting on his bottom bunk, pulling on his ill-fitting boots, when James staggered into the barracks.

"I still don't know how you do it," he wheezed as he passed his friend and pulled himself onto the top bunk a few rows down.

The barracks was an open-plan tent filled with twin-level bunk beds in a twelve-by-twelve grid with single-file walking room between each. Two simple wooden chests sat at the foot of each bunk bed, one for each occupant. Each bunk had a single pillow, a thin inner sheet, and a thick outer sheet that scratched and itched with its coarse fibres. A door at one end led outside while the door at the other end led to the showers. A smaller tent had been hastily erected with crooked piping, from which sprayed unheated icy water.

James groaned atop his bunk as he massaged his thighs. "Kill me now."

"Better get used to it." Samuel chuckled. "Sergeant told me we are running with packs tomorrow."

James rolled over and stared at his friend. "Full gear?"

Samuel shrugged. "Guess so."

"Oh, for pity's sake," James moaned, falling back onto his bunk. "That man's a monster."

Samuel stood and pulled his white linen shirt straight as he fastened the last buttons. His linen pants were of the same colour, as was a simple woollen forage cap that sat peaked on his head. A slight, but painful muscle spasm made him grimace as he bent over and opened the chest allocated to him. He reached inside and pulled out a thick, grey, wool greatcoat that he pulled over his shoulders. At night, the tent grew warm with so many sleeping bodies, and it was comfortable under the twin blankets. During the day, however, while it sat empty, it turned bitterly cold. Samuel hurriedly belted his coat shut, his breath misting in the frigid air.

"Still think you look ridiculous," James sniggered. "What would your ma and pa say if they could see you now, all dressed up in whites?"

Samuel bowed low. "They would say what a gentleman their son looks."

Both boys laughed and shook their heads at the strangeness of it all. A week ago, they were in ill-fitting, often threadbare clothes, up to their ears in mud and muck. Now, they looked better than anyone did at the annual winter's ball, save the town crier, of course.

"Better get moving," Samuel called out to James. "You'll stiffen in this cold, and we have target practice now."

James muttered a series of curses, but with a groan, climbed down and staggered to the showers.

"This is the bayoneted musket," the drill sergeant said, holding a blade-tipped rifle high in the air. A worn leather box hung at his hip. His voice was loud and commanded both attention and obedience, as did that of all the senior army men. "This is your first true love."

A man in the crowd before him sniggered at the words.

"Corporal?"

"Yes, Drill Sergeant?" a man standing a few feet away replied.

"Bring that man to me."

The corporal stepped forward and pushed his way through the assembled men, who stumbled over themselves to hurry out of his way. He grabbed a man's arm and yanked him forward.

"Now, just wait a bloody—"

The corporal's fist stopped the man's protest and broke his nose. He clutched at his bloody face as the officer dragged him out of the shocked crowd.

The man howled as blood streamed down his face. "He broke my nose!"

"Corporal?"

"Yes, sir?"

"Did you break this man's nose?"

"Sir, I was educating him in the manner in which a soldier must conduct himself, and it would appear his face is not up to the task, sir."

"Very good, Corporal, stand at ease."

"Sir!" the corporal said and let go of the man, who dropped to the ground as the officer resumed his position.

The drill sergeant looked over the crouching man to the assembled men.

"You are not at home. You are not in your village or town or farm or whatever other shit of a place you lived in, being looked after by your missus or your ma. You are in the army now, and in the army, there are rules. You do not speak unless told to do so. You do not move unless told to do so. You do not think unless told to do so." The drill sergeant squatted in front of the bloodied man, who stared back at him. "The only words that come out of your mouth are 'Yes, sir!' 'No, sir!' replies to orders given to you. If you are not replying to an order given to you, you are not speaking." He leaned close to the man. "Do I make myself clear?"

The man nodded.

"Oh, no," the drill sergeant said through ground teeth. "That's not right. You must not have understood me, did you?"

The man shook his head in bewilderment.

"Let me explain myself," the drill sergeant said in a flat, menacing voice. "Everything I say to you is an order. Everything. I tell you to shit, it's an order. I tell you to eat your shit, it's an order. What do you say when I give you an order?"

"Yes... Yes, sir," the man replied, his voice shaking with a toxic mix of fear, hurt, and embarrassment.

"So, have I made myself clear?"

"Yes, sir," the man said.

"Do I make myself clear?" the drill sergeant repeated louder.

"Yes, sir."

"Do you need further education?"

"No, sir."

The drill sergeant nodded and rose, gesturing back into the crowd. "Get back into place."

Shaking, still clutching his nose, the man climbed to his feet and rushed back into the cowed crowd.

James and Samuel cast quick glances at one another but did not dare say a word.

"Now," the drill sergeant continued, "this," — he held the rifle high in the air once more — "is your first true love."

Not a single person made a sound.

The drill master nodded with satisfaction. "You will love this rifle more than anything you have ever loved before because this will keep you alive."

The drill master pointed the rifle at the assembled men and swept it across his audience.

"Once you have finished your basic training, you will be deployed to the front lines. You will be in harm's way. You will be fired upon. The thing that will save you is being able to fire your weapon before the other man fires his, fire more accurately than the other man, and fire more times than the other man. You take too long to aim, you die. You miss your shot, you die. You take too long to reload your rifle, and you will die. Do I make myself clear?"

A mumble of *Yes, sirs* responded to his words.

"Do I make myself clear?" he yelled.

"Yes, sir!" came a louder chorus.

The drill sergeant smiled. "Well, then, rookies, we are going to get on well." He held the musket in the air. "When entering into combat, you will follow explicit orders to prepare and fire your weapon. We will drill every day in loading and firing. Once you are assembled, you will hear the words: 'Platoon, load by separate words of command,' at which point the fugleman will step to the front and will lead you through the drill. Fugleman, step forward!"

A soldier stepped to the front and saluted the drill sergeant.

"Today, I have the honour of doing this myself and giving you all a taste of what will become second nature to you. You will say these words and run through this drill in your sleep until it is seamless." The drill sergeant took a deep breath. "When you hear the command *prime and load,* you will make a quarter turn to the right and bring your musket to the priming position as so." He nodded to the fugleman.

"*Prime and load!*" the fugleman bellowed, and the drill sergeant turned to his right at the command, holding his rifle horizontally with his left hand on the swell of the stock and his elbow resting against the weapon's side. His right thumb was against the uncocked hammer, and his right elbow pressed the rifle's butt against his body.

"Note the pan," the drill sergeant called, referring to an L-shaped piece of metal that sat in front of the rifle's hammer. "This will be open if you have already taken a shot, and the frizzen top section that covers it will be tilted forward." He indicated that part of the pan. "As you can see, the pan is closed as we have not taken a shot, and so the next order is to open this."

"*Open pan!*" the fugleman ordered, and the drill sergeant pushed the frizzen forward with his right thumb, exposing the pan.

"*Handle cartridge!*"

The drill sergeant promptly dipped his right hand into the box on his right hip and withdrew a single slender paper tube with a twisted top with his first three fingers. "Pull a cartridge out like so," he said, turning to show the assembled men the paper cartridge clutched in his fingers.

"Place it between your two front right teeth and tear off the twisted end like this." The drill sergeant placed the cartridge between his teeth and bit off the twisted end. He held the now-open cartridge in his hand and again showed it to the men around him.

"*Prime!*"

The drill sergeant shook powder from inside the cartridge into the open pan before placing his outstretched third finger and little finger on the frizzen and pulling it upright, closing the pan and trapping the powder inside. His right hand continued to slide back up the rifle until it rested behind the hammer with his third and little finger curling around the bottom of the rifle stock.

"*About!*"

The drill sergeant half-faced to the left and slid the rifle through his left hand as it was lowered vertically, and the butt placed between his heels with the barrel between his knees. He then tipped the rest of the cartridge powder down into the barrel.

"Now, men," he said in a muffled voice as the paper end he had bitten off the cartridge was still clenched between his teeth, "there is a musket ball in this cartridge." He turned over the cartridge and pushed it down the barrel before taking the paper from between his teeth and pushing that after the cartridge. "Don't forget the paper," he called out. "You lower your rifle without it, and that powder and musket ball will slip straight out of the barrel, and this will all have been for nothing."

"*Draw ramrods!*"

The drill sergeant took hold of the tip of a metal rod that hung just below the musket barrel with his right forefinger and thumb. "You see this?" he bellowed. "This is a ramrod. You use this to push down all that you have just stuffed down your barrel." He drew the ramrod that grew wider toward its hidden end, reversed it, and pushed its larger end about an inch into the barrel.

"*Ram down cartridge!*" the fugleman ordered, and the drill sergeant firmly shoved the ramrod as far as he could down the barrel.

"*Return rammers!*"

The drill sergeant pulled out the ramrod and returned it to its resting place below the musket barrel with his right hand. He then pushed the rifle to rest against his left shoulder, his right arm parallel to the ground, his right fingertips touching the base of the affixed bayonet, and his left hand holding the rifle body. "You now have a loaded rifle, men."

"*Make ready!*"

The drill sergeant lifted his musket up, his left hand on the rifle stock. His right hand moved and pulled the hammer to full cock before grasping the wrist of the musket. He smiled at the men that stood before him. "I would move out of the way."

The assembled men stumbled over each other to make a gap in their lines before the soldier.

"*Present!*"

The drill sergeant lowered the rifle, bringing the butt onto his right shoulder as he moved his left hand to grip the rifle just above the hammer sprint. He stepped back with his right foot and bent his left knee. His forefinger rested on the trigger as his eyes stared down the barrel.

"Fire!"

A sharp crack came from the rifle with a burst of smoke, and several men started, cursing and chuckling embarrassedly to themselves afterward. The drill sergeant lowered the rifle back to its loading position.

He stared at each man standing around him. "You will all practice loading and firing with powder every day until you can fire four times in a minute."

James stared at Samuel. *Four times a minute?* he mouthed.

Samuel shook his head wide-eyed.

"What is more," the drill sergeant continued as he strode up and down before the men, "in battle, you will not be given orders for each step of the loading and firing process. So, pay attention! In battle, you will also form-up in ranks. Each rank will stand behind the other. The first rank will fire while the others stand ready. After you have fired your weapon, you will march to the back and begin reloading. The second rank will step forward, aim and fire together. After firing, the second rank will march to the back. All following ranks will do the same. This you will repeat until the order to charge is given." The drill sergeant grinned. "And that is where the real fun starts."

Samuel shook his head as he struggled to process the breadth of information just communicated. "How are we supposed to remember all that?" he whispered to James, who also just shook his head.

Chapter Twenty-Seven

"The winter has been short, thank the Shepherd," an overweight middle-aged man declared with a smile. The neat curls of his thick yellow parson's wig brushed his shoulders as he turned and gestured around him at his fellow ministers sitting on both sides of the room.

"Farmers are reporting more crops than normal have survived the cold, and the harvest ahead looks bountiful!"

Booted feet stomped the wooden-panelled floor, and voices rose in support.

Smiling widely, the minister sat as another in the opposite section stood and waved a handful of papers aggressively toward the men sitting opposite.

"While we all rejoice nature's bounty and congratulate her on a mild winter, I would like to hear more on what the government is doing about the shortage of food stuffs and vital supplies we face because of this war between our neighbours. Supply lines are either hindered or broken entirely, and this conflict shows no sign of cessation any time soon."

The prime minister rose from where he sat in the centre of the first long pew on his party's side of the chamber. "The honourable fellow from Tinker Town" — sniggers rose from his party as outrageous calls of inappropriateness came from their opposites at the use of the common nickname for a lower-class area of the city — "might want to enlighten the house on the shortages he is suffering at this time."

The prime minister smiled broadly. "I would imagine his treasured Terrsud claret is in short supply," he remarked, igniting guffaws from his party and louder calls for his censorship from the opposition.

"More," the prime minister continued, "I hear the agricole tulips his wife spends such an inordinate amount of money on are proving scarce, and—"

The noisy verbal combat escalated between the two parties.

The prime minister raised his voice over the din. "And, Mr. Speaker..." He turned to the man sitting at the end of the chamber between both sets of ministers and below the raised dais, upon which sat the ceremonial throne of the king that had never been sat upon. "What can we do about the lack of sour dessert apples from West Eros?"

The prime minister turned to his party and put a hand to his brow. "Will someone please tell me how to live without dessert apples!"

The chamber descended into chaos as ministers from both sides leapt to their feet and jeered at their opposites.

"Order!" the speaker yelled. "I will have order!" The man hit the table before him with the small hammer of his office.

A resounding *boom* echoed around the chamber and achieved what the speaker had been unable to do. The ministers glanced worriedly at one another.

Again, the deep resounding crash filled the chamber, and the ministers turned to one another in confusion as the prime minister looked at the speaker of the house, who shook his head.

The sound of moving chains came from the other side of the vast double doors that had been ceremonially sealed when the House started its session, chains that were to remain in place by law until session had ended and the speaker formally announced its conclusion to the guards on the other side.

The doors swung open.

The prime minister was unsure what shocked him more, the doors being opened or a member of the foot guard striding into the chamber in full ceremonial uniform complete with bearskin, a long deep-burgundy-coloured guard's coat, and bayonet-tipped rifled musket. The foot guards were the primary garrison for the capital and responsible for the military security of the monarch. Martin had never seen them enter parliament.

A deep foreboding started growing inside him. "What—?"

The foot guard slammed the rifle butt onto the chamber floor, silencing the prime minister. His rifle against one arm, the other arm rigid by his side, the guard stood tall and unmoving and stared past the politician. "His Royal Majesty, King Edward."

His proclamation made, the guard grasped hold of the rifle's forend with one hand and swung the weapon to rest against his shoulder as he stood to attention.

The sound of marching feet came from the hall beyond the chamber doors, a slight rhythmic beat that swiftly grew louder until the sound of pounding boots filled the room.

As the stunned ministers watched, twelve armed foot guards marched into the chamber and formed a corridor.

King Edward strode between them, another two dozen foot guards following behind him. Cradled in his arms was a gleaming broadsword.

Several ministers stood and looked at one another in shock.

"Your Majesty, what—?" the prime minister began.

"You will be silent, sir!" the nearest foot guard barked, his eyes hard as he glared at the politician.

Martin's mouth opened and closed without sound as words escaped him.

"Ministers," the king began, turning about him to look at each in the chamber, yet studiously avoiding the prime minister. "Return to your seats."

Martin stared at Edward.

A few ministers sat, but most found themselves unable to move, and many were unable to express what they felt or thought.

As one, the rifles of every one of the twelve foot guards forming the corridor around the king aimed at the men filling the chamber.

"I will not ask again." The king's voice quivered.

All the ministers swiftly took their seats.

The prime minister took a step toward the king. "Edward, what is—"

The foot guard who had first entered the room swung his rifle to aim at the prime minister's chest. "You will back away, sir!"

The prime minister put his hands in the air and retreated, his eyes flicking between the foot guard and the king.

"Take the room," the king commanded.

The guards behind the king quick-marched into the chamber and took positions around the room, each facing the nervous politicians.

The king walked between the rows of seated ministers at a measured pace, each footfall firmly placed with painful conviction, until he faced the speaker of the house. The speaker rose from his seat and openly trembled before the monarch.

Edward swallowed several times before he could speak. "Mr. Speaker, you may now step down. Your duties are no longer required."

The speaker stared open-mouthed at the king, then dared a furtive glance to the prime minister, who just stared at Edward wide-eyed and open-mouthed.

"I-I stand relieved, Your Majesty," the speaker stammered before bowing and walking away from his seat. He hesitated at the chamber door and cast confused glances between the king and the armed guards before departing.

The king walked forward and ascended the dais upon which he had never stood before. He paused a moment before the throne, and then sat and stared out at the incredulous faces before him. One hand gripped the other, knuckles gleaming white beneath his skin.

"As King of Southcastle," he proclaimed formally, "I claim the right to wield the Blade of the Chamber. As the wielder of the Blade of the Chamber and as monarch, I hereby invoke royal reserve power and dismiss the prime minister from office."

All eyes turned to stare at the prime minister.

"Edward, please don't," Martin whispered.

"The prime minister will now be escorted from the chamber."

Two foot guards moved to stand on either side of the former prime minister.

"Sir, you will walk with us from this place," one ordered.

Martin stared at the king. "What are you doing?"

King Edward looked at him for the first time, and Martin saw only cold determination in his eyes.

"What I must. This is the right thing to do." The king took a deep breath as Martin was led away. "Ministers, we have watched the West attack our neighbours, and we have done nothing. Contrary to what we have been told, I believe they have ambitions on our lands and our people."

Edward gazed around him. "I am declaring war on Royaume d'Occident." He paused for a moment before standing and pointing his sword at both sides of the house. "I trust I have your total support, sirs. I have dismissed one minister today; I can easily dismiss more."

Nanaya found the king wrapped in a fur cloak sitting in the garden. She paused at the doorway and regarded him. Head bowed, back bent, and shoulders rounded, the king looked exhausted. He was trembling.

And this has only just begun.

As if sensing her nearby, the king turned around and smiled thinly at her. "Lady Nanaya."

He sounds tired. His eyes are red and swollen. He has been weeping. She walked into the garden to stand beside him. She lifted her small white hoop skirt as she walked. The fabric hung from narrow rings as it fell to the floor and did not extend from her hips as larger hoop skirts did.

"It's done." Edward sighed.

Nanaya nodded. "I heard."

"I am sure you did." The king cleared his throat. "Troops will be made ready in the next few days."

Nanaya nodded. She walked out into the garden and looked around her. "It used to be like this, you know."

"What did?"

"The land around the tower. Migru was the town that used to be there in the Kharsaanu Saquutu region. It was full of lush forests, soil so rich with minerals that crops thrived even in the harshest winters or summers. It was the envy of every other region in Darisam. I remember—"

The king's eyes filled with tears, and her next words escaped her.

"I'm tired, Nanaya," the king gasped. "Before. Before I was so certain it was the right thing to do, but now... I've denounced someone I trusted without question, and in doing so, lost my dearest friend." Edward's voice wavered more with each word. "I've declared war on a vastly superior force, and I will be sending thousands of sons and fathers to die in a foreign land far from their homes."

He took a shuddering breath and blew it out slowly. He shook his head. "Southcastle will be crippled for generations to come even if we win, and we will be overrun and occupied by the West if we lose. Whatever happens, the lives of my people, the people who it is my duty to serve and safeguard, will never be the same, and everyone will suffer." Tears dripped from Edward's face. "Everything is broken."

Nanaya placed a hand on his shoulder in reassurance.

Edward shook his head. "I don't understand. I don't understand any of it."

Nanaya stared at the broken man before her.

I'm sorry, Edward, but I must do whatever it takes.

She watched as the king pulled a half-full vial of amber liquid from somewhere beneath the cloak. He uncorked it and poured the rest into his mouth, wincing as he swallowed. A sharp bitter-sweet smell came to her. It was the medicine the royal physician gave the king when his moods were darkest. It would calm him and eventually put him to sleep, but he would suffer a terrible headache and nausea in the morning.

The night was silent, full of thought.

After a moment, Edward regained some composure. He wiped away his tears.

Nanaya placed a hand on the king's shoulders. "We cannot allow whatever is out there to reach the tower. We must do whatever we can to try and stop it. You have done the right thing."

Chapter Twenty-Eight

édric Myon, Commander of the Royal Guard, rapped his knuckles against the door.

"Please enter," came a call from inside.

Cédric grasped and twisted the iron doorknob and strode into the room beyond.

Diers sat behind a small writing desk facing the door; General Bron stood to one side of it.

The general gestured to an empty chair in the centre of the room. "Close the door and sit, Commander."

Cédric's pulse quickened at the prospect of being alone in the small room with both men. Word of what the general had done in the practice grounds had swept around the guards, and so too had the total lack of censure that had come from the archbishop.

The commander's eyes darted to the other man. Rumours of these people, the Chosen, had also spread. Healed by the archbishop, these former lepers were said to be able to do things no normal person should be able to do. Ever since they had relocated from their former leper colony in the quarry to the basilica, there had been tales of strange occurrences in the capital, people inexplicably falling ill, objects moving of their own accord, strange unexplainable apparitions, and more.

Cédric felt his breath catch as he locked eyes with Diers. He was the leader of the Chosen, given he was the first leper healed by the archbishop. He was rarely seen away from the archbishop's side and never alone. Nothing was known about his life before he was healed, and nothing had been learned about him since. As the commander stared into eyes that were beyond cold, that just did not seem to be human, he realised it was more than not just knowing who he was—he didn't know *what* he was.

Cédric closed the door with a shaking hand and took the empty seat.

"Commander," Diers began with a smile that did not reach his eyes.

Cédric regarded the man. He could not read him. There was no hint of what he was thinking or about to say, and his voice did not hold any emotion. Cédric swallowed, his throat dry. He did not know whether the general or this man scared him more.

"There are going to be some changes here," Diers continued. He looked at the general and nodded.

"The Royal Guard is being reabsorbed into the army," Bron said.

Cédric felt his jaw fall open as he stared at the general, unable to speak.

"My father was in the Royal Guard and his father before him," he gasped. "The moment I was offered a place within its ranks was one of the most special moments in my life!" He looked from one man to the other, but neither said a word, they just stared back at him.

"But... but," the commander stammered. "But, why...?"

"The king is dead," the general said. "He has no wife or children. There is no need for a royal guard."

Cédric shook his head. "There is a cousin, and—"

Diers shook his head. "No longer. The princess and her family were murdered."

The commander's eyes widened at the words as his mind raced.

"And a number of other relations have also seemed to have suffered accidents," General Bron added with a slight smile. "There is no royal line anymore."

Cédric shook his head as he tried to make sense of what was being said. "There is no royal line?"

The general shook his head. "None. And without a royal family, there is no need for a royal guard."

Cédric stared at the general silently.

"As you are aware, the Church stands in place of the Crown at this time," Diers said.

"Until the war is over," the commander said.

"Of course," Diers said. "Given the environment, the archbishop believes it is appropriate to move into the castle from the basilica."

"The military agrees with this," the general said before the commander could say anything. "For the archbishop's increased protection."

"The Chosen will be relocating with the archbishop, where we will continue to form his personal guard."

"The military agrees with this also," General Bron said.

The commander shook his head. "But these, these *Chosen* are just people. For the Shephard's sake, they were lepers just a few months ago! How can they think to protect him?"

"Oh, Commander," Diers said in a soft voice that raised the hairs on the back of Cédric's neck. "You don't think that we are *just* people, do you?"

Cédric felt his breath catch, and his hands started to tremble. He felt very vulnerable in the room alone with the two men.

"Thank you for your service," Diers continued, "but you are no longer needed here in the capital. The Royal Guard is formally disbanded. Effective immediately."

"What, uh, what will I do?" the former commander asked. "I have entitlements, and—"

"Not anymore," General Bron said.

A loud knock came from the door, and Cédric jumped at the sudden noise.

"Come," the general called.

Two soldiers entered the room and stood at attention.

"You are back in the army now," Bron said. "Your skills and those of the rest of the Royal Guard are needed by your country in this war. You depart for The Fringe States tonight."

Chapter Twenty-Nine

Margaret sighed as she read the latest internal missive.

What a mess.

She dropped the report onto a pile of others she had recently read and stared up at the ceiling of the small room.

He should never have dismissed Martin.

She picked up a curling piece of parchment and dropped it after reading the first few lines.

Edward cannot do this.

The queen consort took a deep breath and reached for a blank sheet of parchment. She took the quill from its inkpot and hesitated while she thought.

This was far easier when Martin was around. What was he thinking?

She recalled Nanaya's recent frequent meetings with her husband.

It's her. I know it.

She clenched her teeth.

A knock came at her door.

"Come," she called.

A member of the palace staff opened the door and bowed after entering. "A representative from parliament wishes to see you, Your Majesty."

"Thank you," Margaret said as she shuffled some papers together and made some room on the table. "They may enter."

The man dipped his head and left, closing the door behind him.

Moments later, the door opened again, and a nervous-looking middle-aged man entered. "Your Majesty," he said, bowing low before holding out a sealed roll of parchment. "Your Majesty, messages from parliament."

Margaret nodded slowly. "These have been delayed and infrequent recently," she commented. "How are things without Martin?"

The man wrung his hands. "Your Majesty. Well, ah."

The queen consort smiled and indicated one of the seats facing her. "Please take a seat and be comfortable."

"Thank you, Your Majesty," the man said as he took the offered seat.

"Now," Margaret continued, "please tell me how parliament fares."

"Your Majesty, there is a great deal of confusion and consternation at the moment. The king has removed the prime minister and the speaker from office, and we are weaker for it. Indecision and argument grip the house. I cannot see how we will be able to act."

Margaret nodded. She pursed her lips as she thought for a moment. "Martin and I had an arrangement," she said finally. "I am sure this was known."

The man winced. "Your Majesty. I must tell you many remain troubled about that and wish to see a more... traditional situation in place. Many feel recent events provide an opportunity to reset matters and revert back to the way things were in King Alfred the Fourth's reign."

Margaret nodded. "I understand, however, those many forget the state Southcastle was in because of the way it was governed during that time. No, the arrangement works and is good for the kingdom."

"Your Majesty—"

"Sir." Margaret's eyes flashed with intensity as she interrupted the man. "There will be no further discussion on the matter. The arrangement stands by royal decree, the king himself has stated that matters of state are to be referred to me, and in his name, I will direct them."

"Yes, Your Majesty, but exactly what matters of state?"

Margaret stared the man in his eyes. "All of them."

"Your Majesty—"

"All of them, sir."

The parliamentary representative started wringing his hands again.

Margaret raised her eyebrows. "Was there anything else?"

The man shook his head.

Margaret indicated the parchment he still held. "You may leave that here and depart. I expect an immediate return to regular correspondence and collaboration."

The man stood, pulled straight his clothes, and bowed before departing.

Margaret picked up the scroll but paused before opening it.

It was all her now. She squared her shoulders.

I can do this.

She unsealed the parchment.

Chapter Thirty

Samuel lay on his bed, unable to sleep.

Tomorrow, I am going to war.

Around him came the hushed voices of men. Some were excited, boasting about their prowess and marksmanship. Others were trying not to dwell on what was coming, and the hushed sounds of sobbing and praying echoed around him blending with the mocking calls from those full of bravado.

The training had been relentless, and the days had become an endless exercise of exhaustion. His life had become drills, marches, target practice, physical training, followed by more drills and more target practice from before sunrise until after sunset. Blood blisters everywhere had initially made it painful to walk or hold anything, so intensive had the incessant training been. By the end of the first week, though, they had learned that nothing stopped the drills, and blisters had grown over blisters until the pain just became something they all had to deal with.

That first week had not been the hardest; the second and third weeks had. Things were new that first week, painful and hard and unsettling, but still novel and carrying with them a sense of adventure.

When the second week delivered the same as the first week, and then the third week yet again more of the same, the mood had distinctly changed. Men and boys alike wept for their families, for home. There had been fighting, there had been punishments. There was even a rumour that someone had been killed trying to return to his farm. Those weeks had been long and brutal and had broken many of them. After that, though, resignation and acceptance had come in varying degrees. This was their lot now. There was no escaping this.

And tomorrow, we go to war.

Samuel thought back to the farm. He thought about riding the fields at dawn and again at nightfall, watching the sky come alive with colour as the day began and ended. He thought about his mother and father. He pulled his blanket around him, screwed his tearful eyes tightly shut, and wondered if he would ever see home again.

Far from Samuel, but where he was headed, a Chosen gasped and staggered as intense sensations gripped his body. He opened his mouth and let out a low moan, clutching his belly.

Several soldiers glanced his way, but there was fighting nearby, and they were focused on joining the killing.

The Chosen grunted, his eyes watering as it felt like flames were searing his insides. He was about to cry out in pain when the inferno collapsed and changed into a flood of raw energy. It flashed through his body, and he felt himself grow stronger with its passage. He stood tall and laughed in wonder.

Adaru felt a sudden light-headedness, and then a rush of intense heat swept through his body. His skin prickled and beaded with sweat. He swayed a moment, reaching out and leaning against the nearest wall as he caught his breath. He closed his eyes and shivered as energy pulsed inside him. He sighed with pleasure and satisfaction. The Chosen were growing stronger as the energy of Kur inside them was fed by the violence and death of the war. That meant he, too, was growing stronger through the connection that he held with each of them. He smiled.

Part Two

Everything has the capacity for wonder and horror in equal measure.

Circumstance and nurture can influence which direction is taken, can exaggerate it, and can even alter that direction.

When that happens, everything changes.

When horror is turned to wonder, the most amazing things can be achieved. What once destroyed or laid low can vitalise and strengthen. Life and hope are renewed.

But when wonder turns to horror, when innocence is corrupted, the world darkens, and hope is crushed under the terror that is unleashed. Pain, death, and despair reign. Life... Life ceases to have any meaning.

It is my belief, however, my desperate belief, that any such change is just for a moment in time.

Everything I have seen tells me that, in the end, a thing's core nature truly dictates what it is, and no matter the circumstance or influence, that fundamental nature will always return. It can be buried, it can be smothered, but it can never be erased.

Even the most lost may return to us.

Nanaya

Chapter Thirty-One

Something was bothering Samuel. He could not articulate what it was, but something was not right.

"Do you hear that?"

He turned to the man who had spoken. His mouth was open, and he was staring up into the sky, a hand cupped to one ear. "There. Getting louder."

Samuel frowned but tried to find what the man was referring to. After a moment, he caught it. A rhythmic pounding that was steadily growing louder. He frowned harder as he tried to make sense of it, and then noticed that he could not only hear it, he could also feel it. More men were turning this way and that, trying to identify its source.

Samuel's eyes widened as he realised what it was.

Cavalry charge.

"Form ranks!"

Samuel's heart hammered as he rushed to obey the order. The engagements so far had been at great distances. In each there was enough time to load, aim, and fire their weapons. He did not think he had shot anyone in any of those battles, and to the best of his knowledge, no one else had either.

This was different. This time they were being attacked.

The men around him chanted prayers of strength and preservation as they jostled themselves into position. He and James stood in the third rank.

A breath of wind caressed Samuel's cheek with an icy finger. His palms were slick with sweat. He craned his neck around the men in front, but all he could see was the tree line at the edge of the dusty plain they stood in.

Someone sobbed.

The smell of piss was rich and pungent, some of it from those who had just lost control of their bladders, some of it from those who had wet themselves days ago, and their clothes now stank.

This is not like before, Samuel thought, his heart pounding. *This is not exciting, this is scary!*

Young and old, veterans and fresh recruits alike, all scrambled to form lines. There were about seventy-five men assembled into two platoons. The one Samuel was in was mostly composed of men he had trained with. The other was one they had joined on reaching the front lines. They were pushing forward into enemy territory, aiming to join with groups of other platoons advancing from other directions to form a battalion that would then take on the main enemy force.

Samuel's rifle vibrated in his trembling hands. He forced himself to take deep breaths, blowing air out between pursed lips.

Is this what it is going to be like now?

"Stand fast, I tell you!"

"Oh no, oh no, oh no," the man next to Samuel gasped.

"Prepare to load!"

Samuel clutched his musket tightly and tried to calculate how many cartridges he had left, not daring to lower his eyes from what might be approaching.

"Load!"

The young man turned to his right, opened the pan on his rifle, and then pulled a cartridge from his hip box.

"Oh no, oh no, oh no."

Samuel glanced at the man beside him and saw a wet patch blossom on the front of his pants and stretch down his left leg.

I don't like this!

Samuel gripped his musket as tight as he could to stop his hands from shaking violently. It only served to make his whole arm shake.

"Damn it!" James swore as he dropped his cartridge to the ground.

"Leave it and get another!" Samuel said as he tore the end off his paper cartridge and saw his friend start to bend down.

Wide-eyed, James nodded and reached inside his box again.

Samuel shakily poured a small amount of powder from his open cartridge into the priming pan, spilling the powder all over his weapon and the ground. His whole body was shaking, and he was barely able to close the rifle's frizzen and trap the priming powder inside as he prepared to fire. He could hear distinct hoof beats now, a sound that was steadily growing louder.

"Oh no, oh no, oh no," the man beside Samuel panted loudly, his eyes wide.

"*Company!*"

More than one man had dropped his ramrod and was scrambling in the mud to retrieve it.

"*Ready!*"

The enemy burst from the tree line. Two dozen men in sand-coloured soft armour, only their eyes visible above shemaghs wound around conical helmets tipped by dark plumes. Each gripped his mount's reins in one fist and waved a long, curved blade high in the air with the other. Billowing quilted fabric stretching almost to the ground covered their horses.

"*Fringers!*"

Now free of cover, the horses raced toward them, covering the distance impossibly fast.

Seven, maybe eight hundred paces, Samuel thought in a strangely detached way.

"*Aim!*"

The men in the front ranks swung their muskets to point toward the galloping enemy.

"*Steady!*"

Six hundred.

A man panicked and fired, startling his companions, who fired instinctively.

"*Rotate ranks!*" the lieutenant yelled to replace the spent rifles with loaded ones. "*First to back, second line move to front! Move!*"

The front line turned and rushed to the back, bumping and shoving their way past their comrades.

Four hundred.

James and Samuel were now in the second line.

The man beside James was still frantically trying to load his rifle, his hands shaking uncontrollably just like Samuel's own.

Three hundred.

The man beside Samuel openly wept, black powder on his lips and covering his trembling hands.

Samuel could see the whites of the riders' wide eyes above their veiled mouths.

Two hundred paces.

"*Commence firing!*"

The first rank opened fire, a deafening volley that sent plumes of smoke into the air, obscuring the surging enemy.

A horse screamed as it was shot, the ground trembling as it fell.

Those in front of the two young men turned and raced between them.

They were now in the front line.

Samuel and James brought the butt of their muskets to their shoulders and fired blindly. The pounding of hooves thundered louder and louder until, with a cry, James fell to his knees and covered his head in an instinctive need to protect himself, dragging Samuel down with him.

The cavalry smashed into their formation.

Samuel stared open-mouthed as the man beside him was smashed from his feet and pounded to a bloody pulp by horses' hooves.

James screamed.

Samuel screamed.

The cavalry burst through their lines and raced beyond for a moment before turning back toward them.

Samuel stared at James. There was no way they could reload before the cavalry returned. A musket on the ground caught his eye. It was cocked and ready to fire, the man it had belonged to was a broken ruin mashed into the mud. Samuel swept it up, sighted down its barrel, and fired.

A horse shrieked as it was shot, and as it fell, it clipped the one next to it, which stumbled and then also fell. The horses behind them had nowhere to go and ran into the downed animals, tumbling to the ground, their riders crushed beneath their crashing bodies. The following cavalry were forced to pull up sharply, and that gave the soldiers the time they needed.

A man next to Samuel fired. It was Gerald, the innkeeper of The Plough, the young man realised with surprise. The horsemen hauled their horses around and fled the battle.

Samuel stared after them, his empty musket still clutched in his hands. "What happened?"

Gerald started cheering. He took a shuddering breath. "We lived."

Samuel's hands shook so hard that his rifle slipped from his grasp and fell into the mud. He stared open-mouthed at the slaughter surrounding him.

Silence.

Samuel's legs gave way, and he fell to his knees. He realised he was panting, each breath ragged and wheezing. He tried to calm himself, but it only seemed to make things worse. His vision started to dim at the edges while it became impossibly bright at its centre.

"James!" he managed to cry out before he collapsed, and darkness took him.

It had been a long three-day march, but the ridge they had been aiming for was now in sight and growing closer. The army still travelled through forests and farmland, but both were noticeably thinner and far less lush than what the men were used to in the West. The farther east they travelled, the more desolate the land became.

"We'll get there just after dark, I reckon," James sighed as he looked at the ridge. He switched his rifle between hands. "Be glad to put this down and take my boots off, I tell you." He chuckled without the slightest cheer, his eyes a little too wide and staring.

Samuel nodded; he was tired. He glanced up at the sky. The sun had been hidden behind thick clouds all day, and so he was unsure what time it was. He was pretty certain the light was growing dimmer, though, and so he guessed it must be around early evening. They had been marching since before first light, and although that wasn't new, the intensity of that last engagement had left not only him, but a great many soldiers, both physically and mentally shattered.

James nudged Samuel and motioned to a man ahead of them. He was talking to himself as his hands moved up and down his weapon, fingers opening and closing the pan with each stroke.

"I think a few more deserted," James whispered. "I can't find a few that were with us before."

"How many now? Two dozen?" Samuel replied, to which James nodded.

A man to Samuel's right suddenly turned and began to walk away. A few nearby soldiers hastened to him and directed him back to the others. He changed direction to walk back alongside the main group without any comment.

"I swear, I never saw anyone!"

Both young men turned to look in the direction of the raised voice. A man was gesturing to his arm that was bound in cloth from elbow to shoulder. "I must have slipped or something. I did not see any riders!"

"He is convinced he did that," James remarked. "He still swears blind there was no attack. How can that be?"

Samuel shook his head. He could not remember much of the fight, but at least he knew it had happened, not like dozens of others who could not recall it ever happening, even though most of them had a number of injuries to say otherwise.

I wish we had a Chosen with us.

Samuel had heard of them on the way to the front lines as others drafted into the war from closer to the capital had joined them. The stories varied. Some said they were skilled apothecaries, others that they were nothing short of miraculous saints. All, however, agreed these men and women healed wounds and restored vitality and strength.

We could all do with a Chosen's touch about now.

Samuel dismissed the thought. The Chosen had only been dispatched to the first platoons to enter the war, not to the streams of raw reinforcements looking to join them. The young man hoped they joined with a battlegroup soon that had Chosen. Everyone needed healing of one kind or another.

"Keep moving!"

He sighed. Wishes for another day. Today, he had to keep moving forward, no matter how weary he felt.

Despite the men's anxiety and lingering shock, or perhaps because of it, Samuel thought, their lieutenant had driven them mercilessly onward, pushing them to reach a ridge identified as a solid defensible position as fast as possible. There, he had declared, they would find some rest, could change their clothes, and wash their current rancid uniforms.

As they neared their destination, they had merged with others until hundreds, if not thousands, made the final stretch toward respite on aching, weary legs.

A shot cracked the air, followed by a scream. Two more shots followed, and with them, the sound Samuel had come to know too well of a body falling lifelessly into the mud.

"Load!"

Men glanced around themselves in confusion.

"Get ready!" James yelled at a man nearest him as the man stared blankly ahead, his mouth hanging open.

More shots filled the air, and more bodies fell.

"Company!"

Many men tried to organise themselves into ordered lines, but their attempts were hampered by both those who were focused on their weapons and those unable to do anything as their minds unravelled in the face of more violence.

James stepped forward to help the motionless man beside him, but the back of the man's head burst in a bloody spray, and he dropped to the ground.

"*Ready!*"

James stared at the body. "That's Michael from Dion. I saw him at the winter festival once," he said in a flat voice. "I saw his da, too. Young to be a da, I remember. Don't think I ever saw his ma, though. She didn't come into—"

"*Aim!*"

Samuel gripped his friend's shoulders.

"*Commence firing!*"

A volley of gunshots snapped around them.

"James, don't lose it now!"

James stared at Samuel for a moment. "Yeah, yeah, of course, Sam," he managed and pulled out his ramrod to start loading his rifle.

Gunshots filled the air, as did grunts and cries of pain as more men around them fell to enemy fire.

Samuel could not see the enemy, so he just pointed his rifle toward some trees and shot.

A man beside him swung his rifle from one side to the other, unsure where to fire. He grunted as a shot took him in the neck, and he fell next to Samuel, clutching his throat as blood spurted between his fingers and sprayed across Samuel's uniform.

Men were firing blindly all around Samuel before rushing to form the rear line and frantically reloading. The smoke from so many muskets firing filled the air until each man stood alone, unable to see who stood beside him.

Someone a few feet away from the two young farmers screamed as the round misfired in his rifle and exploded in his face.

"Who is it?" James said as he too fired blindly ahead of him. "No one is supposed to be here! This is our ridge!"

"*Cease fire! Cease fire!*"

All but two men stopped firing, most crouching for fear of an enemy shot coming in their direction.

"*Cease fire, mongrels!*"

Panting breaths, groans from the injured and dying, and the

squelch of boots shifting in the mud filled their ears, but there was no sound from any enemy.

Samuel had no idea how many men had died. All he knew was that the gunfire had stopped.

The smoke began to clear as a light breeze swept around them.

"Probably an advanced force," the same officer's voice from before declared. "We make for the ridgeline as fast as we can. We secure that and anyone coming up here—"

"*Sir!*" someone shouted.

"*Up there!*" another yelled, pointing ahead of them.

Samuel turned his eyes to the ridge and watched as dozens of dark forms appeared on the rise, their bodies silhouetted against the darkening sky.

"They have the ridge!" James said in a voice rich with raw terror. "Our ridge. They have our ridge!"

Samuel turned his head to take in the long ridgeline where more and more enemy soldiers were appearing. He stared at the steep drop the land took from the narrow ridge.

"That's going to take a long time to climb," he gasped, "time that they are going to be shooting down on us."

"*Prepare to load!*"

"We can't assault that, right?" James asked. "That's just suicide!"

"By the Shepherd, they got cannons!"

Samuel turned at the words and watched as every tenth and eleventh man on the ridge stepped away to make space for the fat-wheeled weapons.

The Western army was too far away to fire and could just watch helplessly as the opposing force prepared.

"Fringers don't have cannons."

Samuel looked at the man who'd spoken. "What do you mean?"

The man gestured at the ridge. "Unless I'm very much mistaken, that's Southcastle. The south has reinforced The Fringe States. This just got a lot harder."

"*Forward double-time!*"

James and Samuel had no choice but to obey as the men around them picked up their pace and they were swept up in the crowd.

James pointed at the ridge. "We can't hope to storm that!"

Samuel breathed hard, his heart pounding in his chest.

The cannons roared.

One. Two. Three. Four. Five. Six.

A high-pitched whistling and a deep *whooshing* filled the air. Something spinning wildly flew overhead.

"Oh, mother of the Shepherd, it's chain shot!" the officer said with genuine fear in his voice.

Samuel started when he realised the officer was jogging beside him. *"Run for the ridge!"*

Everyone began running as fast as they could.

Samuel felt the ground shudder and heard the dull thuds as whatever the cannons were shooting hit the ground. Screams filled his ears, together with some kind of slashing, breaking sound.

"Why are we running toward the cannons?" yelled James as he ran alongside his friend.

"Have to get inside their range," an older man running nearby shouted back.

Boom, a cannon barked.

The old man gestured up at the ridge with his musket. *"They can't—"*

The man was obliterated with a sudden high-pitched whistle and rush of air. One moment he had been there, the next he was gone.

Samuel staggered to a stop and was knocked from his feet by the men running behind him, who cursed as they stumbled and fell before righting themselves and running onward.

James pulled Samuel to his feet, and they both stared where the man had been. Bits of body and chunks of dirt lay there. They raised their eyes and looked wide-eyed behind them. Churned, bloody ground stretched ten feet wide from where they stood and continued behind them as far as they could see.

"What could do this?" James gasped.

They heard that strange whistling and both looked up. Two

tumbling, spinning, half-cannon balls linked by a long stretch of chain flew over their heads to pound a handful of running men into the ground and rip apart a dozen more, then bounce back into the air before dropping and repeating its slaughter. The two young men stared in dreadful wonder as it dropped and obliterated soldiers, then bounded up only to drop and dismember more, again and again.

"So that's chain shot," Samuel whispered.

Both looked to one another, and then took off for the ridge as fast as they could.

Chain shot fell around them as they ran, ripping apart vast numbers of the surging army. With every BOOM of a cannon, the Western soldiers cast wide-eyed, furtive glances at the heavens as they ran. It was pointless, for even if they caught sight of a shot coming their way, it travelled too fast for them to avoid, yet they did it all the same.

As they neared the foot of the ridge, the enemy rifles started to fire.

Chapter Thirty-Two

A dull whine.

A scratching at the edge of his mind.

An ache that started... somewhere, and then stretched to everywhere.

Why so dark?

A tiredness. A deep and thick and relentless tiredness.

An itch.

A pop.

Grey.

Why is everything grey now?

Not an itch. A sting.

Not a pop. A crash.

Not a sting. A pain.

Not a crash. A thunder.

Samuel opened his eyes and winced as a sharp pain stabbed out from his side.

Men ran wildly in a thick rolling fog of gun smoke, either trying to find cover or trying to flee. Some succeeded, finding a depression to hide in or running beyond the reach of the muskets and out of the firing path of the cannons. Many did not, and he watched them fall.

Some collapsed elegantly as a single shot took his life, others jerking horribly as multiple shots drilled multiple bodies in puffs of red blood.

Many men tried to reload their weapons, and some succeeded. Those who did not were peppered with gunshot or brutally destroyed by chain shot.

Samuel reached down, and as his fingertips brushed a rough bandage, liquid fire ignited inside, and he groaned.

"Don't touch!"

It took a while, but the pain ebbed, and when it did, he opened his eyes and gazed at James, who was watching the chaos around them. They were sitting in a small depression at the foot of the ridge. James's rifle was loaded in his hands, and Samuel's was also loaded beside him. A satchel of cartridges lay nearby.

"We can't take this ridge," James said with the brevity of a man who has thought long and hard over the decision. He took one last look over the brim of the depression, then moved to Samuel's side.

"There was shrapnel in your side. It was not that much. It was poking out. I got it."

Boom, a cannon above them roared.

James glanced around. "I reckon our best bet is to get away from here and find a place to rest up, but I can't see a thing. Have no idea where anyone is."

Someone ran, screaming, past where they hid, and both young men ducked until the sound had faded into the chaos of war.

A gunshot came from somewhere nearby, and another man screamed; he did not stop, however, and his screams grew in pitch and intensity.

"If the enemy is looking for us, that will bring them," James said.

Samuel nodded. "We run."

"We run," James agreed.

Samuel grunted and hissed with pain as James helped him to his feet. Using the butt of his rifle to help steady himself, Samuel clambered over the edge of the depression. Both crouched for a moment as they tried to find their way through the thick smoke.

"There," Samuel managed, nodding to his left. A moment of clear air showed the edge of a tree line.

A volley of shots erupted from somewhere nearby.

"The enemy has come down from the ridge," Samuel said through clamped teeth.

James nodded. "Do you need to lean on me?"

Samuel shuffled forward a little, then grinding his teeth, he took another two steps. Panting, gripping the side of the musket so tightly his knuckles gleamed bone-white, he shook his head. "I can do this."

James gestured ahead. "Good, this is loaded," he said, levelling the rifle at his waist. "Let's go."

The distance was short, but the journey seemed to last a lifetime. Smoke continued to roll down from the cannons, joining with that from the muskets of both sides to blanket the world in a thick, billowing greyness that filled the mouth with ash.

They stumbled blindly, trusting themselves not to deviate and stopped often as men ran and cursed and fired around them. At one point, they crouched on the ground as a handful of Southcastle soldiers materialised from the gloom beside them. The man nearest them did not register their presence, walking within a foot of where they hid and continuing onward without the slightest of glances. Within two steps, he had disappeared once more into the gloom.

Breathing hard, James helped Samuel to his feet, and they moved as fast as they dared through the dead.

"Please!" a man begged in a strange, slurring voice.

Samuel jerked as a hand gripped his ankle and nearly sent him sprawling.

"Please?"

The town crier from home lay on the ground with blood covering half his face. One eye was swollen shut and caked with blood, as was one side of his head that looked crooked and misshapen. He gripped Samuel's ankle and tugged, his single open eye wide and vacant.

"It's Piers!"

Samuel stared at the man they had known for as long as they could remember.

"Please," he slurred.

"We have to help him," Samuel said.

Piers was home. There was no question in Samuel's mind. "Take him. Help him."

James slung his rifle over his shoulder and pulled the town crier onto his shoulder. "Shepherd, he is heavy!"

"We need to move!" Samuel urged.

Grunting with effort, the three figures dragged themselves through the smoke and death and then into the trees.

"Have to keep going," Samuel said through clenched teeth. "We need to get far away."

Piers had passed out and was a dead weight, though breathing shallowly, so James at least knew he was still alive.

James nodded. "Let's keep going."

The three men disappeared into the woods.

Chapter Thirty-Three

"How badly?"

Harold Cornsten, the Secretary of War, shook his head as he regarded the map covering the table before him. Wooden blocks of various sizes and colours represented the numerous battles and engagements they were aware of.

"Very badly. We have always paled before the Royaume d'Occident's military strength. The foot guard has our finest weaponry, flintlock muskets with smoothbore barrels, but these are few and far between, whereas the entire Western army is armed with the weapons. Our infantry mostly have arquebuses with matchlock firing mechanisms. All it takes is a downpour, and our army is severely compromised."

The king's heart pounded. He took a faltering breath. He could feel an anxiety attack rearing its head. In the past few weeks, they had become far more frequent than ever before.

I need some more tonic.

"I don't follow," Edward muttered as he tried to rub away sudden tension across his brow with his fingers. The pain in his head had not abated for days.

"Matchlocks require a lit match," the secretary explained, "whereas flintlocks have a flint ignition mechanism, no flame needed. Without a flame, the matchlock will not fire. A heavy rain will see our men slaughtered."

The king's eyes widened. "By the Shepherd! What are we doing about that?"

The secretary spread his hands. "We are starting to produce flintlock muskets, but until now, there has not been a need to push ahead with their development. We just don't have enough to equip our men, and it will take a long time to scale-up production."

Edward rubbed his temples more vigorously.

There is so much to do, so much to consider and be aware of.

His head was pounding. He was taking more and more of his medicine, and consequently, he felt as though he was always being thrown from despair to pain with bouts of restless sleep between.

"Why did I not know this before the start of the war?"

Harold grimaced. "There really was no need for you to know, Your Majesty. The prime minister was well aware, and plans were afoot to improve production, but he believed there were other matters that were more important for the budget to be spent on. Domestic initiatives. War was a very remote prospect."

I need to do something... What do I do? The king screwed his eyes closed. *Margaret. Margaret will know what to do.*

"Is there any good news?"

Harold hesitated, his face growing troubled. "Yes and no." He indicated a ridge. "Do you remember that scouts reported a major Western force making for this ridgeline? And that if they took it, they would have a near unassailable position with a clear path for reinforcements. This would be a foothold from which things would have escalated very swiftly?"

Edward nodded as he remembered and seized upon his recollection. "Yes, I commanded forces to intercept. We had artillery on the field near that position." The king scowled for a moment. "I think there was discontentment at my decision, but I can't remember why..." He blinked away the memory and licked his lips nervously. "Tell me, did we win?"

The secretary took markers indicating nearby Southcastle forces and moved them to the ridge, then he took those representing Royaume d'Occident and tossed most to the corner of the room. "We got there first and broke them. The force is now scattered."

"Yes!" A thrill of relief at finally hearing good news washed through Edward, easing his anguish as a soothing balm. "We need to capitalize on this." He felt excited, bouncing from his previous low to an almost euphoric high. "Yes, we can do something! Let's—"

"We can't do anything, Your Majesty," the secretary said dejectedly.

"We need to rally and push through—wait, what?" the king asked as the secretary's words registered.

"We took the ridge, but in doing so, we massively weakened our positions here." He pointed at a particular area of the map where he had taken a Southcastle marker and moved it to the ridge. He then gestured to the other places that he had moved a Southcastle marker from. "And here, and here and here.

Edward's high wobbled.

"We won a major engagement, but it left us severely weakened. We have reinforcements on their way, but Royaume d'Occident's will arrive first." Harold moved several new enemy markers sitting within the Western kingdom's territory to inside The Fringe States's border. "Their conscription efforts are pushing new troops into the war every day. This is a numbers game. Rifles, both ours and theirs, are not very accurate at the best of times. Battles are won and lost by the volume of shots you can throw at the enemy and, when it comes down to it, the number of men in a bayonet charge. Our weapons don't have bayonets. Whatever way you look at it, the numbers are on the West's side."

Anxiety reached up and pulled Edward into its embrace. His hands shook.

The secretary rubbed his eyes, and then gestured at a significant collection of shapes sitting just inside the border between The Fringe States and Royaume d'Occident.

"This is Fulton's battalion." Harold stared at the blocks. "Fulton and I have known each other for twenty years. I was at his daughter's wedding." He took a deep breath. "The last report said his support company was almost gone, as were two of his three rifle companies. That was two days ago."

He pointed to another collection of shapes deeper inside The Fringe States. "Walter Spencer leads this battle group, one of our finest commanders. Last report had him in full retreat."

The king stared at the bleak picture before him. He knew the war had not been going well these past few weeks, he just had not realised how bad it was.

What did I do...?

The scope of disaster was too much. Chaos was everywhere.

"Breathe," he whispered to himself.

Harold pointed to several shapes off the coast of Royaume d'Occident. "*La Fureur*, a one-hundred and ten-gun, three-deck equivalent of our first rate ships of the line, sails with seven support vessels. Five of our ships are already resting at the bottom of the ocean after engaging them. For now, our navy has pulled back and sits in the waters between The Territory and The Fringe States."

Edward gripped the edge of the table. "You paint a grim picture," the king muttered through clenched teeth.

"I paint a clear picture, Your Majesty," the secretary of war countered. "We cannot win this war. We are outgunned and out-strategized."

"The Fringe States will fall?" Edward managed between deep breaths as he tried to ease his pounding heart.

"Will fall? They have already fallen, My King! Their military was no match for the West. They may have caused trouble for them in the past, but those days are long gone. Recent years have just seen border skirmishes and minor engagements with individual territories and their respective armies. The Fringe States were crushed by the weight of a unified Royaume d'Occident armed force. Only the introduction of our soldiers has prevented a total collapse and offered resistance to the West's advance. Our troops tenuously hold some ground here and there, but our lines are buckling."

The king gestured to the map and the picture of the war it conveyed with a trembling hand. "What can we do?" His voice quivered with emotion.

I need more tonic, he thought. *I can't get through the day like this.*

Harold frowned at the king. "Do? There is nothing we can do that we are not doing already. Unless a miracle happens, our forces will be destroyed, and if what we fear comes to pass, we will be fighting Royaume d'Occident within our own border by month's end."

A painful tightness in Edward's chest was restricting every breath.

We massively weakened our positions. In full retreat. Ships are already resting at the bottom of the ocean. Walls are weakening. I have no men to give. Total collapse. Our forces will be destroyed.

"It is too much," Edward gasped.

"Your Majesty?"

The king waved a hand in the air and turned from the table.

"Your Majesty! Where are you going? We need—"

"It is too much!" Edward rushed from the room.

Chapter Thirty-Four

"Come," Adaru called from his couch as several knocks came from the other side of his chamber door. The door opened, and a thin young man walked in, and then bowed formally. "Lady Marion is here to see you, Your Eminence."

"Show her in, please."

The servant bowed once again and passed back through the doors. Moments later, a slender woman dressed in a pale-yellow, silk, sack-back gown walked into the room. The fabric at the back of her dress was arranged in box pleats that fell from her shoulders to brush the floor as she walked. At the front, the woman's gown was parted and open, showing a pearl-encrusted stomacher and an elaborately embroidered petticoat. Ruffles ran up her elbow-length sleeves, and a hoop petticoat held her garments modestly out to either side. A small linen cap covered her head, though a few strands of black hair had escaped at the sides and back. Lace lappets hung on either side of the cap, almost reaching her shoulders.

It was her eyes that captivated Adaru, however. Their green was so light it was almost non-existent, so her dark pupils were striking, black-rimmed off-white pools. The result was a gaze of unsettling intensity.

"Archbishop," Marion said with a bowed head and a deep curtsey. Her eyes met his. "If that is how you wish to be addressed."

"Whatever do you mean?"

Marion rose to her full height and walked around the room, inspecting its contents. "You are no holy father of the Church."

"What am I, then?" Adaru asked, regarding her intently.

"After what happened in the quarry I could, well, feel you. You were a presence inside the archbishop. So, you are not natural." The woman gave a small, husky laugh. "But then again, neither am I anymore, am I? You saw to that."

Adaru smiled. "Indeed. Do you have any idea what you are?"

"I know what I am not. I am not sick, and I am not weak." She smiled, but it was almost a sneer. "All my life, I have been both. Despised, abused, punished for a condition that I never asked for. Whatever you did to me has changed everything." Her eyes sparkled with sudden intensity. "Now I am strong, and I do not care what you are or how I am like this. I only celebrate that I am like this. Now, I will do what I want, take what I want."

"Very good," Adaru purred.

Marion smoothed the front of her dress again. Adaru assumed it had been a long time since she had worn such a thing, if ever.

"What do you need from me?"

Adaru's eyes narrowed at her words, and she smiled back at him. "You remade me, remade all of us. It had to be for a reason."

Adaru nodded. "I need you all to play a part in this war and what is to come."

Marion pursed her lips as she regarded him. "Like what?"

"How goes your training?" Adaru asked, ignoring her question.

Marion's eyes flashed, and her mouth tightened, betraying her anger over her question being ignored. "It goes fine.".

Adaru reached out his hands. "Take them."

Marion hesitated for a moment before reaching out and grasping his hands. She gasped as a jolt of energy shook her.

"In order for you to be able to do what is needed, I need to make a few further... adjustments."

Marion wailed as another burst of energy ran through her body. Her skin prickled as if burnt, and her organs ached as if bruised.

"This will be a little unpleasant, but when I am done, you will be much more powerful than you are now. You said you wanted to take what you wanted. Well, this is how you will be able to take it all."

Marion took a deep breath and gripped Adaru's hands tighter.

Adaru's eyes shone brightly, and Marion felt liquid fire flood her veins from where his hands touched hers. She ground her teeth and moaned, sweat erupting from her brow.

She locked her eyes on Adaru. "More."

Adaru smiled and did just that.

Chapter Thirty-Five

"I don't think he is doing so well."

James looked to the town crier lying in the root-ripped hollow of the felled tree. Sweat beaded his face even though it was cold enough for their breath to steam, and he twitched uncontrollably. His eyes had never regained their focus, and he stared vacantly straight ahead.

"Yeah," James agreed with a sigh.

"What do we do? He is getting worse."

James shrugged. "What can we do? We gotta keep going 'till we can't, 'till he can't."

"Let's get going, then," Samuel said with a sigh of his own.

Together they pulled the vacant town crier to his feet, Samuel grunting as the healing wound in his side sent tremors of pain through his body.

"I got him," James said, shouldering the man's weight.

Samuel nodded and pulled open the leather cartridge box belted to his hip. He stared at the blank holes in the fifteen-cartridge wooden block. "I've got seven left. You?"

"Eight or nine, I think," James grunted in reply as he shifted the big man's weight.

Samuel loaded his musket and half-cocked the hammer. "You good?"

James rolled his eyes. "Good enough."

Samuel leading, they continued their slow plod to find safety.

It had been two days since they had escaped the battlefield. Two days of little sleep and an exhausting, chaotic dance of hiding one moment and moving as fast as they could the next as they fled the Southcastle army.

Samuel's stomach growled loudly, reminding him all they had eaten in the past few days was a handful of berries and new tree leaves foraged the night before. He closed his eyes for a moment, rubbed them with one hand, and then looked around him.

I think we are still heading northwest. It was almost impossible to tell with thick cloud cover and unchanging terrain. *I hope we cross back into Royaume d'Occident soon.* He closed his eyes again and sighed.

When he opened them, two Southcastle soldiers were standing in front of him.

Their backs were turned as they talked animatedly to one another, their voices having covered the sound of the Westerners approaching.

Samuel stopped and crouched. He put his hand out to signal James to do the same, but his friend did not see and walked into him, sending all three of them falling to the ground with a crash of broken bushes, crunch of brittle undergrowth, and growled curses.

"What—?"

"Shut up!" Samuel said as he clambered to his feet.

The soldiers were running toward them, weapons raised. Unlike the cartridge box each young man carried, the Southcastle soldiers had their rifle ammunition held inside small, sealed containers that hung from a leather bandolier worn diagonally over each man's shoulder, across their chests to their hips. Each dangling container contained the exact amount of a single shot.

Samuel cursed and cocked the hammer on his loaded flintlock as one of the soldiers fired.

Wooden splinters puffed from a nearby tree as the shot missed by a good ten feet.

Samuel fired at the man, who fell back yelling in pain.

The remaining Southcastle soldier swept his arquebus up, closed his eyes against the expected flash of ignited powder, and fired.

He too missed.

The soldier, Samuel, and James held their breath and stared at one another.

The match on the soldier's gun smouldered, sending curls of smoke into the air.

Samuel was the first to react and leapt forward to use his flintlock as a spear. He rammed the bayonet into the Southlander's stomach, who dropped his weapon and fell to his knees, crying out in pain.

James jumped up and brought his rifle over and down onto the enemy soldier, spearing him at the base of his neck.

The man slumped forward, dead.

Both young men stared at the body, breathing hard.

"Shooting is one thing," Samuel said. "That... that was very, very different. I don't want to do that again."

"We need to move," James managed shakily.

Samuel nodded. They both looked to the other Southcastle soldier, who was still crying out, holding his wound. Blood stained his uniform in a wide bloom around where he had been shot. Both James and Samuel knew they had to finish him. Samuel shakily reloaded his weapon and walked up to the soldier. He aimed at the man's head as he looked up and tried to plead for his life, raising bloody hands imploringly.

Samuel closed his eyes and shot.

After a moment to catch his breath and try to forget what he had just done, Samuel returned to James's side. He handed his friend his gun. "I'll take him," he said shakily as he pulled the town crier to his feet and put the older man's arm over his shoulders.

James nodded and began loading the weapons.

Chapter Thirty-Six

"Do you feel it?"

Diers chuckled. "Of course. It's like lightning through my veins."

Marion took a deep breath, closed her eyes, and exhaled. "I'm stronger. I can feel it."

Diers nodded. "Same." His face tightened with remembered pain. "It was not pleasant, though."

Marion involuntarily shuddered and then physically shook herself as if doing so could discard the memories of what Adaru had done to her. "I don't just mean what he did," she clarified. "Things feel different."

"He said the environment would change once we were here and training together. He also said the war would further change things, but—"

"But they were just words, and we didn't know what they meant," Marion finished for him. "Do you also feel him, now?"

Diers nodded. "I couldn't understand it at first. It is almost as if when Adaru changed us further, a piece of him stayed inside of us."

Marion's lips curled with distaste. "I don't like it."

Diers shrugged, then his mouth twisted into a thin sinister smile. "I like what he has done. I feel powerful."

"Who else did he do this to?"

"Just you, me, and Antoinette." Diers shivered. "Antoinette was disturbing before. I wonder what she is capable of now. She keeps to herself, barely talking to any of us. She is so... distant."

It was Marion's turn to shrug. "I don't care for her." Her eyes sparkled. "Let's see what I can do."

Diers eyes widened. "Now?" He looked around him.

The Chosen were sitting in a wide landing on the second floor that a tall, bifurcated staircase led to. The wide bottom flight rose from just past the main palace entrance, then split into two narrow flights that turned to either side and led to the second floor. Several couches, chairs, and tables sat in the area that was a meeting location for those who visited the palace.

Marion smiled thinly. "Now." She rose and walked to the balustrade that curled around the gap in the floor above the staircase. She trailed her fingers along the polished wood as she gazed down at the people walking below.

"What do you have planned?"

Marion did not turn to Diers; her eyes roamed the men and women below until they settled on a woman standing off to one side. "That one." She closed her eyes and took a deep breath.

The woman raised a hand to her throat. She frowned as she tried to understand what her hand was doing. Her fingers curled around her throat and clenched it tightly, eyes widening in shock. A slight smile parted her lips even as she began to choke. She fell to her knees, gasping. People came running to try to help as the woman continued to strangle herself, her nails digging bloody furrows in her skin. The smile remained on her lips.

Marion let out the breath she had been holding and opened her eyes. The woman's hand fell away from her throat, and her smile vanished, to be replaced with a horrified realisation of what had just happened as she dragged ragged breaths into her lungs.

Marion turned to Diers and smiled. "Last week, I could only do that when I was much closer, and it was more of an effort to force someone to do something." She licked her lips. "Now I can... make someone want to do what I want, and after a while, they want it, too. It's like I change a bit of them."

Marion watched the woman tentatively reach for her throat again before hurrying away.

"She will never be the same, you know. I think when I do this, I put a little bit of my power inside them. It keeps changing them long after I stop. It would not surprise me if she strangled herself in a few days or weeks." The woman's eyes turned thoughtful. "I wonder what would happen if I put more power inside someone, kept changing them. I wonder what I could do to someone..."

Chapter Thirty-Seven

Nanaya stood alone on her balcony, staring out past the mountains and into Royaume d'Occident. She could feel every use of Kur's energy like the slice or stab of a blade.

Just like before. I did not know what it was back then. None of us knew what was happening. That allowed things to escalate, and we nearly lost everything. Never again.

She weighed what she was about to do. She needed to know more about what was out there, and she could not do that from Southcastle. She needed to be in the West, and as soon as she crossed the Kafifi Ranges, whatever had escaped the tower would almost certainly be able to sense her.

And not just what has escaped the tower. If he is still alive, he will also be able to sense me.

She set her teeth together, and her eyes grew hard.

I must know what is happening. I must know how to stop it. Whatever the cost.

She took a deep breath and nodded as she made her decision. Closing her eyes, she summoned her power and released herself from her body. Once more, she raced across Southcastle and from there over the Kafifi Ranges, and then she was in Royaume d'Occident.

Adaru was taking a slow walk outside in the cool night air when he felt it. He abruptly stopped and turned to stare out over the crenulations cut into a parapet wall toward the south. Somewhere in that direction he had felt something emerge, a power of this realm.

"A guardian," he whispered. "I thought they were dead."

He stared to the south, feeling the guardian coming closer before turning and making his way to his chambers. He closed and locked the door before sitting cross-legged in the centre of the room. Closing his eyes, he prepared himself to face whatever was coming.

Nanaya stared at the men and women in the Château Occidentale's basilica courtyard, each trailing stretching shadows in the lamplight that kept back the night.

In her ethereal sight, the black power of Kur bled off them as dark streaks of foulness that stained the air as they moved an oil-like residue that remained even after they had moved on.

It is so much worse than I feared.

She watched those in the courtyard play with this vile power inside them, torturing helpless castle staff by inflicting sudden pain or manipulating their minds or bodies.

Why am I not affected by this use of their power?

She scrutinised the men and women, using her affinity with this realm's energies to delve deeper into what they were doing.

Their power is some sort of hybrid of both realms. That is why it does not hurt me as much as the use of undiluted energy from Kur.

Something caught her attention, and Nanaya turned to find a woman approaching her. The woman's long, dark hair hung around her face like a frame within, which burned two bright violet eyes. Nanaya recoiled in horror. This woman boiled with a sickly glow.

"Antoinette!" someone called.

The woman ignored the cry. "There is something here…" she whispered as she advanced on Nanaya.

"Antoinette, we must leave!"

The woman swung to stare angrily at the source of the voice, and as she did, Nanaya fled.

Adaru felt Nanaya flee and breathed easier.

It did not attack. Interesting. It is either not ready or confident enough to face me and the Chosen.

He thought for a moment.

If there is one, there may be more.

He remembered what had been done before to eliminate the threat the guardians had represented.

I wonder if he is still alive.

Adaru closed his eyes once again. This time, he strained his senses, reaching out into the world for something created a thousand years ago that also held Kur's energy. He eventually felt it. It was faint, but unmistakable.

"Good." He sighed. "He is still here." Opening his eyes, he unlocked his door and called for a Chosen.

"Yes, Your Eminence?" a young man asked as he rushed to Adaru's side.

"Make travel preparations for early tomorrow morning. I am planning a small journey. I want to leave before first light. Inform Marion she is to accompany me."

Nanaya slammed back into her body in Southcastle and collapsed, exhausted, on the floor. She lay there panting for a moment before pushing herself up.

That woman sensed me!

She took several deep breaths to slow her pounding heart.

Nanaya walked to her balcony doors and threw them open, then strode out into the cold night air where she took several deep breaths. She recalled the woman who had felt her and the wrongness that had filled her. She remembered how many others there had also been filled with the power of the other realm.

How can anything stop this?

Chapter Thirty-Eight

"I think you need to sleep, my love."

King Edward stopped rubbing eyes he had not realised he had been rubbing and turned at the sound of his wife's voice. He found her standing in the doorway.

"I just need to" — he yawned widely — "look over the papers; there is so much happening."

Margaret walked into the king's personal study. Set within the royal private quarters, the study had been a room commissioned by Edward's father. Originally a walk-in storage space, he had changed the room into a compact workspace with a sturdy desk, a small couch, a floor-to-ceiling bookcase, and a thick fur rug. It was a room that he could access at any time of the night and continue to work.

Edward looked around the room as his wife moved closer.

"I never liked this room. Whenever I woke early as a child, I would find my father here, and always I would be greeted with a gruff order to go to my mother and leave him alone. A sleepy ask to just sit on his lap was always ignored, a tearful need for a cuddle brusquely pushed aside." Edward sighed. "Now I am in it most nights and into the early morning. Just like my father."

His wife laid a hand on his shoulder.

King Edward shook his head. "I just can't seem to keep on top of everything."

"Leave these for me to look at," his wife said as she sat on the couch. "What can I do?"

Edward shrugged. "I don't know what anyone can do."

Margaret was silent as the king rubbed a stubbled chin.

"I feel trapped," he whispered.

"Talk to me."

Edward stared up at the ceiling for a moment as he collected his thoughts.

"There are things happening outside of my control, beyond my understanding even, that have required me to act, and I have done so to the best of my ability."

The king took a slow sip from his whiskey tumbler. His hand shook slightly. He brought the glass up to his eyes and stared into the swaying, burnt amber liquid.

"Just like my father."

After a moment, he set the glass down and looked at his wife. "I can't see a way out."

His wife nodded. "What happened?"

The king gestured to a paper on his desk. "A report came through from the front." He shook his head. "It's a disaster. Complete collapse. We are falling back everywhere. He took a deep breath, and then took another gulp of whiskey.

His wife leaned forward. "Why *are* we at war, my love?"

The king shook his head.

Margaret leaned closer. "We can extract ourselves. It is not too late. Yes, we have suffered loss, but we can pull back and—"

Edward shook his head. "No, no, we can't. We just can't. Nanaya..." He shook his head again.

Margaret met his gaze. "What has Lady Nanaya made you do?"

The king sighed, rubbing his temples. "I know you don't like her."

"What woman would like another whose figure and looks do not slip over time and who has their husband's ear and attention?"

Edward glanced at his wife, who was staring at him with her eyebrows raised and a tight set to her mouth. She shook her head.

"I have been looking over things," Margaret said in a soft voice as she rubbed her husband's arm. "We have been very good with our policies over the past few years. We can bring our people home and spend on defence."

Edward shook his head, but his wife gripped his arm slightly.

"I know you are worried about the West attacking us, but the only way they can reach us is over the Ranges or by sea. We can bolster the forts and our navel defences. I am sure that—"

"You have not seen the things I have," Edward gasped in a weak voice as he gripped his head.

Margaret was silent for a moment. She stifled a yawn.

No time for that now.

"My love, just remember who you are. You are the king. *You* rule Southcastle, not Nanaya. This is your kingdom by right and by your capability to rule." Margaret reached up to cup his face. "You write your destiny, you write our destiny, and you and only you write the destiny of your people. We must consider that this war is not in the best interests of our people."

Edward was sobbing silently. He took a shuddering breath. "I wish it were that simple."

Margaret sighed. *Nothing can be done tonight except to try to find some peace.*

"Shall I get you some more medicine, my love, and then would you like to come to bed?"

Edward nodded. "Tonic. Yes. Please," he said in a weak voice.

Chapter Thirty-Nine

As the sun rose on a new day, Adaru stood in the midst of a wild, thick woodland a few hours from the capital, laid his hand on a thick, twisted mass of vines before him, and summoned the dark power inside himself. The vines shrivelled and crumbled to ash, withering as their vitality was ravaged to reveal a small, hollow space with a dark shape in its centre. He ducked and stepped inside. A rich sense of rot assaulted him, but it was not the smell of decaying matter. Rather, it was a corruption of this realm that touched him at a fundamental level.

To Adaru, it was the sweetest of nectars, and he savoured it as he looked around at the cocoon of vines.

How ironic that a shell of nature has hidden and protected a thing of death.

Adaru moved to the shape and found it to be a mass of vines even thicker than those that had hidden this space. Each was easily the thickness of his thigh, and they were wound tightly around something, as if clutching it.

Or imprisoning it, Adaru thought. *I wonder what happened.*

Again, he summoned his power and lay his hands on them. These did not fall away, rather they shivered and resisted. Adaru frowned. He could feel the power of this realm pulsing strongly inside them, and it pushed back against Kur's energy.

He ground his teeth and pushed harder, feeling the energy inside him burn coldly. The vines' protests grew weaker until they, too, fell apart, revealing a body wrapped tightly in a tattered cloak. The cloak was a well-made travelling garment of thick cloth that hid the shape of the body underneath. What it could not hide were the foot-long misshapen remnants of antlers that twisted from the head. They had a sickly yellowish tinge to them, and their broken edges were ragged and splintered. The head was turned away from the entrance so Adaru could not see its features, but he felt no need to move it. He remembered the face distinctly, both before and after its change.

Adaru ran his fingers across the cloth, digging furrows in the thick layer of dirt and dust that had settled on the body over the centuries. The sunlight streaming through the opening Adaru had created was clouded with dust motes, creating a hazy, mist-like glow.

The ceiling a few feet above Adaru's head was full of cobwebs, but nothing touched the body.

Adaru lay both his palms on the cloth and closed his eyes. He steeled himself for what he was about to do. Just as he had with the lepers, he reached out with his power and pushed that energy into the entombed body. Unlike the lepers, however, Adaru was not using that power to alter or change. He was revitalising that which had already been changed.

He leaned on the body for hours, feeding it his energy until exhaustion began to take him. His vision greyed, his legs gave out from under him, and he collapsed to the dirt floor. Adaru lay there for a long time as he regained his breath, and he felt a measure of strength return. When he judged himself ready, he clambered to his feet and stood swaying for a moment as a wave of dizziness hit him before turning to leave.

Marion rose from where she had been sitting next to the nondescript single-horse-drawn carriage as Adaru emerged from inside the mass of vines. She watched curiously as he walked unsteadily toward her.

Adaru motioned at the driver of the carriage. "We return to the palace," he commanded in a shaky voice, and then climbed inside and motioned Marion to accompany him.

"So will you tell me what this is all about?"

Adaru turned to her as he settled himself. He stared at her for a moment. "Your eagerness in all things is to be applauded, Marion, but temper it with caution. You may feel invincible, but let me assure you that you are not. Do not let your newfound confidence be your downfall."

Marion nodded and looked suitably chastised, though the rebuke prickled her.

Adaru turned away from her and looked out the window as the carriage picked up speed. "Your power is from another place. I have gifted you with energy from that place and given you the ability to use it."

"Where is this place?"

"Kur."

Marion's eyes widened, but Adaru did not notice.

"It is a different realm," he continued. "There are seals between that realm and here. There are watchers over those seals. They are powerful in the energy of this realm, and they are called guardians."

"Are the guardians still here?"

"I did not think any had survived," Adaru admitted. "I thought they had all been killed."

"By you?"

Adaru laughed. "Oh, no, I was nowhere near their equal back then. Now, closer, but still they were incredibly powerful. No, it was not me. One of their own killed them."

"Who?"

Adaru gestured with his head back the way they had travelled. "The one I just awoke."

Marion stared at him. She had herself at the top of the food chain after her rebirth as a Chosen. This was unexpected.

"It appears I was wrong; a guardian lives, and it is aware of me. Of us. It is a danger to my plans, but now that danger has been addressed."

Adaru's eyes grew distant. "The seals between the realms lay in the foundations of a tower deep in The Territory. That is what this is all about. I need you to reach the tower. The only way to get to it from Royaume d'Occident is either over the Kafifi Ranges and through Southcastle; or through The Fringe States. From what I have learned about this new time, the West and South are bitter neighbours, and fortifications throughout the mountains watch any attempted crossing. Despite superior force, a war with Southcastle will be long, and I am not prepared to wait. The Fringe States, by comparison, are a weak collection of the tribes."

Adaru took a deep breath. "Only the Chosen have a hope to cross The Territory by growing stronger in their abilities, enabling the power of Kur to flow deeply through them. Only then will they be able to withstand the toxicity of the desert."

Adaru smiled. "War was always going to be the solution. The Chosen grow strong through it, and as you all grow stronger, so do I."

Marion opened her mouth to speak, but Adaru held his hand up, and Marion abruptly closed her mouth, her eyes flashing with anger.

"It is time to move. I wanted you to accompany me, Marion, so I can give you your task. After we return to the palace, you will board *La Fureur*. She sails for The Fringe States, where she will support the forward lines, together with the *Dominer* and two other vessels."

Marion's instinct was to argue, to demand a reason why she should travel to the front, but she could not. A part of her was compelled to obey him. She was linked to him somehow. She could feel him as if part of him was inside her. It made her feel violated, but she was helpless. All she could do was nod.

"You will take a couple of Chosen with you to safeguard your voyage," Adaru continued, "though you would, no doubt, be able to look after yourself. General Bron will also accompany you and will take control of all forces once landed. You and Bron will advance to The Territory. As you do, keep testing yourself, keep using your power.

"Once you reach the desert, you should both be ready to cross it and reach the tower." Adaru nodded as he thought through what was to happen. "Despite this guardian, this is all coming together nicely. Antoinette has left for the Kafifi Ranges, where she will advance on the Southcastle forts, and then move on Southcastle itself. That should divert attention away from your landing, Marion."

Adaru steepled his fingers as he thought. "The guardian will be occupied; it will have little time for anything other than its own survival. The battles to the north and the south will keep Southcastle occupied, absorbing their attention." He nodded. "We should be able to march on the tower unopposed."

"And once I get there?"

Adaru's eyes narrowed as he looked at her. "When you get there, I will take you the rest of the way."

Chapter Forty

The tall, yet slight figure stood motionless on the hilltop. Long and curling unkempt brown hair lay around the broken remains of his antlers, a light breath of air catching it and sending it dancing chaotically behind him.

His face was powerfully beguiling, holding both an intense masculinity with its strong, square jaw and a rich vibrancy with its sparkling yellow eyes.

One needed to only look at that face for more than a moment for that beauty to dissolve and be replaced with something terrifying. There was a gauntness about him that suggested he was more than just thin, but that natural vitality was missing completely.

His eyes revealed the real horror, however. They only sparkled on their surface. They were depthless, sickly yellow pools of corruption and decay.

The wind seized the edges of the travelling cloak, lifting it and casting it flapping in the air behind, revealing thin legs clothed in tight dirty pants that had somehow evaded the ravages of time.

A long, thin, curving bow made from bone was slung across his back, its black-and-white marbled ends curling back upon itself to point forward, as if eager to point the way to the target. A leather quiver with a handful of arrows also made from bone, and of the same marbling, was strapped to one thigh; a bulkier leather pouch tied tightly closed was strapped to the other. Two daggers were tucked into his belt.

He stared up at the glowing, pink, evening sky and remembered a similar sight.

~

He licked the blood from his knife and savoured its metallic taste as it slipped down his throat while he stared up at the sunset. His stomach cramped as the blood entered, and he grunted with the pain but savoured the warmth blossoming throughout his body.

A sudden burning sensation ignited on his scalp, growing hotter and hotter. He fell to his knees, clutching his head with both hands.

Bone split and cracked at his touch, and he screamed as he felt his skull quiver with the break.

He brought his hands before his face. In them, he clutched one of his twin thirty-four-point antlers. The end of it was blackened as if rotten, and black tendrils stretched out throughout the bone.

He sat staring at it as his scalp soothed. He reached up and felt the jagged edges of the foot-long remains of that antler.

A part of him howled in despair.

He smothered it.

He was not that person anymore.

Taking the antler in both hands, he snapped it, then threw each piece as far as he could.

A weak groan came from his feet.

"Stop struggling, Ninsar."

His voice echoed the turmoil within his body. The magnificent baritone strength of his former self that had filled whoever heard it with courage and fortitude was now laced with a dusty rattle that incited fear and anxiety.

The short, stocky woman at his feet wore a cloak of living leaves that were browning and curling as he watched. Her hair was a mass of thin flowering vines, those flowers dropping brittle and dry beside her face.

"Why, Cernunnos?" The word was a pleading whisper from her once vibrant green lips, which were now a dark, dry red, matching the spreading stain in her gut from the knife he had stabbed her with.

He stepped forward and knelt in front of her struggling body.

"You were the best of us." she wept.

"The Cernunnos you knew is dead. I am Sharur now," he said and slashed down with his blade.

A sharp pain speared up through Sharur's gut, bending him over. He hissed with its intensity.

I need to feed.

After a moment, the feeling subsided, and he stood with a sigh and a stretch. He looked at the world. Lush woodland, a sparkling clear blue lake, four towns full of people.

I do not remember them. How much time has passed?

He sat for a moment, collecting his thoughts.

I feel the need to hunt. There is prey for me to find, but the feeling is not strong. It must have gone to ground.

He closed his eyes and settled himself.

It will reveal itself in time.

Chapter Forty-One

Samuel slid his fingers down over the town crier's vacant eyes and closed his eyelids. The pain and confusion that had consumed the man since the battle had been erased, and he now lay content.

"I can't believe he is gone."

The young man fell back against the dry riverbank with a deep sigh. He was beyond tired. He could not remember when he had last slept, last had a drink, last eaten, last thought about anything other than the three of them finding safety.

Two, now.

James stared at the town crier's body. "Do you remember that summer festival where he got so drunk on Mr. Burrow's brew that he kept telling the same story about the miller's wife and the goose over and over?"

Samuel smiled, but it did not touch his eyes. He felt a little numb. "Yeah, that was a funny night," he said.

James nodded but said nothing, his eyes searching the dirt in front of him for answers it did not hold.

The two young men sat without talking for a time, each lost in his own thoughts.

"We should bury him," James said.

The proclamation shattered the indecision and galvanised them. Samuel nodded, and each looked around. They sat in a dry, cracked riverbed. A few fibrous branches, broken sticks, and a scattering of stones lay nearby. The bank behind them rose five to six feet, and the immediate land above was patchy grass and remnant woodland. A few hollowed husks of fallen trees lay among scattered bushes, their skeletal carcasses half buried in the dirt like forgotten corpses.

"How do we dig?" James asked as he searched the surroundings. His mind was blank, unable to reason.

Samuel shook his head. "I don't know."

The two young men looked at the body.

"Maybe we just cover him?"

Samuel nodded, and the two of them collected bits of wood and scrub, which they stacked over the body.

They stared in silence at the makeshift grave. Bit by bit, their former lives and former selves were being taken from them. The covered body personified that, and both were reluctant to walk away. When they did, they would be leaving another part of themselves behind.

And what is taking its place? Samuel wondered.

He was a killer now. He told himself that he had only killed in self-defence, but that did not change the fact he had killed another person.

More than one.

Tears came to his eyes as he remembered taking refuge from the storm in the makeshift shelter at the edge of the farm.

I was so desperate to be anywhere except there. Now, I would do anything to be back there.

It's going to change you. His mother's words came back to him. He had not understood the gravity of them back then. He did now.

James grasped the town crier's loaded musket. He took a long, hard look at the makeshift grave, and then looked away. "Let's move."

~

The smell of wood smoke, cooking meat, and the sizzle of fat dripping into the flames had both young men salivating. They crouched beside a sparse tree and gazed longingly into the enemy camp. Four spits hung over two crackling fires, and on each hung a wild pig.

Two soldiers from The Fringe States turned the meat while two more, and three Southcastle soldiers, sat by the fires, either talking together, cleaning their weapons, or resting.

"Seven," Samuel muttered.

James nodded, trying not to stare at the roasting meat. "Seven. How are we going to get past all seven?"

Samuel's stomach growled. "We have to try. We need to eat."

James stared at the men. "I can't see how—"

"We know two of them patrol together," Samuel interrupted, "so if we were able to—"

"Able to do what? That still leaves five of them, and they probably have far more training than us!"

Samuel shook his head, ground his teeth, and clenched his fists. "We have to try!"

James shook his head. "It's too dangerous!"

Samuel checked the town crier's musket and began loading his own. "If we don't eat soon, we are going to die. We need to try."

James shook his head. "This is madness." His eyes slid to the fire. He subconsciously licked his lips. "You are right," he muttered finally and began checking his weapon.

When both were ready, they began to move closer, creeping between rocks, bushes, and trees until they were on the far side of the fires and hidden by a thick prickly shrub.

"So, what's the plan?" James whispered.

"We wait 'till someone needs to take a leak, and then we stick him."

James stared at his friend, wide-eyed.

Samuel shrugged his shoulders. "We need to eat, James! I don't like this any more than you, but they have food, and they are the enemy."

James shook his head. "I don't like this. I don't like any of this." He pointed at Samuel. "You just talked about killing a man. Not this shooting each other stuff, but going up to a man and stabbing him to death."

Samuel stared back at James.

It's going to change you.

He took a deep breath. "Yes. You're right. I'm just so hungry."

James nodded. "I get it, but we start doing that stuff, and we ain't coming back, Sam."

Samuel nodded. "Maybe we—"

A gunshot shattered the night's tranquillity.

James groaned, but the sound was buried beneath the echo of gunfire and the eruption of noise within the camp.

"I got shot!" James said clutching his stomach.

"Can you walk?" Samuel asked in a quiet voice.

"I think so," James replied in a voice thick with pain. "We need to go!"

The soldiers were cautiously walking out from the camp and converging on their position. Samuel dropped the town crier's rifle and pulled James's arm around his shoulders. They hastened away from the camp as fast as they could and into the darkness.

James staggered, and then fell with a grunt, dragging Samuel down with him.

James panted. "I can't walk."

"We can rest a little."

"No," James interrupted. "I can't walk. I don't have any feeling in my right foot."

Trepidation swept over Samuel as he pulled open James's coat to inspect his wound. The front of his shirt was soaked with dark, wet blood. His breath caught. "James, I—"

"Sam..."

Samuel looked at James, gazing into his pain-filled eyes.

"Sam," James croaked. "Remember back on the hill?" He licked his dry lips. "Remember when we talked about leaving, seeing the world?"

Samuel nodded.

"I was wrong. We should never have left. Wouldn't it be nice to be back there? To never leave there?"

Samuel closed his eyes, remembering that moment. It was a lifetime ago. He thought about his ma and pa working on the farm, and his heart ached as they filled his thoughts. He thought about his warm bed, about freshly baked bread in the kitchen, about his mother's laugh and his father's laugh and about their hugs and both their voices.

"Yeah, James," he agreed, his eyes full of tears. "It would be nice."

When James did not respond, he looked down.

James's eyes were closed.

Samuel placed his ear near his friend's mouth and sighed in relief as he heard him breathing shallowly.

Samuel sat in silence, struggling to understand the right thing to do.

A light rain started to fall.

Chapter Forty-Two

Apart from a handful of foot guards standing at attention in their usual posts, the secretary of war stood in the audience chamber alone with the queen consort. He stared at the woman. "This is not how things are supposed to work."

"I understand, Mr. Secretary," Margaret replied in an even tone, "but nevertheless, this is how things will work from this point on."

Harold cleared his throat. "I would like to clarify this with the king, Your Majesty."

Margaret tsked, and then leaned forward. "How have your meetings with the king been thus far, Harold?"

The secretary of war frowned. "I do not think that I—"

"How constructive have your discussions been with my husband? Is he delivering sound advice and supporting military strategy? Are you enabled to win this war through his engagement?"

"Your Majesty, I—"

"Because I hear that he walked out of a previous meeting, one where it was also shared that his actions had weakened the war effort."

Harold Cornsten opened his mouth to speak but did not get the chance.

"You are aware of the arrangement that was in place between my husband, Martin, and myself?"

The secretary nodded slowly. "I am, however, we are now in a state of war, and matters related to a war effort are handled directly by the king."

"Do you know why the arrangement is in place?"

"Was in place," the secretary corrected.

"*Is* in place, Mr. Secretary," Margaret clipped. "Martin may no longer be present, but this has simply adjusted the arrangement. It has not cancelled it. I ask again, do you know why the arrangement is in place?"

Harold stared at the queen consort for a moment, and then sighed. "I can hazard a guess."

"My husband suffers from melancholy, Mr. Secretary," Margaret said. "He is a smart and prideful man, Harold. How do you think smart and prideful men respond to an acute inability to cope in stressful situations? Particularly when they are expected to excel in such environments by not just every single living person in the kingdom, but the generations who have passed before and were able to handle such situations?"

Harold shook his head.

"They are resentful, Mr. Secretary. Resentful to the point of anger and irrationality. They will assert themselves in random situations without rhyme or reason to prove the world wrong and that they are capable."

Margaret took a breath, and her face softened. "I do not tell you this because I am trying to undermine the king. I love my husband dearly, Harold. He is the absolute love of my life, and I would do anything for him. I am telling you this because I am trying to support him as much as I am able and as much as he needs. I am telling you this because I love our people, and I am trying to do everything I can to make sure we get through this war." She gestured around the chamber. "Do you know why he is not here to receive your latest updates?"

Harold shook his head. "No, Your Majesty."

"He is in bed. I would like to say he is resting, but it is more that he is unconscious. He takes his medicine constantly, and the royal physician has had to strengthen the dosage to the point where the king can barely stay awake longer than a few hours. In those hours, he has trouble concentrating and is fearful of everything to the point of utter inaction."

"What has caused this?" Harold asked, shaking his head in disbelief. "I know the king was a... nervous man, but what you describe—"

"It is the dramatically increased burden of duty and expectation during these pressing times," Margaret explained with a heavy sigh. "It is more than a weight on his shoulders and mind. It is something that is smothering him."

"I cannot believe things are so bad," Harold declared. "I know the king is under pressure, but this is war!"

The queen consort rose from her throne and moved closer to him, stopping a few feet away. She placed her hands together in front of her. "Harold, he cannot cope. The arrangement between Martin, Edward, and myself enabled almost all matters of rule and governance to be managed by the prime minister and myself. Edward was always aware of what was happening and was always informed of directives and policy being enacted, but he was spared the intensity of what it took to reach that point. This was all by his word. He formalised the arrangement, made it law. It enabled the kingdom to not only operate, but to flourish."

She stared at the minister with eyes full of earnest need. "You and I need to work together as Martin and I did. As you have experienced, Edward cannot cope with the pressure of this war, and he is getting worse. If you rely on him, we will lose everything."

"What you are asking..." The secretary of war fixed the queen consort with a firm stare. "What you are asking me to do is to acknowledge and support you supplanting the king."

Margaret shook her head. "No such thing. I—"

"Your Majesty, I respect the intent behind your words, but I must decline what you suggest."

"Harold, you do not understand what you are saying, what this will mean."

"Your Majesty, I am extremely mindful of what I am saying and what it means. Your arrangement may be staying in place with parliament on domestic matters, but matters of war are solely the purview of the king, and I must adhere to that."

Margaret and Harold stared at each other, each firm in their own beliefs.

"I cannot sway you, can I?"

"You cannot, Your Majesty."

"Harold," the queen consort pleaded. "Please listen to reason. The king is incapacitated and—"

"Until such a time as the royal physician proclaims such, parliament is informed and unanimously passes a motion of no confidence, I must do as law prescribes, and that is to report to the king and seek his counsel and direction on all matters relating to the war. I can do nothing else, Your Majesty."

Margaret stared into Harold's eyes and found only steadfast belief that he was doing the right thing. She wanted to scream.

"You risk everything," she whispered.

"Your Majesty, to do what you suggest breaks fundamental principles and keystone law." He shook his head. "Your Majesty, matters of war must remain with the king."

Margaret dropped her eyes to the floor. "Then we are lost."

The secretary of war stood in awkward silence for a moment before clearing his throat. "If there is anything else, Your Majesty?"

Margaret shook her head.

Harold Cornsten bowed, and then departed the chamber as Margaret held her head in her hands.

Chapter Forty-Three

"**A**ction starboard!"

The sailors above deck ran to the starboard rail as the lookout in the crow's nest shouted.

Four black shapes marred the horizon, sailing close to the shore.

"*Give me details, man!*" Captain Henry Marston yelled back up the mast as he strode across the deck, his blue frock coat flapping in the breeze. He could not help a wide smile stretch across his weathered face. "*The Rock* has never seen battle, and I am eager to bloody its hands!"

His lieutenant hastened to the captain's side. "Do we run or fight, sir?"

The captain stared at him.

The younger man looked suitably chastised. "Of-of course, sir." He cleared his throat.

"*Stations!*"

At the lieutenant's cry, everyone on board ran to their designated positions. Below decks, the powder boys ran to the armoury and seized gunpowder, then raced as fast as they could to their designated gun crew on one of the three gun decks while those gun crews prepared their cannons. Signals were relayed to *The Rock's* accompanying vessels, another ship of the line, *The Damsel*, and the frigate *Winter's Fist*.

"We have the weather, sir," the lieutenant said, indicating they were upwind of the enemy.

Captain Marston nodded. "Excellent! Winston, bear down, and let's get the bastards!"

"*Sir!*" the spotter shouted. "*It's the flagship La Fureur with three frigates.*"

Captain Marston grinned. "At last!" He salivated as the dark shapes grew clearer, and he studied their formation. "*La Fureur* and two of the frigates are guarding the other; I guarantee you that's a troopship, which is why they are hugging the coast, probably bound for Safety Cove to reinforce the forward lines." He grinned at the lieutenant. "We can pin them against the coast. No way they can head back out to sea."

"*They are running, sir!*"

The captain shook his head. "They ain't going anywhere; all they can do is run up and down the coast. We have the sea. Order the other ships in line, Lieutenant. Let's get after them."

"*Sir!*"

The captain leaned over the deck railing as *The Rock* turned to chase down the enemy, *The Damsel* and *Winter's Fist* falling in line behind, following in her wake.

"*Full and by!*" *The Rock* lieutenant ordered with that same order repeated across the accompanying vessels.

Seamen scrambled up the rigging to pull the sails in tight and enable the ship to sail as near as possible to the direction of the wind. With a mighty lurch forward, the great vessel picked up speed, followed closely by the others.

Marion stared out across the water at the enemy ships. She groaned. "Damn Adaru for making me take this voyage," she muttered as she tried to control her rising nausea.

She ground her teeth as she stared at the Southcastle ships.

"My Lady, perhaps we should retreat below decks?"

Marion glanced at the man who had spoken, a Chosen.

"No, leave me," she said and used her power to push the command into the man.

"At once," he said and rushed away.

Marion smiled. She looked around her at the other sailors on the deck. She had tested herself against them all during the voyage, and all were now in her thrall.

Kur. My power is from the Deceiver.

The revelation had shocked her, but she had since made peace with it.

It doesn't matter where it is from. It makes me strong.

"We can try to outrun them."

Marion glanced at the general standing beside her. He had been resistant to her power at first, but over the past few days, she had weakened that, and she knew he was now hers. She returned her gaze to the approaching vessels.

"We could run," she said to Bron in a thin, tight voice, "but we are not going to."

Bron grinned.

"Come on!" Captain Marston said as the distance to the enemy ships closed.

"They are coming about!"

Marston watched as the boats ahead changed tack, their bows moving across the wind and slowing their speed to a crawl.

"Yes! At last, I will have my fight!"

"Sir, La Feurer is broad on the starboard bow!" came a shout from above.

Henry watched the Royaume d'Occident ships start moving into line formation and grinned. "Lieutenant Winston, ready about!"

"Aye, sir, ready about!"

Seamen scurried across the boat, preparing the vessel to turn ninety degrees through the wind, preparing the jibs, clearing the deck of any open hatches, and calling below decks for everything to be lashed or stowed. When everybody had completed their jobs, cries of "Ready!" were relayed back to the lieutenant.

"Ready, sir," Lieutenant Winston confirmed when he was satisfied the vessel was prepared.

The captain nodded. "Hard-a-lee, lieutenant."

"*Hard-a-lee!*" the second-in-command shouted, and *The Rock* turned sharply into the wind, followed closely by the ships in her wake, preventing them from sailing straight into the enemy's waiting guns.

"*Lieutenant!*"

Lieutenant Winston rushed to the captain as *The Rock* completed its turn and began to race forward, parallel to the Royaume d'Occident line.

The two men watched the Western vessels react to their manoeuvre, preparing to sail once again.

"Not today," Henry said. He turned to his lieutenant. "Maintain course and speed, Mr Winston, and signal *Winter's Fist* that I want to double on *La Fureur*. While that bitch is still trying to get her speed, *The Rock* will move ahead and then swing around to the far side of *La Feurer* while *Winter's Fist* attacks from this side. *The Damsel* is to harry the other vessels while we, by the Shepherd's good graces, cripple the flagship."

Lieutenant Winston stepped closer to his captain. "Sir, I must say this is precarious, indeed. If we concentrate our fire just on *La Fureur*, *The Damsel* risks being overwhelmed by the frigates."

The captain shook his head. "That troop ship will not engage lest she lose her precious cargo, and those other frigates are two-decker ships of, I would say, no more than fifty to sixty guns. They are no match for *The Damsel*. Besides, as long as we come at them correctly, they will fall into each other's firing arcs and spend a good amount of time manoeuvring so they don't hit one another. *The Damsel* will have free reign. No, Lieutenant, this is not precarious at all, this is a gift from the Shepherd!"

Marston ground his teeth as he stared across the sea at his prey. "I

am not going to let this opportunity pass, Lieutenant. I want *La Fureur.*
I want her bad. Carry out my orders, man."

Lieutenant Winston paused for a moment before nodding. "Of
course, sir."

Henry ignored his second-in-command as he hurried away and
prepared to signal the other vessel. His heart was beating fast and hard.

At last, she fights!

"Damned West." Richard, and five other men he had worked with for
the past few years, gathered around their designated gun carriage on
one of *The Rock's* decks.

The gun barrel lay cold and silent between two thick and weathered wooden cheeks, mounted on a thick, cylindrical trunnion that
allowed it to be raised when needed to hit its target. The massive
weight sat on four small trucks, the wheels enabling it to roll backward
after firing, and then roll forward back into position after reloading.

As the gun captain, Richard crouched by the base of the breech,
and another man stood behind him, ready to take the gunpowder once
it arrived. Two men stood off to one side, picking up handspikes, ready
to push the carriage into position, once loaded. Two other men moved
to the front of the gun, one grasping a long pole tipped with a wet wad
of wool called a sponge, the other a long ramrod.

"Ready!" Richard shouted, as did every other gunner on every deck.
As he always had, Richard whispered a prayer to the Shepherd as he
looked at the red-painted interior of the gun port.

Several other men did the same. They were painted red so that any
blood-spray from men injured in battle or cannon failure would be
hidden. The idea was that it helped the gun crews maintain their nerve,
but the reality was that the red paint only served to remind the men
that death was never far away.

"Hard-a-lee!"

The Rock turned sharply once again, but this time toward the enemy vessels. She was ahead of *La Feurer* by several ship lengths and raced to cross her path even as the enemy flagship tried to run and keep her guns trained on the Southcastle vessel.

"All hands to general quarters!"

The distance between the vessels shrank dramatically as *The Rock* sliced through the water. As they came within two thousand feet, *La Feurer* opened fire. Thunder pounded from the Western flagship as her cannons opened up, thick smoke billowing from her gun ports and merging to create a growing, obscuring cloud around the ship's masts.

A boy no older than eight years of age, carrying a bucket filled with packets of gunpowder wrapped in cartridge paper, ran up to the man behind Richard. He pulled a packet from the bucket and gave it to the man, then winked at Richard.

"Good boy, Barry-monkey," Richard said with a smile as the man with the gunpowder joined his two companions. "First again!"

Barry grinned, and then dumped the bucket beside a wooden column standing between this and the deck above. More powder monkeys arrived to do the same for each cannon on this and the other two gun decks.

The man with the sponge thrust it inside the barrel to wipe it clean of any residual embers from a previous firing. Even though the cannon had not yet been fired, the ritual was ingrained in every man, and they all followed every step meticulously.

As the sponge was removed, the man holding the gunpowder cartridge pushed it inside the barrel, and as soon as his hand was clear, the man with the ramrod shoved it home. Richard pushed his pricker, a small length of wire, through the touch-hole in the breech of the gun to feel for, and then pierce, the packed cartridge, shouting "Home!" as he pierced it.

"Shoot your guns!"

The command echoed through the deck, and the man who had loaded the gunpowder pushed a wad of old canvas into the barrel, followed by a round shot, and then another wad.

Richard took a deep breath. *"Ram!"* he called.

The man loading the gun stepped aside so his companion with the ramrod could shove the contents to the back of the barrel.

"Keep her so!" Captain Marston shouted as cannon balls flew through the air around the Southcastle vessel.

Damn them for being the first to fire!

"They are going for the sails, Captain!"

Henry glanced up at the rigging. "They always do, Lieutenant. It'll be a lucky shot indeed to do any damage at this range."

"But, Captain, the range is decreasing as *The Rock* closes. They will surely hit us soon!"

Captain Marston ground his teeth. "We'll get her, don't you worry!"

"Heave!"

Along the gun decks, men holding handspikes levered the rear of the gun carriages sideways as the rest of each team pushed them forward until they rested against the ship's bulwark, and the barrel protruded out of the open gun port.

"Ready!" came a discordant chorus of voices throughout the three gun decks.

Anticipation filled the gun crews as they waited for the order to fire.

Marion closed her eyes and reached toward the crew of the opposing ships.

Let's see just what I can do. She reached into a man on the rigging of *The Rock.*

Cut the line.

The man heard her words and momentarily shook his head, confused by the unexpected thought.

Marion pushed a sliver of dark power inside him and used it to twist his thoughts.

He frowned. *Maybe becalming the ship would not be such a bad thing.* He smiled as he cut the lines he held.

Marion swept through the crew, one after another

Stop it.

Cut it.

Put it down.

Throw it away.

Sit.

Hit him.

Jump overboard.

~

The priming horn full of priming powder fell from Richard's hands. He stared at the powder scattered on the deck next to the cannon. He did not know why he had dropped it. He looked around him and found powder scattered everywhere and other men staring open-mouthed at where they had thrown their priming horns. He staggered as the deck tilted beneath him.

What is happening?

~

Marion opened her eyes and watched as the Southcastle ship's sails drooped, the vessels listing and falling out of formation without anyone steering them.

The cannons of *La Fureur* roared.

Henry was thrown from his feet as *The Rock* was bombarded. He could taste blood from a split lip and felt a broken tooth with the tip of his tongue from where he had hit his head on the deck. The splintering of wood filled the air, and the captain looked up to see a mast break and sag against its rigging. His eyes widened.

This can't be happening!

Winded, a high-pitched whine filling his ears, Richard picked himself up from the gun deck. He tried to blink away dust and blood that ran from a deep cut on his scalp into his eyes. A gaping hole had been torn in the side of the ship near him, and he stared out across the churning water to *La Fureur*. There was no sign of the gun carriages or crew that had sat there.

Dazed and confused, he turned and found bodies lying in the debris and spilled priming powder. Flames climbed the pillars between the decks.

Flames. Powder.

"Barry," he gasped. "Barry, we need—we need, to clear the powder." He shook his head, trying to restore his vision. "Barry, the fire. It will explode. Barry?"

He stared around him, trying to find the boy, and his eyes widened in horror. Barry had been pinned between a pillar and the broken remains of another gun carriage smashed from its placement. Blood dribbled from the corner of his mouth.

"*No!*" Richard said in a hoarse, rasping voice as his horror-filled eyes met the wide, agony-filled eyes of the young boy.

Unable to draw air into his lungs, Barry lay with his mouth open in a silent scream.

~

267

General Bron took a deep breath. Among the salt of the sea and the acrid, burnt smoke of gunpowder, he could taste pain and suffering excreting from the ship. His mouth watered, his body trembled. The acuteness of the agony was like a fine wine. He smiled as he heard the orders to fire the cannons once again.

Barry stared up at Richard. The pain had gone now. He was just tired.

Richard cradled Barry and saw the son he had never had. His eyes were wet with rich memories of the time they had spent together and lost dreams of what might have lay ahead, but which had been so cruelly torn away.

"Pa?" Barry managed with what air he could fill his lungs with.

Richard smiled through his tears. "No, son, but I am here."

Barry never heard him. His eyes were open, but lifeless.

Richard looked around him as the ship shook. Men with bloody wounds screamed as they fought to live, yelling to one another and cursing the world as they tried to push gun carriages through debris to rest up against the ship's bulwark. Richard watched them in a strange, detached way as he laid a hand on Barry's head.

La Fureur and her companions fired again.

Shells smashed into the Southcastle ships, tearing ragged holes through hulls and pulverising masts to splinters. Spilt powder ignited, and explosions rocked all the vessels. *La Fureur* and her coterie withdrew as the Southcastle ships burned. *The Rock* and *The Damsel* were destroyed, their shattered remains slipping beneath the waves while *Winter's Fist* limped away, seeking refuge back in Southcastle.

Chapter Forty-Four

The prisoner touched where the shot had punched through his flesh and winced at its tenderness. He stared around himself. He was in a narrow stone cell with a small, barred window in one wall.

"How am I here?" he whispered. His eyes widened. "And who am I?"

He screwed his eyes shut and tried to remember. A name came to him.

"Baraka. My name is Baraka."

A memory burst into his mind with vivid clarity.

Waking as a storm broke overhead, turning onto his back in a muddy hollow, and stretching his mouth as wide as he could so he could catch raindrops in his parched throat.

Baraka shook his head.

What is happening to me?

Leaning forward, he placed his head in his hands and wept. As the tears came, so, too, did earlier memories. He remembered shivering with cold as he descended the tower's stairwell. Before that, he recalled journeying across the desert, marvelling that he was still alive after a week of travel.

Memories of his life up until the moment he entered the room with the lectern in the tower were full and lusciously detailed. After that room, however, it was like someone had taken a hammer to his mind and not just broken it but shattered it.

Desperate for some comfort, he dove into the memories before the ruins, embracing warm familiarities of his past. Baraka the treasure hunter. Baraka the wild youth, always getting into trouble. Baraka the lover.

He shuffled over to the window and stared out through the bars. He was high up with broken rocks below. The world ahead swept away to a bustling city and then to fields beyond. A light breath of wind caressed his face and brought with it the smells of city life.

Where am I?

Baraka closed his eyes and took a deep breath. He gripped the bars in hands of bones thinly clothed in dry skin.

One day, Baraka, you will be special like your father.

His mother's voice resurfaced from the past, and it was not alone. As if summoned by his mother's words, a blurred shape appeared in his mind, indistinct at first, but slowly resolving into a tall, bearded man.

Father!

It was Baraka's only memory of him. He wore a pearl-coloured, hooded robe and was looking down at him with bright blue eyes that were warm with love and sharp with wisdom. Baraka's baby arms reached up for him.

I wish I could have known you, Baraka thought as tears filled his eyes. He was so tired, so absolutely spent and beaten in both body and mind.

A sharp ache throbbed in his chest.

His father gazed upon him with absolute tenderness. Baraka fell into those eyes, and as he did, the ache inside him intensified.

Adaru dropped the quill to his new desk as he felt a surge of this realm's power nearby. He closed his eyes as he oriented himself and tried to find the source of the sensation. His new office chamber was in the area of the palace formerly occupied by the late King Louis, and he was still acclimatising himself to his new environment.

Baraka gripped the window bars as his body began to shake.

Adaru leapt from his chair as he felt energy building around him. It was like the thickening before a storm. It was like the world was pausing before something momentous was to happen.

The crystal wine glass fell from Nanaya's hand to shatter on the floor, startling everyone seated at the table in the intimate dining room near her quarters.

Impossible!

"My Lady, are you well?" King Edward asked.

For a moment, Nanaya could not speak, her heart pounding with the intense familiarity of what she had just felt. It had been a spark. An ignition of this realm's energy.

Something burst inside Baraka. Liquid fire flooded his body, and he threw back his head and howled.

Adaru threw open the door to his chambers.

"Eminence?" a Chosen standing outside his door asked in concern.

Adaru ignored him and rushed down the corridor. Whatever was happening was happening in the cells.

Baraka... of course! Surviving the journey across The Territory. Surviving so long without food and water. Preventing me from possessing him, relegating me to a passenger. I am such a fool!

~

Baraka howled as his body burned from the inside, but while the fire seared, it also renewed. Like fresh growth after a fire, his body rejuvenated. What was sickly thin and wasted now swelled thick and strong.

~

Nanaya rushed from the dining room, grasping her skirts and pulling them up high above her ankles so she could run along the hallway unencumbered. She ran into a small reading room and raced without hesitation toward two tall, narrow, open doors that led to a small, secluded balcony. Panting for breath, she stared out at the Kafifi Ranges, toward Royaume d'Occident where she had felt something rich in this realm's power manifesting.

Maybe I am not alone. Maybe there is hope.

~

Adaru ran through corridors, leapt stairs, and ricocheted off walls as he rushed to the palace gaol. Bursting from a doorway, he ran across the busy courtyard, ignoring the startled looks of all present as he raced to the prison tower. He shouldered the door open, shoved aside the gaoler, and leapt the steep stone steps two at a time.

~

Baraka gripped the bars tightly and howled as fire surged through his veins. The bars bent and twisted in his fists.

The tortured sound of twisting metal and grinding stone came from somewhere ahead, and Adaru summoned power ready to use.

Baraka stared out of the ragged hole he had created by tearing the bars from the wall. He took a breath, and then leapt, falling to the courtyard very far below.

He landed, unhurt, in a crouch, his impact crushing the stone paving under him and shattering all stone within a ten-foot radius. He raced across the courtyard and out through the fortified gate. He did not know where he was going, but he felt something pulling him south, and so he ran in that direction.

As he ran, he felt whatever had awakened inside seep into every part of his body, and where it touched, it both seared and energised, as if cleansing and reforging his body. He stumbled often as revitalisation swept through his limbs, but each misstep shifted into energised leaps and stretched powerful strides.

As Adaru neared the prisoner's cell, he saw bright light blazing through the small cell door hatch, far more than there should have been. He grasped the doorknob without bothering to look inside and wrenched the door open.

Moonlight shone through the hole in the wall where the window had once been. Adaru let his power dissipate.

This was... unforeseen.

He pursed his lips.

We must move faster. We are so close.

Footsteps pounded on the stone behind him, but Adaru did not bother to turn around. He could feel who it was.

"Something... unexpected has happened," he said before Diers could speak. "I need some of the Chosen to spread through Royaume d'Occident and find the prisoner who escaped from here."

"Of course," Diers said without question. "Pierre would be my first choice to coordinate. He likes to hunt, and the power has awakened some interesting abilities in him that will enable him to find the prisoner."

Adaru nodded absently. His eyes narrowed. "We need to move faster." He nodded to himself, and then turned away from the broken cell and began walking away. "Walk with me, Diers. We need to begin the next phase."

Chapter Forty-Five

"My King?"

Edward stared at the map, trying to make sense of it. The fog was thick in his mind today.

Harold Cornsten frowned. "My King?"

There is so much going on everywhere, the king thought.

"Ah, so..." The secretary of war said, turning away from the king and facing the other members of the war council that were present in the room. "Let us discuss the situation in Eros?" He cast a glance at Edward as the others agreed.

The king's eyes roamed the map.

So many men everywhere.

"The forts are well prepared should any force come over the mountains..."

The voice faded away as Edward struggled to think. It was a distant struggle, one that he barely registered. The medicine saw to that. He was not shaking now, the paralysing, suffocating anxiety had been replaced with a numb indifference.

"...not enough men on the front line." Pieces of conversation came to him. "We just need more..."

Edward stared at the representation of the Kafifi Ranges. It was the mighty arm that curled protectively around his nation. He remembered visiting a number of the forts as a child. Solid fortresses that stood watch over Southcastle's borders.

~

He stood on one of Fort Stalwart's bastions and stared at the road leading to the fortress's portcullis-sealed main entrance. Bordered by impassable rock, the road wound straight up a sharp incline and turned back upon itself many times as it traversed the mountainside.

"No force has ever invaded Southcastle through the mountains."

Edward turned and looked at his father. The thin, balding man was staring at his son.

"And now that we have our first star fort," King Alfred the Fourth continued, "no one ever will." The king gestured around them. "The introduction of artillery into the field of battle has meant that forts have had to change, Edward. You see how Stalwart is flat and polygon in shape. It has low thick walls specifically designed to withstand cannon fire, and a wide ditch surrounds the fort, so anyone looking to climb those walls is exposed to higher-placed gunfire." The king indicated the space they stood in. "These triangular bastions stretch out at each corner between curtain walls rather than the flat, high towers of the older forts, avoiding the creation of dead zones, and enabling cannons and soldiers to fire unobstructed." He nodded to himself. "Fort Stalwart is strong, son."

Edward nodded.

The king took a slightly wheezing breath that triggered a series of wracking coughs. The king panted slightly after they had passed.

"When you are king," he said when he had caught his breath, "you should convert the other forts to this design. With these on one border, and The Territory on another, you will only need to concern yourself with the coast."

The prince nodded. "It is strong, Father."

"Yes, and can be held by few men."

Suddenly, things became clear. Edward could see the solution.

"What if we move men from the forts?"

The room fell silent.

"Excuse me, Your Majesty?"

The king turned to face his secretary of war. "We need men?"

Harold glanced at the other members of the war council. "Ah, yes, Your Majesty."

"The forts are strong, I..." Edward licked his lips and closed his eyes for a moment as a quiver of dislocation swept through him. He felt lightheaded and detached. He breathed in deeply, savouring the tranquillity. He wished every moment could be like this. It nearly was, but there were still times when the demon inside seized him. He held himself in the peace of this moment.

An awkward cough made him open his eyes. He blinked a few times as the light was suddenly a little too bright, and he saw the secretary of war staring at him. He looked worried and more than a little confused. The king looked past him and realised the rest of the war cabinet was also staring at him.

"Did you say something?"

"Ah," Harold began hesitantly. "Ah, I was not sure I heard Your Majesty clearly."

"Oh." Edward smiled. "I said move men from the forts."

Harold glanced again at the war council, and then back to the king. "That would be... unwise, Your Majesty."

"The forts are strong," Edward whispered.

"Your Majesty, the forts are the only things standing in the way of the West, should they have ambitions greater than The Fringe States. We cannot weaken them."

"The forts are strong," Edward repeated.

"Yes, Your Majesty, but—"

"...and can be held by a few men."

Edward nodded to himself. This felt right. "Move all men from the forts except the bare minimum." He turned away from the minister and started to walk away.

"Your Majesty!"

"From all the forts," the king called over his shoulder.

Chapter Forty-Six

Diers watched the congregation bow their heads as the service finished but cast wide-eyed glances at one another and clutch each other's hands tightly.

The fear is palpable, Diers thought. *You can almost taste it.*

As the people began shuffling reluctantly out of the basilica and back to the hardening, frightening world outside, the Chosen who had been standing around the edges of the crowd asked several to remain seated. No two were the same; different ages, male and female, and from different walks of life.

When all others had left, the Chosen closed the doors, and Adaru walked out from the shadows. "These are the ones?"

The seated men and women glanced at each other uneasily as Diers nodded at Adaru. "No families, few friends, inconsequential social and professional standings. Easily made to vanish."

"Begin," Adaru commanded.

Diers nodded, and then closed his eyes.

All the remaining practitioners' eyes widened as their bodies stiffened, and they were unable to move.

Adaru smiled. "Good, your skills have come along nicely. Hold them immobile for me," he said as he also closed his eyes and summoned his power. He sighed with the exquisite agony searing his insides as he let the unnatural energy surge.

"I watched this be done at the tower," Adaru said in a strained voice. "The one that did it was called a skincrafter. He created an army."

Adaru ground his teeth and reached out with both hands toward those sitting immobile in the pews, curling his fingers as if grasping hold of something. "In time, I may need the same, but for now, I think things to stalk the streets will do. Things to ensure the environment here is how we need it to be and to keep the people quelled. Afraid." The tendons and muscles in his arms bulged and strained against his skin as if he pulled at something.

The eyes of the immobile people widened further, and if they could have screamed, they would have as they felt a terrible pressure building inside them, a tension pulsing in their bones and their skin.

$$\backsim$$

Nanaya felt what Adaru was doing as a violent tearing in the depths of her being. It ripped her from sleep, and she lay wide-eyed, sharp bursts of pain cramping her insides.

$$\backsim$$

"Hold them still." Sweat streamed down Adaru's face. "Watch and learn."

The faces of the powerless people twisted into animalistic snarls as Adaru exaggerated their violent and base desires.

"Yes!" Adaru exalted, and then he reached deep into the people before him.

As one, the men and women began to violently shake, and their bodies began to twist and change. As Diers watched, their limbs deformed, stretching and twisting. He saw their faces distort as jaws elongated, craniums shrank, and bony growths erupted from their temples.

As if sensing his attention, each looked at him and met his gaze. Their eyes were opaque white orbs where tendrils of darkness curled and twisted across their surfaces.

Adaru slumped into a crouch with his hands on his knees, panting.

Diers stared at the transformed people, now nightmarish creatures as they slunk from the pews to stand before Adaru, staring at him in utter subservience.

Adaru took a deep laboured breath. "Well, that was harder than I expected." He regarded the creatures before him. "But the results are what I hoped for."

"You said that these would help make the environment how we need it," Diers said. "What did you mean?"

"As the energy of Kur swells here, this realm will push back against it. We are unnatural. Kur should not be here. The fundamental energies of this realm will try to eradicate it, but if we change the environment so that it is attuned to energy of Kur, then we are protected and it is those of this realm that will be afflicted on our ground."

Diers gestured to the newly created creatures. "Did you see what I did?"

Diers nodded.

"Do you think you can do it?"

"I... I am not sure."

"Practice. As much as you need to."

Nanaya rose from her bed and took a deep, shaking breath.

It is all happening again.

The woman walked out onto her balcony and stood for a moment, breathing the chilly night air, allowing its icy freshness to fill her lungs and its frigid caress to wipe away the vileness she had felt trying to smother her.

The power in the West. It is so strong.

But it was not just the West. She could feel the power of Kur being used in the north, and it was growing stronger every day.

And every day it gets closer to The Territory. How long until it is strong enough to reach the tower?

Nanaya took a deep breath.

Southcastle will lose the war. I must act. I must try. No matter the cost. I cannot afford to stand by any longer.

Chapter Forty-Seven

General Bron stood looking at the scout as he made his report, but he did not hear a word the other man said. Blood pounded in his ears, and his heart thundered in his chest.

All he wanted to do was to rip the man, limb from limb.

He clenched his fists and ground his teeth as the man continued to speak, watching the scout's eyes widen as he saw the general's anger rising. Over the past few weeks, the general's body had swollen. He was all muscle now and stood a little over eight feet tall with arms almost as thick as a slender man's torso. There had been a brief moment when he had been concerned about his body's changes, but that had been quickly extinguished by the savage inhumanity that consumed him.

The general took a step forward, murder on his mind.

"General."

Bron ignored the voice.

He wanted blood.

Marion stepped in front of him.

He glared down at her, nostrils flaring as he panted with violent desire. She had replaced the modest, but impractical hoop dress that she had worn on the sea voyage for male garments at least a size too large for her tightened about her waist by a thick leather belt. They made her appear even more petite than usual, however, she stood undaunted before the massive brute.

"General," she repeated. "You are needed in the prisoner tent. More persuasion is required for them to tell us their numbers and placements."

General Bron glared at her for a moment before abruptly turning away and heading back into camp.

Marion watched him go, ignoring the scout's grateful gushing and wondering if there would be any prisoners alive after Bron had finished with them.

She dismissed the thought. The general could kill whoever he wanted, what she needed was to get to the tower, and for that she needed the protection of the army. At least until she reached The Territory. Until then, an unseen shot or a stealthily rammed knife could kill her just as it could anyone else. Once in The Territory, it would be a different story. She could feel how strong she had become and was confident she would be able to survive in the desert.

Marion turned away, dismissing the scout with a flick of her hand. She held no official authority in the camp, but the use of her power had made everyone subservient to her.

"'*Ware the camp!*"

She turned at the lookout's shout and walked to the hastily erected wooden wall to see what had caused the commotion.

The wall had been built from felled trees and reached ten feet high with a trench filled with sharpened stakes dug at its base. The forward elements of the Royaume d'Occident army had gathered behind that wall. Over the last few days, they had been joined by various regiments and battalions fighting their way through The Fringe States until they were now a few thousand strong and growing every day.

"Where?" Marion demanded of the lookout as she reached him. He stood on a crude, raised platform that allowed him to peer through gaps in the top of the wall. She stepped up and joined him.

"There, My Lady." He gestured beyond the wall, and then stepped aside so she could see.

Marion peered through the wall and saw a man staggering toward them, dragging something behind him. As she concentrated, she could make out that what he pulled was some sort of litter.

The sound of footsteps behind her turned her around. The camp commander and several men sat mounted and ready to ride out.

"By your leave?"

Marion smiled. She nodded, and each saluted to her as other men pulled open a space for them to leave.

As Marion watched, the mounted soldiers galloped toward the lone man. As if the sight of them stole his last strength, the staggering figure collapsed and lay still.

She watched as the soldiers surrounded him, and then dismounted and studied him. After a while, all but one of them remounted, pulling the man's limp body up onto a horse and making their way back to camp. The remaining soldier began dragging into nearby bushes whatever the man had been hauling.

"What is it?" Marion asked the camp commander as he returned.

He gestured behind him. "Kid was pulling a dead body behind him. Made a litter from two rifles and both their greatcoats strung between them. Pierre is getting rid of it now."

Marion nodded, then gestured to the body hanging over the horse in front of the soldier. The soldier pulled aside the cloth covering the young man's head. The face underneath was wrinkled by dehydration and framed by a patchy, scruffy beard.

As Marion gazed at that face, she felt something. The man was little more than a boy. Even in his haggard, withered state, there was something tragic about him. An innocence destroyed. Something inside her connected to that.

"Bring him to my tent. I will look after him."

Chapter Forty-Eight

Margaret picked up a message from Alexander Miller, the Southcastle sheriff. Her face creased into a frown as she read, that frown deepening and hardening into a scowl by the time she had finished.

"Oh, by the Shepherd," she whispered. She rose from behind a desk littered with reports and messages from around the kingdom. "Edward, what have you done?"

The queen consort pulled open the door to the room she used to work through the operations of the kingdom and crossed the corridor to the Great Chamber. A private dining and living space for the royal family, the room was almost twenty feet long and wide. Overlapping pastel rugs covered the floor, and several finely upholstered settees and armchairs sat in the centre of the room. Finely carved cabinets and writing desks stood against the walls between tapestries and paintings of landscapes. It was also empty.

She walked through the room to a door in the far wall that led to the main bedchamber. She opened this and found the bedchamber empty, apart from a member of the palace staff.

"Your Majesty," the woman said, curtseying.

"Have you seen the king?"

"He departed for the main audience chamber a while ago, Your Majesty."

Margaret groaned under her breath and swept from the room.

She strode through the palace, the message from the sheriff clutched in one hand, and her mind racing.

The Officer of The Chamber was standing by the closed audience chamber doors near two foot guards when Margaret arrived.

"I would speak with my husband."

"Of course, Your Majesty," the Officer of The Chamber replied and passed through the audience chamber doors, closing them behind him. After a moment, the doors opened, and he bade her enter.

Two women and a man were standing before the king.

"The Queen Consort," the Officer of The Chamber formally announced before departing.

Edward smiled at his wife and motioned for her to approach and take her seat by his side.

"Please," he said to the people before him, "continue."

"It's Charles and my boys," a woman sobbed. "This war... they're working all hours, and there is no let up," she continued in a broken voice. "The docks are just so busy. Ship repairs, refitting, resupply. It never ends, and with many of the workers on the front line, they are each doing the work of two or three. This week, I ain't seen my Charles. He maybe gets an hour or two to camp at the dock before he is up again. My boys are almost the same."

Edward nodded thoughtfully. "Thank you. Thanks to all three of you. I knew that hearing what is really happening in the kingdom during this time would be valuable. Rest assured, I have taken note of your concerns, and I will be taking action."

The three people stumbled over themselves, thanking the king before being led away.

"Holding audiences with the public about the war effort?" Margaret asked as she reached the king.

Edward nodded, then he grimaced and massaged his forehead with one hand. "There is so much to do," he muttered.

His hand dropped to his lap, and he stared into Margaret's eyes.

"Did you know that the volumes of food and materials we are pulling from our regions are leaving entire villages depleted of stores that were to last through the months ahead, and families cannot find wood for their fires. We are starving our people to win the war!" His eyes flashed. "We must do something!"

Margaret sat down slowly next to her husband and reached out to touch his arm. "My love, you must rest. Remember, I can—"

"Yes, but I can, too!"

Margaret was taken back not just by the king's abruptness, but also by the wild intensity of his voice.

"You are not well," she said slowly. "Please let me help you as I have always done. Leave these things to me and—"

Edward slammed his fist down on the arm of his throne. "I can do things!"

The king and the queen consort stared at each other. Edward slowly unclenched his fist and his teeth. "I can do things," he repeated but in a calmer tone.

Margaret held up the message from the sheriff. "Alexander Miller sent this to me."

Edward stared at the paper, frowning.

Margaret leaned forward. "Edward, you ordered young men, barely more than boys, into the city watch!"

Edward's frown deepened, and he rubbed his head. "That does not sound right. They need men, and so I ordered men into—"

"Edward, all the men are at war! The only ones left are those too young to serve, and they are causing problems." Her eyes filled with concern. "My love, you are not making sound decisions. You need to rest and let me look after such things."

Anger and resentment surged in Edward, and he hissed through his teeth.

Margaret leaned back in shock.

The king clenched his fists and screwed his eyes shut as he fought to control the explosion of emotion that was a whisper away from consuming him.

"Your Majesty," the royal physician called out as he rushed from the alcove he had been standing within, hands fumbling in the pockets of the robes he wore. "My apologies, I missed informing you that your tonic is due. Please accept my apologies."

Edward's hands unclenched, and he stared at his physician in confusion. "Did we not just take the tonic recently?"

"It was actually a while ago, Your Majesty," Bernard replied as he pulled out a stoppered vial and offered it to the king. "Time also slipped by me, please accept my sincere apologies."

Edward frowned but nodded and took the vial. "Strange," he muttered as he unstoppered the glass container and downed the contents, "I was sure...." His face twisted in disgust. "That tastes vile! What is that? That is not the usual tonic!"

The royal physician placed his hands together and dipped his head. "I apologise, Majesty. I was missing a few ingredients. The effect is still the same." He shrugged his shoulders. "The war is causing havoc with many supplies. I have managed to find most of what I was missing, however, and I can assure you that the next tonic will taste more like what you are used to."

Edward's eyes widened slightly as a shiver of icy euphoria washed through him, eradicating his previous emotions and leaving only bliss-ful, blossoming warmth and calmness. He blinked his eyes as he worked moisture into his suddenly dry mouth. "What was I saying?"

Bernard smiled at his king. "Your audience has finished, My King. May the staff escort you to your chambers for rest?"

Edward stifled a sudden yawn and nodded with a sigh. "I am quite tired." He turned and smiled at his wife. "See you soon, my dear." He rose as Bernard waved several staff over, and together, the staff and the king left the hall.

"Tonic?"

The royal physician shook his head. "His Majesty does not like referring to it as *medicine*."

"And the strange taste?"

"It is something a little different. It will calm his nerves and allow him a deep restful sleep."

Margaret threw her hands in the air. "What is happening to him?"

Bernard sighed. "He is growing a tolerance for some of the medicine's elements." He grimaced. "His condition, the melancholy, is suppressed, and his mind is calmed, but unfortunately, this also means his thinking is somewhat cloudy. The real concern is what you have just seen. His temper. His control over it is slipping."

Margaret dropped her head to her hands. "What can we do?"

"I will keep a close eye on his dosage, but its effectiveness is now very much in question. I will do what I can to calm his nerves and allow him to sleep." The royal physician shook his head. "I am really not sure what else I can do, Your Majesty.

Margaret sighed. "Do what you can."

The royal physician bowed and departed.

Margaret took a deep breath and prepared herself to continue with the running of the kingdom.

Chapter Forty-Nine

Baraka sat in the back of the inn with the hood of a tattered cloak that he had recently stolen pulled over his face to hide his features. A bowl of cold, untouched, watery soup sat before him, a piece of uneaten stale bread to one side of it and an untouched tankard of watery, cloudy ale to the other. A scattering of coins was also on the table and was all that remained from the purse he had also stolen.

The inn was in a small Terragricole hamlet, and while the local settlement was small, the main travel route to Southcastle was nearby, and its proximity brought many travellers looking for a place to spend the night off the main road. Consequently, Baraka was able to dissolve into the chaotic mix of people filling the inn, and sitting silently in the far corner meant the serving women were too preoccupied with those demanding attention closer to the bar to bother him.

Head bowed, he stared at his clenched fists under the table. Sparks spat between his fingers, and he closed his hands again.

What is happening to me?

He cast a furtive glance around him, but everyone was too involved in their own affairs to pay him any attention.

Baraka stared at the food and drink on the table.

I've hardly eaten or drank since escaping the palace. A stolen handful of vegetables, a loaf of bread, a mouthful of pooled rainwater. Why am I not hungry? And sleep. Or lack of it. I've slept maybe a couple of hours a night. Why am I so refreshed?

He shook his head as he flexed his thigh and bicep muscles.

Stronger than ever.

Baraka grasped the tankard. He took a long drink. The ale had a sour taste and left a strange oily residue on his tongue, but he managed a few deep gulps before replacing the tankard on the table. A distinctly unpleasant aftertaste was left in his mouth, and he decided he would not pick it up again. Baraka regarded the soup and saw that it, too, had an oily film on its surface.

Maybe not.

Even though his hands were clenched, he could feel the sparks in his skin, like little needles incessantly stabbing him. He clenched his fists tighter and looked around him to try to take his mind off what was happening to him.

It was then he noticed that the inn had become quieter.

The general rowdy din of friendly banter had been replaced with a sombre growl of distrust and fear. Baraka shuffled uncomfortably as he felt sudden anxiety seize his heart and mind.

The people crowding the space between him and the bar thinned as some took their seats, and others just retreated to corners and alcoves where they felt more comfortable.

Through the spaces between people, Baraka saw two Western soldiers standing by the door, barring anyone from leaving, and he glimpsed at least one more moving through the inn.

Nausea washed over him, his stomach clenching and bile rising in his throat. He shivered as he felt his very being repulsed by something nearby.

A hush fell over a far corner of the room. Baraka craned his neck to see what was happening and glimpsed a slight man with dark hair pulled back into a tight tail, dressed in a high-collared dark coat.

"Chosen."

Baraka turned toward the man who had spoken. He was crouching down, trying to make himself as small as he could, as was his companion. The two men leaned closer together.

"Did you hear about Fier?"

His companion shook his head.

"They refused entry to the Chosen, said they were unnatural. Said what the archbishop did was not right, that it was against the Shepherd. A Chosen turned up a few days later and stood outside the town gates. Word is he just stared at those gates, but no one could leave. Then the fires started. I heard the screams of those sealed inside were louder than the stones of the buildings that shattered in the fires."

Baraka tracked the Chosen around the room by the way people shrank away from him. As his eyes followed the man, he became aware of two things: The first was that his nausea, the intense cramping wrongness assailing his body, was coming from the Chosen. The second was that the Chosen was moving toward him, sniffing the air as if following a scent.

The needle stabs of pain over Baraka's body intensified as the Chosen circled closer, as did the intensity of the sickness he felt inside. Whatever was happening to his body was also reacting to this Chosen.

A man nearby cast furtive glances at the Chosen closing in, and after a quick gulp of ale, made a run for the door.

"*Hold!*"

The inn fell silent at the Chosen's shout, and the guards at the door half-drew their swords as they stared at the man rushing toward them. Wide-eyed, the man staggered to a stop and desperately looked around for a way out as people moved away from him.

The Chosen walked up to him, his bright eyes narrowing. The man cowered under his gaze, retreating timidly until his back was against the wall and he could move no farther. The Chosen stopped a foot away from the man, his eyes intent on him, and even though he was easily a foot taller, the man shrank before the Chosen.

"What crimes have you committed, I wonder," the Chosen whispered. "What makes you so fearful, so eager to run?" He abruptly turned away. "It's no matter. You are not the one I am here for."

Baraka's body trembled with pent-up energy. He could feel it snapping under his skin.

"Hey, you all right, lad?"

Baraka jerked at the voice and turned to look at an old, bearded man staring at him.

"You sick or something?"

Baraka clenched his teeth to stop them from chattering. "Why do you ask that?" he managed.

The man gestured at Baraka's face. "Your eyes are all bloodshot."

The sharp stabs of pain all over his body intensified and forced a sharp cry from his lips.

The old man got up from his chair and moved away from Baraka. "Somethin' ain't right, son; you ain't well."

People around him were staring at him now and pointing at his body.

"What's happening to him?" a woman asked her companion.

Baraka looked down at his body and saw sparks bursting from his dirty clothes. He unclenched his fist and watched the sparks dance along his fingers.

The people around him cursed, falling over themselves and upturning chairs as they tried to get away from him.

"I think we have found what we are looking for."

Baraka turned to see the Chosen walking toward him. His eyes blazed unnaturally bright, a stark contrast to the dark haze that seemed to be seeping from his skin and surrounding him.

Baraka reacted instinctively and threw a hand out toward the Chosen. The sparks of energy spitting around his fingers came together in a ball of crackling white light laced with red flames. It surged from his hand and slammed into the Chosen, hurling him from his feet even as it wrapped itself around his body.

The Chosen screamed as his hair and face momentarily burned in the pure power that twisted around him, as if eager to find vulnerable places to attack. His scream of pain changed to a shout of defiance, and the darkness surrounding him deepened, smothering what was attacking him and extinguishing it.

He crouched and hissed at Baraka, his once long hair reduced to stubble, and his face now a half melted mess of swollen and burnt red flesh.

People were fleeing the inn, either rushing out of the main entrance or climbing across the bar to escape out the back.

Baraka shook as he faced the Chosen. If anything, he felt more energy inside himself than before as if the confrontation was somehow generating it. His fists were clenched, but that no longer stopped the sparks which were dancing madly all over his body.

The Chosen jerked both arms out toward him with a piercing cry, hands outstretched and fingers spread. The darkness surrounding him swept along his arms and surged toward him. Baraka bowed his head and threw his arms up to protect his face.

The sparks surrounding him flashed, and he was bathed in brilliant light. The dark energy splashed against it and was rebuffed, dissipating as it came into contact.

The Chosen stared at Baraka with wide eyes.

Baraka was filled with anger, a deep utter hatred for the man before him that consumed him and seared away all conscious thought. His lips pulled back as he snarled, his face twisting to show what he felt. His hands snapped open by his sides. The Chosen, together with three surrounding tables and a dozen chairs, were hurled back to crash into and smash through the wall behind.

Baraka took short, hesitant steps forward, his face still locked into a snarl as he advanced. The man shakily tried to rise from within the rubble that had been the entrance to the inn, but seeing Baraka walking toward him with a promise of violence etched on his face, the Chosen reached toward him, and darkness started to form on his fingertips.

Baraka ground his teeth, and white fire engulfed the man. He howled as he burned, writhing in torment as his skin blackened and split. Baraka raised his arms, and the fire intensified, becoming a blinding, raging inferno, the Chosen's voice escalating into a high-pitched shriek.

The people who had been inside the inn were cowering around the scene, hiding behind bushes, trees, and other nearby buildings. A collective gasp erupted as the energy burning the Chosen surged, and many scattered, fleeing to find somewhere safe from the madness unfolding.

The Chosen fell silent and toppled lifelessly into the crumbling masonry.

Baraka walked up to the edge of the inferno and stopped, staring at the blackened body. Just as the energy he had unleashed churned inside him with unabated violent desire, so, too, did his emotions. He could not think clearly. His heart pounded, his breath came in ragged gasps. He fled into the trees.

Chapter Fifty

The sun burned his bare back as he placed the last stone in the wall. He stood and stretched, knuckling the small of his back and groaning as his spine cracked. He wiped the sweat from his face and took a deep breath.

One wall fixed, only two more to go.

"Do you want a hand, Sam?"

Samuel turned at the voice.

James stood in the middle of the field in his dirty, ripped, and bloody soldier's uniform. He cocked his head to one side and stared at Samuel with vacant eyes. "Do you want a hand, Sam?"

Samuel woke from a deep sleep and stared in confusion at a dirty yellow sky. A muted sun vainly tried to shine through what looked to Samuel to be smoky clouds, but the best it could do was cast a ghostly, twilight glow.

Turning his head, Samuel realised it was not a sky he had been looking at, but rather the interior canvas of a tent. He lay on a raised pallet in almost the centre of the enclosed area. Beside him was a small wooden stool, and beyond that, what looked like a bed that was raised from the ground as he was, clothes of different colours and sizes lying atop one another. A chest with a crooked lid that did not properly close sat next to the bed. A few feet away sat two mismatched wooden chairs and a small, chipped wooden table with a broken leg that stood on some stacked, rough and scavenged stone. A handful of papers lay on its surface.

Samuel took several deep breaths. He felt a tightness across his chest and a tenderness beneath his ribs like something inside was bruised or swollen.

"You are awake."

Samuel turned his head to the other side at the sound of the voice.

A small woman with long dark hair, dressed in ill-fitting male pants and an off-white shirt with its sleeves rolled up, walked through an opening in the tent. She stopped a few feet away from where he lay and regarded him. Samuel could not help but stare at her vivid green eyes, which seemed to glow with fierce intensity.

"How do you feel?"

Samuel licked his lips. "Thirsty."

The woman nodded but did not move to bring him any water. "What else?"

"I have a headache." He shrugged. "Other than that, I feel fine." He frowned. "How do I feel fine?"

The woman sat on the foot of his bed. "I healed you."

Samuel shook his head. "I don't understand."

The woman walked toward him and sat next to him on the bed. He flinched as she raised her hands toward him, and her lips curled into a slight smile.

"I healed you once, and no harm came to you."

Samuel regarded her warily for a moment. There was something about her that compelled him to believe she was sincere. He nodded and closed his eyes.

The woman placed her hands on the crown of his head and closed her eyes.

Samuel felt heat under her hands, and as it built, he felt a similar heat building at the base of his spine that spread to other parts of his body, his crotch, his navel, his heart, his throat, and then it collected between his eyes. That heat continued to build until beads of sweat appeared on his brow, and he winced at the sensation that was building to a sharp pain.

"Nearly there," the woman whispered.

Sweat was now running down his face, and he opened his mouth to tell her to stop when the heat rushed to his crown and left his body. He felt weak with the sudden release. A shockingly cold, sharp, icy sensation swept down through his crown back down into the parts of his body that a moment ago had been filled with heat. As that cold swept through his body, it brought with it a stinging sensation that rippled through his body, across his skin, through his muscles and tendons, and surged within his blood.

The cold sensation ebbed, and as it did, it took away Samuel's strength. He yawned widely and loudly, closed his eyes, and he fell into a deep sleep.

When Samuel woke, he saw Marion seated beside him, staring at him intently.

A sudden surge of strength pulsed through him, and he gasped as goosebumps rippled over his skin and flickers of almost-pain sensations sparked on every nerve. His heart pounded, and he panted as slight shakes wracked his body.

When it finished, Samuel was left panting with sweat slicking his body.

Marion took a deep breath, and then looked up and met his eyes. "How are you feeling?"

Samuel's stomach growled.

The woman raised a hand. "Of course. That will go in time." She rose and left the tent.

Pushing himself to sit upright, Samuel realised he was naked under the thin blanket covering him. Looking down at his body, he could see every rib distinctly. He pushed away the blanket, and his heart dropped as he saw his pelvis starkly prominent and his legs sickly thin and wasted of muscle. A sound came from outside, and he pulled the blanket back around himself just as Marion returned with a man behind her, carrying a covered wooden tray. The smell of charred pig seized his senses, and he salivated so much he dribbled from both corners of his mouth.

The woman gestured for the covered tray to be given to him, but when it came close, Samuel snatched it and threw the covering cloth to one side, revealing slabs of juicy meat and two trotters lying in a bloody jus. He stuffed his mouth with the meat and chewed just enough to break it apart so he would not choke before swallowing.

The man who had brought and offered the plate moved toward him, and as he neared, anger surged within Samuel. He snarled and bared his teeth, glaring at the man, who backed away in shock.

A husky chuckling came from one side, and Samuel swung to growl in its direction. The slender woman was smiling as she looked at him.

"Easy. Eat. Relax. No one will take that away from you."

Samuel stared at her mistrustfully and shovelled more meat into his mouth, its juice running down his face to drip from his chin.

"I will leave you to eat and probably sleep," she said. "I will see you after."

Samuel snarled at her.

She chuckled again. "I like this change in you. Enjoy this. This is making you stronger. Embrace this."

Samuel ignored her and ripped at the meat.

The chain shot rebounded into the air from the mud and rushed toward the terrified soldiers. They had nowhere to run, and it tore them apart in bloody explosions of flesh.

Samuel stared at the broken remains of bodies. He knew them all. Around him, the men who had escaped the chain shot were pushing themselves to their feet, whispering prayers to the Shepherd for their salvation.

Boom!

Samuel turned to stare at the ridge where Southcastle soldiers were camped and firing at them. Another chain shot pounded into the ground nearby and nearly knocked him from his feet. He opened his mouth to shout a warning, but there was no time, and it spun wildly past, massacring the men beside him and covering him in their blood as they came apart.

Samuel rubbed his eyes free of sleep and pushed himself up to sit in his bed. He could still see the men being ripped apart as dark shadows at the edge of his vision, as if they refused to die with his dream.

He shuddered and swung his legs over the side of the pallet and stood. Everything spun, and white sparks appeared at the edge of his sight. He half-sat and half-fell back onto the pallet and took several deep breaths as the dizziness faded.

He felt her before he saw her.

It was like a building thickness of sensation. It was hard to describe. He just knew she was close and coming closer. The feeling of her grew and grew until she walked through the tent.

Marion smiled as she entered and saw Samuel looking at her. "You can feel me, can't you?"

Samuel nodded, but then shook his head. "I don't understand."

"Do you know me?"

"I don't think so. I don't remember you."

"Do you feel that you know me?"

Samuel stared at the woman. He knew he had never seen her before, but there was something inside him, a feeling he did know her.

Marion walked up to his pallet, wrinkling her nose as she neared. "First, you need to bathe." With that, she turned and left.

Samuel took a moment, and then stood once again. The light-headedness returned, but much less than before, and after a moment, it dissipated. Wrapping his blanket around himself, he shuffled to one of the wooden chairs in front of the broken table. After a few breaths, he shuffled through the papers sitting on the table surface. A few were provision reports, the state of supplies for the camp, including details of what had been foraged and hunted over the past few days. It was the other papers that interested him. They were maps through The Territory.

I don't understand. The Territory is impassable. Why would anyone want a map through it?

He felt her returning. That knot of awareness grew stronger as she neared. He had managed to shuffle back over to his pallet by the time she walked through the tent opening, followed by two men carrying a metal bath with steam rising from within.

The woman directed the men to place the full bath near his pallet, and then curtly gestured for them to withdraw.

She looked at him for a moment after they had gone, an intensity in her eyes that was acutely unsettling. After a moment, she turned and began to walk out as they had done.

"Get in," she called over her shoulder as she left. "You'll feel amazing."

Samuel stared down at the recently packed dirt where James had been buried.

Gone.

"He was a friend?"

Samuel glanced up at Marion and nodded. "My closest."

Neither spoke for a while. The wind shook dry tree boughs and rustled bushes, filling the air with scratching and scraping. The sounds of the camp were a light background buzz punctuated by random spikes of metallic clashes or raised voices.

"Why can't I feel that, then?"

Samuel turned and frowned at Marion. "Feel what?"

"That you have lost your closest friend? I can't feel anything from you."

Samuel shook his head. "I'm still getting used to this thing, you feeling what I am feeling."

Marion smiled and nodded. "It's new for me, too."

Again, there was a moment without talking.

"I don't understand why I cannot feel anything," Samuel explained. "James was my childhood friend, we were as close as brothers. I know I should be weeping, but I can't because I don't feel anything."

Marion stepped closer. "You don't feel anything?"

Samuel shook his head. "Nothing. He is gone. That's that."

Marion placed a hand on his shoulder and turned him around to face her. "I know you feel something."

Samuel stared at her, unable to form the words.

Marion closed her eyes and tilted her head back as she took a deep breath. "There it is. I feel it." She placed her other hand on his other shoulder, opened her eyes, and stared into his. "I feel it, too."

Samuel searched her eyes for answers. "Why can I not feel anything else?"

"Anything other than...?"

"You. There is nothing apart from you. There is no feeling about anything apart from you."

Marion moved in closer, toe to toe. "And how do you feel about me?"

Samuel's heart pounded, his breath quickened. "Everything. I feel everything for you."

Marion's mouth twisted into a slight smile before her lips parted, and she moved even closer. "Show me," she commanded as her lips sought his.

As their lips touched, a hunger unlike anything he had ever experienced consumed Samuel. It was not that he wanted this woman, not even that he desired this woman. He ached for her from the deepest part of his being.

They fell to the ground, tearing at each other's clothes.

Chapter Fifty-One

Adam Jameson, Commander of Fort Stalwart, ground his teeth at the sound of another cannon ball striking the wall near his command room. He finished the message he was writing, rolled and wax-sealed the parchment before handing it to the waiting messenger. "As fast as you can, man."

The messenger saluted before hurrying away, sliding the rolled parchment into a waxed tube as he walked, which he then stoppered and tucked into his leather satchel.

The commander stood from behind his desk, tugged his pale ivory shirt straight, and then pulled his rich burgundy overcoat from a wall hook and slipped it on before following in the messenger's footsteps and leaving the chamber. A soldier fell into step behind him.

The corridors he travelled were narrow, low-ceilinged, and made from solid stone. As such, they were quite claustrophobic, but thankfully, all quite short.

Another cannonball struck the outer walls with a deep crash.

Adam growled.

"Sir?"

"I've spent forty years stationed at forts in the Kafifi Ranges, and in all that time, no one has dared attack the south through the mountains. Now, three weeks away from my retirement, they decide to test us."

Slamming his palm against the door at the end of the corridor, Commander Jameson left the calm, dim, muffled chambers of the fort's centre and strode into the frantic, deafening, bright inner courtyard.

Tall walls arranged at sharp angles stretched around him, on top of which gun crews hastily fired and reloaded cannons.

A man ran over to him as he strode into the gravel space.

"Peter," the commander shouted above the boom of fired cannons. "Did the messenger get away?"

The harsh smack and echoing thud of wall impacts, together with sharp cracks of rifle fire, filled the air before the other man could speak.

"Yes, sir," the man said swiftly, in a moment of relative quiet.

The commander nodded and gestured to the walls around him as he continued to walk. "How do we fare?"

Peter shook his head. "Not good." The bombardment started again. "The men who were pulled from here for the wall effort would have given us more warning and been able to fend them off while we prepare. The enemy was on us before we had a handful of cannons loaded to defend ourselves."

"Fire!"

Jameson looked at the gunner that had just shouted and the cannon that had then roared. "Are they in range?"

Peter shook his head. "Not quite, but almost. Bad news is that we seem to be within the limit of their range. One out of every seven of their shots hits us, and I don't have to tell you how good that is at extreme range. If they advance, then I don't dare to think what we would be in for. The only thing preventing their guns from getting closer is a sporadic barrage from ours. Even so, their men are scouting for weakness."

As if to punctuate the point, a volley of gunfire came from men manning a far corner of the fort as they dissuaded enemy soldiers from coming any closer. As the enemy scampered away, the soldiers ran to a nearby cannon, dropped their muskets, and began to load it.

"This is where we are, sir. We don't even have enough men to both man all our cannons and stand ready at the walls."

The commander nodded. "We can't ride out at them as they will scythe us down as we approach, just as we would do the same if they approached us. We are stuck in this position. Have faith though, Peter, no force has ever taken Stalwart, and when the messenger brings our reinforcements, the day will be ours. Besides, our supplies are considerable, and I doubt the enemy has enough shot and provisions for a prolonged engagement."

"Sir!"

Peter turned at the call from the wall.

"Someone is walking out from their lines toward us!"

"Cease fire!" the commander ordered

Peter and Adam rushed across the courtyard, climbing up a steep set of steps to the nearest curtain wall, and then making their way to the bastion that projected out at the fort's corner.

The commander stood at the front of the bastion and stared down at the West's force. Field cannons were arrayed one behind the other across two horizontal stretches of the road leading to the fort. Dozens of plainly garbed boys and men that formed the gun crews, and dozens more brightly, smartly dressed soldiers filled the gaps between the guns and stretched behind them.

A lone figure walked from the armed force toward the fort.

"I can't see a flag?"

Commander Jameson shook his head at his second-in command. "Me, neither." He squinted at the figure walking toward them. Wrapped in a thick great coat, there was little to see apart from the distinct absence of a white flag of truce.

"This doesn't feel right," Adam grumbled. "Signal everyone to stand ready. Arm all weapons."

Peter nodded, his eyes also glued to the advancing figure, and started barking orders that returned everyone to a frenzy of motion.

The commander raised a hand to his brow to shade his eyes as he stared.

A light gust of wind swept around the person walking toward the fort and caught strands of long dark hair, casting them into its face. The figure rolled its head, and then jerked it to one side to flick the hair away, a very feminine gesture.

"I think that's a woman!"

The woman continued to walk toward them along the twisting path, one step calmly and confidently placed after another.

"She is almost within cannon range, sir," Peter said under his breath.

The woman lifted her arms in the air.

"What—"

A sudden tightness gripped Adam's chest before a searing agony erupted deep inside him. He moaned and dropped to one knee. Dimly, he heard cries of shock and pain echoing around him. "Peter?"

Peter collapsed beside him, clutching his chest, his eyes wide and begging for an explanation for what was happening.

Sharp searing streaks of fire pulsed through Adam's body as he tried to pull himself up on the bastion. When he crested the tip and could see over, he saw the woman was almost at the gates. He dragged his eyes behind her and saw the Western force was following.

The pain in his chest intensified, and Adam collapsed, cracking his head against the stone. His vision blurred for a moment, and when it returned, Peter's open vacant eyes stared back at him.

Adam tried to push himself up, but his body refused. The pain swelled, and he tried to scream, but there was no breath in his lungs. As everything dimmed, he realised the world had become very quiet. His faint, rasping breath was everything and in between, nothing.

His breaths dwindled, his awareness constricted.

The last thing he heard was an explosion that shattered the fort entrance.

Chapter Fifty-Two

The travel-dirty messenger trudged past Nanaya without even seeming to notice her. She was walking toward the audience chamber as he was leaving it. A battered and weathered wide-brimmed leather hat was pulled tight onto the man's head, long, dark and greasy hair falling from under this and hanging limp around his shoulders. Dirt and grit dropped to the polished floor with each of his steps, dripping from the bottom of his waist-high leather coat, scattering around the muddy prints left by his riding boots.

In stark contrast, Nanaya was dressed in a pristine, pale-yellow dress with a modest hoop that pulled the fabric out to either side.

Something about the man made Nanaya pause. "Stop."

The man staggered to a halt and stared at her. His eyes were wide. His bottom lip was quivering.

The image of him standing there dirty and fearful reminded Nanaya of a moment in the past where another had been equally dishevelled and similarly shaken. Then it had been Ki-ní-te, a teacher at The Academy. The old man had held a special place in her heart because his meditations had eased the anxiety that had plagued her as a young woman and helped her unlock her powers. She remembered finding him staggering among the dead in the aftermath of the massacre at The Academy. He had looked like this man did now. Lost. Terrified. Broken.

The cold woman Nanaya had become in the years since thawed as she gazed upon the messenger. *It's not just about stopping Kur. It's about saving people like this man.*

Nanaya stepped forward and laid a hand on his shoulder. "What has happened?"

"Fort Stalwart's been attacked. It still stood when I left to get rein-forcements, my lady. But..." The messenger shuddered, he dropped his eyes to the floor, and he took a deep breath. "I was along the road here when the screams started. Such terrible screams. The West could not have gotten inside the walls, so I don't understand what could have happened."

The messenger looked up, and Nanaya could see tears in his eyes. Sobs wracked the man's thin body, and his head dropped. "I am ashamed to say I didn't turn back. I just put my head down and rode as fast as I could."

Just as I have put my head down and pushed as hard as I could.

Nanaya felt something that she had thought long lost. Compassion. *I have become consumed by my duty and loss,* she thought. *I have forgotten myself. It's not just about stopping Kur, it's about saving this realm. There is no point in stopping Kur if this realm burns to do so.*

"Do not be ashamed," she said softly. "There was nothing you could have done, and besides, if you had turned back, you would not have been able to tell us what happened. You did your duty."

The messenger nodded and wiped away his tears with a dusty hand, smearing dirty streaks across his face.

Nanaya gestured for a nearby guard to approach. "Accompany this man to the servant's hall and make sure he has everything he wants to eat and drink," she commanded before turning back to the messenger with softening eyes. "Do you need a place to rest?"

The messenger smiled thinly. "Thank you, my lady, but I just want to go home and hold my wife and kids."

Nanaya felt a lump in her throat. She nodded. "Do that, treasure every moment with your family. There is nothing more important." She turned to the guard and gestured to him. The guard invited the man to follow him, and then departed for the servant's hall. She watched the man leave.

I must stop this.

She strode into the audience chamber.

The chamber was devoid of the usual petitioners and nobles, which was strange for this time of day. The secretary of war stood to one side of the throne, gesturing as he spoke. His staff stood next to him, talking earnestly among themselves. Standing patiently to the other side of the throne was the Southcastle lord mayor and sheriff, together with two aides."

"Queen Consort," Nanaya said as she saw who sat on the throne, interrupting the secretary of war, who turned to look at her. She looked around the room for Edward. "Where is the king?"

Margaret stared at Nanaya with cold hard eyes, watching her as she crossed the chamber. "He is resting." She returned her eyes to the secretary of war. "Please finish."

"*The Rock* is destroyed. *Winter's Fist* has limped into dry dock, and we need to repair her and a number of other ships and return them to the war as fast as possible, but..." He shook his head. "Your Majesty, the king has intervened and, well, I am without manpower. Schedules have been rearranged or are now just missing, and there are men either refusing to work or not being where they are supposed to be." He rubbed his templates. "Everything was tightly organised, yes, pushed past the limit, but these are trying times. Now..." He shook his head again.

"So, Mr. Secretary," Margaret said in a tight voice, "do you now understand me?"

Harold's shoulders slumped. "Yes, Your Majesty. I am afraid I do. I wish I had listened to you before."

"So do I."

Harold turned as Nanaya approached. "My lady."

"Secretary," Nanaya acknowledged. "I have just heard about Stalwart."

The secretary nodded. "A battalion has just been sent to support the fort."

Nanaya pursed her lips. "It will slow them down, but they will still come."

"They are some of our finest, kept back from the war effort to guard the palace and for situations just like this. I would hope they would do more than just slow them down," the secretary of war said.

Nanaya shook her head. "You have no idea what we are facing." She turned to Margaret. "I am going to do my best to stop this."

The queen consort cocked her head to one side. "What will you do?"

Nanaya took a deep breath. "Whatever I can," she replied before turning and departing the chamber.

Chapter Fifty-Three

A few moments later, Nanaya was standing in her room wearing a plain linen dress. She placed the fingertips of one hand on the moss-green stone set into a sliver of pearl dragon scale that hung at the centre of her necklace. She smiled fondly as she remembered it being given to her, then she took a deep breath and used a sliver of energy to reach through the stone. It blazed an intense bright green, and the air before her shimmered and distorted before dissolving into a doorway leading into a dark space. Nanaya walked through without hesitation.

Frigid air invaded the simple fabric of her dress and seized her body the moment she crossed the threshold. She shivered with its caress. She stood within a vast underground cavern that the palace of Southcastle could have easily sat within. Patches of glowing moss stretched up the tall, natural walls and illuminated the space. The sound of falling water echoed around her and came from a thin stream of water sliding down one wall to disappear into the uneven rock floor. Stalagmites clawed their way up toward the water's source while stalactites reached back down as if taunting their cousins to try harder.

The woman turned and regarded the archway through which she had just entered. It was carved into one wall with the twin of her stone set in its face at its apex. Both stones glowed lightly, and as she placed her fingertips upon her stone, she felt its steady pulse.

Turning back around, Nanaya looked to the cavern's centre. A mound of dark green rock and even darker green crystal twice as tall as she was sat there. It glowed lightly just like the stone in her necklace.

She walked toward it, the sound of each step echoing around her. She cringed at the noise. The snap of her shoes against the stone floor brought an acute and unwanted disruption to the serenity.

Nanaya stood before the stone mound and stared at it for a moment. It had been a long time since she had last stood here.

The cuts on her body from the battle at the tower were starting to heal, but her emotional wounds over the loss of her friends and allies were still raw.

The stone elemental Ki lay in the centre of the room, unmoving. The journey from the tower back to her sanctum under the Kafifi Ranges had taken almost the last of her strength.

Nanaya shook her head. She did not know why she thought of the massive elemental as a she, but it seemed right.

"You are safe, Ki. Heal."

Ki's immense form shuddered in response.

Nanaya sat down beside the elemental.

"We won... but at what cost," she whispered.

"Annungal is gone, Gibil is gone, Ninsar is gone, Ishkur and his sisters are gone, Ki will need to heal for centuries, and Cernunnos...." Her eyes filled with tears, and she wrapped her arms around herself. "He is gone, too. Lost to me forever."

Nanaya reached out and lay a hand on the elemental's still form. "Heal," she whispered. "I will watch over the nexus."

The memory faded, and Nanaya lay her hand on the stone just as she had back then. She closed her eyes.

"Come back, Ki. I need you."

Nanaya willed her power into the stone on her necklace, feeding it with the energy of this realm. The stone began to pulse softly. "My friend," she said. She leaned forward and placed her forehead on the stone. "I need you to wake. Come back from your deep rest."

Baraka felt something new amid the churning energy and emotions flooding his mind and body. He stopped in the middle of the woodland he had been passing through and tried to understand what it was.

Nanaya felt a low, slow pulse under her palm. The stone trembled and began to glow. Dust filled the air as it was disturbed from where it had lain for centuries. The sharp grind of stone shifting against stone reverberated around the cavern as the mound of rock and crystal began to move. It began to split, its top half rising and its sides pushing outward. Thick fingers uncurled from the ends of those sides, and above them, a roughly oval head of green quartz lifted, sheltered protectively between high, thick shoulders. That head turned toward Nanaya as it rose.

"Ki," Nanaya said, smiling.

The stone being continued to uncurl until a humanoid shape, easily ten feet tall, stood looming over her. Her body was a massive, rich deep-green form that radiated immense strength. As her awakening drifted around the chamber in ever lessening echoes and reverberations, Nanaya stepped back from the elemental and bowed.

"Welcome back, Ki."

The elemental lowered herself to one knee, each movement filling the air with rough sounds of grating stone, until her head was level with the woman's. Her face was featureless, yet Nanaya knew she was somehow looking at her.

"The tower has been breached," Nanaya said. "The power of the other realm is here once again, and it is growing. I need your help, my friend."

Ki remained crouched, regarding her for a moment before standing once again. She raised her arms and regarded herself.

"I know you are still healing from what happened before," Nanaya said, "and I would not have woken you if I did not have to, but I do not have any other options."

Baraka's breath quickened. What he felt was a sense of alignment. Without understanding what he was doing, he reached for that feeling.

Ki abruptly turned away from Nanaya to stare at a sudden distortion in the air beside her.

The woman's eyes widened, and she backed away.

Impossible!

Nanaya breathed heavily as she felt fear caress her with its icy touch.

Nothing should be able to reach here except Ki, or through the stone.

The distortion trembled, and then dissolved inward to reveal a wide-eyed, luminescent, bearded young man staring back at her.

Baraka gazed into the hole in the air that had appeared a few feet away from him. His eyes locked with those of the slight woman standing in its depths. She took a tentative step toward him, and instinctively his hands clenched into sparking fists.

Nanaya's breath caught as she watched brilliant white energy surround the man.

He is the one I felt, she realised.

"Wait!" she said, throwing an outstretched hand toward him.

~

A memory flashed into Baraka's mind.

The Chosen jerked both arms out toward him with a piercing cry, hands outstretched and fingers spread.

Baraka did not wait to see if this woman was also going to attack him. With a roar, he hurled his power at the woman.

~

Nanaya had the barest of warnings, a sudden thickening of the air as if a storm had descended and was about to unleash itself. She pushed a protective barrier around herself, but the force of Baraka's strike smashed her from her feet and hurled her back to crash against a wall of rock. She fell to the ground.

~

Baraka strode toward her, his eyes blazing bright with energy.

Nanaya wheezed a ragged breath. "Wait!"

Baraka stepped through the portal and into an underground cavern. He spared a brief moment to take in his surroundings before advancing on the prone woman.

Something slammed into his side and stole his breath away, flinging him to crash against another of the cavern walls. Unlike Nanaya, however, he rebounded from the impact, landing on his feet at the foot of the wall. The nimbus around him intensified as he clenched both fists and searched for the source of the attack. His eyes widened as a giant humanoid mass of glowing stone came toward him, each step shaking the cavern.

Baraka snarled and fell into a fighting crouch, his body glowing brightly.

Ki rushed forward, raising a massive stone fist.

Baraka ran to meet it, raising his own glowing fist.

The two strikes came together in an explosion that shook the cavern.

Ki was hurled away from Baraka, smashing through stalagmites as she tumbled across the cavern floor to rest amid a mass of broken stone.

Baraka stood blazing like the sun.

Crunching stone echoed around the cavern, and Baraka watched Ki rise to her feet and start to walk toward him again.

Baraka felt an unwrapping within his mind. Before, his use of the power inside him had been instinctive and without thought. Now, the knowledge of how to consciously do it revealed itself as if it had always been there, just hidden until the right moment to reveal itself.

White fire enveloped Ki.

The elemental stumbled, falling into a protective crouch and tucking her head under her massive arms.

Ki pulled her arms away from her face and stood tall. Baraka's flames of rage danced all over her, yet she appeared unhurt.

Baraka threw more of the same power at it, smothering her body in its flames.

Ki did not even flinch. She took one step forward then another and renewed her advance on Baraka, clenching her fists tight.

Baraka pushed more power at Ki, squinting at the brilliance of the firestorm he fuelled.

Ki strode forward and threw a punch at the man.

Baraka put his arm up to block, but the impact was colossal and hurled him across the cavern to crash against the far wall. He shook his head as he pushed himself up to his feet. He looked up to see Ki rushing toward him and pulling her left arm back to strike.

The punch lifted Baraka off the ground and slammed him into the rock wall again. He had not even begun to slide down its surface before Ki hit him again, and then again, and then again.

Cocooned in white energy, Baraka was protected from most of the blows, but as the barrage continued, the concussive blasts from each mighty impact began to take their toll, and he grew listless. He tried one last time to force the rock creature away, but again, the energy he thrust at the stone being did not have any effect. Ki hit him again, and consciousness fled.

Sharur stared at where the portal had hung in the woodland.

Where does that go?

Closing his eyes, Sharur sat cross-legged on the ground and took a deep breath.

This prey is rich in the power of this realm. I must have it.

His thoughts turned to what he had seen through the portal just before it had closed.

Rock. A cavern.

He turned his face toward the east.

The mountains.

He licked his lips.

This will be a good hunt.

Chapter Fifty-Four

Samuel gripped his smoking musket as he marched out of what was left of the village. Burnt-out buildings and broken bodies lay scattered everywhere. Men, women, children.

"Shoulder your firelock!" an officer ordered as the men left the outskirts and entered the surrounding farmland.

Samuel raised his weapon upright, barrel facing outward, its butt flat against his hip, and the weapon body resting on his left shoulder. He touched the leather cartridge box at his hip, making sure it was secured. Men all around him were doing the same. Marion had wanted him close to the general and herself in the command group, but he had felt an overwhelming urge to be with the rest of the men. To be face to face with the enemy.

But was this the enemy? Yes, they were Fringers, but this was a village. They were not soldiers.

He breathed heavily. He was full of surging emotion.

I need Marion to heal me, he thought. His mind cast back to the last time he was healed.

"Southcastle reinforcements have gathered with what remains of The Fringe States's forces," General Bronsaid, striding into the tent.

Marion sat naked, brushing her hair, but nothing indicated he was interested in the slightest.

"How far away?"

"Can't be more than twenty miles." The general raised a fist in the air. "Victory will put The Fringe States in our hands."

Samuel rose from the bed where he had just lain with Marion. His pounding heart had nothing to do with his recent lovemaking. "We need to face them."

Both figures looked at him.

"Your pet needs to know his place."

Samuel clenched his fists as he glared back at the man.

The general noticed and did likewise. Bron was immense now. He stood over nine feet, his broad shoulders stretching wider than two normal men, and his biceps easily bigger than the thickest thigh muscles. His nostrils flared, and his eyes widened and sparkled as he squared-off to Samuel.

"Stop that, General," Marion commanded before standing and walking to Samuel. She raised a hand to the young man's face and turned it toward her. Leaning forward, she kissed him deeply before looking back at Bron. "Samuel is indeed mine, but I would refrain from any name calling. He is changing quite rapidly now."

The general's smile carried no warmth or mirth; it was a wicked expression of desire. "I look forward to seeing just how much he has changed." He waved a hand dismissively in the air. "For another time. We march within the hour."

Samuel had ignored the exchange between the two. "I need to fight."

Marion chuckled and stroked his arm. "I can imagine. I want you close though, close to me."

Samuel shook his head. He felt full of pressure, fit to burst. "You don't understand. I need this."

Marion pursed her lips, then nodded. "You are changing fast. Well, if you are going to be in harm's way, then I think a little more... enhancing is needed to make sure you come back to me." She laid her hands on his crown and closed her eyes. "Let yourself out, General. Samuel needs me."

If the general said anything, Samuel never heard it, as all he could think about was the heat Marion drew from his body and the cold she replaced it with.

Samuel felt himself stiffen with the memory of their second lovemaking that had taken place after Marion had finished her healing. The first time she had healed him, he had felt tired, nauseous even. After the third or fourth act of healing, the reverse had happened; he had felt energised and revitalised. He shrugged away such thoughts. Now was not the time.

Now is the time for killing.

No shock followed his thought. There was no disturbing clash between who he was and what he was becoming. Somewhere over the last few days, he had let go of who he had been and embraced who he now was.

He glanced at the men around him and saw what he presumed were mirrors of his facial expression, grim determination edged with an eagerness to fight. An eagerness to kill.

Since he had arrived, the camp had swiftly swollen in number as more and more Western troops had found them. From those fleeing defeat to battalions victoriously forging onward, the number of gathered soldiers had increased until when they broke camp, hundreds of platoons strode out to find the enemy. Each man had been rearmed and healed by the Chosen, each now desperate to take the lives of those they faced.

Samuel breathed harder and harder as he tried to maintain his composure, his hands clutching his rifle white-knuckled.

A rider appeared from the tree line ahead and came charging toward them, galloping across a grassy piece of land with his horse's hooves tearing at the ground and flinging sod behind. The men around Samuel fell into crouches, and muskets were loaded and raised, ready to fire.

The rider leapt a small stone wall to land in a freshly furrowed field, its rider crouched low against its back as he urged it onward.

"One of ours!" someone shouted as his colours became clear and most, but not all, weapons were lowered.

Samuel recognised the man who had spoken as Gerald Thatcher, the innkeeper of The Plough. Seeing someone from home snapped him from his rage and desire to kill. He stared at Gerald as the man watched the rider. His face was far from the happy, welcoming expression Samuel was used to. It was tight and hard, eyes gleaming.

What is happening to us?

The rider angled his mount to the left of Samuel and toward where the general and Marion sat on their horses behind the assembled soldiers. They were surrounded by a handful of personal guards. Two drummers and two fifers, part of a fife and drum corps, had also recently joined them and stood with the soldiers, ready to walk with them into battle. The men beside the general and Marion twitched and grimaced, wanting to join their comrades rather than remain where they stood.

Excited whispers and hushed words rippled around Samuel and grasped his attention. "What is it?" he asked the man next to him, who gestured into the trees.

"They're in there."

Samuel felt a thrill of adrenaline rush through him at the words. An eager anticipation of battle consumed him, and he forgot all about Gerald and home.

"Look!"

Samuel's eyes searched the landscape in front of him.

At the edge of the tree line, a lone Fringe States soldier emerged. Then another. Then a dozen, each jogging forward individually, without any formation or organisation. As Samuel watched, a unit of Southcastle soldiers walked out of cover and into the open in a single line, their long, deep burgundy guard coats in stark contrast to the muted, dusty pastels of The Fringe States soldiers.

Officers with voices too distant to be heard yelled out orders, and

Samuel watched as more enemy men appeared in line formations. Two, three, five ranks.

"Form ranks!"

As the men formed up, Samuel could not help himself and pushed his way into the front line, staring down anyone who took offence and daring them to confront him.

Officers walked out to stand in front of the assembling men, twelve in total with a drummer every third man, their tall snare drums hanging on their hips. They stood out from everyone with their reversed colour uniforms, deep-blue facings and bright yellow coats.

"Prime and load!"

The drummers played a short roll to carry the command to those who could not hear.

The Western soldiers began the process of reloading. Samuel, like many others around him, did it without thought now, smoothly sliding through the motions of each step without pausing for the next instruction. He had his weapon ready in moments.

The Fringe States-Southcastle combined force advanced. It was a ragged army, a random assortment of uniforms and weapons emerging from the trees in varied preparedness. Samuel stared at them and saw desperation and anxiety. It was a last stand.

A different roll peeled out from the drummers, and Samuel felt his blood surge as he recognised it as the order to advance. As one, the drummers began a steady beat.

Rifles held horizontally at their waists, the West advanced to meet their enemy.

Samuel licked his lips as he marched forward. His eyes darted to the officer just ahead, who strode in time to the drums just as he did. The officer gripped the pommel of an unsheathed, slender sword that he held point upward, a snarl on his lips, and his eyes never wavering from the enemy.

The last Fringe States and Southcastle soldiers left the tree line and joined the assembled lines. Officers ran forward from within their ranks, each gesturing expressively to the men around them. As Samuel watched, the lines shuffled into tighter formation, and one by one, the officers disappeared back into the ranks.

The drums around Samuel began pounding faster, and he, like everyone around him, was swept up into the rhythm and picked up his pace.

The first enemy rank facing the Western army dropped to kneel on the damp ground, their rifles held vertically like those who stood behind them.

"Gonna get yours," the man beside Samuel said, and the young man found himself smiling at his own eagerness for the fight.

Closer and closer, they strode toward battle. Indistinct figures became clearer until Samuel could pick out individual features of the men facing him.

The drummers changed their beat, pounding the order to *Make Ready*. Samuel's breath caught as everyone around him abruptly stopped. He cocked his musket but kept it pointing up.

A shout echoed from the Fringe State and Southcastle lines as the Western army made ready for battle, the rifles in the enemy's first and second ranks dropping to point toward the advancing soldiers, the second rank aiming over the heads of the men kneeling in the front line.

Samuel both heard and felt the soldiers behind him shuffling with nervousness. In such a formation, the army they faced would be able to fire far more shots than they could, given the second line was free to fire at the same time as the first.

Another cry came from the men facing Samuel, and plumes of smoke burst from their weapons, together with rolling waves of dozens of sharp cracks as the Fringe States and Southcastle front lines fired.

The man next to Samuel collapsed with a cry of pain as did several others, but the casualties were light. The men of Royaume d'Occident were at the very limit of the enemy's range, and the weapons were horribly inaccurate, even in close quarters.

The Fringe States and Southcastle soldiers, however, were very much within the range of the West's superior guns, which were also far more accurate.

The drums sounded the order to present, and Samuel lowered his weapon to target the enemy.

One breath.

Another volley came from the enemy as their third rank replaced the second that moved behind to reload.

A handful more Western soldiers fell.

Two breaths.

Fire! the drums pounded.

The Western guns spat death, and dozens of the Fringe State and Southcastle soldiers fell.

Some of the men around Samuel turned and left the front line to make way for those behind them to take their place, but many refused, including Samuel himself. He stood his ground as a man behind him growled, and he calmly reloaded as those who had joined the front line with loaded weapons fired.

Dozens more men ahead of him fell.

The ranks behind the kneeling Southcastle soldiers continued to rotate and fire as those in the first line reloaded. The Royaume d'Occident force, however, was starting to fire less frequently as more and more men refused to leave the fight and walk to the back line.

It should have been disastrous, but not only was the inaccuracy of their enemies at this range failing to punish the West's crumbling discipline, the West's far superior arms were starting to exact a terrible toll, and their inability to hurt their enemies, together with mounting casualties, was undermining the Fringe States and Southcastle soldiers. The bodies were starting to pile up around the second line, and as the men in that line tried to make way for their comrades and retreat to reload in safety, they began to stumble over their fallen brothers. More than one gun misfired as soldiers tripped and fell.

Samuel watched the chaos and death growing in front of him, and his mouth went dry as his heart beat harder. Desire gnawed at his mind, a need to throw off the control and restrictions weighing down on him and run wildly into the fray.

The drums around him pounded as guns fired and the screams rose. More than one drummer had discarded their ordained rhythm and was now smashing often-splintered sticks to a frenzied beat of their own making. It was discordant and chaotic, and it was perfect to Samuel's ears.

Acrid smoke filled the air, creating a bitter, fluctuating veil that swept over the field of battle. Soldiers on both sides started to lose sight of one another, at first an obscured weapon or face, then losing sight of each other for longer and longer periods of time, until the world became a churning, choking maelstrom. Voices, gunshots, drums, everything became muted.

The fog of war consumed all.

"Can anyone see anything?" Samuel shouted, receiving negative yells in response. He ground his teeth, fruitlessly searching the smoke for any sign of the enemy.

"Damn this."

He glanced around him. He could just make out the men nearest. He stared at them, and they stared back, all of them burning with a building, pent-up need for violence.

The young man nodded as he made a decision. "I'm going in."

The man to his right smiled eagerly. "Bayonet charge?"

Samuel grinned back and nodded.

"Ha ha! *Yes!*"

The man behind him stopped growling as he sensed the change in mood from the men around him.

Samuel turned and looked him in the eye. "Bayonets, pass it on."

"Yes!" The man laughed and repeated the call to the men around him. In moments, the Western guns fell silent.

Samuel levelled his musket so the firing lock was just above his waist and its bayonet pointed out at chest height. He pulled the weapon close to his body and took a deep breath.

Time stopped.

Snapping, stabbing sensations washed over Samuel's skin. He felt as if he was standing upon a precipice. Every step of his life until now had taken him to this place, and now, he stood at a critical point in time. He breathed hard and licked his lips. Somehow, he knew that whatever he did now would irrecoverably change him. He stood at the point of no return. He shivered with anticipation of what was to come and felt nervous energy fill him to bursting.

Samuel opened his mouth and screamed, giving voice to the eager fury that had been growing inside him. One by one, the men around him screamed their own release until their voices combined into a roar of impending violence.

The Fringe States and Southcastle lines heard the terrible sound, and what little remained of their courage fractured. Hands shook, and guns stopped firing, as heads turned, and they looked at one another in fear.

Samuel took a small step forward, then a longer stride, then two, then he was jogging forward, and then he was running as he screamed, hundreds of men screaming with him.

For what seemed like an eternity, there was only the smoke that filled the air and the voices of his comrades that filled his ears.

A Fringe States soldier materialised out of the gloom less than a few feet away. He was younger than Samuel, his face smooth and without stubble, a few wisps of dark hair sprouting from his chin. His walnut eyes were wide and scared as he stared at his extinguished match and tried to come to terms with the fact he was not able to use his matchlock. He jerked as he became aware of Samuel and held his weapon horizontally across his body to try to protect himself.

Samuel thrust his bayonet forward.

The long blade passed over the boy's matchlock and buried itself into his chest. The boy fell back as Samuel jerked his musket back into a ready position.

All around him, the other men were doing the same, stabbing and spearing their way into the enemy lines.

The boy Samuel had just struck tried to stand and dragged Samuel's attention to him. Samuel stabbed again, but this time, the blade took him in the eye and sliced up into his brain. He collapsed, lifeless, among the other dead.

Samuel looked around him. The Royaume d'Occident troops were savagely attacking the Fringe States and Southcastle soldiers, many of whom had either dropped their matches or held useless extinguished ones in their shaking hands.

It was a slaughter.

Samuel hacked his way into the enemy ranks, stabbing and slashing. Blood soaked his clothes and dripped from the edges of his coat. It covered his face in wild streaks and ran into his mouth to stain his teeth. He swallowed it and savoured its metallic taste.

Thrust. Breathe. Slash. Breathe. Kick. Breathe. Punch. Breathe. Thrust. Breathe.

He lost himself in the killing.

He kicked an officer off the end of his bayonet, the old man stubbornly gripping the end of his musket.

When he looked around, there was no one left to kill.

He stood in the midst of a field of corpses. They were piled atop one another, broken and bloody. Here and there lay a Western uniform, but they were few and far between. Rare deep-blue flowers in a barren, bloody red world.

Samuel fell to his knees, exhausted in both body and mind. Without anyone to fight, Samuel found his rage abating. As it left, he felt a dim sense of horror at what he had just done, as if the thirst for violence had been suppressing it until now. He stared around him at the bloody bodies, unable to process how he felt, unable to understand what had just happened, what he had done.

Marion found him there a long time later, kneeling vacant-eyed among the dead. She walked forward, but he did not move as she approached. She placed her hands on the crown of his head and pushed her power deep into him, far more than she had before as she sought to drown the last vestiges of the man he had been and mould the man she wanted him to be.

Chapter Fifty-Five

When Baraka came to, his vision was blurred, and he was unable to move.

He tried to rotate his wrists and twist his head, feeling hard, sharp rock graze his skin with each attempt. He blinked several times, and line by line, contour by contour, his sight started to return. Abstracts shifted into defined, yet depthless shapes, and then finer layers of detail emerged in his surroundings, until he saw the creature of stone stared unblinkingly at him a dozen feet away and the woman standing beside it, touching her head tenderly.

As he tried to dispel the fog that clouded his thoughts, the events at the inn burst into his mind, demanding attention.

White fire engulfing the Chosen, who howled as he burnt until he fell as a charred husk.

Baraka's eyes filled with tears as his heart filled with revulsion. "What have I done?"

"Don't worry. Ki is unharmed, and apart from a sore head, so am I."

Baraka stared at the woman. "It's not that. I..." Words escaped him. He pushed aside the memory of killing the Chosen. "I am sorry I attacked you."

"Try not to dwell on it. When your power is unleashed, it can be impossible to control without the correct training. It's a form of mania of sorts and can last hours or weeks, it is impossible to know. It has passed now, though. When you next feel compelled to use it, you should not lose control."

"I don't understand what has happened."

The woman stared at him for a moment, and then turned to the rock figure. "I think he has calmed. You can release him."

Baraka felt the bonds holding him loosen. He looked down to see bands of stone that had been encircling his body flow back into the rock wall. He rotated his head and cracked his neck, rubbed his wrists, and took a deep breath. "Can you tell me what has happened to me?"

The woman gestured to a small stone table and two chairs that Baraka had not noticed before. She sat and smoothed her dress as Baraka took the seat opposite her. "This realm is full of vibrant energy. Some of us are born with more of that energy than others and have the ability to wield that energy. In my age, we were called kishpu. Today, people call us magicians, sorcerers, and the like. I thought I was the last of my kind here, but it would seem you are like me. My name is Nanaya."

"Baraka," he replied, introducing himself. He shook his head. "I still don't understand what is happening to me. I am no magician." He put his face in his hands and rubbed at his temples. "I don't understand any of this. Ever since that ruined tower—"

"The tower?" Nanaya interrupted, her eyes sharp and intense. "In The Territory?"

Baraka nodded. "Yes, though little more than a ruin that—"

Nanaya placed her hands on the table and leaned toward him. "Did you step inside? What did you do? How did you get there?"

Baraka frowned as she stared at him. "What does it matter?"

Nanaya shook her head. "It was you."

She slammed a fist on the table, rose, turned, and walked away. "The one thing I never considered, the one thing that could survive The Territory long enough to reach the tower: Another like me." She rubbed her eyes and sighed. "I thought I had covered every situation."

She fixed him with a piercing gaze. "Why were you there? What took you to the tower?"

"I was hoping to find something of value. That's what I do, I take jobs to find antiques."

"But into The Territory?"

Baraka nodded. "I know, but I had no money and no other options."

Nanaya gazed at Baraka as she pondered his words. "Tell me what happened at the tower."

Baraka shook his head. "I don't remember a lot of it. I climbed the outside and entered the ruin through a door near its top." Baraka licked his lips again, remembering the long, arduous climb in the unforgiving sun that had dried his throat.

"I walked half-buried corridors, searched barren rooms until..." He frowned and had to look away as his memories were scattered at this point.

"Until?" Nanaya pushed.

"There was a room." He shook his head and frowned. "It's hard to remember."

"Did that room have a book on a stone lectern in its centre?"

A scratching sound that gnawed at the edge of his mind. A pressure building in his head.

Baraka shivered as he nodded.

"When you left the tower, you took something with you," Nanaya said.

Baraka stared at her, frowning.

Nanaya stood and began pacing. "Something was sealed in that book. If only we had been able to investigate what was happening in those rooms. We were all so spent at the end, and the effects of the nexus sealing, the backlash that poisoned the land, was fresh and powerful. The most we could do was seal those chambers, and then we had to flee."

Nanaya shook her head. "What is done is done, no use wishing it had been different." She returned her gaze to Baraka. "Whatever was in that book possessed you, used you as a means to leave the tower." Her eyes narrowed for a moment. "I cannot sense any taint of Kur on you, so it has moved on."

"The archbishop."

Nanaya glanced at Ki before returning her eyes to Baraka. "Tell me."

Baraka closed his eyes and rubbed his brow. "I have vague recollections of the journey from the tower. Snap images of eating, or being wet and cold, or stumbling and twisting an ankle. In between them are nightmares." Baraka shivered.

"It was like I was compelled to reach the archbishop. More. It was like there was something inside me, controlling me. I have these fleeting moments of clarity as I was forced to travel almost the entire width of the continent." Baraka shook his head. "I remember meeting this archbishop and then... then I woke up in a cell, and whatever was inside me was gone." Baraka swallowed. "I was told I had murdered the Western king, but... But that wasn't me!"

Silence.

"Then?"

Baraka sighed and sat cross-legged on the floor. "And then something happened. I was exhausted, I felt full of despair and hopelessness, and then, suddenly, I was filled with this, this energy. I don't know what or how I did it, but somehow, I tore a hole in a wall and escaped, leaping down a fall that no one could have survived."

Nanaya nodded. "Something in the tower possessed you and retained enough of a presence after it had left you for this archbishop that it was able to direct your actions. It used you to kill the king. I suspect that doing so, controlling you, was the trigger for your power to awaken."

Nanaya's eyes narrowed as she thought. "It makes sense. It used your body to escape the tower and find what it wanted, another vessel in a position of power that it could use to achieve its ambition of returning to the tower once it was strong enough to do so. It would explain why those others that carry the energy of Kur inside them were at the basilica."

"Chosen," Baraka said. An image of the man burning in the fire he had conjured filled his mind. "I fought one." He could not bring himself to say that he had killed that person, too.

Ki abruptly stretched to her full height, her head looking up and turning around, searching.

"What is it?" Nanaya asked.

Ki gestured above.

Nanaya's eyes also turned to the cavern ceiling. Her eyes widened. "It is as I feared. There is a taint born from the power of the other realm, from Kur moving through the mountains. I doubt it is the archbishop, more likely one of these Chosen. It must be heading for Southcastle. We must stop it."

Baraka stared at Nanaya for a moment before shaking his head and turning away "This is not my fight."

"You must help us!"

"I do not have to. I didn't ask for any of this."

"And you think I did?"

Baraka swung back to stare at her with hard eyes. He jabbed a finger at her. "I don't care what your situation is. I had my body stolen from me and my mind raped. I have been tortured. I have been made to commit murder. I have—" He gestured at himself. "I have had powers erupt inside of me that I could not control and that made me kill again."

His hands clenched into white-knuckled fists. "Ever since I entered that tower, my life has not been my own, and now, when I am starting to gain an understanding of what is happening and regain some semblance of control over myself, you try to take that from me and make me participate in your war—"

"This is not my war! I did not start this, and I desperately want nothing more than to be rid of it!" Her lips trembled with barely restrained fury. She took a moment to calm herself, though her fists were now clenched just like Baraka's, and she was breathing heavily.

"I was thrust into this when they took my husband." Her eyes grew distant "And when they murdered my daughter."

Her eyes refocused, and she stared at Baraka. "Even after they took everything from me, everyone alive that I cared about, I still could not live my life. I needed to stand watch and make sure nothing like what happened could ever happen again. My life has not been my own for over a thousand years, so forgive me if I am not sympathetic."

Baraka dipped his head. "I am sorry for the legacy of the past that haunts you." He shook his head. "But it is not my legacy, and I am not bound by the ties that bind you. I do not want anything to do with this, I just want to go home—"

"The home you knew no longer exists."

Baraka stared at Nanaya, frowning.

She took a breath and softened her tone. "There will not be a Fringe States when this war is over. It will either be a territory of Royaume d'Occident or, more likely, it will be a ruined wasteland."

She took a step closer to the man. "This war is a front for whatever has possessed the archbishop, and as it wages, it is destroying everything. That Chosen is heading for Southcastle, and they will not be able to stop it. It will be a massacre, and as the killing continues, the thing that escaped the tower will grow stronger and stronger. We must stop that Chosen. If we do not, what possesses the archbishop will become strong enough to return to the tower."

She took Baraka's hands in her own. "I understand you want your life back, I really do, but there are so few of us that can stand against this. You are one who can, and with your help, we may just stand a chance of defeating it. If you choose not to... If you choose not to, then it wins, and we will die. Everything will die. There will be no place to hide and no second chances."

Baraka met Nanaya's eyes for a long moment before he shook his head and pulled his hands away from hers. "I am not a fighter. I am just a treasure hunter. I have no place in any war."

"You *are* a fighter," Nanaya said. "A treasure hunter is a hard living in the best of places, and The Fringe States is not the best of places. It is a harsh place that breeds tough people. I can see in you a fierce determination to never give in, to never give up."

"I am no warrior." Baraka placed both hands on his abdomen. "And this power inside me..." The memory of the Chosen screaming as he burned filled his mind.

Nanaya saw a tremor of revulsion sweep across the man's face.

"It terrifies me. I have no idea what I might do." He raised a hand to his eyes as he recalled the sparks of energy that had spat around his fingers, then merged to form a ball of crackling white light laced with red flames. He clenched his fist.

Something Nanaya had said came back to him. "You mentioned another realm before. Kur. Is that where the thing that possessed me, and now possesses the archbishop, is from?"

Nanaya took a moment to think about what she was about to say. "You know of Kur from the Church of The Shepherd?"

Baraka nodded. "But I am not a believer."

"Kur exists. There are things there called gallus that are hate and violence incarnate. Is what possessed you one of them? I don't know." She took a deep breath.

"Over a thousand years ago, a group of us managed to stop the gallus as they tried to cross from Kur to here. The tower you entered was the site of the gallus's incursion into this realm, the seals between Kur and here are there. When the seals were healed, the land around the tower was infused with energy from Kur. It has made it fatal to anything of this realm. As powerful as you are, even you would have succumbed to the effects of The Territory over time, so whatever possessed you needed to escape. Since then, it has been slowly growing stronger and preparing to return to the tower to become even more powerful."

"How?"

"I believe that whatever has possessed the archbishop will try to break the seals again so it can absorb the power of the other realm that will be released. We cannot allow that to happen. If it does, once again the gallus will be able to cross, and this time, there is only Ki and myself to stand against them."

Something occurred to Nanaya, and she stared at Baraka. "You said you fought a Chosen before. Why did you do that?"

Baraka thought for a moment. "I am not sure I can explain it. There was a wrongness to him. It did more than disgust me, it triggered something in me. Something inside me wanted to end it. More than wanted. I longed to eradicate it."

"It was the power of Kur," Nanaya explained. "It should not be in this realm, and your being was reacting to it." The woman put her hands together. "Something inside you compelled you to fight Kur that time. I am asking you to help us fight it again. It should not be your fight. It should not be my fight, but someone has to stand against it, and there is only us. You and I, we have had so much taken from us. We have not been able to live our lives the way we wanted, but we can take a stand. We can regain control of our lives and we can fight back. Please, help me stop it before it is too late."

Baraka did not want this. He desperately wanted to go back to his former life.

If they are not defeated, there will be no where you can call home.

He remembered the feeling of the Chosen. A vileness.

This is not my fight!

But it was. Something inside him did want to end them.

The more he thought about it all, the more he realised he fundamentally wanted to end everything touched with the energy of this other realm. He desperately wanted to deny this truth, but he could not. Something about them ignited this deep inner need.

And there was more.

He remembered growing up in the streets of Eptimi among the gangs, thieves, smugglers, and worse. In order to survive you had to band together with others, and when a threat surfaced, running away was not an option. Running allowed it to threaten you again in the future. Standing against it was the only way to make sure it never came after you again.

With your help, we may just stand a chance.

Nanaya had been right about him. He had never given up before. He had never run away.

How can I start now? How can I turn away from people who need me? A threat I can stand against? A threat that I know I must stand against.

He looked at Nanaya.

I can walk away.

He sighed.

He knew he could not walk away, just as he had been able to turn his back on someone who needed his help in the streets of Eptimi.

I don't have to do this.

But he knew that he did have to.

"I don't want this."

Nanaya shook her head. "Neither do I."

Baraka closed his eyes and sighed. "I will fight."

Chapter Fifty-Six

Antoinette shivered with the remembered pleasure of the fort massacre as she rode through the pass to Southcastle.

A sharp *crack* and *crunch* of shifting rock brought her attention back to the present. Massive slabs of stone detached themselves from either side of the narrow pathway and slammed together with a force that knocked people off their feet and set horses panicking. Other Chosen, together with a handful of unfortunate men and their horses that had been between them, were crushed.

An officer turned to shout an order, but the words dissolved into a desperate scream as the ground fell from under him, and he disappeared into a deep fissure that had not been there moments before, and which abruptly sealed over him.

The ground attacked them. Spikes surged from the ground to impale those walking over their space, lifting them dozens of feet in the air, shrieking through the lifeblood bubbling from their lips. Chunks of stone bigger than a man split from the rock walls to pulverise the soldiers beneath them and batter field cannons to uselessness. Men and horses screamed in terror as they were attacked, and there was nothing they could do about it.

The rock the centre of the army was travelling over rose, throwing men in all directions. As it grew, it formed into a rough, squat, humanoid shape with massive shoulders and thick arms that ended in three-fingered fists. Those fingers curled in the air as they left the ground, and its head swung one way, then the other, to regard the scattered soldiers.

Antoinette mustered her power as the elemental formed.

The giant rock creature staggered backward as something speared its upraised arm.

Antoinette scrambled out of its shadow, half running, half stumbling, as it stared at its arm falling limply by its side. A small dark thorn was embedded in its bicep. As Antoinette gazed at the sentient rock, she saw spider webs of black lines snaking their way out from the wound and stretching across its arm.

The boom of a cannon firing snapped her attention back to the army around her, and she saw smoke from a field cannon that a handful of men had bravely made ready to fire. She watched the lead shot hurtle toward the rock figure, but it struck an invisible barrier and shattered.

The rock giant staggered again as another small black shard burrowed into its chest.

A woman appeared beside the rock creature, her long, blond hair billowing in the light wind. Antoinette could see a bright nimbus of energy surrounding her.

Antoinette turned toward the nearest gun crew readying its cannon and pointed at the woman.

A blast of white energy hit the cannon before she could speak. It exploded, debris smashing and breaking the men servicing it. The Chosen fell to her knees, crying out as bits of broken wood and metal pummelled her and sliced deeply into the arm she had raised to protect her eyes. She swung around to stare at a bearded man haloed in white flames of raw energy.

His eyes met hers.

Pain erupted all over Antoinette's body as white flames engulfed her. She screamed as she fell to the ground and hid her face in her hands as she burned.

Baraka felt torn as he stared at another burning Chosen, the power that was killing her writhing around his hands. His head told him what he was doing was right, but his heart told him it was wrong.

He still did not understand exactly how he was able to use the energy inside him, but flashes of understanding were coming whenever he had the urge to use it.

Shouts and gunfire turned his eyes, and he saw Western soldiers firing on Nanaya. They carried with them an essence of the same taint as the Chosen, and his inner turmoil was quashed with the absolute need to cleanse this place of their presence.

White fire blazed in his eyes, and he unleashed his wrath. Waves of terrible churning power erupted from his body to sweep over the army. Men screamed as they burned, dropping weapons and rolling on the ground to put out the flames.

A sudden cry of pain pulled Baraka's eyes to Nanaya, and he watched her fall to the ground. He ran to her, his inferno extinguishing as his attention switched to the woman.

She was breathing hard, blood on her lips. A white shaft webbed with dark veins was embedded in her chest, and Baraka could see black corruption seeping out of it and spider-webbing through her flesh.

She gasped. "He has found me," she said through bloody lips.

As Baraka crouched next to her, he saw her eyes widen and stare at something behind him.

"He is here!" Nanaya whispered, and her eyes flooded with tears. "Oh, please no. Not again. I cannot do this again."

Baraka spun around to see a tall, lean figure walking toward him, wearing some sort of broken horned helmet. As he continued to look at it, however, he realised the helmet was the remnants of antlers protruding from its head. A long, fitted cloak and tight pants accentuated its gauntness. As Baraka watched, the figure raised a curved bow, and in one fluid motion, knocked an arrow, aimed, and fired.

Power surged within Baraka. He felt an urgent need to push that energy outside his body, and with that need came an understanding of how to do it and what it would do. A protective shield of rippling energy enveloped himself and Nanaya. The arrow struck the barrier and ricocheted off.

Nanaya gasped. "How did you do that?"

"I wish I knew," Baraka said without turning around as he watched the archer stop and silently regard him. "I don't know how I am suddenly able to do these things. It is like a moment of need unlocks something inside me. I know what to do and how to do it without thinking."

The archer blurred, and then disappeared.

"He is hunting," Nanaya managed between hacking coughs and gasps for air. "You won't be able to see him while he hunts."

A titanic groan sounded behind Baraka, and the ground shook violently. He glanced behind him and saw that Ki had fallen to one knee, her head bowed, and her body shuddering. Her stone body was now falling to a bleached white around the wounds, and Baraka suspected that if he touched it, the stone would be brittle to his touch. Something flickered at the corner of his vision, and he spun around just as the horned figure materialised and fired at him. Baraka caught the arrow between two hands, slapping them together just as it passed between them.

The moment his flesh touched the shaft, immense pain flooded his body, but it was not his pain, it was a memory of pain buried in the arrow. It sliced deeply into him, dragging its ragged claws through his being, and his vision blurred.

Baraka threw the arrow down and snarled, hurling fiery energy at his attacker, but the archer tumbled to one side, evading that fire.

A sound caught Baraka's attention, and he spared a glance to his right. Southcastle soldiers advanced around a bend in the road, smoke curling from raised matchlocks. The soldiers cast scared glances at the rock monster, many also looking uneasily at himself and Nanaya.

Baraka returned his eyes to the archer and saw it look at the soldiers and then to Baraka glowing with power. Its form rippled again and lost substance. Baraka could just make out a disturbance in the air that raced away.

The remaining Royaume d'Occident soldiers tried to fight back against the newly arrived Southcastle soldiers, but they were heavily outnumbered and did not last long.

"Please."

Baraka crouched over Nanaya. "What can I do?"

She gestured to the shaft buried in her chest. "This is filled with energy from Kur." She panted with the effort of speaking, sweat running down her face. "It is smothering my power, and I can feel its corruption inside me. You must pull it out." She closed her eyes as a wave of pain rushed through her.

Baraka took a deep breath and closed his eyes. He put his hands to either side of the arrow but could not bring himself to touch it.

Understanding blossomed inside his mind.

I don't need to touch it to pull it out. Without knowing exactly what he was doing, he used his power to pull the shaft from Nanaya's body.

The clatter of the arrow on the ground in front of him opened his eyes.

Nanaya was visibly healthier, her skin without its former black corruption.

She smiled thinly, her eyes beginning to close. "Thank you." She raised a limp hand.

"Please. Help Ki."

Nanaya could not finish the sentence and collapsed, unconscious.

Chapter Fifty-Seven

Adaru could not feel Antoinette. He reached for her presence, feeling for the connection between them, but there was nothing.

He opened his eyes.

Unfortunate, but she was always a diversion.

He pursed his lips as he thought of her loss, then lay back in the hot water and sighed.

The mix of eucalyptus, sandalwood, and rosehip oil filled his nostrils as it soothed his skin.

He raised an oil-coated arm out of the water. It was grey and mottled with white blemishes the size of fingerprints that stretched from his fingertips to his neck.

This body is dying.

Adaru slipped his arm under the water.

Kur's energy is killing it. When the tower is mine, I will have an endless supply of all the power I could ever want. I will make myself a new body.

When the water grew cool, he climbed from the bath, and took a gown from a nearby servant to wrap himself within and dry himself as he wore it. A Chosen stood at the bath entrance, and she bowed to him as he approached before opening the door. Another Chosen on the other side bowed and walked ahead of Adaru as he left the bathhouse, the other Chosen walking behind him.

The bathhouse was within the inner palace rooms on the lower floor, and so Adaru could travel to and from his chambers without leaving the security of the fortified building and the protection of the Chosen. Servants and guards stopped what they were doing and bowed their heads as he passed, not daring to catch his eye.

Adaru smiled.

Château Occidentale was as he wanted it.

Broken.

Even so, he dared not move in public. For all his power, this body was very mortal, and an arrow, a musket shot, or even just a well-thrown rock could kill him if he was not prepared, and he had come far too far, endured and sacrificed far too much for it to end now.

Especially now when the prize is so close I can almost taste it.

So, until the time was right, he buried himself within the palace and surrounded himself by those unwaveringly loyal, the Chosen. Born of his power, they were connected to him on a deep, intimate level, and he held a fundamental domination over them.

When he made it back to his chambers, Diers was waiting for him as he had been instructed.

Adaru indicated that the Chosen should remain outside.

"How are things progressing here?"

"They are as you have instructed," Diers replied. "I have changed more people here in the capital, though not, of course, as well as you have done. They prowl the streets at night, killing and feeding the terror of an already frightened populace. The Chosen here grow stronger in this environment. The people who were able to have left the city, but they are few. Most have nothing outside of their lives here and so are tied here. Those who have left take tales far and wide of what this place is becoming. No one that does not have to visit Château Occidentale does so."

"Excellent. This city is our sanctuary. Continue." He then closed his eyes to settle himself and reached for Marion.

Hello, Adaru.

Adaru frowned as Marion's flat, indifferent voice filled his mind, and a sense of her presence touched him.

Report, Marion.

We push through The Fringe States. Resistance is scattered and broken. I expect we will be able to start crossing The Territory within the week.

Adaru nodded. *Good. I will contact you as you start to cross.*

Marion's presence mostly evaporated, though a faint echo of her remained.

Adaru could feel her, together with Diers, by virtue of their shared connection. "Leave me," he commanded Diers.

The man bowed reverently and departed, closing the door behind him. Adaru sat in the silence for a moment.

He smiled.

So close.

Chapter Fifty-Eight

"How is she?"

Baraka turned at the voice and watched a slightly gaunt man approach along a path winding through the garden, a place Baraka had been summoned to soon after he had arrived with Nanaya. The man wore a simple shirt and plain pants, but they were of fine quality. He wore a crown, and his eyes were dark, tired, and troubled.

Baraka bowed.

"Nanaya was gravely injured," Edward said as he walked between tall ferns. "You remain at her side. How is she?"

"She rallies. She looks better every moment. I think she will recover."

The king nodded as he came to stop beside him. "Who are you, Baraka?"

Baraka chuckled. "A very good question."

Edward frowned at him. "If the accounts of my men are to be believed, you have the same powers as Lady Nanaya does, something I did not think was possible, and which makes you either a powerful ally or a formidable enemy. I also have reports about a *rock monster* that accompanied you both and fought on our side."

The king shook his head and his composure slipped. A haunted look appeared in his eyes. "These are strange and terrible times." He took a deep breath. "I ask you again, who are you, Baraka?"

The world slowed as Baraka paused to think.

Can I trust this man? Can I confide in him things I do not even understand myself?

Moments of revelation like this, where a hidden truth is laid bare and all semblance of secrecy and of protective cover are discarded, direct destiny, and the weight of this moment hung heavy around the two men.

Baraka opened his hand. A dancing white flame sprang to life in his palm, startling Edward, who hastily stepped back.

"This happened when I was in Château Occidentale. It continues to grow stronger."

The king's eyes were wide. "Awakening powers, rock monsters... There is so much happening that is beyond my understanding." The king wearily rubbed his eyes. "I am trying to make sense of everything, but it seems like every time I think I am getting a grip on something, something even more fantastical happens and" — he swallowed and licked his lips — "things have been difficult. I..."

His voice trailed off, his eyes grew a little clouded, and he sighed. He closed his eyes and remained silent for a while. After a moment, he gasped and opened his eyes, turning back to Baraka.

"I am sorry, where was I?"

Something is wrong with him, Baraka thought as he looked into the king's wide and slightly confused eyes.

"You were saying there is a lot happening at the moment that is difficult to understand."

Edward frowned. "Was I?" he asked. "It is so hard to think at times." He yawned. "I apologise. I get so tired presently." He rose and started to walk away, then turned back and smiled wearily at Baraka. "It was good to meet you. Thank you for looking after Lady Nanaya. I have never met anyone quite like her, I..." He frowned. "Did I already say that?" He shook his head, turned, and walked away.

~

Baraka sat cross-legged on the floor of the apartment that had been made available for him. He stared at the leather roll that contained the arrow he had plucked from Nanaya. He unwrapped it, careful not to touch it. His eyes traced the black spider web taint that ran across its surface, lingering on the twists and grooves in the white material beneath.

When he had touched it before, the echo of pain he had experienced was profoundly intimate in a way he could not understand. He licked his lips with nervous apprehension. Something about the arrow called to him. He had to know what it was.

Baraka took a deep breath and grasped the shaft with both hands.

Agony consumed him.

His first instinct was to let go, but instead, he made himself grip the arrow tighter, snarling through the pain. He felt a heat building inside, a warmth that grew and filled every part of his body. His vision blurred, the world distorting as the pain consumed him. The room wavered, trembled, and then shattered. Images flashed in his mind. A pillar of fire. Barbed tentacles bursting from a sea. A young boy raising his hand to stop the blade that was about to strike him. A dark stone tower. A blood red dragon opening its mouth to hurl fire. His mother smiling as she held a baby.

The images abruptly left him, and he found himself standing in a room with curved, bare, stone walls. Light spilled from its far end, where one wall was missing. A deep blue sky speckled with clouds filled the space. He staggered as a wave of dizziness assaulted him, and rubbed the sides of his head to ease away a pulsing ache. When he had recovered, he walked toward the opening and the sky beyond.

He emerged from the room onto an uncovered platform that stretched a dozen feet to a thick, raised edge. As he walked to that edge, he saw he was surrounded by a rough ocean, its white caps startlingly bright against its dark depths. He peered over the edge of the platform and stared down a ragged cliff face that disappeared into the water far below. The crash of waves against the cliff, and the raucous calls of seabirds, filled his ears.

"Baraka."

Baraka turned back to the room and watched the shape of a man walk toward him from the shadowed interior. He balled his hands into fists and tried to summon his power.

Nothing happened.

There was nothing to summon. The pool of energy inside him was not just empty, it was absent.

"You are not physically here, so you cannot use your power," the man explained, as if reading Baraka's mind.

He emerged into the sun, tall, dressed in ivory robes, with bobbed silver hair and a closely cropped and oiled silver beard.

Baraka instantly recognised him.

"Father!"

He also remembered his name.

Annungal.

The man had an expression of pure joy and deep affection. Its intensity touched Baraka, however, he did not really know this man. His father had left him when he was so young, so he hesitated to go to him. The man saw his reaction, and a shadow of sadness washed over his face. He smiled thinly and nodded.

"There is a lot to say."

"You left when I was so young," Baraka said.

"I had no option," Anunngal said with a voice full of regret. "It was Cernunnos, or at least what he had become." His eyes filled with sadness. "Leaving you and your mother was the hardest thing I have ever done, but it was the only thing I could do to keep you safe. Even though years had passed since your mother found me and nursed me back to health, I was still weak, and there was no way I could have protected you from him. He was still hunting, and he would have found me. Found us."

Baraka sighed. "I thought you just left us." He shook his head. "Everything I thought I knew... Things are different now." He snorted and raised his hands before his eyes. "Things are so different now."

"I cannot begin to imagine what you have been through," Annungal said, "but I will help you as much as I can."

Baraka gestured around them. "Where am I?"

Annungal motioned to one side of the ledge, where two solid wooden chairs sat with a thick round wooden table between them, on which stood a tall, crystal decanter full of a rich, orange liquid. Baraka would have sworn the ledge was empty moments ago.

"You are in my mind, or rather, our minds have connected. This" — he gestured around him — "is a memory of a place where I spent some time. A sanctuary. When you reached me, I took us here." He indicated one of the wooden chairs. "Please, sit."

Baraka sat on a rich, opal-coloured cushion he was *sure* had not been there before. "How have I reached you? I was just holding an arrow and—"

"What was it made of?" his father asked.

Baraka shook his head. "I'm not sure. They were white. Not wood and not stone. Almost—"

"Like bone?"

Baraka nodded.

"Interesting," his father murmured. "Somehow, they have enabled you to link minds with me. It is something that some of us can do."

"Us? Who is us?"

The world shuddered and dimmed for a moment.

Baraka looked around. "What is happening?"

"The link is dissolving." His father leaned forward. "You must visit Ki. I am in her cavern. I travelled there after I left you. Even though your mother tended to me, I was still injured, and I could not go back to The Citadel. It was the only place I could hide and heal. Do you know where the cavern is?"

Baraka considered for a moment, and then nodded. "I travelled there, somehow. I am not sure I can do that again, but I can... feel that place. I think I can find it."

His father opened his mouth to speak, but the world shook again.

"There is no more time. I wish I could prepare you, but this—" He took a deep breath. "Come and find me, and we will talk."

Everything went black.

Sharur stared out over the rocky precipice into the Kafifi Ranges.

It burned being there, he thought as he stared at the mountains. He licked one arm as if soothing a wound. *Like the rock and stone were attacking me.*

Sharur growled as he rolled an arrow between his hands. *In all the years since I made these, I have never lost any. Now there are only five.*

The failed hunt ran through his mind. He threw back his head and roared in frustration, a loud, shrieking howl that echoed through the mountains surrounding it.

Those in Southcastle who heard the distant, wild sound shivered and rushed inside the nearest building.

King Edward stared out to the mountains with wide eyes as his goblet of wine crashed to the stone path of the elevated garden.

Nanaya twitched and moaned in her deep, healing sleep.

Sharur let his howl die, and for a moment, just sat staring at the arrow. An image of the blond-haired woman filled his mind.

The kishpu... Why is she familiar?

He stood and pushed the arrow into a weathered quiver to re-join the others. *It does not matter.* He patted the leather. *Five will still be enough, and when I am done, I will carve more.*

Chapter Fifty-Nine

The protest started with a whisper.

"I can't stand it any longer," the mother said, tears streaming down her face.

She had gotten home maybe six hours ago and collapsed into bed and an exhausted sleep. She had awakened, fearful of missing her next shift, which had then changed to a general anxiousness about the state of her life, which had then led to how she was now, sitting dishevelled at the side of the road, sobbing, and unable to bring herself to carry on as she had been.

"Mary, darling, are you well?"

Mary wiped her eyes and turned at the voice. Her friend Catherine sat beside her.

"What is wrong?"

Mary's lips trembled. "After Charles left for The Fringe States it has just been me, Walter, and Emily keeping things going. For a while, my son and I managed to do both the tailoring and the clothes stall at the market while my daughter took up more shifts at the munitions factory."

The woman took a deep breath to steady herself. "Then the trouble at the docks started. You know, people not turning up and supplies going missing. When the militia was enlarged, they found there wasn't enough men, what with them all away in the war. Walter had been drafted.

"Then supplies to be sent to the front went missing." She held a piece of paper up in one hand. "I got this today. Non-essential businesses are to close. Our tailoring business was started by my father, and I've had the stall since before the kids. Emily and I have also been ordered to work at the factories."

Mary fell forward, crying her despair into her friend's shoulder while Catherine patted her back and spoke soothing words. She cried for a long time until she was empty and spent. She took several shuddering breaths and wiped her eyes.

And saw a handful of people around her.

Mary stared at the men and women, each with eyes of aching misery.

"I never see my wife," a middle-aged man said. "I miss her so much."

"I work so much I can't remember what life is," a woman said between sobs.

Mary felt the tightness in her chest lessen as she saw that she was not alone. More people spoke of their despair, and as they did, others stopped and joined the growing crowd.

"Something has to be done!" Dozens of voices erupted in support.

"This is no way to live!" Voices cheered.

"No one listens! No one understands!"

Mary stood. "We need to tell them."

Those nearest heard her and nodded.

She nodded back to them, finding strength in their agreement. "We need to tell them!" she repeated louder.

Her words were carried throughout the crowd, every person hearing them nodding and stating their agreement.

"*To the palace!*"

A chant began, and the crowd swelled.

More and more people stopped what they were doing and turned back from where they were going to join the mass.

"To the palace!"

With a roar, the crowd moved with unified, determined purpose.

Chapter Sixty

Samuel plunged his bayonet into the Southcastle soldier's throat and forced it deeper into the man's chest. The soldier shrieked as the blade speared his body, but Samuel just smiled and leaned close to the dying man, his ear next to the soldier's bloody lips as his death gasp escaped them. The man fell back, pulling Samuel's musket from his hands.

Throwing his head back, Samuel laughed loud and hard, and then, wild-eyed, he searched for his next victim.

He was deep in the enemy lines, Southcastle troops surrounding him, but none dared approach. He cast around him for someone to fight, but those not engaged diverted their eyes and hurried away as best they could.

Grinning, Samuel ripped the dead soldier's sword from its sheath and continued killing, slashing around him with wild abandon. More and more fell to his blade, and with each death, the need to kill grew until it consumed him.

Blood dripping down his face, the enemy officer's sword gripped white-knuckled in one hand, Samuel slaughtered every enemy in sight. Hacking into the back of a man trying to run from him, Samuel heard a noise close by. He ripped his blade free from the howling man and swung.

And buried his sword into James.

Samuel stared wide-eyed at his friend as his eyes glazed over. He knew it could not be James, but there was something in the face now falling away from him that made him think of James.

Maybe it was the same colour eyes that were now vacant just like James's had been at the end. Maybe it was the same colour and length of hair that was pulled back just like James wore his hair. Maybe it was the awkward way he stumbled as life left him just like James used to stumble when tired or drunk. Maybe it was all of it.

Whatever it was, it stopped Samuel cold. His arms dropped heavily to his sides as he stared at the young man's body collapsing before him.

The battle raged around Samuel, but he stood immobile and apart from it.

James.

The battle around him vanished as he remembered his friend James looking after him and leading him from the field of battle as the South-castle cannons destroyed their lines. He remembered James helping him look after the town crier, and then them both burying him.

He remembered James lying dead on the makeshift pallet as Samuel dragged him ever onward.

The clash and *crack* and *snap* of the fighting surrounding him quieted, and then vanished, replaced by the cries of the dying.

Samuel blinked his eyes and breathed in deeply, his nostrils filling with the stench of defecation-laden and bloodied dirt.

Something wet and hard hit his face, staggering him backward. He glanced down to find a bloody severed hand at his feet. He looked up and watched General Bron striding toward him.

Little remained of the man he had once been. Round shouldered, his head hung forward over great slabs of chest muscle on a small, but thick stump of a neck. His shoulders were half again higher than a standing man's head. His arms were wider than a portly man's waist and hung curled at his side as if they refused to straighten.

The general's eyes were wide, bloodshot, and fixed on Samuel, his breath hissing between gritted teeth as he strode closer. He gripped a broken blade in one hand, the fingers in the other repetitively curling into a fist then uncurling into an open claw with nails that tapered into sharp points.

The melancholy that had settled over Samuel evaporated, and the bloodlust surged once more. He smiled and crouched into a fighting stance.

Bron roared.

It was a frustrated, angry, animal vent of unfulfilled desire.

The general leapt forward, arms and legs pumping as he raced across the battleground. As he neared, he swung his broken blade.

Samuel darted to one side, and the sword ripped the air apart where he had stood. He swung his own sword, and it clashed against what remained of the general's armour.

They warily circled each other.

Bron leapt at Samuel, slashing with his blade as he clubbed with his fist. Samuel ducked and rolled under the blows, swinging up. Bron howled in pain as Samuel's blade sliced across his unprotected abdomen.

"*Stop!*"

Samuel's blade dropped from open fingers, and he stepped back from the general as his vision greyed, and a rushing sound filled his ears. He shook his head to clear his eyes.

Bron stood a similar distance away from Samuel, also trying to clear his head, growling and struggling to raise his sword as if his body was sluggish to obey his thoughts.

A slight figure was walking unhurriedly toward them both. As Samuel's vision cleared, he saw it was Marion.

"There are enough people to fight. You can leave each other alone."

Bron snarled as he managed to raise his blade and started to walk toward Samuel with his fists clenched tightly.

Marion flicked a hand at him, and he fell to his knees.

"Enough, General."

Samuel stared at Marion. "How?"

"I have... grown in power," the woman said. "I can do a lot now." She turned cold eyes to the general, who was still looming over her even though he was on his knees.

"Remember that. I will not be as gentle next time." She returned her gaze to Samuel and gestured at him. "Come."

Samuel stood and walked to her side. She turned without a word, and they walked away from the general, who glared at them from his place in the bloody mud.

"We near the end," Marion said as they walked to a small stream. "Stay away from Bron."

"I can take him."

Marion chuckled, and then regarded him intently. "Strip."

Without hesitation Samuel began discarding his clothes until he stood naked before her.

Her eyes roamed brazenly over his body. "You have grown strong," she purred. "The power has worked wonders on you." She nodded to the water. "Bathe," she commanded.

Samuel dutifully waded into its shallows.

"We are so close now."

"Close to what?"

Marion pursed her lips as she regarded him. "Yes, you should know." She looked up into the cloud-filled sky. "Adaru is sending us to a tower to secure it for him. The power that fills me and has strengthened you comes from him, but he is not the true source. There is a portal to another place at this tower, that place is where the power comes from. Adaru means to use it to become stronger."

"But you don't intend to give it to him, do you?"

Marion chuckled again. "No, I do not intend to give it to him. I do not trust him. We are all tools he has forged to get what he wants. When he has it, what use does he have for us?" She shook her head. "No, I will not give this power to him." She looked at Samuel, her eyes sparkling with intensity. "I will take it for myself."

Samuel nodded. "And I will help you."

"Yes. You need to always be by my side. When the time comes, I will need you."

Samuel lifted a clenched fist out of the water. "I am yours."

Marion smiled and began to lose her clothes. "Yes, you are." After stepping out of her dress, she walked into the water and into Samuel's arms.

Chapter Sixty-One

"I thought I heard something."

The sound of her husband turned the queen consort away from her contemplation of a small apple tree newly planted in this corner of the garden. She looked at a man who had fallen a long way from who he had been. A patchy beard covered a face with a yellowish tinge, and wide, frightened eyes stared out from dark, wrinkled pits. Her heart clenched at the sight, and tears came with the knowledge that there was nothing that she could do for him. She turned away and wiped her eyes.

"What is it?"

"You should be sleeping, my love," she managed after a moment.

"I feel good. Awake. My mind does not have the fog it usually has," Edward said as he came to stand by her.

A raised voice came from somewhere beyond the edge of the garden wall.

"There it is again!" Edward said. "What is that?"

Margaret gazed at her husband as she thought about how to explain what was happening, but she could not think of any other way to tell him.

"It's the protest."

"Protest? Who is protesting? What for?"

"Southcastle is protesting," Margaret replied. "About the war and the hardships they are facing."

Edward shook his head. "No, that cannot be. My people do not protest!"

"Things are... difficult for a lot of people at the moment," Margaret explained.

Please, do not push any more. Please, just go back to bed.

"What difficulties?" The king felt himself growing angry. "What hardships are my people facing?" He clenched his fists. "Margaret, you should have told me—I could have done something. I could have—"

Margaret could not help herself. "You have done enough!" She turned away.

Please, just go!

"What do you mean?"

Margaret screwed her eyes shut. She could hear the genuine confusion in his voice. "Please, Edward. Please just go and rest. I can—"

"What has happened? What do you mean *I have done enough?*" The king's voice fell away as memories pushed through the weak effects of his medicine. He heard himself reorganising supplies out of the capital to help the regions, but in quantities that would leave the capital barren. "Why would I do that?"

Margaret heard his words, and she reached out in a desperate need to comfort him. He shrank back, his eyes full of uncertainty.

Edward remembered intervening at the docks, ordering widespread restructuring of workloads despite the repeated protests of the clerk of the cheque. "It seemed like the right thing to do," he muttered, but he knew now what he had done, the chaos he had caused. He had been so sure, so proud of himself, that he had done the same to the factories.

"Oh, by the Shepherd."

"Edward, it's all right, please."

The king staggered away from his wife's concern. Reports appeared in his mind's eye, and their contents resurfaced. Shops closing down. Homelessness rising. The Church unable to hand out food because there were too many who needed it.

More raised voices came to his ears, together with cries of anger and pain.

"I did it." Edward stared at Margaret, his eyes full of distress. "I caused it all." His hands were shaking.

"Oh, my love," Margaret said, stepping toward him.

Edward turned away from her and fled.

"Edward!" Margaret called after him, but he just ran faster.

The queen consort buried her face in her hands and cried as the sound of unrest outside the palace grew louder.

Nanaya brought the small green leaf to her nose and sniffed. There was a distinctly citrus smell, quite like orange.

Smells like orangespice.

She nibbled its edge, and her eyes watered as a fiery hot spice burst in her mouth.

Yes, orangespice!

Nanaya spat out the rest of the leaf and blinked away her tears. She snapped a single leafy stem from the small shrub and dropped it into her woven basket next to a handful of other herbs, berries, and a selection of root vegetables. With a satisfied nod, she stood and brushed loose dirt from her coarse fabric pants, then walked away.

She glanced up at the sky. The sun had already fallen behind a thick bank of cloud, and dusk was approaching. She quickened her pace. While she had no reason to fear this place after sunset, she also had no desire to stumble around in darkness. Home beckoned, and she was eager for its embrace. She moved into a loping jog.

From the clearing where she had found the orangespice sheltering beneath a weeping tree, Nanaya jogged through several copses of trees and rolling hills. She hugged a small trickling stream for a while before turning away and crossing open grassland and heading toward a dense wood. Once under the woodland canopy, she lost what little light remained in the day and ran in mottled darkness.

Ash were the dominant trees here, but their finely divided leaves still allowed some light to reach the plants beneath them, and so the twilight world she travelled was thick with multiple plant layers. Smaller ash trees formed most of the layer directly beneath the canopy, interspaced with sideways-growing hazel trees and shrubs. Ivy and ferns climbed through the underbrush and connected it in thick cords to the canopy above. Leaves, broken branches, and other woodland debris lay thick under her feet while rich green moss covered the blocks of stone that randomly protruded from the wood floor.

Nanaya weaved her way through the trunks and stalks and shrubs barring her way until she reached home. As it came into view, she slowed to a walk and smiled, savouring the pleasure this place gave her.

Home was a vast weeping tree called a twisted elm that grew in the space where several ash had fallen to lightning strikes. The twisted elm got its name from the way its boughs not only drooped until they touched the floor, but also the way they curled around and on top of one another to create a wide, dense, wooden shell surrounding the trunk.

Nanaya's twisted elm had stretched and spread in its clearing to dominate the space, easily twenty feet high with a diameter almost the same.

Ivy grew all over its outside and reached into the canopy in several distinct, tall columns that were hollow in their centre and carried smoke from the fires that burned within the twisted elm's shell. Small, delicate, pink, yellow, and blue flowers dotted the lush green shell, as did pockets of a bright, yellow-green, wolf lichen variant that kept away rodents.

An oval door nine feet tall and four wide sat recessed in one side of the shell, but this door had not been shaped and fitted into its sculpted frame. This door had grown organically. Supple vines were its hinges, and its edge rubbed smoothly against the branches that formed the doorway.

Nanaya smiled as she looked at her home. Ninsar, you did so much for us, *she thought as she so often did when she regarded the home the guardian had shaped for her and her family.*

The great door opened as she approached, and a tall, broad-shouldered figure filled the opening, twin multi-point antlers stretching wide from among the thick, long mop of brown hair on his head and curling into sharp points as they rose to form a powerful majestic crown. His face was chiselled with a pronounced jaw and cheekbones. Two gleaming emerald-green eyes shined beneath thick brown eyebrows. He smiled.

"Nanaya." His voice was a rich baritone.

"Cernunnos," she replied, smiling broadly as she gazed upon her lover, her husband, and father of her child.

Nanaya woke with tears in her eyes as the image of Cernunnos as he had been before he had become Sharur remained vivid in her mind. She curled into a ball and held herself as she wept.

After her tears had been spent, she took a deep breath and wiped her eyes before gazing around her. She lay on soft ivory sheets in a stone room with a high ceiling. It took her a moment to realise this was her room, and she was lying in her bed. She pushed herself to sit up and grunted as a sharp pain lanced across her chest. She tenderly touched the skin just below her left collarbone; it was raw, warm, and tender to her fingertips.

She heard footsteps rush across her living area toward her bed chamber. Her chamber door opened, and a member of the palace staff peered around its frame. She stepped into the room when she saw Nanaya was awake.

"My Lady, I am glad to see you are awake."

Nanaya smiled. "Thank you." Her face grew serious. "Where is Baraka?"

The woman frowned. "I am not sure who that is, my lady."

"Blue eyes, dark-haired with a dark beard."

"Oh, the man from The Fringe States. I think he left, my lady."

Nanaya's heart fell. "Did he say where he was going?"

The woman shook her head. "Not that I am aware of, but I could ask if anyone knows."

Nanaya sighed. "I had dared to hope his strength would turn the tide." She shook her head. "No matter. It is what it is. We do what we can." Nanaya swung her legs over the side of her bed and stood, swaying as a bout of dizziness swept over her.

"My Lady!" The woman reached out to grasp her arm.

Nanaya fell back onto the bed.

"You must rest."

Nanaya shook her head and started to rise once more. "There is no time I must stop—" The room spun, and she clutched her head with her hands, trying to make it stop.

"I will call for the physician."

Nanaya opened her mouth to argue, but the room spun again, and she collapsed.

Chapter Sixty-Two

The ground sloped down from where they stood, the same stone-filled, sparsely covered terrain they had travelled for the past few days. Ahead, what little grass remained grew thinner and thinner as the ground it clutched dissolved into sand until there was only desert.

The Territory.

A tiny, distant part of Samuel was filled with wonder at the sight of sand stretching to the horizon. *Just like in* The Romance at the Palace.

The young man stumbled to a halt as a wave of dizziness washed over him. An image of James lying motionless on his makeshift pallet momentarily filled his mind before being replaced with flashes of his mother and father, of fields and livestock, of repairing fences, and of a night sheltering in a broken building from a storm. Flashes of what his life had been.

Pain ignited in Samuel's head. The world shattered, fragmenting into colourless shards that crumbled to dust. The pain filling his head intensified for a moment before vanishing, and as it left, it dragged away all the warmth and comfort his memories had held, leaving behind a cold, hollow bleakness.

"You must tell me if that happens again."

He turned to look at Marion, who stood behind him, wisps of dark energy curling around her hands, which she lowered from where they had been held near his head. He had never noticed that before.

"I need you focused, Samuel," she said.

He took a breath and nodded. "Nothing before matters."

Marion stared at him for a moment before gesturing at the land before them. "Can you feel it?"

Samuel returned his gaze to The Territory. The sand swept out as far as he could see, building the farther the young man looked, until it formed huge unblemished hills and valleys. "Feel what?"

"Close your eyes and concentrate."

Samuel glanced sideways at the general standing nearby. As ever, he was staring at him with violence in his eyes. His huge fists were clenched into thick, solid masses that made his arms look like two hammers, each the size of a grown man.

"I'd rather not."

Marion looked at him, and then the general, and chuckled in that throaty, husky sound that excited the young man and made him want nothing more than to be with her.

"Ignore him. I will not allow him to try and harm you."

Samuel glanced at the general one more time before closing his eyes as Marion had told him to. "Concentrate on what?"

"On what the land feels like," Marion said. "Feel it. Reach into it."

Samuel knew what she meant. It was something that came with being a farmer. Every piece of land smelled and felt different. Moisture, minerals, local fauna and flora, animal habitation and passage. It all combined to create a unique, distinct identity. He felt for the identity of The Territory.

Stinging, snapping, and stabbing.

Samuel jerked his senses away and scrubbed his arms as if they had been stung a thousand times. As he did, something inside him reacted to the sensations and eased his sense of discomfort. The sensations were still there, but now more like an irritated nettle rash than a painful sting.

"You will do fine," Marion said as she watched Samuel stop rubbing his arms.

She looked at the force in front of her. The passage through The Fringe States had been bloody and the pace relentless, and that had taken its toll. The army she rode at the head of was a fraction of the size it had been before. There were no mounted units; they had fallen long ago, slaughtered as they rushed ahead of the main force, mad with bloodlust. There were also no drummers or fifers, some being killed by the enemy as they ran madly against them with nothing more than their instruments, others murdered by their comrades in flashes of savage anger. What few cannons they had managed to maintain had been discarded long ago, their crews abandoning them in favour of fighting up close with the enemy.

Leadership and organisation had also waxed and waned over the past months. Officers had long since given up any pretence of maintaining order and fought shoulder to shoulder with the rank and file. Command had thus devolved to a simple arrangement: Marion wanted to move forward, and the general made it happen. He moved through the camp as an alpha, an apex predator among other predators. He barked commands, and they were the law that all followed

Marion gestured to the troops. "Many will not make this passage, but we, Bron, and enough of the others will. What is in this land is also in us. It will not be pleasant, but neither will it be fatal. Not to us. Not anymore." Marion stared off into the distance. "The tower is out there. The thing that this has all been for." She fixed Samuel with a piercing gaze. "It is ours to take." She turned to Bron. "General."

Bron raised an arm in the air and let loose an animal roar. "We move!" His words sounded strange as if he was having difficulty saying them.

Men growled back, many screaming with excitement and eagerness for more violence.

Samuel breathed heavily, swept up into the intense storm of ferocity.

Marion smiled.

The army made for The Territory.

Chapter Sixty-Three

Baraka stood before a vast wall of stone in the Kafifi Ranges, his hair dancing in the wind.

How do I enter?

Just as before, need unlocked knowledge, and Baraka knew what to do. He closed his eyes, placed a hand on the stone, and pulsed a single world into the rock.

Ki.

He felt an immense ancient presence uncoil under his palm. The wall before him rippled and fell in on itself, to reveal a narrow passage leading into darkness. Baraka walked forward, and the stone came back together behind him to seal him inside the mountain.

Time did not exist in the silent darkness that absorbed every footfall, every breath. The only noise was in his mind as his thoughts churned, trying to make sense of what he was doing. Little by little, the blackness softened, and the way ahead became clearer until a soft glow grew in the distance.

Baraka emerged into Ki's cavern and found the elemental waiting for him. She stood in the centre of the cavern, staring at him. The young man could feel ancient, immense power radiating from her.

"I am here to see my father."

Ki raised one thick arm and pointed. As Baraka looked in that direction, a section of the far wall rippled and fell in on itself, revealing a descending stairwell. Baraka glanced back at Ki, but she remained silent. Walking forward, the young man started down.

The stone walls of the stairwell glowed and illuminated the descent. After a while, Baraka saw that the stairs ahead curled away to the left and out of sight. As he continued, a brightness came from ahead that eclipsed the glow from the walls, and Baraka heard the faintest sound of running water.

The sound grew as he descended until a thunderous noise filled his ears. He turned around the corner of the stairwell and found the last steps disappearing into the moss-covered floor of a huge, light-filled cavern easily twice the size of the one Ki resided in above.

Water poured from several gaping holes in the cavern roof to form a wide, pulsing and shimmering curtain that ended in a lake seven acres in size, filling the far end of the cavern. Water also fed the body of water from several smaller holes in the other sides of the cavern.

Ivy-like plants dangled from the high roof, swaying in a light breeze that ebbed and flowed through the space. The air carried with it a faint odour of sulphur, together with a delicate sweetness and a touch of sharp spice that merged into a surprisingly pleasant, natural aroma.

The cavern floor rose and fell in haphazard waves with light depressions and small mounds covered with thick, lush moss. Groups of stalactites and stalagmites were scattered around the space, including pillars between the ground and the ceiling, formed where both had met and merged. Most were covered by moss and lichen and resembled tree stumps, some partially hidden behind sheet-like flowstone that curled around them like protective hands.

As Baraka looked around him, he saw the source of the light. All around the cavern, including on the walls and in recesses in the ceiling, were quartz crystal clusters that glowed with a delicate white light and gave the cavern a natural brightness.

Baraka marvelled at the underground world. Everything came together to create a semblance of a rolling, above-ground landscape.

"Amazing, isn't it?"

Baraka recognised the voice. He looked in its direction and saw his father walking toward him. Annungal smiled, but then stumbled, catching himself by holding onto a nearby pillar of stone.

Baraka hurried forward until he was at his side and helped him sit.

"Thank you," Annungal said in a voice thick with weariness. "I have been... asleep for a long time. It will take a little time to regain my strength." He smiled tenderly and raised a hand to stroke the side of the young man's face. "You are a man."

Baraka felt tears welling in his eyes. For a moment, neither spoke, each just gazing at the other.

"Perhaps a good place to start," Annungal began, "would be telling me what has happened to you. How did you come to meet Nanaya and Ki? What is happening in the world?"

Baraka took a deep breath and recounted everything that had happened to him since scaling the tower and everything Nanaya had told him.

Annungal's eyes widened. "Whatever has possessed the archbishop cannot be allowed to reach the tower."

"Nanaya said the same thing."

"Is she well?"

"She was healing when I left. We were attacked, something that was able to disappear or hide itself."

Annungal's face fell, his eyes full of sorrow. "Cernunnos, or rather what was Cernunnos. Sharur, they called him after they had changed him. The Hunter." Anunngal rubbed his brow as if trying to ease a sudden pain. "Did Nanaya tell you?"

Baraka shook his head.

His father stood and walked to the edge of the lake. Baraka walked with him and found, with surprise, that it was teeming with different-sized fish.

"Cernunnos and Nanaya were lovers," Baraka explained. "They started a family together." He took a shuddering breath. "The kishpu took him. They corrupted him, changed him into a killer." He stirred the waters with one foot, watching the ripples. His eyes grew distant.

"It was such a terrible time. Cernunnos. The breaking of the seals.

The massacre of The Academy. The murder of our queen." He sighed and shook his head. He gestured ahead of him. "Let's walk."

They made their way around the lake.

"Everything changed," Annungal continued. "When the seals were broken, the gallus of Kur were able to cross. I feared it would be the end of everything. Together with Ki, Nanaya, and a number of guardians, we stood against them, but we were losing. In order to stop them, I entered a nexus, a place where the realms are close to one another and within which the seals between this realm and Kur can be found. I managed to heal those seals and stop the gallus from crossing, but when I did, a vast amount of energy was released. I was struck, and when I came to, the land around the tower had been replaced by The Territory and hundreds of years had passed." Annungal smiled fondly. "A short time after, I met your mother."

His expression became firm. "We must go to the tower. We must protect the seals. If they are broken, then what is in Kur will be able to cross again. I have been asleep for so long that I need a little time to prepare myself. While I do, you will need to get something for me. There is an artefact, a sword that contains the energies of this realm. That blade is anathema to anything touched by Kur—we will need it."

"Where do I find it?"

Baraka's father narrowed his eyes. "It was not with me when I woke. I do not believe it was destroyed, so I can only assume that either when I entered the nexus, or somehow when the energy was released by the seals healing, it was left behind. If it was, then I know Nanaya would have safeguarded it. I can think of only one place where she would have taken it. The clifftop sanctuary where I took you before when we linked. I can take you there, and you must go now. We need to get to the tower as fast as we can."

Baraka took a deep breath and nodded.

His father closed his eyes, and as he did, Baraka felt the air around him change. It was like a swelling of intensity that also carried with it a sharpness and a sense of vibrancy. It swept from his father to a far wall. As Baraka watched, an archway appeared on that wall with a glowing green stone at its apex. The space inside the arch shimmered and rippled as if it were liquid rather than stone.

His father opened his eyes. "Ki's cavern is linked to the clifftop sanctuary. You can reach it by passing through the portal."

"And I return the same way?"

His father shook his head. "You must go straight to the tower. We must safeguard the seals."

"How do I get there from this clifftop retreat?"

Baraka's father laid a hand on his shoulder. "When you are there, reach out to me. Link our minds. I will show you what you are."

Baraka frowned. "What do you mean?"

"It is... hard to explain. It will be easier to guide you through it. Now, we must not delay. Go through the portal and retrieve the sword."

Baraka stared at his father for a moment longer, and then nodded. Taking a deep breath, he walked toward the portal.

Chapter Sixty-Four

Nanaya clutched the thick cloak tightly around herself as a chilly breath of air swept out from the Kafifi Ranges and grasped her body. She had travelled here as soon as she had woken. She stood on several slabs of stone that formed a rocky outcrop and stared into the distance toward where Royaume d'Occident lay.

This is it.

The ground shook beneath her feet for a moment before rock and stone flowed up and into the shape of Ki, deepening to a rich green as it moved. The elemental dipped her head in greeting, and Nanaya did likewise.

Ki gestured toward the West.

"Yes, I can feel the corruption. It is spreading."

She returned her gaze to the hills, mountains, and rolling landscape around her.

"These Chosen are everywhere in the West, and whatever the thing that has possessed the archbishop is doing, it is spreading the taint of Kur. It is thickest in Château Occidentale. That place feels alien to me now." She turned and looked in a different direction. "And The Territory has been breached. I have felt a powerful Chosen and others tainted by the energies of Kur cross into the desert. We have no more time. We must safeguard the tower, and then we will deal with what is in Château Occidentale. If we can."

Ki stared at her for a moment longer before dipping its head. The elemental gestured at the horizon.

"Yes, with all speed. I will come as fast as I am able, but first, I must retrieve the sword. We will need all the help we can get."

Ki's form began to dissolve back into the ground. After she had departed, Nanaya stood alone for a moment before placing her fingertips on the stone hanging around her neck and preparing to travel to a place she had not visited for a long time.

Chapter Sixty-Five

"This is the second week of rioting, and it appears unabated; if anything, things are getting worse."

Margaret threw her hands into the air as she stared first at the Southcastle sheriff, and then at the lord mayor. "This could have been avoided if those inexperienced young men had not been added to the constabulary ranks. Their heavy-handedness has exacerbated the situation."

The Southcastle sheriff winced at the words. "But the king—"

Margaret sighed and rubbed her brow wearily. "I know." Her hand dropped away, and she stared with hard eyes at each man.

"No more. No more meetings with the king without my presence."

Both men glanced at one another before nodding.

The lord mayor cleared his throat. "The violence has been low, the looting sporadic, and the property damage minimal. I would see this as a major civil disturbance rather than a riot. The people of Southcastle remain loyal, Your Majesty. It is just the pressure of the war effort that has been exacerbated by supply and workforce pressures."

Margaret took a deep breath. "Suggestions?"

"I am confident about how your people feel, Your Majesty," the lord mayor said. "We need to show them we are concerned for their well-being, and more than anything, that we are listening to them and will help them. I would recommend a public gathering to listen to them and speak to them all. Perhaps the king—"

"Not in his current state," Margaret interrupted.

The sheriff also shook his head. "I cannot risk the king in such a way in these times."

"I concur."

The voice was deep and full of command and came from Arthur Stableman, the captain of the foot guard, who had, until now, been standing silently just behind the throne. He walked forward, his sharp hazel eyes moving between the lord mayor and sheriff.

Like the guards who walked the palace and stood at attention within the audience chamber, a long, deep-burgundy-coloured cloak hung from his shoulders. Unlike those guards who wore bearskins, he carried under one arm a plain metal cavalry helmet with a foot-long spike rising from its crown, and from which hung a horse-hair plume of approximately twenty-inches. He wore a plain metal cuirass, and a short sword hung at his hip in a worn leather scabbard.

"I have guards spread across the city, and I have doubled the number here in the palace. It will be... problematic to mobilise more to ensure the king's safety, if he were to be placed at risk in such a situation." He looked at Margaret. "And the queen consort is correct. The king's, uh, illness, has—" He grimaced. "May I speak plainly, Your Majesty?"

Margaret nodded.

"We are in this situation because of the king's current state of mind. I do not think it prudent to have His Majesty make speeches at this time."

The three men looked at one another awkwardly, and then to Margaret.

"I agree," she said. "I wish I had answers for you all. Lord Mayor, Sheriff, do what you can to safeguard our people and the city. I will talk with parliament and try to determine a way forward."

Chapter Sixty-Six

Nanaya stared out across the water, watching the ocean swell, its rippling surface rising and falling with majestic power. She closed her eyes and took a deep breath, filling her lungs with the fresh air, her nostrils flaring with the rich smell of the sea and memories of the last time she had been here vivid in her mind.

The blade felt heavy in her hands.

My friends are dead. Esharra and all of Darisam is destroyed.

Her head dropped. She wanted to weep with despair, but she had no more tears to give.

She fell into a chair near the platform's edge and stared at the undulating ocean. The crash of the waves was the only sound she heard. She let it fill her and tried to drown in its depths, but escape was denied to her.

Everything and everyone is gone.

She raised the blade before her eyes and stared at its brilliant unblemished surface in exhausted despair.

What's the point of safeguarding this? He is never coming back.

She let the sword drop, and it hit the stone with an impossibly loud, medium-pitched chime that made the air vibrate and her body tremble.

Nanaya turned her head and looked to the south, where the continent of Lam lay, the land she had just fled from.

The east would be totally destroyed now, she thought. Nothing except the tower will survive. Ki's energy flows through the Mountains of Ul, and that should protect the south. As for the rest... She shook her head. Who knows how far the shockwave will travel. The south may be saved, but it will almost certainly flow around the edges of the mountain range. The north will be decimated. The lush forests, and all the living creatures that call them home, will be destroyed as far as the shockwave reaches. Perhaps it will not touch the West...

Her mind was filled with an image of her home in the twisted elm, blackening and shrivelling as the corruption sweeping from the nexus hit it.

Her face fell into her hands. *So much destruction. So many dead. Nothing will ever be the same.*

After a moment, she picked-up the sword. Her knuckles gleaming white as she gripped it, and her brow furrowing as she squeezed her eyes closed.

I will not let this happen again. I must safeguard the nexus and keep watch over the tower. This I vow. She opened her eyes and once again she stared at the blade, but this time her gaze was sharp, full of intense conviction.

There is only me now, and I will need every help I can find. I must keep this safe. Just in case.

Nanaya opened her eyes and made her way across the stone platform, then walked into the chamber yawning beyond. As soon as she crossed the threshold, the temperature noticeably changed and became warmer, though there was still no physical barrier to the outside, and fresh breaths of air stirred the leaves of various plants dotted around the room's interior.

The natural cave origins of the chamber were still noticeable by the surrounding bare and weathered stone, however, a round stone table occupied the centre of the room, and stone chairs topped with velvet cushions surrounded it.

A thick, dark-brown, fur rug lay under the table and stretched almost to the far interior corners.

A series of continental maps hung on one wall, and the other was covered by a full bookcase that stretched almost to the ceiling. A narrow opening at the back of the chamber led deeper into the cliff.

Nanaya walked around the table, lingering at each seat as memories of those who had sat in each came to her. Ishkur, the temperamental guardian able to channel the power of storms, grumbling at being there. Beside him, the first of his sisters, Im, who could manipulate air, frowning at her brother's muttering. Beside her, their younger sister, Aru, who could control water and who was ignoring both of them. Ki, one of the four great elementals, the manifestation of stone and the sculptor of this place, sat silent and motionless beside Im. The guardian Gibil sat to Ki's right, a master of fire tossing sparks between his fingers, fidgeting with nervous energy. Two more chairs completed the circle, hers and the other for the dragon Annungal.

"Did my father sit here?"

Nanaya swung to face the source of the voice, energy leaping to her fingers.

"Baraka?"

The young man walked into the light.

"How did you get here?"

Baraka gestured to the table and walked around it to take a seat.

Nanaya stared at him, her mind churning.

How did he get here?

Baraka gestured for her to take her seat, and she was taken aback by the strength he exuded, the confidence in every movement.

He has changed. What has happened?

"A lot," Baraka said.

Did I speak that aloud?

Baraka pulled a seat out next to hers and sat.

Annungal's chair.

"Is the sword here?" he asked.

Nanaya blinked. "How do you know about the sword?" Her eyes narrowed. "And how are you here? There are powerful wards on this place that ensure only I can enter."

His father's parting words as he travelled here came back to Baraka.

Do not tell Nanaya about me. She will have many questions if she realises I am here. She needs to be focused, and you both must get to the tower as soon as you can. I will be there as soon as I am able.

"I have learned a lot," Baraka said. "We need to get to the tower fast." He gestured around him. "Where is the sword?"

"I thought you had left."

Baraka shook his head. "I said I would fight. I just had something I had to do."

Nanaya frowned. "How do you know about the sword?" Her frown deepened. "How did you know about this place, and what makes you want to get to the tower?"

Baraka thought for a moment. "I have... knowledge I didn't have before. I don't know how to explain it. I know about the seals, and I know we have to protect them. Please, the sword. We need to get to the tower."

Nanaya pursed her lips. She rose from the table. "Come," she called over her shoulder as she walked toward the narrow opening in the far wall. "Let us retrieve the blade."

The two figures walked through the opening, and then descended a spiral stone staircase that lay beyond. A doorway opened in the wall partway down the stairwell, leading to another room that also opened onto the world through a natural overhanging cave, though this one was smaller and far narrower than the one above, and because of which, the chamber was darker. A thick rug lay across virtually the entire floor, and a four-poster bed, covered with multiple blankets reaching down to the floor, sat with its head against the wall opposite the cave opening. Two paintings hung on the other walls, one of a dense woodland setting with a vast overhanging tree in its centre, the other of a walled city with a pillar of stone rising from its centre topped with various buildings. Two wardrobes, several chests, and a mirror were also in the room. Nanaya and Baraka continued down past that room.

The stairwell ended at a small landing with two rooms, one an empty storeroom and another with the only door Baraka had seen so far. Nanaya turned her back to the rooms and placed her hand on the stone wall. The green stone in her pendant glowed brightly, and the wall rippled before dissolving, revealing a windowless chamber. Several torches hung in sconces on the walls and burst alight as the wall vanished.

Shelves and alcoves had been scooped out of the stone, and in them sat objects of every description. Books, scrolls, carvings, and much more lined the walls.

Baraka's attention was on a long sword that hung horizontally on the far wall. It had a two-foot-long, two-handed grip with a slight circular guard that appeared to be formed from a single piece of ivory. The blade was just over four feet long and pearlescent with intricate contours giving it the appearance of being made from overlapping scales. They glowed as if filled with energy. The blade slightly curved up and away from its body. There was an undeniable majesty and strength in its smooth, naked lines.

Baraka was drawn to it and could not help stepping closer.

The blade shook, and then jerked off the wall and into Nanaya's hands. It blazed with power, and an aura of energy surrounded her. She gasped as powerful energy rippled through her from the artefact, and when she swung to face Baraka, her eyes blazed with power and intensity.

"Now, you will tell me what is going on."

Chapter Sixty-Seven

Bloodshot eyes in sunken dark hollows on pale faces stared back at Adaru from broken windows. Children whimpered as fathers held them close with trembling arms, mothers huddling close to their families, vainly seeking the warmth of human presence. Most had managed only a few hours of sleep over the past few days, many had also not eaten.

Adaru smiled.

What had been a person, but had been transformed by Diers, slunk out of the darkness and loped toward him. Adaru reached out his hand, and it nuzzled his palm.

Adaru gestured idly, and the thing his Chosen had skin-crafted scampered back into the darkness.

Adaru closed his eyes and took a deep breath. He could almost taste the terror in the city. The widespread dread, the savage killings caused by the things the Chosen had created were making him stronger. He could feel the energy of Kur inside him responding to the new environment.

The sound of confident, purposeful footfalls brought Adaru's attention to the end of the street. A female Chosen strode into view, followed by a handful of nervous city guards. She stopped on seeing him and bowed low, the guards practically prostrating themselves. He dipped his head, to which the Chosen bowed again before continuing on her rounds, the guards keeping as close as they could to her.

Adaru nodded satisfactorily as he looked around the deep shadows of the wide street, then turned and walked back toward his residence.

A Chosen waited at his iron gate entrance and bowed formally before opening it, then closed it after he had passed and the Chosen resumed his watch.

Adaru walked through silent corridors, considering his next actions. His mind was set when he opened the door to his chambers and found Diers waiting as he had instructed.

"Your Holiness," the Chosen said, bowing.

"We advance on the tower," Adaru said. "We are days away from the end of this." Adaru stared firmly at Diers. "I will need to prepare myself for what is to come. Ensure I am not disturbed."

Baraka gestured at the sword. "That is not your blade, it is my father's."

The woman's eyes widened. "Annungal is your father?"

Baraka nodded.

"But how can that be?"

Baraka grimaced. "It is complicated."

Nanaya stared at him.

"We do not have time for this," Baraka said.

How do I explain without revealing that my father is in Ki's cavern?

"I am learning more every day," he began. "Knowledge from my father is coming to me as my powers grow." He thought back to what his father had said about the sword. "As it is here, I am assuming you found my father's sword either after he entered the nexus or after he healed the seals. Is that right?"

"After he entered the nexus. We went down into the catacombs where the nexus was and found it there. How do you know that?"

Baraka tapped the side of his head. "Please, let us get to the tower, and we can discuss it after."

Nanaya regarded him for a moment before lowering the sword and nodding. Together, they returned to the upper chamber.

Baraka stood on the precipice of the cliff and stared out to sea.

When you are there, reach out to me. Link our minds. I will show you what you are.

When he had touched the arrows, he had linked minds with his father without any conscious thought. Somehow though, Baraka knew how to do it again. He reached out with his mind.

Father.

A presence blossomed.

Son.

You said you will show me what I am? What did that mean?

Let me guide you.

Baraka took a deep breath.

"Baraka?" Nanaya called. "Is everything all right?"

What do I do? Baraka asked his father as he turned to look at Nanaya and nodded.

Until this moment, you have harnessed the energy of this realm and released it externally. Now, you must feel the energy inside you and release it internally. This will complete your transformation.

Transformation?

I can feel your apprehension, Baraka. I understand. Trust me when I say there is nothing to be concerned about.

What will happen to me?

You will change. How you are now is just one side of you. You need to release the other.

I don't know. I am unsure.

Even as he thought the words, however, Baraka felt his apprehension ease. Something about what his father was saying felt right, and he could feel a warmth inside as if the energy inside him was reacting to the words.

Feel the energy inside you and allow it to expand through you.

How?

Feel around your energy. Can you feel its edges?

Baraka focused on the well of energy inside himself.

Yes.

Good. Now, feel into the energy and push it against those edges. Push the energy outward. You need to break those edges. You need to release the energy inside yourself so that it fills you.

Baraka focused on the well of energy inside, submerging himself and becoming one with it. He no longer saw the clifftop sanctuary or Nanaya. His senses were filled by the energy within himself. He could feel currents and eddies within its vitality. He could also sense a hardness surrounding him. He pushed against his confines, surging against it like an ocean swell. He felt the barrier that held him fracture. He pushed again, and it collapsed.

Nanaya took a step back as the young man's bright blue eyes blazed.

Well done, my son. Be at peace. This is your final awakening.

Baraka was at peace. What was happening felt right. He became aware of his body again and could feel the energy inside him stretching and filling every part of him. His body began to glow as power seeped from inside, ribbons of energy wreathing him.

Nanaya staggered back, covering her eyes with her hands as the light became blinding.

Baraka's body shimmered. His form flexed, trembling. He could feel himself changing, but it was not distressing, in fact he felt a sense of relief as if something suppressed was finally uncaged.

Nanaya fell to her knees. She could feel energy blazing before her and formed a protective shield around herself.

Baraka swelled in the heart of the inferno, his body enlarging.

Nanaya watched with squinted eyes from between her fingers as Baraka's head shifted. It elongated, stretching forward as flesh began to grow from his raised arms, falling as a thick curtain that connected to his torso.

Nanaya could only see his body as the faintest of outlines in the stark brightness of the nimbus of power that surrounded him. She could see it swell, now standing far wider than he had, and over twelve feet high and continuing to grow.

Baraka's mind expanded. Who he had been was still there, but now there was so much more.

The energy surrounding Baraka flared, and Nanaya was forced to turn her head aside.

Nanaya.

The voice pounded into Nanaya's mind. It was undeniably Baraka's, yet it held an intensity that had not been there before.

Look at me.

Nanaya hesitantly lowered her hands from her face.

A dragon stood before her.

Nanaya fell back, power leaping to her fingertips.

Do not be afraid, Baraka's voice said in her mind, the words soothing her fear.

Nanaya stared at the mighty beast.

Its body was covered with pearly scales streaked with thin red lines that glimmered in the sunlight. Two long thin horns stretched up and back from the top of its head, and Nanaya could just make out small spines running down its back. Bright blue eyes blazed with immense inner power, and trails of steam curled from its nostrils as its mighty body swelled and contracted with loud ragged breaths.

"Anunngal really was your father," Nanaya said.

Baraka dipped his head.

Adaru was sitting cross-legged on the stone floor with his eyes closed and the backs of his palms resting on his knees when he felt Baraka's transformation.

His eyes snapped open as the final stage of Baraka's awakening assaulted his senses. He took a moment to regain his composure, and then closed his eyes once more and concentrated.

It was like back home, but more so, Samuel thought as he stared up at the night sky.

A few wisps of patchy grey clouds stretched thinly over a field of stars. Some shone brightly like mature flowers at their prime, while others were growing buds of future potential. All stretched from one dune-marred horizon to the other. Back at the farm, there were more hills and trees than here, but the experience was the same. It was magical.

A sharp temple pain snapped the young man from those thoughts back to the now.

Magical? Farm? Samuel shoved such thoughts away. They had been happening more and more since he had killed that young man who had reminded him of James. He shook his head and tried to clear his mind.

Samuel sat cross-legged on a coarse rug atop a tall sand dune within whose hollow they had made their camp. The blade he had taken from the officer in a battle he could not remember how long ago, lay across his lap. It comforted him to hold it. Below him milled what remained of their army. There were maybe a hundred of them now, and all except himself and Marion were little more than animal-like savages. They snapped and snarled at one another when left alone, but when the general was present, they bowed their heads and meekly followed his direction.

And that direction was ever onward, deeper into The Territory.

They carried few supplies, and their water was almost gone, yet the orders were always to push onward and never a consideration of turning back.

Samuel frowned. *When was the last time I ate or drank?*

The sun had risen and set at least three times since they had last rested. He flexed the muscles in his arms. *I feel stronger than ever. This is not right. I am not right.*

The jarring thought spasmed into his consciousness as it had more and more over the past few weeks. He ripped the thought apart as he had every other time it had surfaced and sought a rediscovery of self in the smouldering intensity of emotion that always boiled in his core.

He found it, but it was not the same. Some element of doubt persisted.

Samuel stroked the flat blade of his sword and found a measure of solace at the touch of the metal. So many had died to this sword, so much blood spilled that the metal was now a deep grey, as if it had drank from the lives it had helped end. His fingers traced the strange lines that had begun to appear in the metal, and he felt the incessant sense of doubt inside him dwindle before a sudden surge of overwhelming power that filled his mind and body.

Bron roared as he backhanded a soldier, knocking him flying through the air to land in a moaning heap. The general pointed farther into the desert and roared again. The remaining soldiers finally began to dismantle what stood for their camp. The men obeyed less and less each time they stopped. Tonight, the general had needed to kill several men as examples before they finally erected Marion's tent. Tomorrow, Samuel doubted that would work, but it did not matter, they were nearly at the tower. He had seen it this morning, a blemish against the skyline, a man-made mark in the featureless world of The Territory. They might not even stop tomorrow night, just push through.

Samuel felt Marion pull at him and rose without pause. He sheathed his sword and curled the rug into a roll and tucked it under one arm as he trudged back to her tent.

He did not know what to expect when they reached the tower, but it was inconsequential. Marion needed to get there, so that was all that mattered.

Bron.

The general stopped and swung around, searching for the source of the voice.

"What is it, General?" Marion called out to him.

Bron ignored her as he tried to find who had spoken to him. The remaining soldiers ran away from him, trying to put as much distance between themselves and the volatile general.

It is time, Bron.

Unbridled savage rage consumed Bron. The need to kill was everything.

He tore apart the nearest soldier and used his limbs to bludgeon several others to death.

"General!" Marion shouted. *"Stop!"*

Bron leapt among the remaining soldiers and lashed about him with razor-sharp talons.

Samuel drew his sword and stood in front of Marion protectively, but terror filled him even as he moved. There was no way he could stand against Bron like this.

Blood streamed down Bron's body as he savaged the men around him.

Now!

Every bone in Bron's body snapped.

Bron screamed and collapsed to the sand.

~

Adaru reached into Bron through the bond created when he had started the general's change.

~

Dark energy seeped from Bron like a haze of dirty smoke that twisted and curled in the air as if alive. It stretched and reached for the bodies of those the general had killed, lifting them into the air, and then pulling them toward him.

Bron absorbed them.

The soldiers' flesh melted into Bron's body.

Bron screamed.

Bron swelled.

Marion stared open-mouthed at what was happening.

Massive before, Bron swelled to giant proportions. As he grew, he drooped forward, and his arms lengthened as they bulked, so that his knuckles rested on the ground. His skull thickened, stretching the skin of his face until it split with a spray of blood, and pale eyes stared out of deep pits.

Bone pushed against the skin from the inside before bursting through all over the general's body. It curled in on itself as it pushed outward to embrace his bloody pulsing flesh and muscle. Where bone met bone, they fused until the general was encased in dull ivory armour. Shards of bone pushed out from along his arms and legs to form dozens of spearpoints stretching over his hands, their ends tapering to sharp points.

When the changes ceased, where there had been a man, now crouched a terrible trembling horror bathed in blood and gore. It rose and surveyed the world around it.

"General?" Marion whispered.

Bron turned his skull-face toward the Chosen and stared at her with white, bloodshot, pupil-less eyes as he breathed hard.

Samuel gripped his blade tighter.

Bron dropped his gaze to look at the young man for a moment before disregarding him and lifted his head. His bone-jaw cracked open as his chest swelled, and then he shrieked. The terrible sound sliced through the air with its wrongness, and the realm shook with his presence.

～

In another place, another transformation was complete, but this was pure and wondrous to behold. Nanaya tentatively approached the dragon.

At that moment, Bron's scream of rebirth reached the clifftop. Baraka and Nanaya both turned to stare toward The Territory from whence the sound came.

Baraka raised his head and roared back in defiance.

～

Go now.

Bron leapt forward toward Marion. Samuel stood firm before her and raised his blade. The creature reached for them and snatched them both in one hand before the young man could react. Bron surged forward and galloped off toward the tower, his free arm as well as his legs pounding the ground as he moved.

Chapter Sixty-Eight

King Edward walked out into the garden, the sound of civil unrest filling his ears and making him grip a length of rope tighter while the words of his father filled his mind.

There is a difference between holding the position of king and being a king, Edward. Being a king is being selfless, living a life not for yourself, but for your people. Your needs are nothing, your people's needs are everything. What you want only holds value if it is what the people want or if it gives the people what they want. You serve your people, you devote yourself to making their lives easier, happier, better.

Edward sat heavily on the ground under a tree with long, high boughs.

His people were not happy, their lives were not easy.

I have failed.

The faces of the secretary of war and the Southcastle mayor filled his mind. Each was looking at him in confusion, but he saw past that to what lay beneath.

They know I can't do this.

Bernard Forges, the royal physician, appeared next. He held a vial of medicine out to him, but the pity in his eyes did not come from compassion, it was born from disappointment.

The foot guard and the palace staff tried to hide their emotions, but Edward could see their disgust.

How can I come back from this?

He took a deep shuddering breath and stared at the rope in his hands.

Everything has come undone.

He could see it in his wife's eyes. He had failed her, too.

"Edward, please don't." Martin's plea as he removed him from office filled his mind as did his horror-filled eyes.

I thought I was right, but look at what I have done. In the end, it was me who destroyed everything. It is me who has doomed my own people.

Something crashed outside the palace walls, and the shouting became louder.

Edward wept. He wept for everything he had done, everything he had lost, and everything he had become. After a moment, the painful eruption of misery was calmed by a soothing balm of clarity.

I am not going to get better. The melancholy. It has me now. No tonic will ever be able to free me from it.

He raised his head to stare at the outer wall.

So many have lost so much because of me. I must take responsibility. I must pay for what I have done, and in paying the price, pave the way for someone who can make it better.

He stared at the rope in his hands as his father's voice filled his mind.

Your needs are nothing, your people's needs are everything.

He raised a hand before his eyes.

My fingers are not trembling.

He took a deep breath.

I do this for my people.

❧

"My love, are you here?" Margaret called as she walked into the garden. "The foot guard said you were here."

Her mind was on the events of the day. Food and supplies were now flowing into the capital from the regions, and there seemed to be a lessening of tension in the streets. She walked around several large bushes that formed a screen around a part of the garden.

"*No!*" She screamed as she saw the body hanging from the tree branch.

"*Edward!*" She ran to the body, grasping its legs and trying to lift it. "*Help me!*"

Foot guards came running through the garden. They dropped drawn weapons when they saw the king hanging from the tree and rushed to help the queen consort. Together, they managed to get the king down to the ground, but it was obvious there was nothing anyone could do.

Margaret looked into Edward's vacant dead eyes and howled.

Chapter Sixty-Nine

Ki rose from the last unblighted stone of the Kafifi Ranges at the edge of The Territory. Crystalized rock glowing a deep green with elemental energy swept up dozens of feet like a thick vertical waterfall and formed her head, broad shoulders, torso, and then her feet.

Ki took a step forward, but recoiled the moment her foot touched the sand. She stared into the depths of the desert where the tower stood. She looked to the ground again.

Gemstones, crystals, and veins of the strongest metals were drawn from the deepest layers of the world and flowed up and over her. They twisted through her form and wound over her face and body to create a glittering helm and suit of armour. It would protect her as she travelled through the poisonous land.

With a mighty leap onto the sand, she raced toward the tower.

Part Three

"Duty drives me. When I am weak, it is duty that makes me carry on. What about you?"

"Redemption. The hope that something good I will do will atone for all the wrong that I have done."

Overheard conversation in The Citadel between Zababa and Annungal.

Chapter Seventy

"Marion, are you hurt?" Samuel shouted as Bron pounded across the desert.

He grimaced as the fist he was held within tightened at the sound of his voice. He felt Marion's body shift behind him.

"No, but Bron is about to be."

NO.

Marion gasped as Adaru's voice burst loudly in her mind, and as it did, a pressure erupted in her head. He had spoken to her before, but it had not been like this. His voice was louder, closer, and it felt different, like he was not trying to reach her, but like he was beside her.

Leave Bron. He is taking you where you need to go, and he will guard you while you are in the tower.

Marion ground her teeth and tried to generate her power regardless.

No, Marion.

Pain burst in Marion's mind, and she slumped back against Samuel.

"*Marion!*" the young man called, but Marion could not answer as each breath she took sent spikes of pain through her body. Samuel could do nothing more than stare at the tower as it grew closer.

The black monolith was ominous in its silent dominance of the landscape. Samuel had changed much since the war had started and rarely felt fear anymore. He certainly did now. The tower held a sense of malice. It seemed to emanate from the stone structure, and the closer he came to it, the more it assailed him, until he could not stop himself from trembling, and he felt his breath catching in his chest.

Before long, the tower was looming over him. Samuel cursed as Bron jumped, the great fist holding him tightening around his body and squeezing a pained grunt from him as his breath was squeezed out. The tower rushed toward him, and he closed his eyes, thinking that he would be crushed against its surface.

Bron smashed into the tower, his free, taloned hand punching into the stone as his clawed feet also gouged into it. Samuel opened his eyes as the creature the general had become hung there for a moment, twisting until he found himself able to fill his lungs again. He was about to call out to Marion when Bron started to move.

Hauling himself up, Bron lifted a foot free before ramming it back into the stone some feet up from where it had been. He did the same with his other foot, and then pulled his hand free. For a moment, Samuel felt himself start to fall back, then Bron jabbed his claw forward and back into the stone, pulling himself close to the wall. Step by step, jab after jab, he climbed up the tower.

Bron scaled the weathered ruin in no time. Gripping the ragged top, he swung up the hand that held Samuel and Marion and dropped them onto the tower's upper level before falling back to the desert sand.

Samuel fell and landed hard on a wooden surface, the air bursting from his lungs. He rolled onto his knees and elbows, gasping until he had regained his breath. A moan from nearby turned his head, and he watched Marion pushing herself up to sit, tenderly touching a swelling red blemish on the side of her face.

Marion winced at the flash of pain triggered by the touch of her fingers, but it was not her face that troubled her.

Something does not feel right...

"Marion?"

Samuel's voice shook her from her thoughts. She waved her hand dismissively as she spat a mouthful of sand from her mouth and pushed her inner concerns to one side so she could concentrate on the current situation.

Samuel looked around. They were lying on a section of what would have been the floor of a level within the tower, but was now a pitted, broken roof for what remained of the structure. Across a gaping hole stood an open door with a descending stairwell beyond. Samuel peered down through the hole to the floor below and found little more than mounds of sand. He returned his eyes to the doorway.

"I guess we go through there."

Marion stood and dusted herself off as she regarded the gap between them and the small bit of floor that lay by the stairwell. She took several steps back, and then ran and leapt over the hole. She landed with a slight skid as her shoes slipped on a fine layer of sand. She peered inside the doorway, and then strode inside.

Samuel leapt over the gap in the floor and hurried to her side.

It grew darker the lower they went, but Samuel was still able to see. The sense of foreboding that had gripped him ever since they had come near this place still lay on him, and he fought against a smothering and suffocating feeling. He drew his sword and gripped its hilt tightly, taking some comfort in its solidity.

Side by side, he and Marion descended into the tower.

Adaru saw through Marion's eyes.

He had used the connection between them to push his awareness into her. He now saw what she saw, felt what she felt.

Just as he had planned.

Everything he had done had been to be here in this way.

He calmed himself in case Marion became too aware of his presence and settled into being a passenger on her journey through the tower.

Bron felt the vibrations through the sand and turned toward their source. He could see a colossal shape in the distance, moving toward him, its body glinting and occasionally flashing in the light cast by the stars and moon.

Bron did not remember anything before his transformation. The general he had been, the decades of warfare experience, and his knowledge and skills had dissolved with his former body. The direction that had come with Adaru's presence had also almost entirely dissolved as he had departed. What was left was a monster of rage and violence with a single remaining directive implanted by Adaru: Stop anything from entering the tower.

He set his taloned feet as he prepared to meet what was coming.

Nanaya sat on the base of Baraka's neck gripping two thin spines. A protective sphere surrounded her and kept the buffeting air away. She watched as the rolling waves of the Helba Ocean were replaced by the sweeping sand dunes of The Territory. A stinging sensation washed over her as she felt the taint of the dead land. She leaned closer to Baraka, her thighs clenching a little tighter around his neck.

I remember traveling like this on Annungal so long ago. That was the day my world changed. Everyone lost to me.

Nanaya shook herself free from bitter memories of the past and cast her mind toward what lay ahead. She could still feel those with the power of Kur ahead in The Territory.

What will we face? A few chosen? An army? At least I can't sense any gallus, so the seals are still whole. For now, anyway. They may have already reached the tower.

As if sensing her concern, Baraka beat his wings harder, and they surged forward.

Nanaya let go of one of Baraka's spines and laid a hand on his neck. She stared at the scales covering his new body. They had a sense of texture as if each was filled with thick white clouds, and their surfaces were speckled with thin lines of varying shades of red. A sheen of faint greens, blues, and yellows appeared as they caught the light.

The power I can feel inside him. It is immense. Even more than his father's.

The desert sped beneath her, and a dark shape appeared ahead of them.

The tower. She dared to hope. *Perhaps his strength will be enough.*

The tower neared swiftly, and movement near its base caught her attention. The speed they travelled at revealed its source almost immediately.

"Look!" Nanaya called.

I can see, Baraka said as he regarded the creature. He, too, was feeling the fallout from the healing of the nexus so long ago, but to him, it was more an inconvenient ache rather than a distinct pain. Without thinking, he pushed his senses toward the creature so he could better understand it.

~

Bron felt something push against his mind from the sky, and his head jerked up to stare at two dark shapes growing steadily closer. He opened his maw and shrieked at them.

~

Movement below caught Nanaya's eyes, and she watched Ki race toward the tower just as she had over a thousand of years ago. Then it had been a vast dense forest that surrounded the structure rather than the desert of The Territory it was now.

I was so young back then and knew so little.

She pushed such thoughts aside; there was no time for that now. She had watched the creature climb the tower and thought that she had seen two figures enter.

They are going for the seals!

Baraka only had eyes for the creature in front of the tower.

It radiated wrongness.

He flexed his wings and marvelled at how natural that was. The raw power of this realm burned inside him as he flew. It coursed through his veins with rich intensity and flooded his muscles with mighty vitality. He opened his mouth and roared.

Bron felt the power of the dragon as it neared. He shrieked and flung a clawed hand out toward it. The spear points of bone on the creature's arms burst free and raced toward the dragon.

Baraka saw the gesture, but only saw the projectiles just before they struck. He braced for impact, but they never hit him. The shards of bone struck an invisible field of energy surrounding him and dissolved. Baraka took a deep breath as more dormant knowledge unfurled. When in dragon form, he could not manipulate the energy of this realm as he could when he was in his normal human form, but instead, that power filled his body and naturally protected him. There was a balance in his forms. His human form was strong in its ability to use the energy of the realms but physically weak, whereas his dragon form was the exact opposite.

Baraka opened his mind to speak to Nanaya, but his words were torn away by a sudden searing pain in his wing. A burning numbness swept outward, and then he was falling. Lifting his wing, he saw one of Sharur's arrows buried in its membrane, black corruption spreading out from it.

He looked around for Nanaya and saw her floating serenely but swiftly toward the sand, cocooned in a protective sphere. *Get into the tower*, he pulsed to her. *Ki and I have our battles out here, yours is in the tower.*

Dread filled Nanaya as she watched Baraka fall. She scanned the desert and found what she had feared: Sharur, rising from a crouch in the hidden shadow of a sand dune. He slung his bow over one shoulder, and then his form blurred as he hunted Baraka. She looked at Ki racing toward the Bron-creature. She looked at Baraka's falling body as he managed to stabilise his fall, and then change to human form and land ungracefully, but safely. *I cannot help them,* she told herself as she settled on the sand and raced for the open doorway to the tower and whatever awaited inside.

Chapter Seventy-One

Baraka used the power inside him to remove the arrow as he had before from Nanaya and Ki, wincing as sharp pain lanced through his body. Finally, it was out, and he used his power to hurl it far from him. He could feel himself fighting against the corruption from the arrow.

He looked at himself. Before he had transformed into dragon form, he was wearing pants and a shirt. Now, he was wearing some sort of robe, pearl in colour with red flecks and marbling.

Just like my father.

He looked around. It was a clear night with a bright half-moon that illuminated the undulating desert in a cold silvery light. He had fallen several hundred metres from the tower, yet its black shadow still stretched long enough to reach him.

Baraka's eyes searched the desert for a sign of Sharur. A piece of knowledge rippled into clarity in his mind, and his vision shifted as his eyes scanned the landscape, not for a physical shape, but for a disturbance in the energies of this realm.

A blurred shape of churning darkness that was somehow darker than the night raced between dunes to his left.

Found you.

Baraka turned to follow it, his body tensing. The shape rose and solidified into Sharur with its bow in one hand and the other drawing an arrow, ready to fire.

Baraka threw himself to the sand as the arrow sliced the air where his chest had been. The shaft seemed to shriek as it passed over him, a hushed scream of agony filling his ears. He flung an outstretched hand in the direction the arrow had come from, and white energy erupted from his fingers to form a spear of burning light that sped through the air, but Sharur had already moved, and the strike soared over the sand before dissipating in the distance.

Baraka scrambled to his feet and scurried away from where he lay, head down and crouching, his mind racing to find a way to fight back.

Sharur raced between the dunes, his feet lightly touching the sand. His awareness was spread wide, senses stretched to their limit. This was perhaps the most dangerous prey he had ever hunted. He smiled with eagerness.

Ki thundered across The Territory, the tower looming before her.

Bron watched the charging stone form. The dragon had been felled by something, and he no longer considered it a threat, so he now focused on what approached. His assessment was dispassionate, a cold stark calculation of strengths and weaknesses as he measured himself against this challenger. Bron's vast bulk swelled as he inhaled deeply, then he lifted his skulled head to the sky and let loose a terrible, piercing expulsion of violent desire before leaping forward.

Baraka stumbled as Bron's fearsome scream of twisted agony and longing filled his ears. He turned the stumble into a dive, rolled back to his feet, and then raced in a different direction to the one he had been heading. He could not devote any thought to the cause or nature of the noise, he was solely occupied with survival.

He crouched as he moved, eyes searching for Sharur.

~

Marion stared at the glowing sigils on the stone that filled the doorway at the bottom of the tower stairwell. She reached out with one hand, and as her fingers neared, the sigils shone brighter.

Not physically, reach out with your power.

Marion felt a ripple of fear wash through her.

You can see this? Where are you?

Before, you released your power and pushed it into others, Adaru continued, ignoring her questions. *Now, release it once more, but push it into the stone. Reach inside the stone just as you have reached inside people.*

Withdrawing her hand, Marion pushed her power into the wall.

Samuel fell to a crouch and shielded his eyes as the sigils blazed intensely.

Harder. The wards are designed to prevent anything from this realm reaching the seals. They cannot stand against energy from Kur. Harder!

Marion closed her eyes and hurled her power at the stone.

The stone cracked like striking lightning, and then all was silent and dark.

Samuel's eyes regained their unnatural ability to see in the blackness. He rose to his feet and approached Marion. The woman was breathing hard but dismissed his outstretched hand of concern and pointed.

Samuel turned and stared at a massive split in the rock that ran from the top right corner to the bottom left. Where it passed through the carved sigils, four smaller cracks had burst from the main fault, each lancing into one of the shapes of power and fracturing them.

"Break it," Marion commanded.

Samuel looked at the stone for a moment before leaning back, raising one leg, and lashing out with his booted heel. The rock shattered.

Marion marched past and through the doorway before the dust had begun to settle.

Wide, cracked stone steps led down from the doorway within a long, narrow stairwell, and Samuel could see everything was carved in a different way and from a different type of stone and appeared far older. He and Marion made their way around the broken rock debris and descended. The world grew quieter as they walked, first an absence of noise, then a suffocation of it.

The stairwell opened after a long descent into an ancient crypt. Dozens of stone pillars stood approximately ten feet from each other and stretched up to merge into a sculpted stone ceiling. Niches were carved into the walls, and Samuel could see stone coffins sitting within their dark recesses. Broken rock from the destroyed barrier above littered the floor, but even without it, Samuel could see a thick layer of dust from the passage of untold lifetimes covered everything.

"There."

Samuel looked first to Marion, and then to where she pointed. At the far end of the chamber, in a wall recess where a coffin should be, there was just a pale glowing mist.

"Can you feel it?"

Samuel could only nod, words escaping him. There was an intensity within the mist, unlike anything he had ever felt before. As he moved closer, that intensity pulled at him, at both parts of him. It pulled at his physical body at a fundamental level that made his muscles and bones vibrate. Whatever was in the mist also pulled to that other part of him, the dark violent part that had been growing inside him, and he felt it swell and threaten to overwhelm him. Samuel panted, he bared his teeth, and clenched his fists.

He turned to Marion. "What do we do now?"

Marion opened her mouth to speak.

Do what you did to the stone before. You must direct your power into the nexus. You must feel for the seals. Break them, and the power of Kur is ours.

Marion took a deep breath. "Now we take the power of Kur."

"You will never have it," Nanaya said from behind them as she entered the crypt and drew the sword.

Ki shrugged off Bron's punches and smashed her head forward. Bron staggered back, but Ki stepped forward and did it again, then again, and again. Blood and bone scattered with each blow. Ki snapped a jab that cracked Bron's jaw, and then stepped forward and spun on the ball of her foreleg, swinging her back arm to deliver a thunderous, swinging back-fist strike. Her knuckles smashed into the side of Bron's head and knocked him from his feet, sending him crashing to the ground a dozen feet away.

Ki strode forward, fists clenched.

Samuel drew his blade and snarled as a wave of hatred for the newly arrived woman swept over him. Step by wary step, she advanced, and as she did, a fierce desire to inflict pain on her grew in the young man.

Nanaya regarded the swordsman who approached, apprehension shifting to concern that shifted to doubt and then trepidation with every step he took toward her. She could feel the power of the other realm inside him and a well of that dark energy within his blade. She could also see a dark vapour seeping from around the energy the woman was using to burrow into the nexus. Those wisps of energy from Kur were twisting and reaching for the young man as if they desired him. When they touched him, Nanaya could see subtle changes in the young man. His face hardened, his eyes grew brighter.

It was not just the young man the energy touched. Tendrils of energy burrowed their way into the sword he carried. It twisted and stretched as if alive, as it drank the corruption of the other realm. Barbs appeared along the blade that now churned with eddies of dark power. The cross-guard and quillons twisted and split to form a claw curling back, as if trying to clutch the young man's hand, and a wicked black spike grew from the pommel.

Everything Kur touches, it corrupts.

Nanaya's fingers flexed on the grip of the sword she held. It, too, was reacting to the power here, and she could feel a stream of vitality and strength flow from the blade into her. Her eyes flicked away from the swordsman to the woman behind him. She stood immobile, staring into the mists, but her face was contorted into an agonising grimace. Nanaya could not begin to guess what was happening to her and could spare nothing more than an idle thought as the man roared and rushed her.

Chapter Seventy-Two

Marion reached into the mist and felt a barrier blocking her way.

It is the seal to this realm, Adaru explained. *Push harder. You must force your way through.*

Marion pushed against what was blocking her and felt it flex.

Yes! Harder! Push your power at it.

The Chosen snarled. She felt the barrier bend farther, giving before her effort, until it suddenly cracked with a dull snap. A burst of energy surged from the mist and almost knocked her from her feet. She saw, however, that most of the energy was drawn into the stone around her. All sense of the barrier had vanished. As if it had a mind of its own, Marion could feel the power inside her reaching towards the mist. A flutter of alarm caught her breath.

No, Marion, let it go. Your power is reacting to the presence of the other realm. Kur is close now. You have broken through the seal of this realm, now use the connection you feel with Kur and find the seal to that realm.

Marion pushed energy into the nexus until she felt it hit another barrier.

Like energies only strengthen the seals. Your power is from Kur, but it is also merged with the energies from this realm. Do what you did to the other seal. It will take longer, but the seal will break.

Marion struck the seal. She struck it again and again, and as she did, she felt cracks and fissures spider web across the barrier. She gasped as tiny slips of energy from Kur escaped and merged with her, and as they did, she felt herself invigorated. The fractures in the seal split wider. Marion felt the energy of Kur close around her and seep inside her, bringing with it a sudden eruption of searing power.

It is mine! She declared ecstatically to Adaru. *It is all mine!*

No, Marion, Adaru admonished. *It is mine.*

Marion felt Adaru expand inside her.

I could have tried to make the journey, Adaru said as Marion felt a sudden pressure at the base of her spine that swept to her groin, and a gasp escaped her lips.

But why take the risk? Adaru continued, his voice filling her mind as she felt him growing inside her. The feeling of him reached her navel, and the pain seared to crippling agony that stole everything and left her helpless.

Marion tried to call out to Samuel, but pain seized her heart, and she fell, convulsing, to the floor, unable to breathe as Adaru filled her throat, and then started to seep into her skull. Pressure built between Marion's eyes, and somehow, she knew she was screaming.

When Baraka came, well, I had never possessed someone before, and of course, I did not know what he was. It did what was needed though, it got me away from the tower when I was not strong enough to break the nexus and certainly not strong enough to stay here in this corrupted land trying.

A line of intense pressure drew itself from between Marion's eyes to her crown. She felt herself shaking violently.

I did better with the archbishop, and after taking him over, I regained my strength, learned about this new time that I had returned to, and began enacting my plan. There was no reason to risk everything trying to reach the tower. Why not have someone else make the journey for me? Why not let someone else take all the risks and take me there?

Marion felt the little bit of her that remained being crushed by Adaru as he possessed her. She felt what was left of her being scooped out of her body. Adaru held her last fragments.

Goodbye, Marion.

Adaru consumed the last vestiges of the woman he had both saved and damned and possessed her entirely.

Samuel staggered as he lost all sensation of Marion, and with it, her absolute hold on him evaporated. The Samuel he had been, the young man who had been smothered to the barest of embers roared back to life. It surged without the suffocation he had not realised Marion was inflicting on him and raged in the freedom it found. It swelled and Samuel split in two, a Samuel who lusted for pain and death, and a Samuel who longed for love and life.

The corrupted blade that had been gripped in his hand dipped.

Nanaya saw the opening as the swordsman's blade lowered, but before she could act, she felt the straining seals between the realms buckle. A protective shield sprang around her moments before she was blasted from her feet.

The tower exploded.

The noise was beyond deafening and stole Baraka's hearing. He saw Sharur smashed from his feet and hurled away, tumbling wildly over the sand dunes before he, too, was struck by the explosion.

Baraka closed his eyes and buried his bloodied face in his hands. Broken masonry shattered around him and a wave of raw energy erupted from where the tower had stood, crashing on him with a violent desire to drown him in its intensity.

He hit the ground hard and it took a long time to catch his breath. When he was able to breath once more and his hearing had returned, he opened his eyes and lifted his head.

Nothing remained of the tower.

The stone from which it had been formed was now strewn all over the desert. Baraka felt lucky that most of the debris had passed over him. He grunted in pain as he stood, and every part of his body howled in wounded protest. Lucky, but not unscathed.

He stared at what had replaced the tower. Where it had stood there was now a column of dark, twisting energy that rose a hundred feet in the air. At its apex hung a body caught in the energy currents.

The ground shook violently, and a thunderous crash filled his ears. Baraka turned to stare in the direction of the noise and watched Ki stride over to the creature that had just been felled and sprawled in the sand. Ki raised her massive fists as she approached, the creature trying in vain to rise.

A torrent of dark energy buried itself into the creature.

Baraka spun to find where it had come from and saw that the body that had been hanging listlessly in the air was now facing Ki, its arm outstretched to somehow funnel the dark energy erupting from the depths of the tower's ruins into Ki's adversary. A nimbus of power surrounded the body, illuminating long hair and a feminine form.

Bron howled and thrashed as the energy buried itself inside him, and then with a roar, he leapt to his feet and hurled himself at Ki. The elemental had just enough time to raise her arms to defend herself before Bron was on her. He pummelled his bone-gauntlet fists into the rock being, each blow smashing shards of her stone form to scatter in the sand, the living glow of each extinguishing as they touched the tainted land. Punch after mighty punch struck Ki, knocking her back a step each time until she lost her balance and toppled to her back. Bron did not hesitate and leapt onto Ki's body, pinning the elemental's arms with his legs and resuming his relentless barrage.

Baraka turned back to the woman channelling the torrent of dark energy and threw his own power against her. Waves of pure brilliant white energy of this realm surged from his outstretched hands and crashed into her. Baraka forced more and more of his power at the woman, feeling his body burn with the raw energy he was bringing forth. He grunted with the effort, energy crawling across his skin. He pushed more, forced more, and vented his anger and pain in a shout that became a scream.

The woman at the heart of the inferno did not burn, she gestured with one hand, and the flames of incredible energies died around her as the power of the other realm smothered Baraka's power.

Exhausted, Baraka collapsed to his knees, and his power died. He stared up at the woman and tried to summon the last vestiges of energy inside him.

The slightest of sounds caught his ear, and he turned instinctively.

It saved his life.

The blade burst from his chest near his shoulder.

Baraka yelled as the blade sliced through him and again louder as the blade was ripped out. He fell onto his back and stared up at Sharur, who stood over him with blood dripping from one of the two, long-blade daggers the hunter held in each hand. Sharur leaned forward and slashed down with both weapons. Baraka felt all strength leave him as he tried to put up an arm to stop them. He could not move and was forced to watch death swing down for him.

Sharur's daggers clashed against a glowing sword.

"Never again." Bloodied and bruised, Nanaya jerked her blade upward and sent Sharur staggering. She glowed as energy from the blade filled her body.

Baraka clutched his chest and tried to both heal himself and attack Sharur, but he was spent and was forced to concentrate just on saving himself.

Sharur rushed forward, daggers blurring in his hands.

Nanaya blocked each strike precisely and unflinchingly. One. Two. Three. Four. Five. Six. Seven, eight, nine, ten, eleven.

Nanaya lashed out with a savage kick and sent Sharur sprawling.

"I will not hide any more. I will not stand aside." She strode toward

Sharur as he rose back to his feet. "I was always the protector, the shield, the defender, but you destroyed that person." She raised the glowing sword. "I cannot change what powers I have, but I have learned how to fight, and here and now, this will end."

Sharur rushed forward with blades spinning, and again, Nanaya danced with him, and the artefact was always there to meet each attack.

~

Ki was dying.

The ground underneath her was unreachable because of the corruption that lay thick in it, so she could neither draw strength from the depths of the world nor escape through it. Her body was covered in fractures that grew wider with every strike the creature landed.

As Bron raised his fists high in the air, ready to strike again, a sound that had not been heard for thousands of years filled the world. It was the roar of an ancient power and a challenge to all who would dare stand against it. The sound stopped Bron's attack. He stared up at the sky, searching for its source.

The roar came again, louder. Closer.

~

Baraka felt something inside him stir at the sound. It touched him in an intimate way, and even though he was filled with pain, the sound brought comfort.

Sharur's eyes flicked from Nanaya to the sky at the sound he had heard before and had never expected to hear again.

Baraka smiled thinly.

Nanaya stepped away from Sharur and also glanced to the sky with the sound sparking memories from a different time. A small spec in the clouds swelled as she watched it come closer.

Could it be?

The roar came again, and it was deafening in its power, dropping everyone except Baraka and Bron to their knees and bringing hands to their ears.

As Bron jumped off Ki's broken body and screamed his defiance, Baraka smiled as the shape in the sky defined itself into a massive pearl dragon.

"Father."

Chapter Seventy-Three

Annungal gazed at the twisting pillar of energy rising from the destruction of the tower with both hatred and despair filling his eyes.

Not again!

Memories flashed in his mind of the two other times he had witnessed the seals broken.

He watched the Nagiru cross from Kur, the flesh of the dead wrapping around the gallus herald as it entered this realm to form the body of a warped feline monstrosity. He shifted to human form. Physical strength would not save him against this. He needed every sliver of this realm's energy to fight against it. His fingers curled tightly around his blade, and he hoped he was strong enough.

The scene dissolved and was replaced with the first time he had faced nightmares from Kur.

A swarm of black shapes burst from the Si Esia nexus and smashed into the protective shields surrounding the dragons. The barriers held, and what touched them dropped charred and lifeless.

Annungal glanced at them even as he continued to pour his energy into his lord Zuen, who was trying to heal the seals. The blackened bodies had wings of various sizes, necks of different lengths and thickness, and heads of different shapes. All of them were an intense deep black, their mouths had wickedly sharp teeth often too long or too many to keep inside their mouths, and in some instances, they protruded from their upper or lower jaws as large tusks or fangs. Annungal shivered in both disgust and fear at what they were.

"Lirum, abatu!" The command from the war-queen of the lirum dragon kind, the red dragons, filled his ears as did the responding roars from the lirum as they opened their dragon mouths and vented fire at those creatures that had survived.

Annungal shook away the memories. His acute eyesight picked out the figures arrayed around the pillar of energy. He could feel the wrongness of that energy as a sharp scratching on his. His eyes fixed on the woman in the air, and with a powerful flex of his immense wings he surged toward her.

Sharur stared wide-eyed at Annungal flying above. A movement at the edge of his vision snapped his attention back, and he was just able to parry Nanaya's sword as she lunged.

Nanaya's eyes blazed with hatred as she came at Sharur. Energy sparked across her body, enabling her to strike harder and move faster. "I remember everyone you killed," she said as she attacked. She stepped forward and swung an up-slicing blow at Sharur, which he parried with his twin blades and danced a little farther out of reach.

"This is for Ninsar." She twisted and spun to strike at Sharur's torso, an attack that he could just turn aside, and he was forced to retreat.

She spun in the other direction as soon as her attack was blocked, using her momentum to strike at Sharur's opposite side. This time, the attack was too fast, and the sword sliced deeply into his body. He howled and staggered backward, his eyes wide with disbelief.

Nanaya's sword blazed brilliantly as she glared at Sharur. Energy seeped out from the sword and began to wind around the woman's body. "You know who I remember most of all?" Power from the blade wreathed her body in churning waves of ice blue. "I remember our child." The energy encasing Nanaya's body blazed, and Sharur shrieked as it started to burn his flesh.

"I remember finding her!" Nanaya said as she strode forward, and Sharur fell back to scramble in the sand. Nanaya's burning eyes were filled with tears. "I remember finding what you had done to our baby, her blood coating the floor and walls. Her eyes wide and dead."

Sharur dropped a blade and held his hand protectively in front of his face. His clothes were ablaze, and his skin was blackening as it burned. The fierce raw energy of this realm was also scouring his insides and roaring through his mind. He howled in pain and dropped his other dagger to raise his other hand in a vain attempt to stop what was happening.

Nanaya brought the sword up and took hold of its grip in both hands, tears streaming down her face. She stood in the calm centre of an inferno of power. She took a deep breath and screamed a wordless terrible vent of unimaginable anguish as she raised the sword, but before she could swing down, Sharur dissipated.

Nanaya stared at where his body had been and howled, falling to her knees and weeping as long buried emotions boiled over her.

The fight between Nanaya and Sharur went unseen by Annungal, who only had eyes for the woman in the air. Tendrils of energy wrapped around her body, and he saw her shiver as she absorbed the power from Kur that seeped through the now-broken seals.

Annungal felt the air around him thicken as the realm reacted to the released energy from Kur. Clouds were forming and a grumbling of thunder echoed across the desert.

The woman swivelled to look at the dragon, and he saw with piercing clarity the evil that looked out from behind those eyes. He had looked upon many types of vileness through his life, including the gallus that had crossed over from Kur. This was not one of them, this had been something of this realm that had willingly given itself to the poison of Kur and become something dark and twisted.

Adaru watched the dragon approach through Marion's eyes. His eyes now. He looked down to the desert floor and watched the creature that had been Bron standing over a badly wounded being of stone.

Just a little longer... He closed Marion's eyes and allowed Kur's energy to fill his new body.

Annungal watched in horror as the woman blazed with dark energy. The power of the other realm was feeding her, strengthening her.

Lightning flashed around him amidst dark churning storm clouds. It began to rain.

For a moment, he considered landing and taking human form so he could use his power more broadly, but he disregarded the notion. Now was not the time for subtle, expansive skill. Now was the time for the unbridled brute force of his dragon form.

He opened his mouth and blasted fire at the woman, consuming her body in raging raw energy. On and on he attacked it until he felt his throat start to burn with the energy's intensity. He let the flames die and looked for what remained as the fire gutted.

The woman hung untouched.

Adaru smiled.

The woman's body convulsed and then distorted. Her head elongated, and several black horns sprouted from her cranium, twisting and tapering as they grew. Her arms swelled with taloned fingers curling to form fists. Her torso bulked, and clothing fell from a now androgynous body, skin blackening and hardening into overlapping scales. Its legs stretched thick with muscle, each ending in taloned feet. A long tail grew from the base of the body's spine, stretching high over its horn-crested head and ending in a sharp barb.

Adaru breathed deeply, filling the lungs of his new body. He opened his mouth to reveal razor-sharp teeth and smiled.

At last, I am strong! No one will ever take anything from me ever again.

Annungal roared.

Adaru turned and watched the dragon beat his wings and race toward him. He summoned the power of Kur and hurled it at the dragon through his outstretched taloned hands.

Annungal snarled as black churning energy erupted from the creature and enveloped him, searing his skin and igniting sharp stabbing pain in his mind. He pushed through the agony and surged forward, opening his mouth and roaring defiance, hurling his own power back at the thing before him.

Adaru cloaked himself in the power of the other realm, wrapping it around like an obsidian shell. The dragon's flames parted on it, but he still grunted with the impact of the dragon's power.

Annungal did not relent and continued to encase the creature in the raw energy of this realm. It forced its way through Adaru's shield and charred his new skin. He hissed with pain and prepared to strike back, but Annungal struck before he could.

The dragon ripped Adaru's weakened shield apart with his clawed feet and snapped at his neck. Adaru threw his head back, avoiding Annungal's lunge. His tail whipped forward, its barb aiming for the dragon's face. Annungal weaved to one side to avoid the strike and clamped his jaws around the tail. He bit down and savagely tore the tip off in a spray of dark blood.

Adaru roared and slashed at Annungal. His claws raked down the dragon's face, cutting bloody furrows, and it was Annungal's turn to howl in pain.

The dragon kicked out with his feet, but rather than attacking, he slammed his heels into Adaru's body and shoved him back, beating his wings to put distance between them even as he opened his mouth and let loose with more power at the creature before him.

Adaru formed another shield around himself, and even though he ground his teeth with the painful effort of holding back the energy barrage, he managed to turn aside Annungal's flames, and they swept harmlessly around him.

"Annungal!"

The dragon glanced down at the shout and watched Nanaya throw his sword into the air.

Annungal's form blurred as he shifted to his human form, and he snatched the blade from the air. As his fingers touched the blade's grip, he felt the energy of this realm inside the artefact fill him, revitalising and strengthening him.

Dark energy rolled out of Adaru like a surging black ocean. It parted on the edge of the blade that Annungal held before him in a fountain of multi-coloured light.

Annungal gripped the sword in both hands and pointed it at Adaru. A torrent of energy lanced out from the sword tip as he channelled power through it.

A memory of Marion's surfaced, and Adaru reached behind him. An object burst from the rubble of the destroyed tower and slammed into his palm. Adaru pulled his arm back, and in his hand, he held Samuel's long, black serrated blade. It twisted in his claw, growing larger. The power from Annungal's sword hit an invisible force around Adaru's sword and was extinguished. Annungal roared with anger and threw himself forward. Adaru let out his own battle cry and surged forward to meet him. Adaru's vast transformed body towered above Annungal's human form, yet when their blades met, Annungal did not flinch.

Nanaya watched the two mighty figures clash high above her. The power of each realm exploded around them as they fought. Each clash of their blades sent arcs of energy scattering across the sky amidst chain lightning seething hatred at the unnatural confrontation as it lanced through the storm clouds.

A sharp pain sliced up through her abdomen and through her heart, dropping her to her knees. *I have already been here far too long,* she realised. Her body was being attacked by the energy of the other realm suffused into every grain of sand.

A grunt of pain brought her attention back to the desert, and she saw Baraka struggling to get to his feet. She rushed to him and found him clutching his side with a bloody hand.

"I... I must help my father."

Nanaya shook her head. "You are in no condition to do anything."

Baraka tried once again to stand, but the sudden pain dropped him to the sand. Tears filled his eyes. "I must help him."

Nanaya looked up and watched as the two figures exchanged a flurry of furious blows. The creature Annungal faced sent a blast of power at the dragon, which he deflected with his sword before doing the same. His adversary also pushed the power aside before they both circled each other again.

"That is his fight," she said. "Neither of us could face that."

The ground shook, and with it came a bestial shriek of victory. Both turned and watched as Ki struggled on the ground beneath the foot of the thing she fought. That creature reached down and grasped one of Ki's arms. It wrenched it up and with a thunderous *crack*, ripped it free.

"No!" Nanaya shouted.

The skull-faced creature glanced her way before throwing Ki's severed arm in her direction. Nanaya hurled a shield around herself and Baraka, and the stone arm bounced off it to land nearby.

Nanaya stared at the thing that had crippled her friend and watched it stand above the prone elemental and begin to rain down blows of impossible strength.

Baraka gasped as he sat upright. "Go help Ki."

Nanaya looked at him for a moment, and then nodded. Taking a deep breath, gritting her teeth against the pain lancing inside her, she summoned the energy inside her. Power from the blade still filled her, strengthening her beyond anything she had ever thought possible. It coursed through her veins and sparked from her skin. A white protective aura glimmered around her. Her hands curled into tight fists, and the nimbus of energy around her flared, its edges becoming thick and hard. She thrust her hands toward the creature.

Bron lifted two huge fists high in the air and smashed them down to crush Ki's head.

They never struck.

A flicker at the corner of Bron's eyes was all the warning he received before the energy struck him. Fuelled by Annungal's artefact, Nanaya's protective aura had become a solid, unyielding sphere of raw power. It smashed Bron from his feet. The initial strike shattered every bone in his torso and sent him hurtling through the air to smash into the side of a desert dune hundreds of feet away. The immediate surface gave way beneath the massive creature, but beneath it was sandstone that had been changed to quartzite in the pressure of the healing of the seals so long ago, and there was no measure of give there.

Bron's body pulverised.

Nanaya rushed to Ki's side.

Fractures spider webbed the elemental's body that shuddered and trembled and threatened to shatter at any moment. Her form, once glowing with a rich green vitality, was now dull and brownish.

Nanaya stroked Ki's stone face with a wet quivering hand.

The elemental turned her head and looked at her. Nanaya gazed into her eyes and felt a connection form between them. Warmth rushed through her body, and a vision filled her mind. She stared at a mountain peak that was the highest in the world. Snow blanketed the jagged landscape of lesser peaks as far as the eye could see, and above, cirrus clouds made from ice crystals streaked the air in gossamer strands.

Three different-shaped figures stood beside one another in a wide depression at its peak. One was a tower of twisting flame. Another was a writhing mass of air laced with pale yellow threads. The third appeared almost a twin to the tower of flame, except its form was a deep-blue boiling and churning body of water.

Enlil, Enki, Nuskil. The elementals.

A smaller figure in brilliant white robes stood in front of them. A sword was gripped in each hand, the ends of each curling back in a hook. They all faced a sixth form with dark skin and wearing robes of depthless black, who crouched in the stark white snow.

Nanaya's arms rose, and she saw they were dark green stone and crystal.

Like Ki... Am I seeing through her eyes?

Suddenly, they were gone, and an immense sprawling castle stood where the figures had been. Dozens of towers stretched up from a thick stone base, each ending in an open flat platform. Various stone domes nestled between the towers, varying in size from two dozen feet in diameter to one in the centre that easily stretched a hundred feet wide and several hundred feet tall.

The image dissolved, and Nanaya was back in the desert.

"What was that?" The words tumbled from her lips in a confused yet wondrous whisper.

A cry of pain pulled her eyes back toward where the tower had stood, and she watched Annungal fall from the sky, the creature diving after him.

Chapter Seventy-Four

Annungal hit the ground hard but was cushioned by a sphere of energy surrounding him. He rolled across the sand as Adaru slammed into the ground where he had landed, his black blade burying itself almost to the hilt where the dragon had been. Annungal flipped himself up and onto his feet, swinging his sword at the creature. Adaru pulled his blade free and deflected the strike, staggering backward with the impact.

Rather than press the advantage, Annungal took a moment to rest, standing, breathing hard. His once fine robes were a ripped and bloody mess, and one side of his face was dark with crusted blood where Adaru had clawed him. It was healing, but the wounds were tainted with the foulness of Kur and were slower to cleanse and close.

Adaru regained his balance, and then circled Annungal warily, twisting the wicked blade in the air with fluid rolls of his wrist.

"You cannot defeat me." Adaru's voice was a deep, grating bass that seemed to shake reality, and the air seemed to vibrate painfully with each syllable.

Annungal attacked.

"I cannot be stopped now," Adaru said, sweeping his blade up. He blocked, parried, and deflected, and then counterattacked, forcing Annungal backward.

"You do not realise what you are doing," Annungal said as he set his feet and turned Adaru's strikes aside. "What you have done."

"Fool," Adaru said as he swung at Annungal's side. "I know exactly what I am doing." He pushed an outstretched clawed hand toward Annungal, and a burst of black power erupted from it. It never struck, however, hitting an invisible shield before Annungal and parting around the wounded dragon.

"I have power the likes of which you cannot fathom!" Adaru swung his sword.

Annungal leaned back as he turned aside the strike, and then stepped toward his enemy, closing the distance between them. He spun on the ball of his front foot and sent his right elbow cracking into the creature's jaw.

Adaru moved with the impact and also spun, sending a savage backhand swing at Annungal's back. Annungal saw it coming and lifted his sword in both hands up over his head to point down between his shoulder blades, where it met Adaru's sword with a loud clash and a shower of sparking energies. Annungal kicked out and hit Adaru in the abdomen, knocking him backward.

"You have nothing," the dragon said as he settled back into a defensive stance. "You think you have taken power? You think you have elevated yourself? All you have done is damn yourself. Kur does not grant anything without also taking what it wants. You have given yourself to the dark realm and the gallus."

Adaru circled Annungal, searching for an opening. "I have given nothing! I am the master of my own destiny now."

"You are master of nothing! You cannot take from Kur what it does not wish to give, and it gives for only one reason: so that it may take this realm."

"I have taken it! I am in control!" He hurled himself at Annungal.

Flashes of energy illuminated the fight in stark and surreal moments of vivid clarity as the blades clashed before the figures were absorbed back into the darkness.

"This is mine!" Adaru said as he swung and slashed wildly. "It is all mine! You cannot stop me!"

Annungal was forced back, step by step, as Adaru unleashed his ferocity. Adaru hacked at him, and Annungal retreated farther as he frantically twisted his blade to block.

The side of his face the creature had clawed burned, and pain pulsed in time with his pounding heart.

Baraka watched the battle and saw his father's arms droop, his movements increasingly unsteady. *He is tiring.*

Streams of oily smoke ran over Adaru's scaled skin, and when he gestured at Annungal, it surged at him.

Annungal was just able to bring his sword up to deflect it with a flick of his wrist but had to weave to avoid the black blade that came for him. His breath was laboured, and every movement seemed slower than the last.

Kataru. Baraka did not know where the word came from, but it was suddenly in his mind, and with it came knowledge. *Gu-ul. To enlarge. Increase...*

"Gu-ul," he said aloud and felt himself drawing energy from the world around. The power inside him swelled.

Another word filled Baraka's mind. *Wussuru. To release.* "Wussuru," he said through clenched teeth.

Energy hit Annungal and knocked him back, staggering.

Adaru shrieked with glee and lunged, but he struck an invisible barrier and was repulsed, thrown dozens of feet to crash into the sand. He leapt to his feet and stared as Annungal was surrounded by a nimbus of bright energy, throwing his head back and roaring with the voice of a dragon.

A line of energy led away from Annungal. Adaru followed it and found Baraka. Power flowed from him into Annungal. Adaru threw a lance of power at the young man.

The lance shattered.

Adaru turned. Annungal was striding toward him. He was healing and revitalising with every step as Baraka sent energy into him. Age lines on his face were disappearing, he stood taller, and his breathing was deep and strong. Even the injuries on his face where Adaru's talons had raked his skin were smoothing.

Baraka collapsed, and the stream of healing vanished.

Adaru hurled power at Annungal, but the energy burst on a protective shield.

Annungal attacked, his sword a blur, sweeping one way then another as he twisted, turned, spun, and pivoted.

Adaru's eyes grew wide as he desperately tried to defend. Dark power seeped from Adaru's skin and swept around Annungal, seeking to smother him, but it dissolved before it could. The two blades clashed and clashed and clashed with increasing speed until Annungal was too fast and darted forward to plunge his sword through Adaru's abdomen.

Adaru screamed as the artefact blazed with power, his dark blade falling from his hands as the energies of this realm, which coursed through the dragon's sword, attacked the energies of the other realm, which were now fundamentally part of what Adaru had become.

"*No!*" Adaru howled as his being began to burn.

He reached for the power of Kur that was seeping through the nexus. It filled him eagerly and rushed to smother the fires the artefact had ignited inside him. The darkness of Kur flooded his body, and he began to change again. It leached away what little humanity remained in the body he inhabited, flesh and bone dissolving into a thick black substance that fluctuated chaotically between solidity and fluidity as he became thoroughly infused with energy from Kur.

Annungal's eyes widened at the dramatic transformation, and terror seized him at what it meant. The power from the other realm, which had been the merest of trickles, was now a raging torrent that would be ripping wider the tears in the seals separating the realms. There could no longer be any doubt that what resided in Kur would be aware of the open path to this realm and would be rushing to cross.

Adaru swelled as the energy filling him pulsed and pushed more of itself into the physical body it was connected to. That power did more than just change the physical form it was feeding, it reached into its mind and began to claw at it.

Adaru felt the intrusion and recoiled from it. He tried to banish it, but it was unaffected by anything he tried. For the first time since he had begun this journey to seize the power of Kur for himself, he felt a sense of powerlessness and panic started to take hold of him.

I am the master of this power!

But he was not.

No matter how much he tried, he could not push back the insidious encroachment of Kur into his mind. He could feel it slipping into his thoughts, and with horrific realisation, understood just how alien Kur was and its innate desire to consume everything of this realm.

Annungal saw the creature back away a few steps, its eyes widening in obvious uncertainty and confusion even as it visibly grew stronger. The creature's body was now a featureless mass of churning dark vapour, though it somehow retained its overall shape. The dragon clutched his blade tighter and took a deep breath as a moment of destiny seized him.

If I wait, this may pass. If I do not strike now, it will just get stronger.

His mind made up, Annungal leapt forward and attacked.

Adaru saw the dragon move and swept an arm up protectively before him. The insubstantial essence his body was now formed of rippled out away from him, becoming more defined as it raced toward the dragon until it was a physical wave of razor-sharp edges.

Annungal brought his sword up to block this new threat, but even though the wave shattered on its edge, what had not broken on the blade passed through the shields encircling him and sliced into his body. He howled as the physical manifestation of the other realm bit deeply and where it lodged inside him, it began to poison him.

Adaru had no opportunity to take advantage and counterattack, he was fighting an all-consuming battle within himself. He could feel the energy of Kur digging deeper, and as it did, he could feel himself becoming less.

No! He wrestled with the power inside him, determined to force it to his will, but it refused to submit. It was like the power had a life of its own.

A terrible realization dawned on Adaru. The promise of empowerment and the allure of ultimate strength that he had been sold on were all lies.

"*No!*" Adaru screamed as the power of Kur tore him apart.

Annungal grit his teeth against the pain inside and again attacked.

Adaru saw the dragon advance, but his body was refusing to obey the few coherent thoughts he still managed. He just managed to thrust his arms out toward the dragon, and waves of dark energy erupted from them.

It crashed upon Annungal but never touched him. The dragon held the artefact before him, and it blazed with power, as if reacting to the intensity of the power of the other realm assaulting it. The dark power evaporated as it met an invisible shield around the dragon, though the force of the impact pushed him to his knees.

Adaru watched Annungal start to rise, but he was dissolving and did not have the strength to do anything about it. With his last remaining strength, he fled his body.

Without anyone pulling at Kur, the dark energy seeping through the nexus receded.

The creature before Annungal shivered, and then was still.

Annungal's eyes narrowed. *Something has changed.*

Diers staggered to a stop in the street as a searing pain ripped across his temples. He dropped to one knee and moaned as the sensation intensified, and an undeniable pressure built in his mind. He pushed back against that pressure, and it lessened a little. It felt to the Chosen as if something inside him was recoiling.

Let me in.

Diers gasped in surprise. "Adaru?" The shock broke his concentration, and the pressure in his mind surged with an intensity that forced Diers to the ground. He fought back against what was happening, and again the sensation lessened.

Annungal warily faced the thing before him. He did not know what had happened, but the creature's eyes had dimmed and were now dark and vacant.

~

Let me in!

Diers shook as he lay on the ground, his body spasming. *What are you doing?*

You are my lifeline.

Diers shook his head and tried to muster his willpower.

Why do you think I kept you close to me? If all else fails, then you are my escape. I will not die.

"No!"

The presence inside Diers surged. *Let me in!*

No!

Diers pushed back. Adaru felt himself being forced out of Diers body.

But I made you! Adaru howled as he felt his connection to Diers fracture.

Diers felt Adaru retreat before him. He mustered every ounce of his willpower and strength into eradicating Adaru from him.

Adaru screamed and hurled himself at Diers. *I will not end this way! This is not my destiny! This is not how things should be!*

Diers struck Adaru with everything he had.

Adaru broke, then shattered, and he was exorcised from Diers body. Without a physical form to anchor himself, the natural laws of the realm asserted themselves, and Adaru's tortured essence was destroyed.

~

Annungal roared as he rushed forward and swung his blade. The lifeless creature did not react, and the sword cleaved through its unnatural form and split it in two. The two halves fell smoking to the sand, twisting as they continued to char with the power of this realm released from the sword. In moments, all that was left were two blackened unrecognisable shapes.

Annungal stood breathing heavily, staring at the remains.

"Father...?"

"Baraka!" Annungal rushed to his son's side. Baraka lay as he had fallen, but to Annungal's relief, he was breathing, albeit shallowly.

"Thank you, son. Without your strength I would not have survived."

Baraka's eyes flickered open, and his lips parted in a small smile before he lost consciousness.

Annungal took a deep breath and looked around him. The sky remained full of clouds, but the lightning and rain had stopped. Debris from the tower lay scattered as far as the eye could see, but nothing else moved. Now that the battle had ended, no sound came from anywhere. He looked at the crater where the tower had stood. Wisps of dark, smoky energy curled up from its depths. The tower was destroyed.

The legacy of the past is put to rest.

Chapter Seventy-Five

Margaret sat in her throne in the audience chamber and stared at the secretary of war in confusion. "I do not think I understand."

The secretary of war shrugged and shook his head. "It makes no sense to me, either."

"On the eve of victory," Margaret said, "you are telling me that when our forces were routed and the West had victory in their grasp, all their remaining forces marched into The Territory?"

Harold nodded. "Every report says the same. The Western force broke our lines, and instead of consolidating their position, they marched into the desert." He shook his head. "It makes no sense. Your Majesty, we have won. Against everything, despite everything, to all intents and purposes, we have won the war."

"I cannot believe this," the lord mayor said.

"This makes absolutely no sense," Margaret said.

The secretary ran a hand through his hair. "They entered The Territory to a man. They didn't leave a single soldier behind. What remained of our Fringe and Southcastle force regrouped and fortified at the edge of the desert as they watched the Royaume d'Occident army disappear into the distance."

The secretary shook his head again. "When no one returned, they sent word and gathered what other survivors they could find. They commandeered the West's vessels that had been left on the shores and sailed around The Territory, but they saw nothing of the Western army. The Westerners must have travelled as far as they were able, and then were swallowed by the sand. One of those ships sailed here to make this report while the others returned to bolster the emerging Fringe States's border defences. We have won, Your Majesty," Harold said with a smile. "We did it."

"Can we really be sure that this is over?"

"No one has ever returned from The Territory, Your Majesty. I cannot speak to their motivation, but facts cannot be disputed. They will not return."

Margaret placed her hand on her trembling lips and nodded as she swallowed. She gasped as she felt both a great weight that had been pushing onto her body and an intense pressure filling her suddenly evaporate.

It is over.

"We—" Her voice quivered. She took a moment to compose herself. "We must make an announcement to the people. We should do so swiftly."

"Agreed, Your Majesty," the lord mayor replied. "The news will be welcomed by your people, especially since the announcement of the king's death."

The lord mayor cleared his throat. "I must tell you that the people of Southcastle know the efforts you have made and that you have directly helped ease the chaos and hardship they have endured. There is a sense of optimism for the future that has been absent since the war started. News of our victory will only increase this and further their support for your coronation. Martin's reinstatement as prime minister has also restored public confidence. Martin has always been well liked by the people."

Margaret turned to a member of the palace staff. "Please send for the prime minister."

"At once, Your Majesty," the young man said and hastened away.

The queen turned back to the lord mayor and the secretary of war. "Thank you, gentlemen, you may depart."

The two men left, leaving Margaret in silence.

It is over.

Her eyes shifted to look upon the throne beside her. She had not been able to give the order to remove it.

I wish Edward was here.

Tears filled her eyes.

Things would be easier now. Edward would be able to cope, would be his normal self. Would have been, she corrected herself. *He is gone.*

Feeling acutely alone, the queen wept.

Chapter Seventy-Six

anaya felt a change in the air and turned.

Annungal, in dragon form, swept across the desert toward her, his wings wide and outstretched.

He pulled his wings up as he neared, and Nanaya had to turn away as the updraft sent the sand swirling against her. When she turned back, he was walking toward her in human form, wearing bright, clean, pearl robes.

"It is done," he said.

Nanaya rushed toward him and threw her arms around him as she hugged him fiercely, sobbing. "How are you here?"

After a moment, Annungal hugged her back.

"How are you here?" Nanaya repeated as she held him. "I saw you die."

He looked at Ki. The elemental twisted her head to look at him. Her body was a dull brown and covered in a spider web of fractures and fissures. Parts of it crumbled and fell with every movement.

"I didn't die," Annungal said.

"But I remember you entering the nexus," Nanaya said. "Then there was the shockwave, and everything was destroyed." She shivered at the memory.

"I managed to heal the seals," Annungal replied, "but I was caught in some sort of backlash—the shockwave you mentioned. I did not die, I —" Annungal saw that Nanaya was frowning. "What is it?"

"They cannot be allowed to return," she muttered.

Annungal's eyes narrowed. "What did you say?"

"They cannot be allowed to return," Nanaya said again. "You said that before you entered the nexus. I just remembered. *Who* cannot be allowed to return? I thought the danger we faced was the gallus?"

Annungal shook his head. "That is something I cannot speak of."

"But—" Nanaya began, but the dragon held a hand up in the air.

"No, Nanaya. I will not speak of such things. Besides, now is not the time."

Nanaya stared at Annungal for a moment, and the silence stretched between them. After a moment, she nodded.

Annungal crouched next to Ki. He pushed his hand into hers and felt the stone fingers curl around his. Annungal felt a constant trembling as he held her hand.

The dragon turned and looked back to where the tower had once stood. "I cannot save Ki," he said in a voice heavy with sadness, "but I can restore the seals as I did before."

"Father."

Annungal turned at the sound of Baraka's voice and saw him struggling to stand. "I must go to my son."

Ki gripped Annungal's hand and tried to rise.

"Rest, Great One," Annungal said.

Ki shook her head, dust and small pieces of stone falling to the sand with each movement. Annungal helped the elemental stand. Ki swayed for a moment, and then pointed at Baraka.

Annungal nodded, and the three of them moved haltingly toward the young man.

"It is over," Baraka said as the three figures approached.

Nanaya stopped with Ki, who collapsed to the sand. Annungal approached his son.

"Not quite," Annungal replied. "I have one thing left to do. I have to heal the seals."

"How?"

Annungal walked to the edge of the crater that marked where the tower had stood and peered down into its depths. "I must enter the nexus."

"You told me what happened the last time you did this," Baraka said. "What will happen when you do it again?"

"I don't know. Maybe the same thing, maybe nothing, maybe something different. There is no way of knowing what will happen."

"But I have just found you again!" Baraka eyes were full of tears. He gestured to himself. "And there is this, what I am. What I can do. There is so much I need to learn, so much you need to tell me."

Annungal placed the palm of one hand on one of Baraka's cheeks. "I must do this, my son. With the seals broken, the way between the realms is open for—" His eyes darted to Nanaya and found her watching him intently. "The seals must be restored," he finished.

He shook his head and wiped away the tears streaming down his son's face. "I wish there was another way, but there is not. I must heal this nexus."

Baraka could not speak. To be reunited with a father he thought dead, and then have him torn away from him again was too much. He rose, grimacing with pain, stepped forward, and embraced his father and sobbed into his shoulder.

Annungal held his son and felt his own eyes filling with tears. He gripped him tightly and wished the moment would never end.

An intense cold that sparked pain in the cores of their being suddenly washed over both father and son, and then was gone.

"What was that?" Baraka pulled away from his father to stare around him.

"Something is attempting to cross over," Annungal replied. He looked into his eyes. "There is no more time, son. I must do this."

Baraka nodded and embraced his father for one last time before stepping back.

Annungal turned and looked at Ki and Nanaya. Ki dipped her head while Nanaya came forward and hugged him. She held him for a moment, then stepped back. "Do what you have to do."

Annungal nodded, then walked back to the crater. He paused for a moment, and then stepped over the edge and disappeared into its depths.

~

"Stay close to me," Nanaya said as she concentrated. "When Annungal healed the seals last time, it created a shockwave that destroyed the kingdom of Darisam and nearly half of the entire continent."

A nimbus of energy surrounded her and expanded outward until a protective dome covered them. It flickered and wavered as Nanaya struggled to maintain it

"I will do what I can to protect us."

Baraka took a deep breath. "Let me—" He swayed, and Nanaya had to catch him to prevent him from falling.

"You have nothing left after giving your energy to your father."

The scrape of sand on stone came from beside her as Ki pushed herself to her feet. The elemental pointed at the crater and ponderously made her way toward it.

"Ki?" Nanaya called out.

Ki shook her head and continued half walking, half stumbling toward the crater. When she reached an area of bare stone at the crater's edge, she turned to face Nanaya and dipped her head.

"Not you, too!" Nanaya said, her voice thick with despair.

As she looked on, Ki began to reduce and seep down into the stone at her feet. Merging with her element in any other place would have energised Ki, but taking the tainted stone here into herself sent veins of dark corruption lacing through her form and leached her of vitality. As her humanoid form shrunk, Ki's essence, together with the stone she had merged with, began to stretch out across the chasm created by the previous explosion of energy from the nexus.

The sand shifted all around the crater as Ki pulled more of the tainted stone from the tower into herself, and then pushed both it and herself out as a growing cap over the gaping hole Annungal had disappeared into. In moments, Ki's humanoid form had disappeared, and the stretching mass of living stone began to slow, yet it still continued to grow over the crater until it reached its edges and curled over, burying itself in the sand.

The sand hissed as it was super-heated and vitrified into a dark, glass-like substance. With an audible sigh, Ki stopped moving. As the elemental's last reserves of energy spent themselves, her body hardened, and its colour darkened to a deep brown, spider webbed with dark veins of obsidian.

Nanaya felt tears running down her cheeks as she tried to maintain the shield around her and Baraka.

Chapter Seventy-Seven

A nnungal landed on the remnants of a floor from the tower. He made his way down through the wreckage, leap after leap, passing smoky eddies of energy from the other realm as he descended until he landed on the ancient stone of catacombs over which the tower had been built.

He could feel Kur through the tear in the seals, its wrongness pulsing eagerly into this realm. Annungal looked for its source, the nexus, and found it, a shroud of grey-veined mist hanging serenely amid the destruction littering the ancient stone. He walked toward it, pausing at its threshold.

One more step, and there is no turning back.

A sudden deathly chill came again, and Annungal knew he could delay no longer. Gritting his teeth, he stepped into the mist.

There was a sudden intense disorientation as he passed through the seal that surrounded the physical realm and emerged into the nexus. This was a place between realities, a place with no boundaries and no physical matter. There was no up or down, left or right, but still, Annungal found himself trying to look around. Nothing changed; there was no sense that he had moved or changed perspective.

Annungal stopped thinking in normal terms. He remembered being in the nexus from before. In this place, there was no normal. To find what he wanted, he needed to manifest it. He focused his thoughts on himself, visualising himself, and as he did so, he felt his wings beating. With the sensation, a perception of solidity came to the void he was in, and he was able to feel a sense of up and down, beyond and behind.

As he had before, the dragon thought about the ruptures in the seals between the realms and the energy of Kur seeping from that place into the one he had just left. Manifested by his thoughts, a dark, smoky, gossamer stream appeared, twisting and churning as it flowed from somewhere ahead to somewhere behind. He turned and looked behind him, finding a crack in the unmarred, perfect void through which the dark energy escaped.

He turned back and peered ahead, finding a blemish in the void ahead, from which the energy stream flowed. Annungal imagined flexing his wings, and as he did, he flew toward the fissure, through which the energy of Kur was passing. As he travelled, he felt as well as saw surges in the energy stream around him. It grew darker and thicker, surrounding him as he moved, until he was struggling against it, fighting to make any headway.

Even so, the tear in the fabric of the void steadily increased in size and detail until he saw the rupture in the seal that held Kur back. It was a jagged tear that led to a place of blackish-green obsidian, through which the dark energy of that place streamed.

"A seal can only be harmed by the energy of the opposite realm," Annungal remembered, *"and it is strengthened by energy from the realm it is linked to."* He summoned his power, reaching deep within his being and bringing forth everything he had. He did not need to try to manifest that energy, it blazed from him as pure energy. He directed it onto the seal behind him, the seal to his realm, and it began to heal as like energies met and it was reinvigorated. He watched as it closed once more.

He turned his attention to the seal to Kur and directed the energy not at the seal, for that would harm it even further, but at the dark energy seeping from it. He carefully shaped his power so that what was escaping was pushed back and against the seal. It, too, began to heal as it was revitalised by aligned energy.

A thicker darkness began to seep from the seal to Kur like a thick sludge.

A gallus is trying to cross!

Annungal opened his mouth and roared. It was more than just sound, laced by the immense power he was unleashing. His roar was a blast of energy that pushed back the gallus and turned more of the escaping energy against the seal. The tears in the seal snapped closed, and the sudden return of the nexus integrity generated a shockwave of primordial energy. Annungal had the barest of moments before it hit him, a moment where he was filled with both love and loss. Then the shockwave hit him, and he felt no more.

Chapter Seventy-Eight

A crash like a sudden peal of thunder was the barest of warnings before the blast came from the vortex. Ki's sacrifice that created the closure over the crater held most of it below ground and prevented it from reaching them, but in doing so caused the shockwave to pass through the stone far beneath where they stood.

The ground heaved and buckled, knocking Nanaya from her feet, and as she fell, she lost control of her fragile shield. A terrible, deep grumbling and a slight trembling began somewhere deep, the noise growing in volume, and the shaking growing in intensity, until both Nanaya and Baraka were unable to even stay on their hands and knees and were being tossed around in the sand.

"We need to get out of here!" Baraka said as a deafening groan came from below them, a sound that echoed up through the sand and rattled his bones.

Nanaya tried to summon her power but shook her head. "I have nothing left, and I have been here too long." Her vision started to cloud. "I cannot last much longer. The corruption in this land is affecting me."

Anything Baraka was going to say was lost as the ground beneath them heaved upward, and then dropped a dozen feet lower, casting the two of them high in the air to crash back onto the churning sands.

Again, the ground beneath them surged upward, but this time far faster and far higher. A violent shattering breaking came from beneath them, and then the ground for hundreds of feet around them plummeted down.

Fractured by the first shockwave from the vortex thousands of years ago, the rock beneath the desert gave way under the pressure exerted by this second blast, and Baraka and Nanaya began falling into a vast chasm stretching down into bottomless black depths.

Nanaya screamed as she fell. She was spent, there was nothing that she could do to save herself.

After everything, this is how I die?

Her breath was forced from her lungs, and several ribs snapped as her body was crushed. Her vision started to dim, but then she felt herself rising, the suffocating grip on her body lessening.

I have you.

Baraka's voice was clear yet laboured in Nanaya's mind. She twisted, gasping with pain as she did so to look up and find herself gripped in Baraka's claws. She slumped in his grasp and stared as a huge area of the desert collapsed.

Baraka fought against being sucked down into the chasm, banking, ducking, and diving to avoid the downpour of sand and stone. He was as tired as he had ever felt yet pushed everything he had into beating his wings. He was so weakened that the protective shield that normally enveloped him barely formed, and he roared in pain as his body was battered and his wings sliced open by debris, a stream of blood trailing behind him as he tried to escape.

A space free of falling debris opened above him, and the dragon made for it, sweeping his wings powerfully to gain some height. He reached it, suffering only a handful of new minor wounds, and burst from the chasm into the calm air beyond. The last storm clouds had dissipated and he soared in a clear blue sky. He twisted and turned as he rose higher, and then flew back over the devastation. Where the tower had stood was now a wide fissure, as if an immense axe had buried itself in the land and split it deeply. Hanging over the centre of the chasm was the nexus that had been hidden under the tower. It appeared as a patch of marbled smoke or mist that twisted and churned to its own currents but never dissipated or lost form.

Baraka soared near it and felt the immense energy contained within as an intense warmth that swam over his skin as he passed.

It is over, he thought to Nanaya, but she was hanging limp and unconscious in his claw. Taking a deep, painful breath, Baraka beat his wings and made for Southcastle.

Chapter Seventy-Nine

The darkness was absolute in the small stone chamber she entered. She knelt as soon as she crossed the threshold and bowed her head. Steam slipped from her lips with each nervous breath, its thin wisps joyously fleeing into the room. She envied its freedom. The silence was oppressive and suffocating, but she endured the anxiety it brought.

The tower is destroyed, the Dannum nexus healed.

The voice that filled her mind was beyond strong. It was dominating. It demanded utter subservience and attention.

She waited for her time to speak. To utter a word without permission would incite terrible repercussions.

It is of no matter. The tower was but one play in the Great Plan. It was a focus for a time, but that time is over. We did not reveal ourselves by supporting this human, and we are not diminished by his failure. We continue as before. You will go to Fōji.

She listened to what was expected of her and smiled.

Chapter Eighty

Arthur Stableman cursed as he pulled on his helmet and ran along the palace corridor toward the courtyard.

It's probably a bird.

"It's getting closer!" a guardsman shouted from the courtyard.

"It must be huge!" another said with more than a hint of fear in his voice.

A really big bird.

Arthur snatched a musket tossed by a guardsman. "Is the queen safe?" he asked as he ran.

"Sir!" a guard responded as he caught up with him. "Now that the protests have stopped. we have moved her to a barracks nearby."

"Good." He had been distraught when hearing of the king's death. He was not going to lose the queen as well.

He ran out into the courtyard and into bedlam. Guardsmen were rushing to the ramparts, gun teams were preparing cannons, and officers were trying to force an order to the chaos. Men were shouting for cartridge ammunition, for gunpowder, for direction, and above all, for sightings of whatever this thing was that was flying toward them.

The captain paused for a moment to take it all in.

"Oh, by the Shepherd, it's getting close!"

Arthur looked at the man who had spoken and ran to where he stood at the ramparts, taking the steps up from the courtyard two at a time. He stared in the direction the guardsman was pointing in.

That's a really big bird.

What flew toward them glittered when the sunlight struck it. *Just like the suit of chainmail in the palace entrance hall when the sun shines through the ground floor windows.*

Arthur watched it fly toward them, its vast wings sweeping the air.

That's not a bird.

"Prepare cannons!" he ordered as he strode forward. "Load muskets and prepare to fire!"

"Sir!"

Arthur turned to a young guardsman who had approached him. "Report."

"It's the cannons, sir. They can't aim that high! They are designed to fire down, not up!"

Arthur stared at the cannons and swore as he saw men struggling to raise the barrels. His mind raced as he thought through every armament and defensive resource the palace had.

Nothing. We have nothing—

"It's coming so fast!"

The captain turned back to look into the sky.

"Shepherd!" he swore as he watched the creature grow with every passing breath. For a moment, he was frozen with fearful indecision, then years of discipline forced him to action. He pointed at the beast.

"Fire!"

Muskets fired all around him, creating a thick cloud of dirty smoke that obscured the dragon.

"Did we get it?"

The smoke was swept away by a powerful burst of wind, and the dragon was on them. Men scattered in terror as its huge pearl body passed overhead, and then banked over the palace to return.

Arthur was captivated by its glittering scales, marvelling at the streaks of red running over its body. For the first time, he became aware that it clutched something in one foot.

Is that a body?

And then it was coming back toward him, and the captivation turned to terror. This time, there was no training that could overcome it, and Arthur Stableman, a veteran of countless border battles and the leader of hundreds of the most highly trained soldiers in the kingdom, was petrified.

The dragon tilted backward as it passed overhead, raising the front of its wings so that it abruptly stalled and dropped to the courtyard. As it fell, its form blurred, shrank, and changed until where a dragon had started the fall to the ground, a man in pearl robes landed with a woman in his arms.

Arthur stared at the woman as the man stumbled toward him across the courtyard.

She looks familiar.

The woman's long blond hair tumbled free from the man's arms. And Arthur instantly knew how he recognised her.

"Don't fire!" He waved his arms in the air as the guardsmen glanced his way. *"It is Lady Nanaya! Do not fire!"*

Baraka sat on a cushioned chair next to a cold chiminea in the garden. A dozen foot guards surrounded him, their eyes never leaving him.

"I have a lot of questions."

Baraka turned and watched the captain of the foot guard walk into the garden. He walked with the slow, confident, prepared gait of a warrior. He stopped a few feet from Baraka and rested a hand on the pommel of his sword.

"Where is Nanaya?" Baraka asked before the captain could speak.

The veteran frowned. "In her chambers," Arthur said. "The royal physician says she is battered and bruised but otherwise well. She will be sore after a good sleep but will recover."

Baraka nodded.

"So you are a dragon?"

Baraka raised his eyebrows as he nodded. "And that's not even the strangest thing that has happened."

Arthur shook his head. "I never thought they were real."

"Me either."

Arthur frowned again and cocked his head to one side as he stared at the younger man.

Baraka waved a hand in the air. "It's a long story. I didn't know my father, he was a dragon—"

"Your father was a dragon?"

"Like I said, a long story." Baraka gestured around him. "Anyway, what has happened here? I hear the king is dead?"

"Yes. It is complicated," Arthur muttered. "The queen sits on the throne now." He took a deep breath. "But at least the war is over, and rumour is that the Western archbishop, who pushed for the war, is missing."

"He is dead."

Arthur frowned again. "How would you know that?"

"My father killed him."

Arthur blinked. "Your father killed the archbishop?"

"Yes."

"Your father, who is a dragon?"

"Yes."

Arthur stared at Baraka. He opened his mouth to speak, but the sound of footsteps caught his attention, and he turned to see who approached. He straightened as he saw the queen. "Your Majesty."

"Arthur," Margaret replied with a dip of her head. She turned her eyes to the man sitting on the ground. "Baraka, is it not?"

Baraka climbed to his feet and bowed.

"Walk with me," Margaret commanded. "Arthur, please remain here with the other guards. I wish some privacy."

Baraka remained quiet as he walked with the queen further into the garden.

"My grandparents were not from Dannum," Margaret said after a moment. "They were from The Confederate States of Ares, islands far to the north of here. I remember the stories they used to tell me as a child of the wonders that existed there. Griffins, sphinxes, unicorns, phoenixes, and more. Magic was well understood there, quite unlike here."

She stopped and turned to face Baraka. "Edward used to talk in his sleep. He spoke of a tower and of a battle against nightmarish creatures. This battle also involved a dragon and a being of stone—the former *you* now seem to be if tales are to be believed; the latter something that sounds like the creature you and Lady Nanaya fought with against the Westerners attempting to cross the Kafifi Ranges." She shook her head. "I don't think I will ever know or fully understand what has really happened, what made Nanaya push my husband—" Her eyes were intent, searching, and there was a sudden sense of vulnerability about the woman. "I have to believe there was a reason for it all."

"There was," Baraka replied. "The archbishop was possessed. If what possessed him had not been opposed, then I believe that nothing in Dannum would have survived." Baraka's eyes grew distant. "We have all lost."

Margaret's head fell and she closed her eyes.

"None of us will ever be the same again," Baraka continued, "but yes, there was a reason for it all."

"Is it over?"

Baraka nodded. "Yes, I think it is over."

Epilogue

He was an ancient among ancients. His angular face was etched with lines born from both the stresses of his duty and the passage of generations. Silver hair, the same colour as his robes, fell to rounded shoulders past silver eyes that had seen the rise of the first civilisations. He wondered, not for the first time, if they would also see the fall of the last.

He closed those eyes as he rested the tips of his fingers on one of dozens of small spikes driven into a world map carved into one stone wall. This spike had been white marble for over a thousand years before recently changing to charcoal grey and then transforming into obsidian. Now it was back to its former white marble.

"The nexus is whole once more. The seals are restored," Zuen declared with more than a little relief in his voice.

Behind him stood three women of the ri dragon kind in blue robes, beside them were two men in yellow. They were of the ti dragon kind. Behind them all were twelve men and women in robes of various shades of red. These were the militant lirum. Those in red each held a different type of weapon, ranging from swords and hand axes to spears and halberds. They had all assembled the moment the spike had turned black, each prepared for battle.

"The queen waits no longer. She demands information. How far were the seals ruptured, Zuen?"

The ancient dragon opened his eyes and turned to face the source of the voice. He stood among the twelve armed men and women, dressed in a rich burgundy robe, his bright yellow eyes shining in a dark-coloured, hairless head.

"Enough for the power of Kur to be released, Zababa, but not enough for a crossing." The lord of the zalag dragon kind turned angry eyes on the lirum. "Your queen played a dangerous game. You know the law. The moment the seals are ruptured, the Kataru is decreed, and—"

"I am sure *our* queen knows the law and has her reasons," Zababa replied. "'Ware your tongue, Zuen."

"It does not matter," Zuen said. "The seals were restored before we could have arrived anyway." He stared at the spike. "This nexus has been troublesome for a time, but I feel its time is past. I sense it has reached its destiny."

The red dragon grimaced. "You sound like Dumuzid."

Zuen's eyes flashed with intensity, and he shook his head. "Do not compare me to that zealot."

"Then do not speak of destiny and such things. Leave that to the fanatic."

Zuen frowned at the other dragon, and then returned his eyes to the spike he had been touching moments before.

"We will need to watch this nexus closely to safeguard it." He turned his eyes to the rest of the map. All but one of the spikes driven into specific locations on both land and sea were white marble. One was obsidian.

Zababa strode forward to stand beside the older dragon. He pointed at the obsidian spike. "This nexus remains a problem."

Zuen regarded the spike set in the middle of a vast ocean far to the east of Dannum. "Fōji. Remember, if it were not for their... unique situation, you would not be holding the weapon artefact that they craft."

Zababa huffed. "At some point, something will have to be done about their *unique situation*."

"We have lost another elemental," Zuen said after a moment.

Zababa shrugged. "It will be reborn."

"She."

The lirum frowned at Zuen.

"The elemental was a she."

Zababa shrugged again.

A sharp chime echoed in the chamber.

Zababa dipped his head. "It is over, and the queen calls. I must go. By your leave, Zuen."

The older dragon dismissed the younger with a wave of his hand. The other lirum turned as Zababa passed them and followed him out of the chamber, the ri and ti leaving soon after, leaving Zuen standing alone before the map.

"It is never over," he muttered.

Small aftershocks still shook The Territory in the aftermath of the chasm's creation. A small stream now ran at the bottom of the deep fissure. It was currently only a foot deep, but the destruction unleashed by the shockwave had released a vast underground lake that, until now, had been hidden far under the desert. The stream was steadily growing deeper, fed by melting ice in the Kafifi Ranges that found its way into the subterranean lake. In time, the stream would grow to be a mighty river, but for now, it trickled contentedly, adding its light sound to the serenity that had settled in the wake of such epic destruction.

A black fist punched through a mound of rubble and shattered the stillness. It uncurled and pushed aside the rock surrounding it, making room for a second black fist to smash through alongside the first, and together, they ripped a hole in the fallen rock. A figure covered entirely in black armour clambered free and stood breathing heavily in the cold shadow cast by the chasm wall. The armour appeared at first glance to be a form-fitting seamless suit of overlapping scales over a lithe yet well-muscled man.

A closer look revealed this suit of armour did not fit its wearer like a second skin, it *was* its skin. The vascularity in its neck, chest, arms and legs, was distinct, and as it moved, the scales covering its body twisted and flexed smoothly. Those scales also covered its face in a featureless, opaque shield.

It stood with its chest heaving and stared around, taking in the stream, and then raising its head to gaze up the walls of the chasm to their distant edge outlined against a dawning sky.

Where am I?

Its breathing slowed, and it lifted one hand before its eyes, staring at the black scales that covered its skin.

What am I?

Something flickered at the edge of its thoughts. An image of a farm briefly filled its mind, the smell of freshly baked bread and the feel of summer sun against its skin filled its senses. A woman's tender voice spoke a name in its mind.

Samuel.

The name resonated.

Is that who I am?

One hand twitched, and Samuel raised it curiously. He needed something. It was like a part of his body was missing. Instinctively, he felt where that part was and reached out in that direction. With a sharp *crack*, a section of the chasm floor split, and out of it darted a long, black, serrated blade. It slammed into Samuel's armoured palm with a loud *smack*, and he sighed.

He now felt complete.

His hand tightened around the sword grip, and he took a deep breath as he gazed at it. Even though he felt complete, the serenity that came with his sword's reunion was the thinnest of shells. Underneath, he could feel a raging storm of apocalyptic wrath, a boiling violence that promised utter annihilation. At the moment, it was contained, but it burned for release.

Samuel.

The sword in his hand dissolved and was replaced with an ageing brown-haired woman sitting on a bed, clutching a mud-stained shirt.

My shirt?

Hazel eyes bloodshot with grief gazed at him, and then she was rushing toward him. A part of him remembered her holding him tightly.

"*It's going to change you,*" she sobbed. *"Please remember who you are. Remember this beautiful boy who is my son."*

The rubble of the chasm floor filled his eyes once more. He reached up to touch his face, and at his touch, the featureless mask that had been there collapsed to reveal what had been smooth, youthful features now irrevocably hardened by brutal experience. Blue eyes so bright they seemed to glow looked around him, and a mop of dark, curling hair fell to below his shoulders.

His fingers touched his cheek and came away wet with tears. His other hand twitched on the sword grip. With a last look around, he picked a direction and started walking.

Thank you for reading

You could have chosen a lot of other books, but you chose mine.

I am humbled.

If you enjoyed the story, please write a review on amazon or Goodreads (both would be amazing) and please spread the word. I'm an indie author and that means I'm pulling all of this together myself. Your support is very much appreciated!

You can also join my newsletter for special offers and updates on, well, everything!

Acknowledgments

There are a lot of people to thank and I am almost certainly going to forget some. Forgive me.

To Rich, Si and Will, the Warhammer Fantasy Wednesday-nighters. You ignited my passion in fantasy. I will never forget those magical nights.

To my developmental editor, Theodora Bryant AuthorsHQ.com. Thank you for the patience and advice that you gave me. You had the unenviable task of making sense of the first draft and working with a first time writer who had/ has no idea. I learnt so much from you.

To my copy editor, Claire Ashgrove, thanks for the polishing and your nuggets of gold along the way. This book is much better because of you.

To my beta readers, you helped take this to the next level.

To patigonart, the cover is epic!

To Kieran, the soul of The Unemployed Gigilos, the greatest garage band of all time. Not only are you an amazing friend, you never stopped motivating me.

Thank you to Magnum and Avantasia for producing music that inspired and motivated me along the way.

Throwing this out to the universe: David Gemmell, thank you for returning my call and inviting me into your home. You inspired me and I hope one day to do justice to your advice. And I finally get Rocky.

Mum and Dad, thanks for putting up with me. I am hard work. You are great parents.

To my daughter. I can't promise not to write as much, but I can promise to play more ball and frisbee.

To my person. Thank you for reading all my drafts including the crap first one and your insightful and supportive comments. Characters and sub-plots lived and died with your words. Thank you for everything x

About the Author

David Cornford has been writing ever since David Gemmell invited him into his home, made him a cup of tea and tried to explain that Rocky was the best movie ever made. Holding Snaga The Sender, looking up at a wall of pistols from the John Shannow novels, he knew he had found his calling.

Born in Canada, raised in England and then let loose on the world, David has lived in India, America and now calls Western Australia home.

When he is not lost to his writing, David enjoys trying to grow every sort of fruit and vegetable and watching anything apocalyptic. He is supported by his wife of unfathomable patience and his bemused daughter who is a pixie-mermaid-fairy.

amazon.com/author/davidcornford

goodreads.com/david-cornford

facebook.com/davidcornford

bsky.app/profile/davidcornford.com

instagram.com/davidcornfordauthor

x.com/dcornfordauthor

patreon.com/DavidCornford